A Time to Grow and Change . . .

Yafatah's face blotched with fury. "That doon't be fair. You put me in a corner. I canna' win. I canna' be a child, and I canna' be a woman. That doon't be fair."

Barlimo chuckled. "Welcome to that celebrated malady called 'growing pains.' It's when you aren't one thing or another for a while. And you feel real uneasy inside all the time. You don't know where to stand with yourself. You get a little scared. Then you take it out on everybody around you. You want them to make the scare go away. But they can't, see."

"Why not?" retorted Yafatah.

"Because," said Barlimo kindly, tousling Yafatah's dark hair, "if they take away your scare, they take away your struggle. And they want you to have your struggle . . ."

Contrarywise

Zohra Greenhalgh

ACE BOOKS, NEW YORK

This book is an Ace
original edition, and has never been
previously published.

CONTRARYWISE

An Ace Book/published by arrangement with
the author

PRINTING HISTORY
Ace edition/April 1989

ISBN: 0-441-11711-2

Ace Books are published by The Berkley Publishing Group,
200 Madison Avenue, New York, New York 10016.
The name "Ace" and the "A" logo are trademarks
belonging to Charter Communications, Inc.

PRINTED IN THE UNITED STATES OF AMERICA

10 9 8 7 6 5 4 3 2 1

With Love
To the Deviant Denizens of Lytheria:
Past, Present, and Future
Especially to Lee Schneider
Who Provided the Refuge in the First Place

Acknowledgments

HEARTY THANKS TO my mother who provided my Big Brother (typewriter) in the nick of time; to my father for his gracious grant in 1984; to Jean Marie Stafford for an early vote of confidence and those wild family dinners which first inspired the Panthe'kinarok; to the late Jane Roberts—teacher, mystic, and pioneer—her husband Rob Butts, and the rest of the regular class rowdies for their blessed spiritual irreverence (especially the "Boys from New York"), to Seth himself for his disarming and devastating model of the Tricky Teacher, to the Sumari for ancient songs that linger just out of mind, to Pir Vilayat Inayat Khan for reminding me of Splendour; to the generous Yellow Springs of Ohio for iron medicine and the concept of *landdraw*; to my editor Terri Windling for early morning coffee and spirited courage; to the countless musicians to whose work I listened while writing— especially to those gentle heretics Ron Romanovsky and Paul Phillips; to my agent Val Smith who has a "soft spot" in her heart for Trickster; to Karen Pauli for Utter Chocolate Decadence; to David Bowie (whom I've never met) for his pied-eyed Jinnjirri visuals; to Professors Bruce Stark and Harold Scheub of the University of Wisconsin-Milwaukee and Madison respectively for Tricksterish lectures on Loki and Uncle Tompa; to Keith Stafford for his insight regarding artistic sketches and his gift of Every-when; to the Room 9 Hearthhags for their female presence and creative heroism; to the Hearth for messages; to Midori Snyder for fight scene specifics; to Charles and MaryAnn de Lint for writerly support when it was sorely needed; to Stephanie for tea; to my sister Sarah for fierce faith; to Kato Hayden for sheer exuberance; to David Piselli for being absolutely Contrary; to Anja for ambulatory walking sticks; to the Coffee Trader of Milwaukee for many hours of conversation and livelihood; to J.D. LaBash for impromptu talks on molecular biology and "selfish DNA"; to Marjorie Shyne and her daughter, Patti, for introducing me to the East Coast ditty "Dicky Dunkin'"; to Judy Frabotti for bringing me the concept of "the group" at the right moment; to Ardvesura

Krafft for sounding my heart during a stolen, fierce week in August; to Kathe Ann for the storyteller's perspective; to the scattered cast of *The Seven Rooms* for patience; to Grace Daley for the pun on her name; to the seen and unseen participants in my Lake Michigan Naming Ceremony for that new dawn; to my Grandmother Marie Walbridge Greenhalgh for "trust fund" teaching; to Mark Arnold for rampant tomatoes and solitude when it was needed; to my gray-haired, gold-eyed cat, Rimble—for his impossible, four-legged displays of claiming affection; to Gary Cone for the meaning of Podiddley; to the outraged, young Afghan woman on the cover of *National Geographic*, June 1985—may you be answered; to my beloved kin, Desiree Luena Bell, for embodying the sweet trueness of friendship; and finally to that irrepressible rogue, Trickster—here's to your great, wild heart and endless Improoovements on my life.

Better known as Divine Meddling . . .

The Trickster's Touch

PART I

He came to her when her world was frozen
And the dormant dreamed of Spring;
He came to her on her own asking
Her need his open door.

His ways cut deep,
His smile sly
And forged in some ancient, secret place—
His black eyes exacting.
He was a summer wind in autumn,
Circling the stillborn house of her soul,
Prying and piercing
Until she reached weeping-blind
For the promise of his unknown.

Stark and hungry for essentials,
Seeking bone and sinew
Under layers of wool and homespun chatter,
He shattered her at Trickster's Hallows
And left,
The wild poison of his thaw
An aching kiss upon her lips,
His touch
Searing.

He was the invited stranger,
The masked reveller of the street.
And she?
She was the Great Fool's common ground;
She was Greatkin Rimble's *He*.

—KELANDRIS OF SUXONLI
circa Jinnaeon

Contrarywise

The Panthe'kinarok Prologue

IN TRUTH, THERE was no eldest or youngest among the Greatkin for they had all emerged from the Presence at the same moment. However, they were a playful family who loved games of pretend almost as much as they loved to create worlds, each of the twenty-seven Greatkin adopting and discarding an endless array of shifting physical forms with exuberant abandon. In time, the Greatkin became such skillful masters of disguise that they confused even themselves. One day, in a fit of pique, Sathmadd, the Greatkin of Organization, Mathematics, and Red-Tape protested vigorously. Her exasperated outburst earned her a moment of unprecedented silence—which she promptly filled with her own opinion. Wagging a finger at her boisterous brothers and sisters, this tidy-minded Greatkin proposed that each of them chose a favorite persona, a *single* Primordial Face that would be immediately recognizable to each other and to all the peoples of their worlds.

"There now," finished Sathmadd, folding her old hands primly in her lap. "Isn't that a lovely idea?"

"Nope," retorted the youngest and most wily Greatkin of them all.

Sathmadd peered at him over her bifocals. "What do you mean *nope*?"

"Just nope," he replied, sticking his chin in the air. The name of this Greatkin was Rimble. Called Trickster by his family, this little maverick was the Greatkin of Deviance, the Unexpected, and the Impossible. Currently, Rimble appeared as a cross between a French fop, a griot, and an urban bagman. Rimble was also uncommonly short. And glib of tongue.

Sathmadd gave her little brother a wary look. "Would you to explain yourself?"

"Oh, *Maddi*," cried another Greatkin with alarm, "don't give Trickster a lead-in like that! He'll have us here all day!" The speaker's name was Jinndaven. He was the Greatkin of Imagination.

Rimble smiled serenely at Jinndaven and got to his feet. "On the contrary, dear brother. What I have to say is brief." He grinned as Jinndaven stared at him in surprise. "Just keeping you on your jingle-toes," replied Trickster nodding at the silver, upturned slippers worn by the Greatkin of Imagination; they were rimmed with tiny, tinkling bells. "No point in doing the Expected," Rimble added with a sly wink. "Now where was I? Oh, yes— Sathmadd's proposal." Rimble eyed his older, gray-haired sister with weary patience. "Maddi, dearest—" he began.

"Uh-oh," she grumbled.

Rimble batted his long eyelashes at her. "Maddi, dearest—a *single* persona is a Boring Idea. Think of what the mortals will do with it."

Sathmadd looked unconvinced.

Rimble paced. Then he stopped abruptly and said, "Mortals enjoy mental boxes more than *you* do, Maddi. They delight in trying to explain us away. Give them the idea that they can recognize us by *one* Primordial Face, and you'll have them calling us things like Muses, Archetypes, and—"

"Goddesses," said Sathmadd dreamily.

Rimble hesitated, stroking his black goatee. "Well, there *is* that." Trickster considered the matter from this angle and said, "All right, Maddi. I accept your proposal. But only on one condition."

"What is it?" asked Sathmadd suspiciously.

Trickster grinned. "That you let me make one teensy, weensy, Improoovement—"

"Oh, no you don't!" snapped Jinndaven.

A chorus of protests from the rest of the family backed up Jinndaven. As far as the Greatkin were concerned, Trickster's improvements were a euphemism for nothing more than thinly disguised Divine Meddling. And everyone, Jinndaven included, had been turned inside-out by one of Rimble's famous remedies at some time or other. Not that the effects of these remedies, these Improoovements, were necessarily bad—at least, not in the long run. They were, however, always extreme; even the most innocuous appearing ones could turn out to be shake-you-to-the-foundation radicalizing. And everyone knew it.

Adoring all the consternation he was causing, Rimble circled his seated family, his footsteps echoing throughout the great hall of Eranossa, the home of the Greatkin. Most of the twenty-seven Greatkin lived at Eranossa all the time. The exceptions to this were the members of that portion of the Presence called The Fertile Dark, or Neath. Rimble himself, being a most subtle and shadowy fellow, hailed from this Divine Down-Under. And it was Rimble's great pleasure to make the shining denizens of Eranossa nervous whenever possible. Like now.

Doing a sauntering little jig in his yellow boots, Rimble walked over to the Greatkin of Imagination and, smiling broadly, said, "I'm only suggesting a small Improoovement, dear brother. So relax."

Jinndaven rolled his eyes. "Only you could make the word 'relax' sound alarming."

"Naturally," replied Rimble, giving his family a small bow. "As always, I'm at your service. And at yours," he added to the enormous hearth at the end of the great hall. The flames leapt high and crackled loudly. Trickster grinned, turning back to his brothers and sisters, his pied eyes—one black, one yellow—glittering. "You see," he said slyly, "even Trickster has an ancient loyalty to the hearth."

No one cared to debate this; the hearth at the end of the great hall was intelligent. It was *also* a direct manifestation of the Presence, the Great Being who had given birth to them all. And according to Themyth, the Greatkin who tended the hearth, Trickster had as much right to serve the Presence as the rest of them. Galling, but true.

Jinndaven pursed his lips. "All right, Rimble. Let's hear this *small* improvement."

Arguing eloquently, Trickster made his point. He explained that as he was the Patron of all Exceptions, it was his right—indeed his very nature—to gleefully disregard this Single Face Thing. Furthermore, since he was the literal embodiment of Divine Shiftiness, the rest of the family couldn't expect to box him in. In fact, they simply *had* to let him get on with his work in the known and unknown universes—namely that of keeping creation moving. After all, he was change personified.

Sathmadd, who also happened to be the Patron of Logic, winced. She saw where Trickster was leading the family. She saw it all too clearly. Sathmadd slumped in her chair and put her gray head in her hands.

Jinndaven turned to the youthful, lovely Greatkin seated to his right. Her name was Phebene and she was the Patron of Great Loves and Tender Trysts. "I don't know, Phebes," Jinndaven muttered. "I don't like it when Maddi gets worried. Means Trickster is up to something."

"But, of course," replied Phebene, her voice sweet and musical. She wore a gown of gossamer, rainbow hues and a garland of wild, green roses on her head. "He's *always* up to something," she added with undisguised affection for pied-eyed Trickster.

Jinndaven rolled his eyes. "You just like him for the weird sex."

Phebene grinned demurely. "Deviance can be fun," she whispered in his ear. "You should try it sometime."

The Greatkin of Imagination grunted. "*Who* do you think Trickster gets his ideas from?" he scolded.

"Then hush, dearest bother, and let's see what Trickster had in mind."

Jinndaven crossed his arms over his chest and turned his scowling attention back to Rimble.

"As I was saying," continued the little Greatkin. "*If* you should find yourselves boxed in someday—stuck with only one identity as it were—then I suggest you provide yourselves with a way out of this difficulty. Me. *Some*body has to embody the Primordial Multiple Personality. For *Presence* sake," he added coquettishly. Then looking insufferably pleased with himself, Trickster added, "Oh come on, you guys—you've *got* to admit, I'm a great loophole. And Presence knows," he said pointedly to the Greatkin of Red-Tape, "*every* system needs a loophole."

Sathmadd looked dubious. "And how do you propose to do this?"

Rimble grinned broadly and played his trump. "By retaining my changeable form, of course. By being the exception to the rule," he added while doing a small contrariwise turn. "By creating the First Loophole in the First System!" Then he began laughing uproariously. "Hoo-hoo!" he chortled. "*Gotcha!*"

There was a stunned silence.

Rimble's logic was brilliant. The Greatkin groaned, swore, and conceded. In this way did Greatkin Rimble retain his changeable guise (*and* create the First Loophole in the First System). From that day forth, no one—neither Greatkin nor mortal alike–could ever predict Trickster's next form. He might appear as a crooked stile, a dance of autumn leaves, or the sensual smile on a stranger's face across the room. Trickster could be anything and anywhere at anytime.

Take this morning for instance: this morning Greatkin Rimble was busy impersonating a small rock on the side of the mountain path that led to their ancestral home, Eranossa. Rimble literally sat in plain view, but everyone at Eranossa was so accustomed to Trickster's subtlety that no one could find him when it came time to call everyone for the great potluck feast of the Greatkin, the Panthe'kinarok. Themyth, the Greatkin of Civilization and the Greatkin who presided at the Panthe'kinarok, sent Jinndaven after Rimble. She reasoned that only the Greatkin of Imagination would come up with the creativity to locate the little rogue. And she was right.

After an hour's fruitless search for Trickster, it finally occurred to Jinndaven to try the obvious. So he looked right in front of his nose. Not ten feet from him sat Rimble.

"*There* you are!" cried the Greatkin of Imagination in an exasperated, out-of-breath voice. Dressed formally for the upcoming Panthe'kinarok dinner, Jinndaven wore a filmy robe of lavenders riddled with small round mirrors. The bells on the tips of his silver slippers jingled as he trudged through the fresh fall of snow on the mountain's trail. As Rimble did not appear to have heard him, Jinndaven knelt beside the small, asymmetrical rock and whispered, "I see you."

Rimble immediately changed into two-legged form. Like Jinndaven, Trickster wore his best clothes for the great meet of his ragtag family, that once-an-age council they called the Panthe'kinarok. However, Trickster's version of Best Clothes was a little different from Jinndaven's—or that of anyone else in the family. To begin with, nothing matched. Furthermore, each article of clothing on Trickster's person hailed from cultures representing every corner of the known universes. The effect was Positively Ubiquitous—and just slightly unnerving.

Naturally, thought Jinndaven as he eyed his bagman brother with a patient expression. He sighed, wiping the sweat of the mountain climb off his brow with a silk handkerchief, thinking that sometimes even the Greatkin of Imagination had trouble keeping up with Trickster. Jinndaven studied the lower half of Rimble's harlequin costume then pulled back warily.

"What's that big bulge under your—"

"*Shhh!*" said Rimble, waving Jinndaven silent with a sharp gesture of his small hand. Everything on Rimble was small— *except* that bulge, thought Jinndaven. Rimble now pointed to a thick tangle of black briars growing a few feet off the snowy mountain trail. Jinndaven stared at the dark briars in silence, wondering what Trickster was seeing that he wasn't.

Jinndaven cleared his throat uneasily. "Uh, what exactly are we doing?"

Trickster grinned. "We're considering ecstasy."

"We're considering what?" Jinndaven asked, staring even harder at the thorny labyrinth of brambles in front of him.

"Ecstasy," repeated Trickster. "Only I'm renaming it Contrary-wise—that's with a 'y' not an 'i.' One of my Improoovements, you know."

Jinndaven looked unimpressed. "Changing the spelling of a word hardly merits the term 'improvement,' Rimble. I mean, how strictly small-time."

"Ha," replied Trickster with a meaningful shrug. "That's all *you* know, big brother. That's all you know."

Jinndaven, who was generally fond of Rimble for the most part, gave his sibling a withering smile. Rimble could be so arrogant at times. "I suppose you plan to *explain* the meaning behind your cryptic remarks?" said Jinndaven.

"In due time," replied Trickster.

Jinndaven's eyes narrowed. "Not even a hint?"

Trickster pursed his lips. "All right, a hint. Contrariwise with an 'i' is a direction, is it not? The opposite way of things, yes?"

"Yes," agreed Jinndaven. "Utterly contrary."

"Well," said Trickster rubbing his hands with glee, "Contrary-wise with a 'y' is a direction, too. Transposably speaking, of course."

There was a short pause.

"That's *it*?" asked Jinndaven with irritation. "That's the hint?"

Rimble rolled his pied eyes. "You're not trying."

"That's because I'm hungry," said Jinndaven starting to get to his feet. "Which is what I came to tell you: Dinner's almost on." Rimble grabbed Jinndaven's arm and pulled him back to his previous squatting posture in the snow.

"Okay," said Trickster. "I'll give you a bigger hint."

"Oh, Rimble—I'm *hungry*!"

"Yeah," snapped Trickster, "and you don't even know what for!"

"What?"

Trickster let go of Jinndaven's arm and folded his hands primly in his lap, his nose in the air. "Tell the others I'll be along."

Jinndaven eyed him warily. "When?"

"When I finish completing the greatest experiment of all time."

Jinndaven bit his lower lip, his curiosity aroused. "Surely you're exaggerating."

"Nope," said Trickster and went back to watching the tangle of black briars. "But what do you care? You're *hungry*," he said in perfect whining mimicry of the Greatkin of Imagination.

Jinndaven swore under his breath. His curiosity had just gained on his hunger. And Rimble knows it, too, Jinndaven thought sourly. Calling on the Presence to protect him from Rimble's meddling—a prayer that had yet to be successful—Jinndaven took a deep breath and said, "All right—I'll play. What's the difference between contrariwise with an 'i' and contrarywise with a 'y'?"

Trickster turned to look at him, his smile broad. "That's my boy," he said nodding enthusiastically. "The difference is a teensy, weensy psychic *shift*. Which translates into Reality as a genetic transpositional element."

There was dead silence. And shock.

Jinndaven stiffened so sharply that he fell over in the snow. He scrambled to his knees, took Rimble by the shoulders and shook him. "A *mutation* on the eve of the Panthe'kinarok?" he cried. "Have you forgotten the mortals? *Have* you?"

Trickster extricated himself from Jinndaven's strong grasp gingerly. "I haven't forgotten anything," he retorted. "Least of all the mortals. In fact, it's them I'm thinking about." He grinned. "I've finally found a way to motivate their 'selfish DNA.' We're talking Fundamental Change. Big Time. Very big time." Rimble shrugged. "One or two more psychic adjustments *here*, and my latest Improoovement will be ready to fly."

Jinndaven frowned, then seeing the look of absolute mischief in Trickster's pied eyes, Jinndaven paled. "What kind of adjustments, Rimble?"

"Well, I just need a little help—"

"What *kind* of help?" asked Jinndaven, wishing fervently that Themyth had sent someone else to find Greatkin Rimble.

Trickster winked at him; then before Jinndaven could bolt, Trickster began humming an entrancing little tune, purposefully punctuating it with explosive laughter and drunken smiles. Jinndaven's breathing turned shallow. He made a hasty ball of his lavender handkerchief and began dabbing frantically at his brow and neck. He tried to get to his feet but was swiftly prevented from doing so by Greatkin Rimble. Grabbing Jinndaven's arm with his strong, claw-like grip, Trickster grinned seductively at the Great-kin of Imagination. Then Trickster farted. The sound of it was so loud that the hapless Jinndaven lost his balance and fell backwards into a snowdrift. This sent Trickster into hyena-like giggles. Then, still sitting cross-legged, Greatkin Rimble began to rock from side to side singing the following verse in an unexpectedly pure tenor, the quality of his voice as sweet and piercing as that of a young boy:

> Will you turn the inside inside-out,
> And be sanely mad with me?
> Will you master the steps of my turnabout,
> And come to my ecstasy?

When he finished, Trickster met Jinndaven's eyes briefly, his expression suddenly wistful. "It's a reel," he said, his voice full of yearning.

Jinndaven, who was used to Trickster's quick changes of emotion, (and terrible puns), replied drily, "A real *what*?"

Trickster instantly shrieked with laughter, threw open his harlequin greatcoat, and exposed a gilded penis sheath two feet long. Pretending to masturbate, Trickster moaned and said, "It's a real hard! Care to come? No? But why not? *My* ecstasy is sobering."

Jinndaven turned scarlet. Well aware that any portion of Trickster's anatomy was subject to change without notice, he stared bug-eyed at the length of Trickster's penis sheath. "I hope you don't intend that thing for *me*!"

Trickster sniffed haughtily, and covered the gilded penis sheath with the black and yellow front of his greatcoat. "Don't be absurd, Jinn. You've neither the courage or capacity."

Jinndaven scowled, his pride stung by his brother's waspish tone. Still, he had to be careful how he responded to this jab of Rimble's. He didn't want to find himself in bed with Trickster. At least not right before the Panthe'kinarok. It would cause talk and there were the mortals to think about. Jinndaven bit his lower lip and shook his head. Tonight of all nights—on the evening of the Panthe'kinarok, he thought raggedly—when the Presence opened the Everywhen, and all things that the Greatkin did and thought translated into Reality! Jinndaven swore. Leave it to *Rimble* to speak of transposition and "selfish DNA" at such a time.

Trickster, who was watching Jinndaven closely, whispered, "Change *can* be inconvenient."

Jinndaven snorted. "Inconvenient or no, I'd like to point out that my 'courage and capacity' are both substantial. For what*ever* you have in mind. I *am* the Greatkin of Imagination," he added with bruised dignity.

Trickster smiled. "I'm sorry, dear fellow," he said patting the bulge under his coat, "but this insertion is not for you."

Jinndaven peered at Rimble's black-bearded face, trying to read the truth or falsehood in Rimble's pied eyes. "So, I'm not the dupe? I'm not the help you need?"

Trickster chuckled. "You sound almost disappointed."

A chill slipped up Jinndaven's spine. "And you're hedging—"

Before Jinndaven could press Rimble further for an answer, Trickster snapped his attention back to the tangle of dark briars before them. Pointing excitedly, Greatkin Rimble cried, "At last!"

Jinndaven looked past Rimble's small hand, his eyes widening with wonder. Rimble's briar patch was suffused with a soft, blue-white light. As the light intensified, the briars turned a blood-brown and gave way, their thorny mesh slowly pulling back to reveal a delicate, crystal-stemmed flower, its white petals still shut.

Jinndaven's jaw dropped in astonishment. "Was this one of my ideas? I don't seem to remember creating any flowers with crystal stems—"

"Will you lower your voice?" hissed Trickster. Then he added proudly, "This is the Wild Kelandris. Also known as the Winterbloom. It's a weed. And it can grow in the worst of conditions. It can even bloom in the dead of winter. Hence the name, you see."

"Yes," whispered Jinndaven. "But who's idea was it?"

Trickster grinned. "It's an Improoovement—on one of yours. A rose, I think you called it?"

Jinndaven's eyes blazed with indignation. "Whatever happened to creatorly consideration?" he muttered under his breath to the twilight and snow and winter wind rustling in the pine trees above him. Then he turned to Trickster, but before the Greatkin of Imagination could tell his little brother what he thought of his meddling, the Wild Kelandris began to emit a powerful pulsing red light. Startled into silence, Jinndaven stared at Rimble's improvement with grudging awe. The crystal stem of the delicate flower filled slowly with crimson liquid. It seemed to be boiling. Jinndaven wondered if the heat or pressure building inside the stem would shatter its crystalline structure. As the molten liquid continued to bubble, a light snow fell softly on the unopened bud. When the large flakes touched the white petals of the Winterbloom, they melted.

"They look like tears," mumbled Jinndaven.

Trickster rolled his eyes. "Sentimental dope. You've been hanging out with Phebene too much."

Jinndaven shrugged. He couldn't help it if the Greatkin of Great Loves and Tender Trysts was his favorite sibling. He liked being around her influence. Phebene made him feel. Jinndaven slid his hand over his heart. He frowned. "Seems you're making me feel, too, Rimble. Very strange, in fact."

Trickster beamed. "I always feel strange."

"No, I mean it. I feel *very* strange."

"Is that bad?"

Jinndaven swallowed, starting to sweat again. "Well, I don't know exactly. I feel—uh—pierced." He winced, pressing against his heart with his hands. "Pierced," he repeated in a whisper.

Rimble pursed his lips, looking very much like a scientist examining his laboratory results. He reached for Jinndaven's handsome face, took it in his small hands and peered intently into Jinndaven's eyes. "Anything else? Any other sensations?"

Jinndaven nodded slowly. "It's almost sexual," he added, glancing nervously at the two-foot bulge under Rimble's greatcoat. "But it's inside. Organic-like—more fundamental somehow. *Inside* inside. And intelligent."

"Presence directed?" asked Trickster.

"Yes. Very—uh—natural. Once you get the rhythm of it. Of the pulse, I mean."

"Ah," said Trickster, and smiled. Then he went back to watching the Wild Kelandris. Jinndaven did so as well, his body straining against the shock of the New coursing through his system. When he could match the greater rhythm of Rimble's improvement, he felt light-headed and free-wheeling. Almost weightless, he thought. Jinndaven grinned unexpectedly. Won't Mattermat be sore when he finds out about this, he thought drunkenly. Mattermat, who was the Greatkin of Inertia and All Things Made Physical, generally scoffed at anything that guaranteed escape from gravity. Jinndaven giggled, his gaze on the flower intensifying.

The crimson liquid inside the Wild Kelandris darkened and thickened. The force of the pressure against the unopened bud of the white flower was so extreme now that Jinndaven gasped against the answering resonance inside his own body. Individual rhythm strained to encompass the universal. Jinndaven took an uncomfortable breath, wishing the Wild Kelandris would hurry up and bloom. He winced. He was beginning to feel disturbed in some way. Deeply disturbed. Maybe even a little crazy.

"Rimble?" he said hoarsely,

Trickster patted him on the arm. "It's the *shift*, that's all. You'll be all right as soon as the Winterbloom releases her flower."

Jinndaven blinked, his sense of time and place fuzzy. "Will that be soon?" he asked in a distant tone of voice. "I would really like it if it could be soon. This is very uncomfortable."

"That's because you're resisting the *shift*. Stop trying to access it as if it were something outside yourself. Turn inside inside-out instead."

"Oh," said the Greatkin of Imagination, struggling to make sense of Rimble's directions. "But—uh—what *is* this *shift*?"

"Has to do with helixes. I think."

Jinndaven blinked. "You think?" His eyes narrowed, as the truth suddenly dawned on him. Too late, he realized that he was indeed Trickster's dupe. And guinea pig. "Blast you, Rimble! This isn't one of your Improvements. This is one of your *untested* experiments."

Rimble smiled sheepishly.

His face furious, Jinndaven grabbed his little brother by the frilly front of his greatcoat. "Why you shit-grinned little bastard!"

"Now, now," said Rimble hastily. "It's not nice to mangle a god. Even if I *am* short," he added.

Jinndaven got to his feet dragging Rimble with him. As he lifted Trickster into the air, he shouted, "Don't give yourself airs, brother dear. You're a Greatkin not a god. Now hear me clearly. You know the word *permission*? I invented it. And I gave you no permission to muck about with roses. You listening, Rimble?"

Feeling Jinndaven's fingers tighten, Rimble swallowed and said, "Oh. Well, perhaps I was getting a teensy bit out of hand—"

Jinndaven shook him. "I should rearrange your face. Make that faces."

Rimble broke out in a sweat. "But don't you want to see how the experiment turns out? *Think* of the mortals, Jinn. Something might go wrong if we don't follow through on this. There's no telling—"

Jinndaven pressed his lips together, his eyes searching Rimble's. He took a deep breath, letting it out through clenched teeth. It was true. There was no telling what would happen if he punched the Greatkin of Deviance during an incompleted experiment. Jinndaven dropped Trickster into a nearby snowdrift. As the snowdrift was a least a foot deeper than Rimble was tall, the little Greatkin began swearing. As he dug himself out, Jinndaven leaned down and pointed a finger in Rimble's face.

"Okay. Fine for now, Rimble. But when this is over, dear brother, you better run. Because when I catch up with you—"

Jinndaven suddenly broke off in mid-sentence, his body shuddering. His handsome face switched gender, changing from male to female and back again. Touching his cheeks, Jinndaven panicked. "What have you done?"

Rimble's pied eyes danced. "It's the 'y' that does it. The 'y' in Contrarywise. Welcome to transposition central. It's a *matter* of pitch."

Naming Rimble every four-letter word he could think of (and the Greatkin of Imagination could think of a lot), Jinndaven tried valiantly to get a psychic grip on his identity, but his normal boundaries of self slipped and slid and would not remain anchored to the here and now. Jinndaven scooped up a handful of snow and mashed it against the bare skin of his neck, hoping the shock of the cold would cause him to return to himself. But it didn't.

"Rimble," whispered the Greatkin of Imagination, "what have you *done*? I'm entering the Everywhen of the Presence. I'm losing control of my Primordial Face. I'm—"

"Yeah, yeah, yeah," said Trickster feigning boredom. "You've been stuck," he said, finally extricating himself from the snowdrift in which Jinndaven had dumped him, "and although it doesn't look like it," he added, brushing snow off his legs, "I'm digging you out. You're *shifting*."

"But Sathmadd's rule. One Face—"

"It's only temporary."

"Sathmadd's rule most certainly is *not* temporary!" cried Jinndaven as his beautiful face changed into three probable versions of the original. The Greatkin of Imagination clapped his hands to his temples, shut his eyes and grit his teeth.

"I am myself!" he whispered. "I am myself!"

"It's only a concept. And it's very inadequate," said Trickster. He sighed. "Resisting the *shift* won't stop it," he added conversationally. "And anyway, I was referring to the *shift* being temporary—not Maddi's rule."

"What?" mumbled Jinndaven, his disassociation from serial time almost complete now. He fell to his knees in the snow, holding his head and rocking. He felt the doors of Everywhen open around him, the rush of probable futures brushing across his face like a cold wind with a hot center. Time restructured itself inside him, moving into a speeded up simultaneity. Jinndaven tried valiantly to stop the process, but the impetus of Trickster's *shift* was too powerful even for him. Rolling his eyes helplessly at Trickster—who was watching him now with unexpected compassion—Jinndaven yielded to the pressure within, his face alternating freely now between male and female according to an inner, organic prompting. Trickster grinned now, his expression now one of fascination and undisguised conceit. He circled Jinndaven jauntily.

"Excellent," said Rimble softly, his pied eyes—one black and one yellow—glittering in the deepening twilight.

Jinndaven groaned, shaking his head. "This—will—translate. This—will—cause—havoc—with—Inertia. Mattermat—will—have—your—ass!"

"Not if *I* have anything to say about it!" retorted Trickster.

"The—universes—" continued Jinndaven, every word labored. He wondered if he were actually speaking. Maybe my tongue is in the way, he thought spacily. "The—universes. Don't—you—realize—?"

Trickster slapped his own thighs gleefully. The sound of it made Jinndaven jump. Then, grabbing the face of the Greatkin of Imagination once more in his small hands, Trickster lifted his chin and said, "Can you *imagine* the effect this'll have on mortals? They could call the process *Shifttime*. Or," he said, wig-wagging his black eyebrows at Jinndaven, "in honor of your supreme sacrifice and *eager* participation here, they could name it after you. They could call it *Jinn*aeon."

Jinndaven frowned. He was having a great deal of difficulty following Rimble's words. Worse yet, Jinndaven had the distinct impression that he was about to be blamed for something that was Trickster's fault and not his. He touched his face gingerly, sure that it would never stabilize again.

Trickster patted his hand. "Will you relax? I *told* you—this is just a temporary condition. It'll pass. If you let it," he added sourly. He peered into Jinndaven's bewildered eyes. "Are you still in there?"

"Sure. The whole gang's here," mumbled Jinndaven. "Who

d'you want to speak to? Oh, and specify past, present, or future while you're at it, will you? We wouldn't want to confuse you."

Trickster chuckled. "No chance of that. I'm the original Multiple Personality—remember?" He smiled cheerily at Jinndaven then glanced at the straining bud of the Winterbloom. "Any moment now," he said to his brother. "Yup—there she goes. I suggest you yield, Jinn. I suggest you yield completely."

"What?"

"Yield!"

Jinndaven blinked, forcing his eyes to focus on the slowly opening bud in front of him. As the white petals unfurled, Jinndaven felt a curious leap of hope in his heart and a steady streaming of raw, potent joy throughout his body. Unexpectedly delighted, Jinndaven turned to this joy in wonder. As he reached hesitantly for it, the joy reached for him with confident, wild desire. It flooded him, irradiating his every cell with an ancient intelligence that spoke of renewal and a wild emergence of the Utterly New.

The Winterbloom continued to flower, the blood-like liquid in its crystal stem now shooting freely into the bud's center. The white petals slowly turned pink along the outside edges then darkened to a glistening, brilliant red. Then a queer thing happened; the center of the Winterbloom began to turn counterclockwise. The effect on Jinndaven was immediate. He gasped, clutching at his heart.

"It's opening. The flower. My heart."

Trickster smiled knowingly. Then he leaned toward the Greatkin of Imagination and whispered, "So choose the self you most want to be, Jinn. Pick the one most precious to you. Go on. Imagine the best of all possible yous—living in the best of all possible worlds. Now's the moment of conscious choosing. Now is the moment of Shifttime—when all things are possible. Stir yourself to excellence. Change the psychic code of all Reality. Insert a new sequence of self."

"But there's nothing wrong with the psychic code of all Reality. Or with me as a person," added Jinndaven crossly. "I'm a perfectly good Greatkin."

"So be a better one," replied Rimble, his expression hard.

"But everyone likes me the way I am. They'll be upset if I go and start imagining myself differently. Especially Sathmadd."

Rimble grunted. "I doubt she'll even notice a change of this kind. She's not very subtle, you know. But enough of that—go on and *shift*. The Winterbloom is nearly ready to fly."

"Flowers don't fly," said Jinndaven stubbornly.

"Impr*oo*ved flowers are liable to do anything," retorted Rimble. "Even the impossible." Trickster inclined his head. "Stop stalling, Jinndaven. You know you want this. Your eyes are so bright I can barely look at you."

"Okay, okay," grumbled the Greatkin of Imagination. Then without further ado, he drew himself up, sifting through a thousand faces until he came to the one most precious to himself. Picking that one, he let that future fill him with purpose. He let that future show him what sequential choices he'd have to make to become this new self. Yielding now to the great good inherent in making the choice to become not only a better person, but the very best he could possibly be, Jinndaven felt himself become inwardly buoyant—ecstatic. His face suffused with a gently psychological radiance, Jinndaven finally relaxed. Suddenly he understood Trickster's great freedom: multiplicity. Everything was again possible—despite the rules. And he was sanely mad—"touched" by Trickster. The *shift*, he thought, that's the wild labor. Labor for a psychic birth.

Movement caught Jinndaven's eye. It was the Winterbloom finally come to term. Like this new self, the blossoming flower now strained against its own roots and yearned for emergence. Jinndaven watched the flower struggle for flight, the entire bloom now beginning to spin. What had once been a rose, thought Jinndaven, was now a Winterbloom. What had been an ordinary flower was now an original. It was wholly new. And somehow, the transformation was contained in the turn.

Jinndaven gasped. "My heart—I think you broke it."

"Nothing else will do," replied Trickster. "Nothing else can induce the turn necessary to support the shock of the new. I said it was hard."

Jinndaven nodded, his eyes still on the flower. Its spin was so swift now that the petals appeared as a white blur. Then slowly the bloom separated from the crystal stem. The stem itself shattered, its pieces tinkling like shards of glass as they fell against each other in the snow. Finally, the Winterbloom lifted into the wintry air and flew free. Jinndaven whooped with delight.

"There I go!" he cried, his voice joyous. "I'm soaring!"

"Mmm," nodded Trickster, his face upturned as he watched the flower sail into the gray sky, its spin emitting a hum that echoed over the mountain and made Trickster smile. Then the flower incandesced. As the sky lit with brilliance, the Winterbloom released a fragrance. Its perfume was so heady, so intoxicating that Jinndaven scrambled to his feet, grabbed Rimble by the hand, and danced a mad jig up and down the steep mountain trail. Finally out of breath, the two Greatkin fell backwards into a drift, making snow angels and laughing.

"Hoo, hooo!" cried Trickster rubbing his small hands with glee. "It works! What an Improooovement, eh?" he added, clapping his brother on the back and jumping to his yellow-booted feet.

The Greatkin of Imagination smiled drunkenly at Trickster. Yessir, he thought, If this was Trickster's ecstasy, he'd come to it *any* time.

Trickster turned a *contrarywise* circle, spinning left. Grabbing the sheath under his greatcoat, he gave his brother a diabolical grin and said, "Now to take my Improovement to where it'll do some good."

"Where's that?"

"Civilization's bed."

Jinndaven's eyes widened. The Greatkin of Civilization was their sister, Themyth. She was also a crone who had only this morning complained of feeling unusually stiff in the joints. Jinndaven swallowed. "You're going to take that two-foot— *thing*—to Eldest? Have a heart. Themyth will probably run screaming from the house. And you complain about *my* capacity for change."

Trickster grinned. "You underestimate our good sister. And besides, Jinn, this wouldn't be the first time I've fucked with Civilization." His expression softened. "Not the first time at all."

Part I:
THE LEADING EDGE

Some fall off and never return,
Some walk the shifting line,
But neither knows the tricksy turn
Of Rimble's Contrarywise Nine.

—A MAYANABI SAYING

Chapter One

FIRST LIGHT: THE between-time of Everywhen when night tarried, day still longed to be, and all Mnemlith listened for the sounds of morning. First light: the rift between worlds when dreams murmured subtle things in gray, and waking minds reached for the distinct colors of dawn. Now was the moment of renewal and eternal return. To consciousness.

The Mayanabi Desert gleamed at sunrise. Amber light played across shifting sands and vanished. Silence. Three heartbeats, and the earth opened. Sound that clattered and gathered speed, hoof against stone. Like a jagged riptide, a green-cowled figure thundered from the gap, his cloak a dark undertow of roiling power that startled. The desert stirred in its sleep, a hot wind running to meet this first wave of Jinnaeon: Trickster's Improvement. The desert air crackled with the shock of the new, and the figure in green came riding into the open on the back of a blue-black mare.

Faster.

The man hunched forward. His name was Zendrak. He was Trickster's Emissary: Rimble's threshold of change. The mare's dark mane whipped his hidden face, and he bent lower to fill his senses with the mare's strong animal smell. Her sweat blended with his, salty and pungent-wild. This mix was a perfume that slapped the mind awake; it was the scent of Rimble's Own.

Zendrak held his olive-skinned hands steady on either side of the mare's reaching, streaming neck. His fingers held no reins. There was no need of them. Nothing in civilization could control this mare. Nothing could constrain her. She was a loan from the Stables of Neath, and she ran to the rhythm of her own fierce spirit. She was the leading edge of Rimble's building crest, her hooves striking the meter for change. She travelled no roads: only the currents of coincidence. Her name was Further, and she was a Power of the Fertile Dark.

Faster.

The Emissary whispered his destination. The words were a hiss on the hot, dawn wind: the Yellow Springs. The mare's ears flicked backward. Her pace never faltered as she turned north toward snow-misted mountains. The thrum of her hooves, the beat of his heart, and it was on to the Yellow Springs: an ancient haven of healing. This was a four-thousand-mile journey, and they would complete it by day's end. Tonight they would position the final piece of puzzle-unasked-for but undertaken long, long ago.

The mare's powerful stride lengthened. They passed through town and valley. The remains of night shattered in their relentless wake. Heads turned, but eyes saw nothing. Tale-tellers yawned over breakfast, and children stumbled out of bed. Some wondered at the sudden shift in temperature and shrugged as they unbuttoned their nightshirts. Here in the southern lands, the air was sweet and warm, and summer still lingered though the months approached Fall. In the north, however, this was not so. There, Autumn made bright festival with the trees, and the people of Suxonli already wore wool.

Zendrak smiled. This was the cusp of the season when change gusted with the wind and colors were crisp. Now the weather was unpredictable. This was nature's *shifttime*—Trickster's Glory. A wild joy overtook the Emissary. He cried out, reckless and alive! Sparks flew, hoof against stone. And Zendrak was riding, riding. He was riding north to Suxonli to bring Summer to one of Rimble's Own.

Faster.

Chapter Two

CRAZY KEL SAT motionless on a mossy, limestone ledge a few feet above the Yellow Springs of Piedmerri. Swathed in her habitual veil and robe of black, Crazy Kel lay her head against her hunched knees and sighed. Her expression remained concealed under the drape of material covering her face and broad shoulders. She opened her startling, pale green eyes slowly, her face strained by an internal turmoil that had caused her yet another sleepless night. She took a deep breath, trying to calm the ache in her chest. This ache was not a physical pain; however, it had a physical location—her heart and lungs. Crazy Kel rubbed her breastbone gingerly and winced. What *was* this ache? she wondered. She had felt it only once before, and that had been sixteen years ago. There had been no answer for it then, and there appeared to be no answer for it now. She shut her eyes again, listening numbly to the tumbling rush of the twenty-feet fall of water directly below her. Crazy Kel smiled sourly.

Crazy Kel—born Kelandris of Suxonli—was thirty-three years old. And as far as the elders of Suxonli Village were concerned, Crazy Kel ought to be dead. It annoyed them that she wasn't.

The woman in black chuckled bitterly. "Strong I am," she whispered in a queer, sing-song monotone, "and strong shall I ever be. I have danced for the King of Deviance, and the bastard made me his *he*."

The ache in her chest intensified without warning. Crazy Kel swore. Gasping for breath, she pressed her forehead against her knees, her jaw clenched. "I draw the Springs roundabout. I cast this pain out and *out*!" When this incantation failed, Crazy Kel sidled closer to a trickle of the copper colored water of the springs diverted from the main by fallen leaves. Crazy Kel thrust her left hand into the iron laden wash, hoping to draw some strength from the minerals themselves. She sucked the taste of it off her dirty fingers, comforted by the familiar feel of the metal flavor in her mouth. "Iron Springs be my friend. Bring the pain of Suxonli to end."

Her shoulders sagged as she wondered just how many times she had prayed for this in the past sixteen years. How long would it take? How *long* would her internal wounds remain raw? She shrugged. The lashes on her scarred back had healed long ago. But her mind? Crazy Kel groaned. Sometimes she was very, very sane. And sometimes she wasn't. Crazy Kel watched the spray from the falls below her catch the light from the setting sun. A rainbow flickered briefly and was gone.

"Don't make promises you cannot keep," she snapped at the Springs. "What was sown in Suxonli, I forever reap."

The rainbow reappeared as if in contradiction. Crazy Kel spat at the Yellow Springs. When the rainbow remained, she bowed her head unexpectedly. She felt ashamed. The Yellow Springs had provided her safe haven since Suxonli had cast her out. She owed the Springs gratitude, she told herself angrily—even on her bad days. Crazy Kel bit her lips under her black veil, listening to the cheery splash of the water. She smiled hesitantly, as if the muscles of her face were unaccustomed to doing so. Then once again, she put her hand in the rivulet beside her, touching it as gently as if it were a lover she had inadvertently spurned. The rainbow lengthened, then vanished.

Night approached. The fading rays of the sun turned dark gold, making the deposit of iron on the rocks below the surface of the Springs appear as bright as a newly minted copper. Crazy Kel inhaled the peace of the place, thanking the Springs again for the long moment of protection they had afforded her. She certainly hadn't deserved it, she thought. But then that was the nature of this place. It didn't judge. It simply gave. Even to the condemned like her; even to a person who had been branded *akindo* and convicted of murder. Which is the same thing, thought Crazy Kel tiredly. She shook her head. Stupid Springs—giving to a murderess. But then, I suppose that's your business, isn't it? she thought at the falls. And what do I know? I'm just an ignorant village woman. And a criminal at that. Her shoulders sagged again with a bitterness that even the Springs could not alleviate.

The Yellow Springs were an ancient place of sustaining spiritual power well known to the locals yet virtually undiscovered by the rest of Mnemlith. Those few who were fortunate enough to drink from the mineral and metal laden water of this hidden place left whispering tales of miraculous cures—both physical and psychological. Lying deep in the black earth piedmont of the Western Feyborne Mountains. They lay half a mile south of Suxonli village—on the other side of the Mazemouth River and just across the border of the land called Piedmerri. Kelandris grit her teeth. She could not remember how she had come to the Yellow Springs. Or who had cared for her during those first months after the Ritual of Akindo. Mostly, she remembered feeling alone. And helpless. Crazy Kel glared at the old scars on her dirty hands, and wondered how she had gotten them. Then she wondered why she had survived the Ritual of Akindo.

It was also a mystery to the elders of Suxonli why Kelandris had not died sixteen years ago when they pronounced her *akindo*: kinless and without soul. The Ritual of Akindo was an ordeal of harsh justice designed to destroy not only the mind but also the body. This had not been the original purpose of the ritual, but the people of Suxonli had forgotten its older significance and meaning: namely, a confrontation with death while still living and a radical release from personal history. The current Ritual of Akindo included a severe beating which was then followed by the ingestion of a toxic dose of an indigenous hallucinogenic substance called holovespa: the whole wasp.

Understandably so, the elders of Suxonli had expected the beating alone to kill seventeen-year-old Kelandris, but her six-foot-four body had proved to be as strong as her stubborn, insolent spirit, and she had survived. As a result, the elders had been forced to continue the ritual, now pouring a killing dose of the drug holovespa into Kel's bloody mouth. This had been carried out by the person whom Kelandris had loved most: her fifteen-year-old brother, Yonneth.

The holovespa itself was a natural substance, a kind of royal jelly manufactured internally by the Holovespa Wasp Queen—intended solely for her larvae. However, the villagers of Suxonli had been stealing this jelly for centuries, making a potent sacramental compound from it. They called it Rimble's Remedy and dispensed it during their yearly Trickster's Hallows—a late autumn carnival of euphoria. The Ritual of Akindo had turned this wild (but essentially harmless) festival of masquerade into a streaming, screaming nightmare of distortion. As per the requirements for *akindo*, Suxonli had given young Kelandris enough drug to synaptically unhinge her mind permanently. They had expected her to kill herself. But Kelandris had not. She had lived—not well, but she *had* lived. Despite Suxonli and its judgement.

The Ritual of Akindo had not been without its effect, however. By the end of that particular Trickster's Hallows, Kelandris had emerged certifiably insane. Left emotionally stripped of all normal ego structures—both positive and negative—Kelandris had collapsed into herself and wandered lost in a miasma of mistaken perceptions and uncontrollable fear. Her body bloody and broken by the beating and her mind savaged by the holovespa, the villagers had left her in a cave on the outskirts of town. Kelandris had been too weak and disoriented even to weep. Everyone in Suxonli had agreed that if Kelandris survived, it would be an utter miracle. Kelandris did them one better. She not only survived—she escaped. But not without help.

After a week of questioning and piecing together everyone's stories of that night, the elders of Suxonli concluded that Kelandris had received aid from someone outside the community. There was talk (especially by Yonneth, Kel's younger brother) that his seventeen-year-old sister had lost her maidenhead the night of

Trickster's Hallows. Yonneth swore that there had been a stranger present—a man who topped Kel's own formidable height by an intimidating two inches. He had also smelled—said Yonneth with disgust—*reeked* of unusually strong horse sweat.

There had been an immediate uproar. Kelandris had not played by the rules. She had added insult to injury; not only had she been responsible for the death of several villagers of Suxonli, but she had also had the bad taste to survive the justice of the Ritual of Akindo *and* escape Suxonli's borders as well. Some months later, someone reported seeing Kel alive at the Yellow Springs in the land of Piedmerri. As the harshness of a Tammirring village meant little to the gentle Piedmerri-born, Kelandris had been permitted to remain at the Springs with no fear of extradition. Surrounded by the Feyborne Mountains, this region was a place of unusually potent and unpredictable *landdraw*. That is to say, the geological matrix of the area was naturally tricksterish. Protected by the seemingly random weather conditions of the mountains that surrounded the Springs, the area was a mapmaker's nightmare. Trails were known to disappear at will, and compasses sometimes spun wildly—the magnetic field of the Feyborne Mountains living up to their name. Very fey. And occasionally very sentient.

Crazy Kel stiffened abruptly. She had acute hearing and night vision—an inadvertent legacy from the holovespa. The veil obscured nothing but the plaintive beauty of Kel's face. Her senses alert, she listened intently to the sound of an approaching child. An adolescent girl, thought Kelandris. Southern Asilliwir born by the queer brogue of her accent. Crazy Kel wondered who the kid was talking to. Then she realized the answer was no one; the Asilliwir girl was talking to herself. Crazy Kel decided to stay where she was—perhaps give the girl a fright if she became too bold or inquisitive. Crazy Kel patted the double-edged knife she wore hidden in the inside sleeve of her right arm and smiled coldly.

As the girl came into full view, Crazy Kel started. The kid was not Asilliwir born at all; judging by the girl's dark hair and green eyes, she was Tammirring. Crazy Kel fingered her knife thoughtfully.

Yafatah, which was the girl's name, was fifteen and an only child. Having spent her entire life without the company of a brother or sister, Yafatah almost always talked to herself when she was alone. Especially when she was troubled about something. Like tonight.

"I be all right," she told herself with more confidence than she felt. "The dreams mean nothing. And me Ma be just worried—that be all." Yafatah lowered a leather water sack to the pool of copper-colored water at her feet. "And it doon't have nothing to do with me being Tammirring. It be just a phase. On account of me getting me bloodcycle so late and all."

Crazy Kel frowned under her veil. Had she heard the girl correctly? Bloodcycle dreams? The woman in black leaned forward, her grip on the hidden knife tightening slowly. Thoughts of Suxonli clouded her mind.

Yafatah, who was busy pouring water, did not hear the soft rustle of Crazy Kel's clothing. The young girl sighed heavily and continued trying to cheer herself up. "And I will na' go to a Jinnjirri-born healer. What do they know, them Jinnjirri? I doon't care if there be a Jinnjirri in me dreams or noo. It be *just* a dream!" she added loudly, fighting back the tears of panic in her throat. She wiped her face hastily. "And that Greatkin. That Rimble. He be noo dream-friend of mine. So what be everyone's *problem*? And Jamilla? Just because I be fond of her—of a *dread* Mayanabi Nomad—oooh, scary, scary," mocked Yafatah. "So what? Old Jamilla be a Mayanabi, *and* she be harmless. And her stories doon't be causing me nightmares. They *doon't*!"

Yafatah bit her lower lip, feeling painfully confused. She was sure the dreams would go away if her mother and the rest of the Caravan Council would just leave her alone. Responding to the darkening twilight, Yafatah's gloom deepened. Then, almost against her will, the young girl felt her mood buoyed by the relentless rush of the Yellow Springs. Brimming with the healing properties of its minerals, the water chattered happily in her ear like a good friend making jokes. Yafatah dipped her fingers in the brilliantly stained pool. She stared grumpily at the Springs, aware that their incessant murmuring made it impossible to feel completely alone. Or frightened. She shrugged, thinking that in a place like this, she was sure a person could untangle the worst of personal knots. Yafatah sighed wistfully, wishing she and her mother could tarry longer in this hidden glen. Scowling, she idly scanned the rocks directly above her. And froze.

So did Kelandris.

Yafatah, who had heard stories from her old Mayanabi friend about a crazy woman living somewhere in the vicinity of the Yellow Springs, swallowed hard. Remaining motionless, she stared at the dark mass on the ledge. Was it a person or just a trick of the twilight? The mass remained absolutely still. After staring at it for several minutes, Yafatah concluded that it must be a boulder or something. She continued filling the water sack—albeit more hastily. When she finished, she glanced back at the ledge. And yelped.

The hunched, black silhouette was gone.

Reaching for her akatikki—an Asilliwir blow-tube—Yafatah hoisted the filled water sack to her shoulder and ran in the direction of her clan's caravan camp. The water sloshed out of the sack as she stumbled down the dark mountain trial and spilled onto her red tunic and pants. She ignored the cold water, her heart pounding in her throat, her akatikki grasped firmly in her left hand. Suddenly remembering that she presently carried only mild sleep darts with her instead of her clan's more lethal hunting type—an adjustment she had made herself after one particularly emphatic dream last week—Yafatah swore softly under her breath. Would a sleep dart hold a madwoman? Especially one as tall as the old Mayanabi claimed this woman was? Yafatah scrambled over some loose rock nearly losing her footing. As she slowed to catch her balance, Yafatah heard them.

She heard wild dogs in the near distance.

Wild dogs that were downwind of her.

Chapter Three

NIGHT HAD FINALLY come to the Western Feyborne Mountains. Zendrak guided Further down the steep forest trail with the firm press of his knee against her shoulder, both rider and horse depending on each other's extreme night vision to see them through the utter dark. Brittle autumn leaves rustled overhead. Squirrels scurried along oak limbs. Acorns and twigs snapped loose and fell to the ground. Further suddenly snorted nervously, her blue-black ears turning backward and forward as she listened to the baleful howl of an approaching wild dog. She came to an abrupt standstill, her haunches trembling. At Zendrak's insistent pressure, leg against belly, she continued her descent. She sidestepped a fallen branch and snorted again, her blue-glass eyes wild with an instinctual fear of the unseen dog; there had been hunger in that howl. Zendrak patted Further's sweaty neck quietly, his touch reassuring but uncompromising. The mare jigged in place; then, prompted by Zendrak, she departed from the main trail. They travelled due west now, moving through the underbrush into a direct line of intersection with Yafatah and Crazy Kel.

Ducking a low overhang of branches, Trickster's Emissary held his left hand in front of his face, testing the air experimentally with his long fingers. He stroked the darkness deftly like a master weaver sorting threads. Then, finding the one he wanted, Trickster's Emissary smiled. In his hands, coincidence was a subtle power. And he enjoyed making use of it. Zendrak tugged the night gently.

The direction of the wind changed to east.

In a matter of moments, the starving cur on the uppermost end of the forest trail picked up a familiar scent: sweaty, fearful horse. Giving voice immediately, the dog signalled the rest of the pack that dinner was imminent. They replied with excited baying. Zendrak grabbed a handful of black mane as he felt Further prepare to bolt. Glancing over his shoulder at the snuffling lead dog, Trickster's Emissary laughed. The trap was laid. He and the mare were its camouflage; Yafatah was the bait. But Rimble's quarry? Zendrak's eyes glittered cooly. Rimble's real quarry was the last unclaimed member of his small Contrarywise Circle: Kelandris of Suxonli. Zendrak pulled his green cowl away from his face. He had waited sixteen years for this night.

Crazy Kel began humming to herself as she climbed down the steep trail that ran above the waterfall of the Springs. So the young girl was from Tammirring, she thought, testing the razor-sharpness of her knife as she walked. *And* she had bloodcycle dreams. Tricksterish ones. Kel's mind slipped into a drowning pool of mad logic, distorted and inaccurate. Tricksterish dreams could mean only one thing, decided Kelandris, the child was a Revel Wasp Queen—like she herself had been sixteen years ago. Crazy Kel stiffened, a new thought occurring to her. So, she thought nervously, the child was from Suxonli. Come to fetch Kel, no doubt. Bring her back and make her stay. For Kel must pay and pay and—

"Springs about! Pain stay out!" whispered Kelandris in sudden panic. Pain, she thought. Calm, now. Think. The knife. The girl. Yes. Do it.

Crazy Kel picked a fork in the trail that would intercept Yafatah before the young girl was in shouting distance of her caravan. As the woman in black slipped between the shadows, she suddenly slowed, her veiled head cocked to the side. She listened to the frantic, unexpected baying of the wild dogs. Crazy Kel swore. She had killed this pack's lead mastiff last week hoping the rest would panic and disperse. Apparently, they had not. Unknown to Kelandris, Zendrak controlled tonight's attack. Rimble's orders. And pleasure. Crazy Kel shrugged. So she would kill again. Yes. A thrust to the young girl's heart should do it.

Yafatah, for her part, had been casting nervous glances over her shoulder for the past five minutes. What had incited the wild dogs to such a frenzy? she wondered. They sounded as if they were very close to their quarry. She swallowed, hoping fervently that she was not it. Sweating with fear, Yafatah tried to increase her speed in the woods. But unlike Kelandris, Yafatah did not know all the twists and turns of this particular glen trail, and she missed a curve. She slipped off the gently sloping embankment, falling to her knees and dropping the water sack. Yafatah cursed her unfamiliarity with the Piedmerri terrain. She left the sack where it lay, and got to her feet.

Still holding her akatikki firmly, Yafatah groped through the dark like a blind person and climbed back on the path. She hesitated. Was it her imagination, or did the baying of those wild dogs sound quite a bit nearer? Truly panicking now, Yafatah sprinted in the direction of her clan-kin. As she rounded the corner, she slowed in confusion. What little night perception she possessed had suddenly been blanked out. She shook her head, peering intently into a large blackness not fifteen feet ahead of her. Hearing the rustle of clothing, Yafatah nearly cried with relief. Surely, here was help—a member of her clan, perhaps? Then Yafatah noticed the height of the figure and stiffened. Heart pounding, she realized Old Jamilla had not lied: the Madwoman of the Springs was real.

Yafatah bit her lip; the hungry baying of the wild dogs seemed minor in the face of this new, immediate danger. Should she shoot the woman with her akatikki? What if she wasn't truly mad? Yafatah's breathing became shallow. If she knocked out the woman with a sleep dart, then the woman would surely be dinner for the wild dogs. That would be murder. Killing four-leggeds for food was one thing. Killing a two-legged out of fear was quite another. Yafatah fingered her akatikki uneasily, And loaded it.

"So you dream of the King of Deviance, too," whispered Crazy Kel. "And do you know, my sweet, what he'll *ask* of you?"

"What?" asked Yafatah hoarsely. She stared into the pitch black, seeing absolutely nothing but darkness upon darkness. "What?" she repeated.

Crazy Kel chuckled. "He'll fuck you, and prick you, and mark you with 'C.' Then he'll put you in his oven and have you for 'T.'" Kelandris laughed uproariously. "That's 'T' for Trickster. He's the Greatkin Prickster."

"I beg your pardon?" asked Yafatah. She had been raised not to use any of "those words" with adult company. "I mean—"

"Oh no," interrupted Crazy Kel. "It's I who must beg *your* pardon. After all, I'm the one who killed you. Rue on rue."

"But—but I be not dead," said Yafatah checking the position of the sleep dart.

"Neither am I," giggled the woman in black. "But I should be. That's the law. According to shit-hole Suxonli."

Yafatah raised the akatikki to her lips, her conscience screaming at her. "I be sorry Kelandris," she whispered, the name of the woman in black suddenly occurring to her. "I do be sorry to have to do this."

Crazy Kel sniggered. "I *think* you should know that Trickster's an old fart. And what's more, I've a knife pointed at your heart."

Yafatah blanched. Her lips inches away from the mouth of the akatikki, she hesitated. Did the woman in black know she was holding a loaded blow-tube? If so, that meant that Kelandris of Suxonli could see in the dark. Yafatah shivered imperceptibly. Yafatah was good with an akatikki—very good, in fact. And at this close range, she was certain to hit the Madwoman of the Springs. However, thought the young girl, it's also possible that Kelandris of Suxonli has a way with knives. And if she throws the knife true? Yafatah took a ragged breath. Then I will be quite dead. Yafatah lowered the akatikki slowly.

"Dying," said Kelandris thoughtfully. "Dying is easy. It's living that's queasy." She positioned her knife for throwing.

"I don't understand, Kelandris—"

The woman in black chortled with new laughter. "Nobody did. So of me they got rid. I am the nameless and the formless. The spaceless and the faceless. Kelandris? Who is she? *She* is the Trickster's infernal *he*."

As Crazy Kel finished speaking, the hunting call of the wild dogs exploded around them. Simultaneously, Zendrak and Further broke through the forest underbrush. The power of the Fertile Dark surged over horse and rider, causing a blue-black charge from Neath to spark along Zendrak's green cloak. Yafatah took one look at the mare's enormous size and the absolute dark of Zendrak's eyes as they reflected in the queer blue light of Neath and screamed. Before she could bolt, Trickster's Emissary reached down and grabbed her by the waist.

This was the cusp of the season when change gusted with the wind—

Not knowing what else to do, Yafatah called to the woman in black for help. "Kelandris," she screamed, "do something—"

But Kelandris of Suxonli remained rooted to the spot, her expression unreadable under her flowing black veil.

"Please!" wept the child, struggling frantically against Zendrak's strong grip. "Kelandris—"

Trickster's Emissary smiled, then, pulling Yafatah toward him roughly, he said, "Change or be changed."

Looking into the face of the man who held her, Yafatah shrieked. His eyes had no pupils. They were as dark and reflective as obsidian. Another charge of electric blue-black light snapped and crackled over Zendrak's cloak then shot down his arms. His fingers discharged the current into Yafatah, who yelped as much from fear as from the intensity of the electrical shock. Just when she had given up hope that she would ever escape this terror, the horseman dropped her to the ground. He sped away. As Yafatah fell sideways, she heard the growling lunge of one of the wild dogs. She also heard the sound of a deft intervention.

The dog howled in agony, its throat cut.

As the cur rapidly drowned in its own blood, the rest of the pack broke cover, baying and snuffling. Yafatah heard the muffled plunge of Crazy Kel's knife once more. Another dog screamed as Crazy Kel continued to notch the night with her terrible skill. Yafatah scrambled to her feet, her akatikki in hand. There were too many dogs—even for the black-robed giant standing beside her. Yafatah squared her shoulders, and entered the snarling fray.

Waiting until one of the dogs attacked her singly again, Yafatah fit her blow-tube with two sleep darts—wishing anew that they had been marked with poison. True, the Asilliwir herbal sleep potion was potent, its effect long lasting. It was not, however, immediate. So two darts were better than one. Yafatah smiled grimly. She would use the same dose on the madwoman beside her, she decided. When this was over. And without warning. Yafatah had seen Crazy Kel's level of expertise with the knife now. She must not permit the woman to take her by surprise. If she did, Yafatah knew she would never survive the night. Hearing a growl to her left, the young girl whirled, sending her darts airborne as she did so. There was a surprised whimper and the satisfying crash of a large dog seconds later. Feeling pleased with the trueness of her aim, Yafatah reloaded her akatikki.

The woman in black swore unexpectedly. Breaking free from the queer, monotone rhyming she had used before, Kelandris said clearly, "I've been stung in the face by something." Then, feeling the unseasonable heat of a certain desert wind, Kelandris added in a more horrified voice, "Greatkin-have-mercy—don't do this to me *again*! Don't bring me your thaw. Don't bring me your thaw in autumn."

Yafatah stared at the woman in black. Kelandris had her hands stretched out in front of her—as if she were reaching for something she could not see.

"He's gone," said the fifteen-year-old girl, taking aim against another attacking dog.

"Who's gone?" asked Kelandris, her voice puzzled.

Yafatah stiffened as the truth dawned on her; Kelandris of Suxonli had not seen the man on the blue-black mare.

The wind changed.

Yafatah wrinkled her nose. What was that peculiar smell? she wondered. Horse sweat and something else. Then her eyes widened. Sniffing the sleeve of her red tunic, she realized she had the smell all over her.

Chapter Four

YAFATAH WAS NEVER certain what happened next. Everything at once, it seemed. The wild dogs of the Feyborne continued their attack, snarling and snapping at the young girl's legs. She fought them off valiantly with well aimed kicks and the sleepy sting of her darts. Crazy Kel did likewise, her knife slick with the blood of the ravenous curs. At odd moments, however, Crazy Kel also complained viciously of a growing numbness in her body—so much so that young Yafatah finally had to wonder if maybe she'd inadvertently hit the madwoman with one of her akatikki darts. Yafatah shrugged. Kelandris *had* mentioned being stung by something very shortly after she'd let the first darts fly. And there had been two in the blow-tube. Yafatah pressed her lips together. Somehow, that man on the big horse was involved in this. Somehow, she thought, sniffing the fingers of her left hand and wrinkling her nose once more. The scent wasn't bad, she decided. Just strong. However, before she could consider the' matter further, chaos erupted around her.

It seemed the calvary had arrived—in the form of ten members of her Asilliwir clan, all of them on foot, all of them carrying torches and darts. Dogs fell right and left. Sometime during the melee, Crazy Kel fled to the woods, her black clothing rendering her all but invisible in the forest shadows. Yafatah watched her leave but was distracted by her mother's glad hug. She crushed the girl to her bosom, her voice choked with the happiness at finding her only child still alive. Her mother's name was Fasilla. She was an herbalist-healer. Unlike her daughter, Fasilla was Asilliwir born; it was from Fasilla that Yafatah had received her southern brogue.

"Child, child—doon't ever frighten me like that again!"

"Well, I didna' *mean* to," replied Yafatah indignantly. She scowled. Her mother made it sound like she'd gone *looking* for the wild dogs. "They came all of a sudden, Ma—from noowhere."

Fasilla grunted with agreement. "Blast these Feyborne. It be just like them to let something fierce bad happen. They be a tricksterish range; they doon't be called Rimble's for nothing!" Fasilla spat on the ground at the thought of Greatkin Rimble and all his mischief.

"But the *Springs* do be good, Ma—"

"For the Piedmerri born, perhaps. But clearly not for the Asilliwir."

"But I can feel their good, Ma," protested Yafatah, all of her native Tammirring-born psychic senses on the defensive. "I can almost hear them talking to me, Ma. If we could stay a little while longer—"

Fasilla regarded her daughter wildly, her irritation with Yafatah's thinking evident on her tanned face. "Ya," she said fondling her daughter's dark hair roughly, "you do be almost *killed* out here. Have you noo thought for your own safety?"

Yafatah stared at the ground. "I just wanted to listen to the Yellow Springs, Ma. I thought they might talk to me about me dreams. That be all."

Fasilla turned Yafatah toward the caravan park and smiled. "Never you mind. We'll see to what ails you come the morning."

"We will?" asked Yafatah, her expression dubious.

Fasilla nodded. "We do be leaving at dawn for Jinnjirri country. For that dream doctor I do be telling you about."

Yafatah said nothing, her green eyes angry and trapped.

Dinner with a southern Asilliwir clan was traditionally a rowdy affair, the meal ending with dancing and musical accompaniment. As Yafatah picked at the remains of sweet beans and jerky on her plate, a few of her adoptive landkin scrambled to their feet and beckoned to her to join them in a fast moving circle dance of all women. Yafatah declined their invitation with a shake of her head. Drums and flutes soon trilled the night with a lively melody. Feeling miserable, Yafatah put her plate aside. She was about to get up and head off to bed when one of the younger clan children grabbed her sleeve and offered the older girl a piece of fresh fruit for dessert.

"Pommins?" asked Yafatah in wonder. "Where did we be getting these? I thought they be long out of season."

"While *you* were being dog meat," replied the child, "we had visitors. One was a caravan out of Speakinghast. Seems you can get *any*thing in a city as large as that," added the twelve-year-old. "Here—take it." She grinned, exposing a hole in her front teeth—one she'd recently acquired in a fist fight with an older brother. "I've had three. One more pommin, and I'll puke." Her name was Cass, and she was from northern Asilliwir, a region known for blunt speech.

Yafatah accepted the proffered fruit greedily. Pommins were her favorite food. Colored like a peach but having the tough skin of an orange, the pommin was an eastern delicacy. Yafatah peeled the skin slowly, exposing the sweet, golden meat of the fruit. She bit into it, wincing in preparation for the tangy burst to come. Scarlet, jewel-like seeds exploded in her mouth, their juice slipping over her lips. Yafatah's eyes danced.

"It do be ripe!" she cried with delight.

Cass put her hands on her hips, her blue eyes annoyed. "What?

Give you a *green* pommin? What kind of friend do you think I am?"

"Mmmm," said Yafatah, nodding her head and taking another large bite. At her passion (and the pommin) got smaller, it suddenly occurred to Yafatah that Cass had not told her who the other visitor to camp had been. She inquired between mouthfuls, wiping her lips with her tunic sleeve.

Cass looked uneasy. "I won't tell."

Yafatah shrugged. "Why?" she asked, her expression puzzled.

"It'll only make you pissy, Ya. And you've been pissy a lot lately."

Yafatah's cheeks flushed. "Thanks. That do be a fine thing to say."

Cass swore. "Your *Ma* said for me to keep my lip closed. I'm just doing what *she* asked me to do, so don't get sore with *me*, Ya. It's not *my* fault."

Yafatah nibbled at the empty peel of the pommin, her expression thoughtful. "It was old Jamilla, wasna' it?"

Cass's jaw dropped. "How in Neath did you figure that out?"

"Easy," said Yafatah in disgust. "Ma forbade me to talk to the old woman this morning. She said she'd tell Jammy off, too, if she ever saw her again." Yafatah sighed sadly. "That do be a terrible thing Ma did. Jammy was me friend."

My only real friend, thought Yafatah in silence.

Cass rolled her eyes, her face contemptuous. The hardness of her mouth expressed all the prejudice her kin felt toward Jamilla's kind, the Mayanabi Nomads. "Why are you *so* loyal to that stupid, old bagwoman?"

"Jammy doon't be a bagwoman!"

"Well, she *wears* nothing but *rags*, Ya. And she smells—"

Yafatah jumped to her feet unexpectedly, sending the pommin peel flying. Old Jamilla *did* smell, she thought in astonishment. And it was a smell a little like that of the dark horseman! Jammy. She had to find Jammy. *She* would understand what Yafatah had seen out in the woods. And she would believe her, too. Not like Ma before dinner, thought Yafatah angrily.

An hour earlier, when Yafatah had tried to tell her mother about the woman in black and the electric-blue charge of the horseman, her mother's face had gotten her "worried look." Then Fasilla had changed the subject, pulling Yafatah into a discussion about their dawn departure for the land of Jinnjirri. In no time Yafatah's waking nightmare had become lost in a mass of details: what provisions they would need, which harness they would use on the pair of gray geldings that drew their wagon, the condition of the horses' shoes versus the condition of the roads they'd be travelling. Yafatah had tried to bring the topic of conversation back to the woman with the knife, but Fasilla prevented her. Yafatah fell into a sullen silence at this point and had refused to speak to her mother for the remainder of the evening. Fasilla, for her part, had put her daughter's ill humor down to sleeplessness and the trauma of having nearly been eaten by a pack of wild dogs. If Yafatah needed to make up stories in order to make herself feel better—make herself look braver—then Fasilla would permit it just this once. After the child saw the Jinnjirri healer, however, all this fanciful fibbing would have to stop. Fasilla, like her daughter, was a very honest person. She was also, like her daughter, very opinionated on certain subjects. Lying was one of them. Truthtelling took courage—said Fasilla on more than one occasion—and, by Presence, she'd raised her child to *have* such courage. Until tonight, Yafatah had never let her down. Fasilla was certain that Yafatah would stop the lying once she felt safe again. Her mother's conclusions had been obvious to Yafatah at the time. And it had made the young girl feel even more isolated than before.

"In which direction did Jammy be going?" asked Yafatah.

Cass bit her lip. "Your Ma wouldn't like it if I told you."

"Yeah? Well, I willna' like *you* if you doon't tell me!"

Cass lowered her eyes. "You're so mean now, Ya. You never used to be this way. Ever since your blood—"

"I canna *help* it, Cass! I canna help it if I doon't be the person I *was*. Why doon't you see that?" she asked tearfully. Choking on the words, Yafatah added, "Jammy do be the only one who lets me be different. The only one."

Moved by Yafatah's desperation, Cass relented. "Okay. Okay. Jamilla went east. The old Mayanabi went east. Into those woods there," she added pointing a helpful finger. "But she was cursing, Ya. She was cursing the whole clan." Cass shrugged uneasily. "You best be careful—she might put the evil eye on you, Ya. And she could do it, too."

Cass was making reference to the fact that Jamilla had pied eyes.

"She just be blind in one of them," replied Yafatah. "That be *all*." Then thanking the younger girl with a hasty squeeze on the arm, Yafatah took off at a run, heading into the dark forest.

"Jammy," she whispered as she fought for a path among the brambles, "please let me find you. Please."

But this was not to be.

Not tonight.

Chapter Five

WHILE YAFATAH SCRAMBLED through the underbrush in the foot-hills of the Feyborne, Trickster's Emissary dismounted from his mare not six hundred feet from where the young girl travelled. Giving Further her freedom, Zendrak patted the blue-black mare softly on the rump and began to climb the trail that ran above the Springs. Further walked away slowly, her head close to the ground, nibbling contentedly on fallen leaves.

Zendrak was in a terrible mood. Crazy Kel was the only woman he had ever truly loved in all the years of his unusually long life. Seeing her again tonight after their sixteen-year separation had stirred feelings he had forgotten about. Passions denied. This was suffering seemingly without end—for both of them. Gritting his teeth, Zendrak continued climbing.

As Zendrak reached Crazy Kel's favorite ledge—one that afforded a good view of the Springs themselves and of the caravans that camped in the vale below—Zendrak heard some-one's throat clear. Taking a deep breath, Zendrak bowed slightly to the small figure already squatting on the limestone outcrop. The figure grunted, stroking his black goatee.

"You're late, Zen-boy," said Trickster.

Trickster's Emissary snorted. "I've had a lot to do tonight, Rimble. As per *your* orders, I might add."

Trickster grinned in the darkness. "That's what I like about you, Zendrak. You're never afraid of earning my displeasure. Most mortals—"

"And I am not most mortals," said Zendrak tiredly. "As you well know."

Greatkin Rimble chuckled merrily. "Are you still holding *that* grudge?"

"My kind have a long memory," replied Zendrak, his voice cool.

"Hoo-hoo," said Trickster, rubbing his chin. "I can see what kind of talk *this* is going to be."

"Short," said Zendrak. "I've been riding since dawn. And I must still cover the three hundred miles to Speakinghast before ten bell-eve."

Trickster giggled. "Ah, lovely Speakinghast. The eastern culture-capital of all Mnemlith. *And* Civilization's pride." He leaned forward. "What a time we'll have there, eh, Zen-boy?"

Zendrak said nothing, his expression unreadable. Finally, Trickster's Emissary spoke. "I hope the time in Speakinghast goes more smoothly than the one in Suxonli, Rimble. I truly hope so," he added, an edge to his voice.

"You threatening me?" asked Greatkin Rimble, inclining his head.

"No," replied Zendrak. "But I *am* warning you. Mortals, you see, take a dim view of gods who make mistakes. Makes them very nervous."

"Well, I'm not a god. Ask Jinndaven, he'll tell you straight out. And since I'm not a god, I don't see what business it is of the mortals if I make mistakes or not. Besides, there's no such thing as a mistake. There's only exploration. Admittedly, *some* ideas are better than others."

Zendrak's black eyes blazed with anger. "You should've known that before Suxonli! Before you hurt Kelandris like that!"

Rimble jumped to his feet, genuinely annoyed now. "You dare blame *me* for what happened in Suxonli? Let me tell you something, Zen-boy—*I* am not responsible for what the villagers of Suxonli did to Kelandris. The Trickster's *he* was prophesied. The villagers didn't recognize the *he*—or train her. And we both know why." He grunted. "Physical reality is so clumsy sometimes."

"Kel has a multiple personality, Rimble! That's more than clumsy!"

Trickster smiled. "Yes, well. Makes Kel a regular chip off the old block, doesn't it? Relatively speaking, of course. But you wouldn't know anything about that, would you?" He chuckled. "*Much*. Oh, cheer up. At least she's alive. That *did* take some doing. On both our parts." When Zendrak said nothing, Trickster added, "Sometimes, my friend, madness is the best possible solution for certain kinds of pain, Kelandris does matter to me, you know."

"Nobody matters to you, Rimble," he retorted. "Nobody but you."

Trickster sighed and changed the subject. "About the other Tammirring girl. The one called Yafatah—"

But Zendrak would not be put off. "My kind, Rimble—we mate for life. Can you imagine that?" he asked bitterly. "Or do you need Jinndaven to imagine it for you?"

Trickster's smile turned sly. He had Zendrak exactly where he wanted him.

Zendrak paced. "Do you understand, there can be no one *but* Kel for me?"

"Good," replied Trickster calmly and returned to the previous subject. "About Yafatah—"

"What about her!" yelled Zendrak, his voice shaking with the rage of sixteen lost years.

Trickster shrugged. "I was wondering if you'd figured out who Yafatah is yet? She has a very definite role in all this, you know."

"I'm hardly in a mood for riddles, Rimble."

"A pity," replied Trickster. "Self-pity, in particular. It can be so boring. Mortals seem *terribly* prone to it. Eh, Zen-boy?"

Zendrak swore. Trickster had manipulated him into an emotional corner. *And* managed to indirectly accuse him of indulging in self-pity. Zendrak ran his fingers through his hair, his expression ragged. "Okay, Rimble, you got me. So who is Yafatah? She's not one of your Contrarywise Nine."

"True," replied Rimble jovially. "Yafatah is something a little bit different. Zendrak is one of the Nine. She's my Crossroads Child."

"Your what?"

"My loophole. My Suxonli loophole," he added firmly. Then Trickster smiled. "She's a gift, you see. A bit of unexpected grace. You must treat her well, Zen-boy. She's important, I think."

"You *think*? I thought you said she had a definite role to play."

Trickster chuckled softly. "Do you think I control the Presence, then? Do you think I dictate policy to Great Being? Decide the outcome of all things before they happen? What's the exploration in that? *I* don't know Yafatah's final destiny. How could I? That's something she must discover for herself. But in the meantime—"

"You'll just help her along?" asked Zendrak sarcastically.

Trickster smiled. "I'll give her a nudge."

"In which direction?"

"Speakinghast."

There was dead silence. "Speakinghast?" said Zendrak in amazement. "Why there?"

Trickster grinned, looking up at the six-feet-six man towering above him. "Because," said Trickster playfully, "I'm *bigger* than you are, and I say so. Will that do?"

Zendrak scowled.

Trickster clucked his tongue in disapproval. "*Such* an insolent man. I swear, I don't know where you get it from. Must be the company you keep."

"Must be," replied Zendrak sourly.

Trickster got to his feet. "Well, you'd better be off soon. You've got trouble of your own to cause tonight."

"Thanks to you."

Trickster shook his head. "Where's your enthusiasm, Zenboy?"

"Suxonli killed it."

"Well, then," replied Trickster, patting the tall man on the hand, "we'll just have to remedy that, won't we? We'll just have to inspire you." Trickster cocked his head to the side and began speaking in a queer, singsong voice, images of change falling from his lips as easily as the copper-colored Yellow Springs fell to the pool below. "Shifttime," said Trickster softly. "Jinnaeon. The white water of time. Those maddened, careening years that mark the Age of Transition. *Shifttime*. Trickster's Folly. When good and evil do a jolly two-step across the same dance floor." Rimble giggled. "And no one can tell them apart. No one except my Nine. The world sleeps, you see. And it's left its backdoor open. Enter Trickster, his yellow coattails flying, his pied eyes flashing.

"Welcome," Rimble continued more forcibly, "welcome riptide at the money-jugular. See the rich scramble? They hear the long scream a-coming and panic. And the poor? The poor learn once again that charity is but a carnival show—a freak phenomenon just passing through. But Greatkin Rimble doesn't care. He strips one and all just the same. *Change or be changed*, he says. But no one listens. So Trickster dances his reel. And he dances real hard.

"Weather goes wild! Summer masquerades as autumn. Lightning bites forest and prairie. Silent mountains heave their guts skyward and blast the land with snowy ash. Rivers gorge, and mud swallows what is precious. Or so it seems." Rimble rubbed his hands together with glee. "Keen! Keen now for civilization. Someone chortles, Zendrak. Who dares? It is the other. It is the reveller, the shrieker in the street. It is the one who must go farther. And farther still. Speakinghast, Zendrak."

The mare's ears flicked backward. Her pace never faltered as she turned east toward the country of Saämbolin. The thrum of her hooves, the beat of his heart, and it was on to proud Speakinghast.

Trickster's turning point.

Chapter Six

IN MNEMLITH, RACE, culture and country were synonymous; such was the impact of *landdraw*. In Mnemlith, land was alive and its *draw*—its regional character—determined a person's hereditary and psychological composition. It also determined the responsiveness of soul to things like the Greatkin. Physical conception was therefore a three-way affair: mother, father, and *landdraw*.

Boundaries between countries were always reckoned by nature—never by politics. Pregnant women were careful not to cross *landdraw* borders inadvertently. To do so would cause immediate miscarriage. The Power of Place formed a more potent umbilical cord with an unborn child than the usual one of flesh and blood. *Draw* was the dominant factor. In utero, a child built its bones and tissue not only from its parents' genes but also from the geological matrix surrounding it at conception. One child might emerge with a personality reflecting the icy remoteness of a nearby mountain range. Another might reflect the placid bounty of a fertile river valley. Furthermore, *draw* made it possible for two Saämbolin-born parents to give birth to a Jinnjirri—provided the mother remained in the country of conception—in this case, Jinnjirri. In certain terms, *landdraw* could be defined as a responsive geological intelligence.

Saämbolin, the country in which Speakinghast resided, tended to produce a native population inherently tidy and emotionally precise. Thus, the landrace of this region—also called Saämbolin—boasted some of Mnemlith's most capable lawmakers, scholars, and administrators among its number. The City of

Speakinghast itself was contained on the east by the vast blue-gray shoreline of one of Saämbolin's great lakes: Lake Edu. Situated in a geologically striated area of the world, the *landdraw* of Speakinghast added a love of organization and systems to the landgift of its people. The residents of the city ran their affairs efficiently and fairly. At least, that's how the Saämbolin saw it.

The Jinnjirri born, however, disagreed.

It was only "natural" that the Jinnjirri should feel this way about their conservative *landdraw* neighbors; the native Jinnjirri came from a country famous for passionate, erratic weather, and geographically shifting borders caused by unstable fault lines. They were Mnemlith's iconoclasts.

In Jinnjirri opinion, the pursuit of permanence and rigid explanations of how the world worked were a waste of time. Not to mention psychologically killing—for them. The Jinnjirri believed that all structures would eventually collapse. Ideas must break ground or be tossed like outgrown hand-me-downs. This was a visionary people, and improvisation was their rule. Often the Jinnjirri were also dissident. Inveterate challengers and debunkers of tradition, this landrace created a naturally occurring counterculture wherever they settled.

The Jinnjirri of Speakinghast were unusually vocal. Saämbolin *landdraw* experts agreed that this unruly civilian population was probably reacting to the ordered, layered bedrock that sat under the city's paved streets and open canals. Their bohemian politics barely tolerated by the slow moving and somewhat reactionary Saämbolin Guild, the Jinnjirri of Speakinghast regularly flouted what rules they could, practicing what they termed "intentional irritation"—for the good of the Guild's soul, of course. Taking their kind natured but merciless crusade for reform one step farther, the Jinnjirri of Speakinghast opened their doors to the city—offering an unconditional sanctuary to the eccentrics of *all* Mnemlith's six landraces. Much to the Guild's dismay, the city took the Jinnjirri offer seriously. In no time at all, the Jinnjirri Quarter attracted a farrago of Speakinghast's most seasoned intellectual and artistic renegades. Cafes regularly opened their doors after hours to the creative and transient. One establishment went even farther.

It housed them.

The Kaleidicopia Boarding House was a three-storey architectural hodgepodge of odd angles and asymmetrical additions. The improvised design was typical of this quadrant of the city and was considered brilliant by the Jinnjirri architects of the day. The Saämbolin Housing Commission, however, logged the Kaleidicopia as "an architectural nightmare" in their books. Crowned by six spires, three domes, a nonagonal diamond-paned cupola, one gothic tower, four brownstone chimneys, and a tri-colored slate roof (green, hot pink, and lavender-blue), the Kaleidicopia caused all passersby to gape. Regardless of *landdraw*.

Known as the "K" by the eight people who currently lived there, the house was the architectural wonderchild of one Barlimo of Whimsiian Sane. A creative genius of modest means, Barlimo was a Jinnjirri of extraordinary cross-cultural tolerance. She collected the rents when her tenants had the money, and she ran the "K" with a loving, but firm hand. Since it was her house—as far as anyone knew—Barlimo also presided over every house meeting. Even the emergency ones. Like tonight's, for example.

The bells of the Great Library of Speakinghast tolled the hour: exactly ten bell-eve. At present, fifty-year-old Barlimo stood in the large kitchen of the Kaleidicopia. A wooden spoon in her left hand, she stirred the meat and vegetable stew in the cauldron that hung in the kitchen's fireplace. She had seasoned the stew heavily with imported Asilliwir curries. The scent had escaped the room and spread throughout the entire house—despite the closed swinging door that led into the Kaleidicopia's common room. Barlimo sniffed her late dinner happily. As she did so, the door behind her swung to and fro. She turned around to see who had joined her. It was Timmer, a blonde jazz musician from the land of Dunnsung. Her long hair hung in a thick braid down the middle of her slender back. Dressed in the aquas of the sea water that made a peninsula of her native land, she was a strikingly lovely young woman of twenty-three.

"Here's the rent, Barl," said Timmer, handing a roll of Speakinghast Guildtender to the Jinnjirri. Barlimo stuffed it in the oversize pockets of her raggle-taggle garb. Timmer sniffed the stew. "What is it?" she asked, clearly offended by the strength of Barlimo's choice of spices.

Barlimo shrugged. "A little of this, a little of that."

Timmer leaned against the counter next to the sink. "Typical Jinnjirri response," she commented matter-of-factly. She eyed the stew. "So how come you're eating late? I thought we were supposed to be having an emergency house meeting tonight. That's what the *note* said on the other side," she added nodding in the direction of the swinging door.

"We're having one," replied Barlimo. "Soon as Doogat gets here."

"*Doogat*," protested Timmer. "Doogat doesn't even live here, Barl. Why in the world does he need to attend one of our house meetings?"

"Don't whine. It's most unbecoming," said Barlimo, crossing the room and fetching more curry. She winked at Timmer, who was watching her with an appalled expression, and dumped the remaining third of the bottle in the bubbling stew. "You don't like Doogat very much, do you?" she asked, continuing to stir her dinner.

Timmer sneezed. "Ugh—my allergies don't like your *cooking*, Barl." The red-nosed blonde pulled out a crumpled handkerchief, adding, "What's to like about Doogat? He's Mayanabi. Same as Po. Ain't *neither* of them got class."

"Exactly," said Po, coming into the kitchen on the tail end of the conversation. "Mayanabi ain't got no class, 'cause Mayanabi don't need it. Not like *some* people we know," he added, referring to her love of fad and fashion.

Timmer's brown eyes blazed. "Shut up, you!"

Po glanced inquiringly at the Jinnjirri who was still calmly stirring her dinner. "Don't tell me, Barl—it's pick on Po night again."

Barlimo tasted her stew. Just about right, she decided, the hot spice terrorizing the front of her tongue. "'Fraid so, Po. Seems you've climbed to the top of everyone's Terrible Person list." She gave him a defeated smile. "Again," she added.

Po, who was a Northern Asilliwir and typically blunt of speech, muttered, "Goddamned asshole house." He looked up. "What for this time? Rent?"

"*Dishes!*" shouted Timmer, glaring at the short, five-feet-no-inch man.

Po crossed his arms over his chest, giving the musician a bored smile. Po—Podiddley of Brindlsi by birth—was an infuriating little fellow even on his good days. A slob by inclination and a criminal by profession, thirty-eight-year-old Po had not been a welcome addition to the Kaleidicopia. The fact that he was also a Mayanabi Nomad had endeared him to some but horrified others—like Timmer. She detested fanatics. Especially religious ones.

"And while we're at it," continued the Dunnsung musician

hotly, "where *is* your rent? Surely you make enough with your street thieving to pay poor Barlimo her due."

"That's *my* business, Timmertandi," Barlimo interrupted cooly. "The financial arrangements I make with each member of this house are private. Understood?"

Po gave Timmer a smug smile.

Barlimo wagged a finger in Po's face. "Don't goad. Otherwise Doogat'll find occasion to box your ears again. And Doogat's arriving any minute."

Po frowned. "Doogat?"

It was Timmer's turn to give Po a smug know-it-all-smile. "Yes, Po—Doogat's coming to the house meeting. In fact, according to Barl, we can't start it without him. Isn't that interesting? *I* find it interesting—"

Podiddley ignored Timmer's jabs, and crossed the room to where Barlimo stood cooking. "Doogat's coming to the *house meeting*? Since when?" he demanded, his blue eyes anxious.

Barlimo grunted, inclining her head at Timmer. "Since a few members of this house took it upon themselves to have you thrown out by the month's end. They had a little vote, you see. Behind closed doors." Barlimo threw a fresh clove of cut garlic into the stew. "It was done quite without my knowledge."

"Or sanction?" said Timmer accusingly, her expression one of utter frustration and disbelief.

Barlimo sighed. It was moments like this that caused Barlimo to privately curse Trickster's Emissary, for it was moments like this that made her wish she'd never agreed to build a house for Rimble's contraries. Much less collect *rent* from them, she thought tiredly. During the past three years, it had been Barlimo's unrewarded task to keep Trickster's Own functioning as an intentional family—without telling them that's what they were. All for the love of a deviant Greatkin, she mused. None save she knew the Kaleidicopia's real purpose. As a result, the rest of the house members wondered daily why honest, hard-working Barlimo didn't toss the little thief out in the street—or into debtor's prison. After all, the little Asilliwir owed her six months' back rent. There was also the matter of Po's bad attitude toward his portion of the household chores. And so on.

Barlimo lifted the steaming, black cauldron out of the fire easily, her strong muscles flexing as she did so. She set the cauldron on an iron rack to cool. Selecting a wooden bowl from one of the kitchen cupboards, Barlimo served herself some curried stew. As she did so, she spoke to Timmer. "Podiddley has as much right to live here as you do, girl. I realize Po's habits of cleanliness and integrity fall far below your own—"

"*And* the house's," retorted Timmer defensively.

"And the house's," agreed Barlimo. "Nonetheless, Timmer, I think you should remember just how destitute you were when you arrived here last winter. You were between jobs and pulling the starving artist routine—"

"I *was* starving!" replied the musician indignantly.

Barlimo smiled. "Then be a bit more charitable, won't you? Like we were to you?"

Timmer scowled at Barlimo and lowered her eyes.

Barlimo pursed her lips. Guilt, she thought drily. Works every time.

Po said nothing, turning his back on both women to stare moodily into the kitchen hearth. The flames crackled as charred wood tumbled gently into a bed of deep ash. "*Is* that why Doogat's coming?" he asked finally. "To reprimand me about the dishes?"

"Who knows why Doogat does what he does, Po?" she replied. "I certainly don't." She shrugged. "He's a Mayanabi Master."

"Yeah," snapped the little thief, "mine."

"So?" asked the Jinnjirri, blowing a cool breath on her steaming dinner.

"So that's a fucking low trick, Barl. You know damned well if Doogat gets it into his head that I'm being disrespectful to the house—or to you in particular," he added, nodding at the colorfully dressed Jinnjirri, "by night's end he'll have me washing *his* dishes, too." Po paused. "Ever *been* to his tobacco shop, Barl? A good housekeeper he's not."

Barlimo smiled.

Timmer sniggered. "I think I'll ask Doogat to take you with him when he leaves. We'll call it Remedial Dishwashing."

Po whirled around, his face furious. "You do that, and I'll smack your mouth!"

Barlimo slammed her wooden spoon against the counter, making both Po and Timmer jump. "We'll have none of that in this house! Do you understand? No physical violence! Clear?" When neither Po nor Timmer answered her, the Jinnjirri stepped between them, slipping her powerful arms around their waists. "Act like children, and I'll treat you like children. Neither of you is too old to be sent to bed without dinner. Translated—you lose your kitchen privileges for a week. And I keep the key to the pantry."

"With the way you've stunk up the kitchen," muttered Timmer, "who'd *want* to cook anything in here!"

The swinging door opened, ushering in an immaculately dressed, dark-skinned, seventy-year-old man. His name was Rowenaster. He was a renowned professor of religious antiquities at the University of Speakinghast. A scholar of impeccable standards, Rowenaster's area of emphasis was Greatkin Rimble. An odd choice for a tidy-minded Saämbolin professor. And everyone on campus knew it. Rowenaster sniffed the air appreciatively.

"What smells so delicious?"

Barlimo grinned. "Finally—someone with taste. Want some?"

"I'd be *delighted* to share in your repast," said the professor gallantly. "How many bowls shall I fetch?" he asked, giving Po and Timmer an inquiring glance each. Po shrugged a "yes." He could take or leave Asilliwir curries. He grew up on them. Timmer, however, sneezed, made a disagreeable face, and fled the room. Rowenaster watched her leave, his expression amused.

"For someone so concerned with what's trendy in town, you'd think she'd display better manners. This *is* Saämbolin territory. The very bedrock of all things civilized."

"Ain't got no class," remarked Po, taking his bowl of curry in his hands and also leaving the kitchen. Barlimo slumped against the counter. Then, without warning Rowenaster, she removed the scarf she wore on her head. A fine spray of Jinnjirri hair fell to her square shoulders. Its shade was mottled red.

Rowenaster stared at Barlimo's hair color in surprise. "What in Neath has made you so angry, Barl?" he asked, watching the Jinnjirri's shifty-tempered locks darken to a burnt scarlet in perfect emotional mimicry of her frustration with the denizens of the Kaleidicopia.

"Same old things, Rowen. Same old things," she repeated, her hair now streaking with depression blue.

In a state of deep meditational creativity, Jinnjirri hair shone a milky opalescent with hints of fiery color from the full light spectrum in each strand. Since the Jinnjirri born hailed from a land of shifting topographical and climatic patterns, Jinnjirri hair naturally changed color with their moods. The process was so completely involuntary and emotionally revealing that the Jinnjirri often wore hats to protect their privacy. Fortunately for the Jinnjirri, their smooth faces were devoid of facial hair of any kind—including eyebrows and eyelashes. Even so, the hatters of Speakinghast enjoyed a booming business, their fashions so imaginative that even members of other landraces were tempted to purchase or barter for them. In any event, a Jinnjirri's removal of his or her hat indicated that the Jinnjirri was willing to risk a fairly high level of emotional vulnerability.

Rowenaster inclined his gray head, clearly honored by Barlimo's unhatting gesture. He ate his stew in silence, waiting for the fifty-year-old architect to speak her mind.

Barlimo took a bite of her own stew, savoring the strong taste of garlic in the meat. Finally she raised her eyes to meet Rowen's. She shrugged and said, "The Saämbolin Housing Commission is sniffing around again. Got more building codes specs today in the mail. We meet none of their requirements, of course. What Jinnjirri house does?"

Rowenaster nodded, his expression thoughtful behind his silver bifocals. "It's an election year, dear heart. And Gadorian's pushing for a second term in office."

"He's going to lose the Jinnjirri vote," retorted Barlimo.

"What does he care?" asked the professor mildly. "Your *draw* makes up a negligible portion of the city population. He's after bigger stakes: the wealthy Saämbolin administrators on University Hill."

"And to think I voted for Guildmaster Gadorian," grumbled Barlimo.

"His wife's nice," remarked the professor. "And I have some pull with her, Barlimo. Perhaps I could speak to her about the Housing Commission. Master Curator Sirrefene owes me quite a few favors," he added, "including passing a certain struggling student some twenty years ago when I had him in my Greatkin Survey class. Made it possible for them to get married."

"Gadorian was your student?"

Rowenaster nodded. "Does seem impossible that our present tyrannical Guildmaster could ever have been a struggling student, doesn't it?"

"Prince of the City," snorted the Jinnjirri derisively. "Where *does* he come up with these ideas?"

"Academic aristocracy is making a comeback on the Hill," said Rowenaster. "It's very trendy," he added with a smile. "Better watch out or we'll have Timmertandi expecting us to kiss her hand when she walks in the room. Students rule, you know."

"Not in *this* house," retorted Barlimo. "This is a pure dictatorship. Mine," she added with a twinkle in her eye.

Rowenaster surveyed the Jinnjirri's hair; it was turning a light shade of good-humored yellow. "That's better," he said.

The door to the kitchen swung toward them. A brown-haired, round-faced girl of nineteen walked into the room. Her movements were timid, her posture poor and lacking a spirit of self-assurance. She was the youngest and newest member of the Kaleidicopia. Her name was Mab, and she was Piedmerri born.

"I'm sorry to disturb you both," said Mab so softly that Barlimo had to strain to catch the words.

The professor smiled warmly at the plump girl. Her *landdraw* was one of natural generosity; thus the people of this race tended to have bodies that reflected this quality. Mab started suddenly when she realized that Barlimo wasn't wearing her scarf.

"Um—maybe this isn't such a good time—" she began.

Barlimo chuckled. "Don't be a goose, Mab. If you're going to live in the Jinnjirri Quarter of the city, you're going to *have* to get used to seeing unhatted Jinnjirri."

"Yes, ma'am," she replied dutifully, her cheeks coloring with embarrassment.

Barlimo shook her head imperceptibly. She still had her doubts that Mabinhil of Matterwise would survive her stay at the Kaleidicopia. Other members of the "K"—Rowenaster included—had taken one look at the girl's innate wholesomeness and predicted she'd last no more than her trial two weeks. But Mab had surprised them all. She had not only passed the mandatory two-week "you-look-us-over-we-look-you-over" period without a snag, she was also the one person who not only paid her rent on time, but also managed to do her own chore load and often part of someone else's. As a result, Mab had endeared herself to all concerned—except Barlimo. Barlimo found Mab's goodness stifling. And manipulative.

"So what can we do for you, Mab?" asked the professor kindly.

"I thought—I mean, isn't there supposed to be a house meeting tonight?"

"When Doogat gets here," replied Barlimo, taking another bite of stew.

Mab's smile caved in.

So Doogat frightens you, thought Barlimo. So does everything else, it seems. The Jinnjirri rolled her eyes and concentrated on her dinner.

Professor Rowenaster regarded Barlimo with interest. "What brings Master Doogat to one of our house meetings, Barl? They're hardly Doogat's usual fare. Besides, this one is bound to be ill-tempered."

"It is?" asked Mab nervously.

"Po's the topic of discussion," said Barlimo. "And I think you know why, Mab. That was some meeting you organized."

Rowenaster stared at the cherubic-faced Piedmerri. "*Mab* called the secret meeting? I don't believe it," he said, genuinely astounded.

"People are just *full* of surprises in this house, Rowen," replied the Jinnjirri, her expression unreadable.

"Yes," said the professor. "I guess *so*." Then he asked, "Is it my imagination, or is everyone edgy tonight?"

"Edgy?" asked Mab with increased uneasiness. She twisted a piece of her shoulder length hair around one of her fingers. "What do you mean?"

The professor shrugged. "Timmer's out of sorts due to a flare up of her allergies; earlier this evening I heard Tree yelling down in the lab before he went off to do the effects for the Merry Pricksters, and Po seems more than a little unhappy that Doogat is coming for a visit."

"Tree was yelling?" asked Mab in surprise. Treesonovohn of Shroomz was a Jinnjirri. He was also the makeup and special effects artist for an all Jinnjirri troupe of actors on the far side of the Jinnjirri Quarter of the city. Tree was usually a very even-tempered soul, his hair remaining a constant green. He also happened to be sweet on Mab, and Mab knew it.

"He got a shipment of damaged furs and soggy flash powders in from the north today," said Barlimo. "They were needed for the Prickster's new play. *Rimble's Remedy*, I think it's called."

Mab smiled broadly. "The one that Cobeth's in?"

"Yes," replied Barlimo, not sharing the girl's enthusiasm.

Rowenaster took a deep breath, turning to Barlimo. "I'll be glad when that little bastard, Cobeth, is finally out of here."

Mab stared at Rowenaster, her expression puzzled. "Did I say something wrong?" she asked. "About Cobeth, I mean?"

"No, no, child," replied the professor hastily. "I was just expressing a personal opinion. Pay it no mind. Cobeth and I go back about ten years. I had him in my Survey class."

Mab bit her lower lip. She was in the professor's celebrated class this term. Mid-term examinations had been handed in three days ago. Mab was dying to know if Rowenaster had corrected her paper yet. She suspected she had done quite well on it. As usual. Mab smiled timidly at the old man. "Um—did you—I mean, have you—"

"The exams are in the next room," said the Professor. "I know I've done Tree's. I can't remember if I've done yours or not," he added with an apologetic smile.

Mab's face paled. "You don't remember—"

"Mab, Mab—you always do this to yourself. Don't *always* assume the worst. Me not remembering could mean any number of things," continued the professor. He chuckled, winking at Barlimo. "Could mean I'm senile."

"That'll be the day," replied Barlimo. "You Saämbolin are notorious for growing old brilliantly."

Rowenaster grinned. "In any event, Mab—you know you're a good student. You haven't made less than one hundred percent the whole term. So relax. And if it'll make you feel better, I'll correct your examination next."

"During the house meeting?" said Mab dubiously.

Rowenaster grunted. "She thinks I can't do two things at once."

"Oh, no, sir—" said Mab hastily, looking so alarmed that both Barlimo and Rowenaster wondered if the little Piedmerri was going to burst into tears.

"Mab," said Barlimo with genuine concern, "he was making a *joke*. Come on, child—lighten up."

Mab blinked, then apparently perceiving Barlimo's comment as a rebuke, she burst into tears and left the kitchen.

Barlimo watched the door swing to and fro in stunned silence. "Did that just happen?" she asked the professor.

Rowenaster took a deep breath. "Someone's hurt that child. And not just once either." He poured himself a glass of water from the tap in the sink. "Know anything about her family background?"

"Mab paints a peculiar, but overall pleasant picture of her folks. Artists of some kind. Bohemian Jinnjirri." Barlimo smiled wryly. "You know the type."

Rowenaster sighed. "Speaking of such creatures—are Janusin and Cobeth coming to this house meeting?"

Barlimo pursed her lips. "Probably just Janusin. He and Cobeth have been going at each other's throats all day in the studio. You know how we Jinnjirri are when we breakup—big floor show. Includes everyone, you know. I'll be surprised if we get through the meeting without *some* reference to their scuttled relationship."

"But no Jinnjirri emotional fireworks, I pray."

Barlimo shrugged. "Well, Jan and Cobeth *are* both sculptors. I suppose there's no telling what could go flying—hammers, chisels, or tempers."

The professor smiled grimly. "Never a dull moment at the Kaleidicopia."

Barlimo nodded at the swinging door and the commons room that lay just beyond it. "Shall we enter the maelstrom?"

"By all means," said the professor, picking up his bowl of curry and following Barlimo into the next room.

Podiddley looked up as the two entered. "Hey, professor," he said with a pleased expression, "you put my question on the exam." The little thief nodded at the pile of neatly stacked papers by the oil lamp on the far wall.

"You're not supposed to be thumbing through those, Po," said Rowenaster with an annoyed frown.

"That's what *I* told him," commented Timmer. She was sitting by the roaring hearth of the commons room, rebraiding her hair. "He's a little light-fingered louse!"

"I didn't take anything!" retorted Po.

"I bet that's what you tell all your marks in the street, too!"

"Timmertandi," said Barlimo sternly, "that's enough."

The room fell into a disgruntled silence.

"Where's Mab?" asked Rowenaster.

"In the usual place," replied Timmer with disinterest. "Sobbing her eyes out in the first floor bathroom. Shall I fetch her?" she asked, her expression bored. Mab's unusual sensitivity to other people's displeasure irritated Timmer. She appreciated Mab's helpfulness around the house but not her constant tears.

"Leave Mab for now," said Barlimo. "I expect we'll have excitement enough when Doogat arrives. Best to let our Piedmerri catch her breath."

Timmer sighed loudly. "Why we have to have *Mayanabi* in this house utterly eludes me."

"That's not surprising," replied Po smoothly.

"Implying?" Timmer snapped.

"Oh, I'm *implying* nothing," said Po with an ingratiating smile at Barlimo.

Barlimo stopped eating her stew.

Po grinned more broadly. "I'm stating without hesitation—

Timmertandi of Belkanon Tuning—that everything eludes *you*. You're a dumbshit Dunnsung."

The room exploded with bad tempers.

In the midst of all this, the front door to the Kaleidicopia opened and closed. A man of medium height and dressed in varying shades of blue entered the front hallway and removed his full length cloak. Listening to the furious round of insults, he started laughing. The sound was deep and genuinely merry.

The room fell silent in surprise.

The man in blue turned around, giving the boisterous denizens of the Kaleidicopia a small bow. When he raised his head to look at each of them individually, his pupilless black eyes glittered.

The Irreverent Old Doogat of Suf had finally arrived.

Chapter Seven

BALDING WITH RUDDY apple cheeks and impossible eyes, Doogat resembled none of the known *landdraws* of Mnemlith. When asked about his point of origin, the man remained secretive, indicating that he had kin somewhere "up north." He appeared sixty-two years old in wrinkles and age spots, but his movements were those of a much younger man. Doogat had one known vice: his meerschaum pipe collection. Carved from a substance known colloquially as sea foam, Doogat's meerschaums were the finest anyone had ever seen. Each bowl was cut with exquisitely carved figures and faces, some of them etched with Mayanabi sayings.

Doogat smiled playfully at his apprentice, Po, and pulled out a bent, black-stemmed beauty of a pipe. Po took one look at the interlocking design on the meerschaum bowl *and* at the nimble-footed figure of a Greatkin pirouetting there and blanched.

"Uh-oh," he mumbled.

"*Now* what?" asked Timmer, throwing another log on the fire.

"That's his Trickster pipe," muttered Po. "When he's smoking that one, there's no stopping him. Po shook his head worriedly, adding to himself, "Oh, I'm in trouble now. Yes, I am."

Doogat grinned at Po, his black eyes unblinking. Then the

Mayanabi Master turned to Barlimo. "This is hardly the whole crew, dear lady. Where are the rest of your deviants?"

Barlimo counted the missing members of the household on her fingers. "Let's see—Cobeth's not coming because he's moving out, Tree will be along as soon as he's finished with play rehearsal—uh, Janusin's out back in the sculpting studio, and Mab's bawling in the bathroom."

Doogat rubbed his clean shaven chin and nodded. "A typical day at the Kaleidicopia. Well, well," he said, crossing the room and plunking down beside Podiddley, "hope I haven't missed anything yet."

"You never miss anything, Doogat," grumbled Po under his breath. Then, looking into the Mayanabi's queer eyes, he added, "Just don't box my ears tonight, okay?"

Doogat lit a match and purposefully charred the top layer of tobacco in his Trickster meerschaum, sucking the bright flame deep into the bowl. "Now why," he asked, blowing out the match, "would I need to do a thing like that, Po?"

"I don't know. But you've done it before—and for no good reason!" complained the little Asilliwir thief, his expression indignant.

"Only as a last resort," replied Doogat mildly, continuing to puff on his pipe. He turned to Rowenaster who sat directly behind him in a large leather armchair, the stack of midterm examinations in his lap. "Professor, what's your opinion?"

"About what?" asked Rowenaster peering over his silver bifocals.

"Don't you agree that students who don't listen should get their ears boxed?"

Po licked his lips nervously. He started to move away from Doogat, but the Mayanabi Master caught his arm and held him fast. Po began to whine. "Doogat—now come on, Doogat—don't do anything—"

Rowenaster cleared his throat and folded his dark-skinned hands over the sheaf of white papers in his lap. "I've never had to resort to such measures, Master Doogat. We Saämbolin are a conservative bunch."

"You've never flunked a student?" asked Doogat.

"Well, yes. But—"

Doogat made a fist and playfully punched the air. "Same thing."

Rowenaster stiffened. "Hitting a student is *not* the same—"

Doogat wagged a finger in the professor's old face. "You're being civilized again, Rowen—I warned you about that. Now observe the direct teaching approach." Then, before Po could flee, Doogat grabbed the thief and neatly boxed his left ear.

Po howled with dismay.

Doogat continued his demonstration of direct teaching without a pause. "Observe, Rowen—see how Po clutches his ear. Po has just remembered that he *has* an ear. That's important. Before any real learning can take place, pupils must be made aware of the tools at their disposal." Doogat winked at Podiddley and blew a lazy smoke ring.

Po, who was furious, scrambled to his feet. "I didn't deserve that!"

"Rimble-Rimble," said Doogat evenly. "You will."

"You can't punish me for something that hasn't happened!"

Doogat made a disapproving sound with his tongue. "That's linear thinking, my boy. Remember what I told you about that."

Po scowled. "You twist everything to your own advantage, Doogat. It's not fair. It's not fair at all."

Doogat chuckled. "Such a complainer." He patted the spot on the rug next to him. "Sit down." Po regarded him warily. "Po—sit!" When Po finally did so, Doogat added, "You know very well, O My Student, that Mayanabi Masters don't always do what's fair. They do what's indicated."

"Yeah, yeah," mumbled Po, "and their ways are mysterious. I read that book, too, Doogs." He slumped, sitting cross-legged.

Doogat cuffed Po gently on the back of the neck and gave the little thief a warm smile. Then Doogat turned to the professor once more and said, "Do you begin to understand a little?"

Rowenaster frowned. "I'm not sure."

Doogat grunted approvingly. "Good. Students who're sure before they're ready to be sure are a waste of my time."

Po stared first at Doogat, then at Rowenaster, and back at Doogat again. "*Professor Rowenaster* is your student, Doogat? Since when?" he asked indignantly, feeling immediately protective of his twelve-year-old relationship with the Irreverent Old Doogat of Suf.

The Mayanabi Master blew a smoke ring. "Since the professor asked me a certain question over a month ago. I'm endeavoring to answer it—Mayanabi style. Using you as my eager assistant, of course. You could call this a rather tricky tutorial," he added, smiling at the pirouetting figure on the front of his pipe.

Po rubbed his left ear gingerly. "I could call it a lot of things, Doogat. Do me a favor, will you? Leave me *out* of the lesson plan. Okay?"

Doogat's expression sobered unexpectedly. "As you wish."

Po's eyes widened in appalled amazement. He swallowed, his voice stricken. "Doogat—now let's not be hasty. I mean, I'm still your student, aren't I?"

"Are you?" asked Doogat, raising an eyebrow. "We'll see."

Mab, who had finally finished her cry in the bathroom, joined the rest of them at this moment. Heads turned to look at her. She smiled weakly, well aware that her face was bloated and red from weeping. Doogat met her eyes without blinking. The effect was so unnerving that the young Piedmerri shrank back. Doogat gestured her over with a motion of his head. Mab licked her lips nervously, her brown eyes pleading for escape. Doogat grunted and got to his feet. Mab's eyes widened. Her body stiffened as she prepared to flee.

Doogat said softly, "Like a frightened doe, hmm, Mab?"

The Piedmerri girl swallowed. "I don't know what you mean, sir."

"That's too bad. I'd hoped you would," he said with a disappointed sigh. "Well, well—I must've misjudged you. I thought you knew something about courage."

"Her?" said Timmer in disbelief.

Mab blinked, feeling more and more confused. She bit her lip, her eyes jumping to the dancing Rimble figure on Doogat's pipe. She recognized Trickster immediately having just had him on the mid-term exam. Although she professed no particular belief in the existence of the Greatkin, it was still queer to be standing face-to-face with a such a fine representation of the Patron of Deviance and Dirty Tricks. In an effort to relieve the tension she was feeling between herself and Doogat, Mab mumbled, "Your pipe, sir—it's very—uh— interesting."

"Isn't it?" asked Doogat smiling broadly. He pulled the pipe out of his mouth, holding it toward Mab. "Come take a closer look."

Mab hesitated. She didn't want to appear rude or—Presence forbid—give Doogat cause to be angry with her.

"Come, come. It won't bite," said Doogat jovially.

"Ha," muttered Po.

Mab glanced at the disgruntled thief. Pressing her lips together, Mab inched toward Doogat, acting as if she were testing the high wire in a circus act. A high wire without a safety net.

Doogat remained motionless, his dark eyes watching her with amusement. Mab took another unsteady step toward Doogat, her fingers reaching for the meerschaum pipe. Her hand was trembling.

Doogat chuckled unexpectedly and moved aside—putting the pipe just out of her grasp. Mab came to an abrupt standstill, tears brimming in her eyes.

"What did you go and do that for, Doogat?" asked Rowenaster indignantly. "Can't you see how frightened Mab is of you?"

Doogat waved him silent with a sharp gesture of his hand. His eyes never leaving Mab's, the Mayanabi Master said, "Try again."

Tears streamed down Mab's cheeks. She wiped them away hastily. "No," she whimpered. "I can't. You'll take it away again."

"You don't know that," replied Doogat evenly.

"It's a—it's a Trickster pipe—I know about Greatkin Rimble—"

"Do you, Mab?" asked Doogat calmly. "Do you really?"

Rowenaster interrupted at this point, holding up Mab's recently corrected mid-term. "She aced the exam, Doogat. You can't do better than that."

"Can't you?" asked Doogat, his black eyes boring into Mab's terror-stricken face. "What if a hundred percent won't do?"

"Won't do?" asked Mab, her expression bewildered. "It has to do. It *has* to, Master Doogat." Mab's crying became very agitated now, a panic growing inside her. "It—it's always been enough. A hundred percent. You can't do any *more*," she wept.

Doogat watched her in silence, his expression unexpectedly compassionate. Without a further word, the Mayanabi Master took Mab in his arms and held her. She struggled half-heartedly, then seemed to give up, her face pale with fear.

"It's all right, Mabinhil," Doogat whispered softly. "Rimble isn't interested in a hundred percent of nothing."

"Wh—what?" she mumbled.

"All that Trickster wants from you right now, Mab," said Doogat brushing a strand of brown hair out of the young girl's face, "is that you try again, hmm?"

Mab refused to look at Doogat, her shoulders sagging.

Po interrupted at this point. "You sure treat *her* nice, Doogs. Me? You just punch *me* out whenever you fucking feel like it!"

Doogat ignored Po's comment and looked over at the professor who had been watching the entire scene with astonishment. "And that's the answer to your question, Rowen. Multiple. Trickster takes the form indicated by the circumstances presented. Thus, I treat Po one way. And Mab quite another," he added, ushering the little Piedmerri over to an empty spot on the couch. Mab sat down numbly, her expression troubled.

"You were just using me?" she asked. "You didn't mean what you said?"

"On the contrary," replied Doogat. "I meant exactly what I said."

"But what was the *question*?" asked Timmer.

Barlimo, who'd been eating her dinner in silence throughout the whole "lesson," now looked up. "Simple," she said, meeting Doogat's dark eyes briefly. "Rowen must've asked, 'What is the nature of Trickster?' "

Doogat smiled. "Very good."

"Yes," said Rowenaster, nodding. "As a matter of fact, Barl, that's exactly what I asked. But what I really wanted to know was what the ethics—"

"Ethics!" cried Po. "There aren't any!"

"You should talk," snapped Timmer, glaring at the little thief.

Doogat turned his attention back to Mab. Touching her cheek gently, he smiled at the trembling young woman and said, "On the contrary. The ethics are there. *If* you know what to look for. Rimble-Rimble."

This was not exactly comforting.

To anyone.

Chapter Eight

WHILE THE TEMPERS of the five house members inside the Kaleidicopia flared and subsided, Master Janusin and his protegé, Cobeth, regarded each other with contempt. The two Jinnjirri sculptors stood in the artist's studio behind the Kaleidicopia, their lean, muscular arms crossed over their chests, their shifting Jinnjirri hair crimson with anger. Cobeth was the first to break the lull in the argument. He turned away from the forty-year-old man who had been his friend, lover, and mentor for the past five years and continued packing his sculptor's tools. Cobeth, a person nine years Janusin's junior, was a particularly skinny fellow. Appearing perennially undernourished, Cobeth's waifish, boyish body brought out the maternal instincts in women and men alike. It helped that Cobeth had large eyes. At once innocent and seductive, such eyes masked his driving need for power. Other people's power. Such eyes spoke of a terrible soul ache; they were a sad, bottomless well that only *you*—and you alone—could fill.

Janusin watched Cobeth put a chisel into a leather carrying bag and rubbed his neck tiredly. He felt exhausted. Drained. He cleared his throat and said, "It's not surprising that you're leaving me now, Cobeth."

"Oh? Why's that?" asked Cobeth, his movements jerky, furious.

"You've run me dry." When Cobeth refused to answer him, Janusin added, "There is *one* good thing about you, however."

Cobeth met Janusin's gaze cooly. "I'm surprised you can remember a good thing about me, Jan. How gracious of you."

Janusin chuckled. "You don't kill your host."

"Oh, I'm a *parasite* now?"

"But I think I know why that is," continued Janusin conversationally.

Cobeth put his hands on his hips, waiting for Janusin to finish.

The master sculptor nodded his head. "You see, you're a very smart fellow, Cobeth."

"Glad to hear it."

"You're an excellent judge of people—you know exactly what they have to give you. And exactly where their breaking point is. Sheer genius."

Cobeth's hair turned a deepening shade of rage.

Janusin smiled. "You're a hustler, Cobeth. Always looking out for yourself first. So you figure—hey, I might need old Master Janusin at some later time. After all, he's got a lot of clout in the city—especially with the rich art patrons. So, we'll cut him. Not badly. But enough to get ourselves free of his influence. Free of his opinions—"

"You have a *lot* of opinions, Janusin," snapped Cobeth.

"Yes, and I'm paid to have them. It's my job, you know. That's why I'm called Master Janusin. Entitles me to teach. Gives you the benefit of my long years of experience. All that good stuff."

"What's your point, damn it!"

Janusin shrugged. "That you've wasted my time. And my time, dear protegé, was not yours to waste."

"I spent *five* years in this stinking—"

"Our contract was for seven," interrupted Janusin, his voice becoming more forceful. "It was a verbal contract of honor." He paused, his hair streaking with frosted blue hurt. He kept his voice steady and added, "But why should I be surprised at this point? You made a worse abuse of the trust I gave you in bed." Janusin laughed sardonically. "What did you call all those little affairs?"

"Desserts," replied Cobeth, his posture defiant.

Janusin eyed Cobeth's scrawny body with amused disgust. "Desserts. You don't need desserts, Cobeth. You need real food. Real nourishment."

Cobeth narrowed his eyes. "Too bad you couldn't—or wouldn't provide it," he said silkily, inclining his head toward the cot in the back corner of the studio. "But then yours *is* a rather bland diet."

Janusin's frosted hair streaked with dark red now. He stuffed his slender hands inside the pockets of his long dress. Covered with delicate needlework and tiny mirrors, the dress glimmered in the candlelight.

Jinnjirri men wearing dresses was a common event in Mnemlith. Hair was not the only thing changeable about this people; they also shifted gender. At a moment's notice, a Jinnjirri could switch from being one sex (and preference) to another. Jinnjirri took gender shifting as a matter of course. The other landraces of Mnemlith did not. As a result, the Jinnjirri usually stayed with their own kind. It seemed remarkably easier that way. Even so, some Jinnjirri were strictly heterosexual or strictly homosexual and expected their lovers to follow their lead and change to the appropriate sex. Janusin was one of these latter; he preferred the homosexual—of either sex—to the heterosexual. Cobeth, on the other hand, preferred the free-wheeling versatility of all forms of sexual experience. During the last year, he had tried to interest Janusin in a little beating and bondage, but the master sculptor had been quietly horrified at the invitation.

Cobeth laughed harshly. "And *you're* working on a statue of Greatkin Rimble? You're not even capable of understanding the first thing about real deviance. Real deviance," he added smugly, "is cruel. That's what makes it so exciting, Janusin. So dangerous. But you? You like your sex safe."

Janusin's breathing became shallow. "I like my sex *loving*, Cobeth."

"Whatever you want to call it," replied Cobeth, picking up a mallet and stuffing it roughly in the leather bag at his feet. "You go too slow. In bed and out of it," he added making reference to Janusin's meticulous teaching methods.

"Certain things are worth learning slowly, Cobeth. It's a shame I couldn't convince you of that. But you always did like your shortcuts."

Cobeth tied the leather bag shut and stood up. "There's a whole world out there. And I intend to have it."

"For dessert?" asked Janusin sarcastically.

"Yes."

Janusin pursed his lips. "And if I tell you that I think you'll starve yourself?"

"Then I'll tell you that your head's up your ass." He glared at his mentor. "If you're trying to undermine my confidence, Jan, you're doing a piss-poor job of it."

Janusin's shoulders sagged unexpectedly. He turned away from Cobeth, staring out of the studio window at the candlelit Kaleidicopia. There was an awkward silence, then Janusin said softly, "I'm trying to save your life, my love. Not undermine your confidence."

"Save my life!" cried Cobeth indignantly. "Who says it needs saving? And who says you're the one to do it?"

Janusin whipped around. "As your teacher, it's my job to see that you learn the art of sculpting—"

"Get this, Janusin! *My* life isn't sculpting. Yours is. Mine isn't." Then he added with disinterest, "Never was. It was just something to try."

Janusin's hair darkened to a burnt blood-red. *"Just something to try?"* he asked, practically choking on the words. "You wasted five years of my life on a *whim*?"

"Yeah, Jan," he replied with an insolent toss of his head. "What of it? Jinnjirri are natural dilettantes. Shit, man—you've been living in this stuffy city too long. You're beginning to sound like a fucking Saämbolin!"

"Because I asked you to make a commitment?" shouted Janusin.

"Where do you *get* these expectations? From that Mayanabi asshole, Doogat?"

A familiar voice interrupted their argument. "Not that I'm

aware of," replied the Irreverent Old Doogat of Suf. He was standing on the threshold of the studio. Janusin wondered how long he had been listening. Then, his face turning color from embarrassment, the master sculptor turned away from both the Mayanabi and his protegé. His hair betrayed him, of course; it shifted to a bright, hot pink.

Doogat noted it but said nothing to Janusin. He turned to Cobeth. "Gentlemen—or women—" he added, glancing at Janusin's dress, "are either of you planning to attend the house meeting? If so, we're ready to start."

There was a stony silence.

Janusin ran his fingers through his spiky pink hair. "I forgot about it, Doogat." He turned around to face them, his expression weary.

Cobeth picked up his bag of sculpting tools. "Well, I didn't. And as far as I'm concerned, everyone at the house can go fuck themselves. I hope I never see the place again."

Doogat took out his Trickster pipe and lit it. Looking at Janusin, he shrugged and said, "Cobeth's *such* a sentimental sort. Warms the heart to be in his presence."

Janusin said nothing, feeling too sad to speak. Doogat had never born any love for Cobeth. But he, Janusin, *had*. And no matter what a little stinker Cobeth had been—or might yet be—Janusin would always love a portion of the man. He knew it was stupid. He knew it made no sense. And he was absolutely stuck with the feeling. For a Jinnjirri, Janusin had an odd core of loyalty in his personality. It had always baffled Cobeth; Jinnjirri never remained long with anything. Or anyone. Jinnjirri shifted relationships as easily as they shifted hair color or gender. It was a natural response to their *landdraw*. But Janusin had never fit that norm. Janusin had expected commitment in his class—and out of it. In fact, by Jinnjirri standards, Janusin had expected the preposterous: monogamy.

Catching sight of Rimble on Doogat's meerschaum, the master sculptor turned to Cobeth and said, "What about the Trickster's Hallows at the house? Are you still planning to attend it? A third of the guests invited are from your list."

Cobeth laughed spitefully. "The Kaleidicopia's idea of a Rimble's Revel is a fucking joke. Nobody in the house would know what to do at a real hallows."

"Would you?" asked Doogat unexpectedly, his voice like ice.

Cobeth shrugged off the Mayanabi's disconcerting, dark gaze, and muttered, "There's a *lot* you don't know about me, old man."

Doogat blew a smoke ring. "Likewise, my friend."

There was a peculiar silence.

Janusin cleared his throat uncomfortably. "Well—uh—we can continue this later, Cobeth."

"There's nothing to continue," replied Cobeth indifferently. "I'm gone when I leave here tonight. *If* I come to the hallows, I'll come with a new lover. Count on it," he added. Then Cobeth opened the door to the studio and walked rapidly away into the peculiarly warm autumn night.

Janusin's hair turned a despondent blue. He covered his face with his hands, trying to hide his tears since he couldn't hide his hair from Doogat's inquiring glance.

"Master Janusin," said Doogat firmly, shutting the door to the studio once more, "I want to talk to you." A fine layer of marble dust swirled into the air from the draft of the closing door and settled around the bases of Janusin's current works in progress.

The master sculptor winced. "I don't think—uh—I *can* talk just now."

"I know," replied Doogat, not yielding, "but it's necessary."

Janusin nodded, shutting his eyes. Tears slipped down his face. "The—" he whispered hoarsely, "—the house meeting?"

"It can wait."

Janusin nodded again, his hair turning a dark, painful blue. "What's the topic?" he continued in a whisper.

"Protegés."

Chapter Nine

TREESONOVOHN OF SHROOMZ was the last straggling person to arrive in time for the Kaleidicopia's late night house meeting. Jinnjirri like Barlimo and Janusin, Tree added a certain artistic bufoonery to the "K." He was not really a tree, but he *did* do his best to impersonate one. A makeup artist of consummate skill, Tree had perfected a greaseless foundation of dark mahogany red. When applied to his face, the color and feel resembled the grainy texture of bark. Neither rain nor soap could remove this staining makeup base.

"And it's a good thing, too," Tree muttered at the gray clouds scuttling across the night sky. The weather was unseasonably warm, he thought, and wondered why. Tree loved the seasons—all four of them. And he didn't see any reason for summer to linger this late in the fall. Temperatures like these played havoc with his wardrobe. He shrugged. "I mean, how am I supposed to *dress*?" he muttered at no one in particular. "I feel *stupid* walking about in my autumn regalia when it's hot enough to wear a summer tunic and sandals!" Tree wiped a raindrop off his cheek with a twiggy finger. The light drizzle glistened on his wild thicket of perennially green hair.

Tree's robe rustled as he walked. Decidedly deciduous, his overtunic was a fantasy of rippling color. Composed of several layers of hand-dyed cloth leaves, Tree's autumn garb matched the red, orange, and brilliant gold foliage of the city arbors. Tree was a walking celebration. To complete the effect, he wore what he called his "Fab Fall" fragrance. This was a heady scent comprising the best of the season: crisp red apples, burning firewood, damp wool, and sweet mulled wine. Being a gifted chemist of sorts, Tree had managed to find a way to keep the scents separate. It seemed that the particular scent perceived depended on the mix of sweat from Tree's body. Thus the side of Tree's neck might smell of burning wood, while the backs of his knees might smell of sweet mulled wine.

Tree's thoughts returned to his former place of employment. "That's *recently* former," he said with disgust. "Like one lousy hour." He kicked savagely at a pile of scarlet leaves on the street curb, swearing at actors in general and at Cobeth of Shift Shallows in particular. "Flaming, cowardly prig," he added. "Where does *he* get off having me fired? The little shift," he said, using the derogatory word for Jinnjirri. "And he didn't even have the nerve to fire me face-to-face. Leaving Rhu to do it."

Rhu was the stage manager for The Merry Pricksters. She was also a personal friend of Tree's. They had known each other in Upper School—the Mnemlith equivalent to grades eight through twelve—and had grown up in the same hometown. Like Tree, Rhu was barely twenty-one. She and Tree had also been lovers during the summer of their ninth-grade year. Jinnjirri children tended to mature early sexually, and as they had a perfect method of birth control— switching gender during ovulation—they usually acted on their maturity.

Hearing the large brass bells of the Great Library ring eleven bell-eve, Tree increased the speed of his walk. He was exactly an hour late for the house meeting. Still, he thought, Barlimo had called it on a moment's notice. And with his schedule at the playhouse—that's *previous* schedule, he reminded himself sourly—they were lucky to be seeing him at all tonight.

"Greatkin alive," he swore. "And if Barl asks about rent?" This was such a glum thought that Tree's green hair turned frosted blue.

Scowling, Tree waited for his mood to improve—and his hair to shift back to emerald green. He sighed. How was he ever going to pay for classes at the University of Speakinghast? He couldn't get a loan; being Jinnjirri born, Tree didn't qualify. Prejudice, he thought bitterly. Saämbolin prejudice.

"That stupid administration. I swear—if Rowenaster defends that pig, Gadorian, one more time!" he said hotly to a watering trough as he passed it. "Oooh—that Guild scum. And we were *so* close to rigging a Jinnjirri scholarship program too." He spat into the gutter. "*Next* year," he promised.

It was Rowenaster's opinion that if Tree spent more time working on his homework and less time on reforming the University Financial Office, he would do quite a bit better on his exams. Tree, however, found the doing of life more interesting than the studying of it. That was why the position at the playhouse had been such a Presence-send. With The Merry Pricksters, Tree could get hands-on experience in makeup and pyrotechnics. And Tree was certain that experience of this sort would impress a future employer far more than a series of straight A's. Tree sighed. He was going to miss working at the playhouse for another reason. The Merry Pricksters were an all-Jinnjirri troupe. As such, the Pricksters had provided Tree with a haven of like-minded individuals—indispensible in a city as hostile to Jinnjirri as Speakinghast was. Tree winced. Well, there was always the "K."

"Greatkin-bless, Barlimo," he muttered. "She could fight the entire Saämbolin Housing Commission and win," he told a sleepy horse standing in its traces. "Barlimo's got the luck of the Trickster. Well, except with Cobeth."

It didn't seem fair to Tree that Barlimo should have to take the brunt of Cobeth's celebrated callousness on two counts. First, Cobeth moved out without giving Barlimo even a week's notice.

Second, Cobeth fired Tree from a job that paid Barlimo one of her rents. Tree grimaced. Barlimo was generous, but she was *not* a charity. And the last thing Tree wanted to do was arrive at Podiddley's status: rent scum-bum.

Tree took a deep breath and let it out slowly. As he turned the corner of Wiscombe Street and crossed to Wise Whatsit Avenue, the chimneys and cupola of the Kaleidicopia came into view. Tree pursed his lips as he walked, thinking about Podiddley's precarious position in the house. That Mab, the newest member of the Kaleidicopia, had called a secret meeting to oust Po was amazing the Tree. It was an utter breach of precedent, and of pecking order etiquette. New members, or newbies—as they were informally called by the senior members of the "K"—were expected to mind their manners and observe the day-to-day workings of the house *before* involving themselves in its politics. The rules existing at the Kaleidicopia were there for good reason. After all, the house was Jinnjirri born—out of Barlimo—and Jinnjirri didn't create rules just to have them. *Not* like the bureaucracy-loving Saämbolin. Tree ran his fingers through his thick hair. Mab really puzzled him. Where did someone as timid as Mab get the gumption to rattle the silent power structure of the house? She must have had a reason, he thought. Tree squinted at the dancing firelight in the windows of the "K" as he cut towards the front walk. Barlimo said she thought Mab had done it to get approval, not because she had a particular conviction about the rightness or wrongness of Po's residency. Tree winced. He hoped this was not true. If it was, he thought sadly, then he would have to reconsider his sexual attraction for the Piedmerri. He disliked wimps.

"I may have to do that anyway," he muttered as he avoided the fuschia colored front door to the house. He headed for the back porch of the kitchen, taking the stone stairs two at a time and adding, "Virgins are *such* a pain. Especially non-Jinnjirri ones."

Tree slipped in the back door of the Kaleidicopia and immediately wrinkled his nose. The scent of Barlimo's garlic curry still lingered in the kitchen. Tree dipped a wooden spoon into the still warm cauldron and tested the stew gingerly. He found it surprisingly tasty and so helped himself; Barlimo always cooked more than she needed, and Barlimo always offered it to those standing about in the kitchen. Tree listened to the strained voices on the other side of the swinging door. His eyes narrowed. Apparently, the house meeting hadn't started yet.

"Good," he whispered to himself. "Then, I'll eat." Tree sat

down at the round kitchen table and continued with his dinner, enjoying the relative peace. It was short-lived; Po and Rowen walked in, both wanting seconds of stew.

Entering the room first, Po took one look at Tree and snorted, "So I suppose *you* sided with Mab? Voted me out like Timmer, Cobeth, and Janusin?"

"As a matter of fact, Po," said Tree with his mouth full, "I didn't side with Mab at all."

"Why?" asked Po in surprise.

"Not for love of *you*," replied Tree drily. He wiped his lips with a napkin. "I just didn't like the precedent."

Po rolled his eyes. "Figures."

Tree shrugged. "I don't have to love everyone who moves in here."

"Only the Piedmerri ones," replied Po smoothly.

Tree's green hair streaked with red.

This brought peals of laughter from Po. The little thief pointed rudely at Tree's hair color and turning to Rowenaster, said, "I *love* screwing him up like that. He's such an easy mark."

"I'll remember you said that, Po," replied Tree. He smiled icily. "Especially if any more money disappears from this house."

There was a dead silence.

Two weeks ago Janusin had put his rent money in an envelope and hung it on Barlimo's door. It had vanished before the Jinnjirri architect returned home that evening from a meeting with the Saämbolin Housing Commission. Everyone suspected Po, but no one had any proof. Just lots of motivation. It was common knowledge that the little thief was six months behind in his rent payments. He still managed to eat, so the money had to be coming from somewhere. Rowenaster had countered the circumstantial evidence by suggesting that perhaps Doogat supplemented Po's income when things went badly in the street. Barlimo had seconded this opinion, but the younger members of the "K" had remained unconvinced. Irate, they had all converged in Mab's room to discuss the possibility of evicting Podiddley.

Rowenaster broke the silence. "Tree—remember yourself, please. You've *no* proof for such an accusation."

"I don't need proof," retorted the crabby Jinnjirri. "The guy's a professional pickpocket. Stealing is second nature to him."

Po said nothing, his fist clenched. He threw his empty curry bowl into the sink—leaving it unwashed—and stormed out of the kitchen.

"Nice," said the Professor, meeting Tree's eyes cooly.

Tree swore, putting his head in his hands. "This just isn't my day," he mumbled through his twiggy fingers. "This just isn't my day at *all*."

Chapter Ten

MASTER JANUSIN WAS beginning to think this wasn't *his* day, either. He pulled out two studio stools, offering one to Doogat. Then, kicking some marble rubble out of the way of the other stool's legs, he sat down, his shoulders slumped. His hair was a frosted black and blue: beaten up.

Doogat noted the Jinnjirri's emotional barometer and cleared his throat. "This concerns protegés in general—"

"And Cobeth in particular?"

The Mayanabi Master nodded. "To begin with, Jan—Cobeth isn't worth your grief."

"Tell that to my heart," muttered the Jinnjirri.

Doogat reached over and rapped playfully on Janusin's chest. "Yoo-hoo, in there? Don't grieve for a weasel."

Janusin laughed drily. "If he's a weasel, Doogat, he's the most talented weasel I ever met."

"Skin-deep."

"What do you mean?"

Doogat relit his Trickster pipe. "Talent like Cobeth's is useless."

Janusin winced. "Uh—Master Doogat—could you maybe wear gloves tonight? I'm in need of a soft touch. I've just spent five years trying to train that useless talent."

"Yes, you did," replied Doogat mercilessly. "And now you can stop."

Janusin hung his head. "It's not that easy. I—uh—still appreciate him."

Referring to general Jinnjirri wantoness, Doogat teased, "I think you *often* appreciate the artist as well as his or her work, hmm?"

Janusin's hair turned a brilliant pink. He smiled weakly,

looking anywhere but in Doogat's direction. "Shit," he muttered. Then, in a gallant effort to get himself out from under Doogat's ruthless scrutiny, Janusin added, "Poor Tree. He's going to hit the roof when Cobeth fires him tonight." If Doogat was surprised by this piece of news, he gave no indication of it. Puzzled, Janusin decided to pursue the subject a little further; "Tree loathes Cobeth, you know." Janusin laughed bitterly. "Tree keeps telling me he thinks Cobeth is an emotional charlatan."

"Too bad you don't listen to Tree."

Janusin swore. "Do you *ever* have a soft touch?"

"Only when it's necessary," replied Doogat, his black eyes twinkling.

"How about now?"

Doogat regarded the forty-year-old Jinnjirri with amused affection. "I believe you have a question for me, Master Janusin?"

The Jinnjirri stared at Doogat. "How in the world—oh, never mind!" he snorted. "I should know better than to ask you a straight question, anyway."

"Who knows," replied Doogat puffing idly on his meerschaum pipe, "you might get a straight answer. *This* time."

Janusin took a deep breath. "All right, all right. Here's the question: Teacher-to-teacher, I'm wondering about Cobeth—"

Doogat nodded encouragingly.

"—I mean, I tried everything I could think of to bring his talent to bear. To get him to *use* his potential. But clearly I failed. After five years his commitment to sculpting remains—as you say—skin-deep. What should I have done differently? If anything," he added in his own defense.

Doogat blew a smoke ring between them. Then he said, "It's the way of the Mayanabi to answer such a question with a story."

"*This* is a straight answer?"

"That depends on your readiness," replied Doogat calmly.

Janusin rolled his eyes. "*My* readiness. Well, I suppose there's no way to know if I'm ready or not, is there?"

"Let the story be the test."

Janusin's shoulders sagged. "I don't know, Doogs—I feel so sad right now. I don't even know if I could *listen* to a story, much less comprehend it on more than one level. My heart is just so—"

"Broken?" asked Doogat gently.

Janusin nodded, a tear slipping down his cheek. "I'm sorry," he said hoarsely. "I shouldn't have asked the question if I wasn't prepared to hear the answer."

Doogat was silent for a moment. "You're very hard on yourself, Jan." He touched the sculptor's shoulder. "Listen to me: good teachers are good learners. And good learners are risk-takers. You with me so far?" Janusin nodded mutely. Doogat smiled. "Now *sometimes* risks turn into what is commonly called 'a mistake.' For the risk-taker—for the learner in the learning process—a mistake is simply a dead-end exploration. Some students turn out to be mistakes. Like your Cobeth."

"But what a waste of time!" said Janusin desperately.

"Not for the good teacher. The good teachers profit from their mistakes. As do the good learners."

"And don't make the same one twice, right?"

Doogat shook his head. "That's unrealistic. The truth is, you're very likely to make the same mistake twice."

Janusin gave Doogat a horrified look.

Doogat held up his finger. "But," he said sternly, "the good learner will recognize the same mistake in half the time. And so on. Until finally, the 'mistake' can be averted altogether. But that can only be done over time—and through painstaking but *informed* trial and error. That's the nature of exploration. Everyone alive makes mistakes. Everyone, that is, save 'The Boy with Intelligent Hands.' "

"What?" asked Janusin, feeling completely confused by Doogat's swift change in subject. "What boy with intelligent hands?"

Doogat puffed on his pipe, his black eyes glittering. "Once," he said with a smile, "there was a young boy born in Jinnjirri. Now his family was Asilliwir born and so were travellers. One day, when this boy was very young, a great storm arose in the mountains where his family was camped. He got separated from them. He got lost. They searched and searched for their Jinnjirri son—but they never found him. So they left the Feyborne broken-hearted.

"Little did they know, however, but their son was not dead. He was alive and living in a village across the *landdraw* border of Tammirring. Now the Tammirring born are gifted seers, but they're not particularly gifted artists. Not like the Jinnjirri and not like *this* Jinnjirri boy. This boy could turn anything into a masterpiece—a stack of toothpicks, a sack of seeds. The world was his medium.

"His new Tammirring family was awed by this ability—so they

• 69 •

praised their Jinnjirri boy loudly and often. As a result, the boy became used to being the only talent around. One day a stranger riding a large blue-black mare came to town. He was a Mayanabi—among other things—and so had seen something of the world. He listened to the villagers tout their prodigy proudly. The man asked to see the Jinnjirri boy. The boy came out to meet him. The stranger frowned. He saw something in this boy that he did not like. Without explaining why, he asked to see the boy's hands.

"The boy held them out, his smile insolent.

" 'You have smart hands, boy,' said the stranger.

"The boy nodded matter-of-factly.

"The stranger smiled. 'They're a curse. You should cut them off,' he said.

"The boy's smile faltered. 'Wha-what?' he asked in disbelief.

" 'You should cut them off,' repeated the stranger. 'You don't know how to use them. On you, they're a waste. In the end, they'll kill you. One way or another.' He leaned forward. 'If you wish to live, if you wish to love— cut them off.'

"The boy was indignant. 'I can't do that. My hands are the smartest part of me. That's what my name means. Yonneth: smart hands.'

" 'For now,' replied the stranger drily.

"The boy regarded the stranger with disdain. 'I'm going to the big city when I grow up. I'm going to be famous,' he asserted.

"The stranger ignored the boy's ambition, looking past him to where the boy's older sister stood. 'Do you love your brother?' he called.

" 'Oh yes. He's a wonderful brother,' she said softly, her eyes full of awe and respect. 'He's a blessing for our family.'

"The stranger's face sobered. 'So are you, my child,' he told her.

"There was a peculiar silence.

"The boy frowned. 'She doesn't have hands like mine,' he muttered. 'You should see her try to paint a picture. *Her* hands are stupid. They make mistakes.'

" 'Yes,' said the stranger with a smile. 'Her hands do not protect her like yours do you. That's because they're empty. What she touches, she feels. Directly.'

" 'My hands feel!' protested the Jinnjirri boy.

" 'Ah,' said the stranger, 'but does your heart?' "

Doogat ended the story here, taking a moment to relight his

Trickster pipe. When he had drawn on it several times, he added, "You see, Jan, like this boy, Yonneth—Cobeth of Shift Shallows didn't come to you with empty hands. He came to you holding tightly to his pride and arrogance. How could you hope to fill what was already filled?"

Janusin took a deep breath. "But that part about cutting *off* the boy's hands—how barbaric."

"The stranger was a Mayanabi Master. His suggestion was radical because one cannot travel the Way of the Mayanabi without experiencing severence from the familiar. What could be more familiar than one's own hands? The stranger's suggestion was really an invitation—he was inviting the boy to become his student. So an opportunity was missed."

Janusin gave a despondent sigh. "Cobeth probably would've missed the opportunity, too."

"That's why I tell you the story," replied Doogat softly.

Janusin rubbed his eyes. "You know, for all my 'appreciation' of Cobeth, I have to say, he could be uncommonly cold sometimes. And secretive. Maybe that's the price for his kind of genius."

Doogat nodded. "Genius uninformed by the heart is brilliant. But it is also insensitive. It lacks empathy. Cobeth, you see, is completely incapable of putting himself in another's situation." Doogat gave Janusin a sad look. "That's why I tell you not to waste your time grieving; Cobeth has no idea what pain he has caused you. How can he? His hands are so full of himself, he has no room for another. And that is his tragedy, Jan. Don't make it yours."

Janusin bit his lower lip. "Pretty strange story, Doogat."

The Mayanabi Master smiled. "Strange to the strange."

Janusin scowled. He was just about to retort when Barlimo came bustling through the studio door, her shawl of many colors slung unused over her back. "It's so damned warm out!" she muttered. Then, seeing the Mayanabi and the sculptor, she put her hands on her hips and said, "What in *Neath* are you two doing out here? I send him out here to fetch you, Jan, and nobody comes back? Come on, fellows. You're holding up the house meeting."

"Who says we haven't been having it?" asked Doogat chuckling.

Barlimo wagged a finger in his wrinkled face. "*I* have other things to do tonight, Master Doogat. Sleep, for one!"

Doogat nudged Janusin. "I think she's cross with us."

The sculptor smiled conspiratorially. "We probably deserve it."

"Probably," agreed Doogat, getting slowly to his feet. As he walked past the glaring Barlimo, he whispered, "Zendrak asked me to tell you that he has a plan for Po; he wants Po to stay at my house for a while."

Barlimo grunted. "Does Po know this?"

"He will."

"Wonderful," replied the architect without enthusiasm.

Po had a vocabulary of four-letter words so rich in imagination that only Greatkin Jinndaven could top him.

"Wonderful," Barlimo repeated.

Chapter Eleven

As BARLIMO, JANUSIN, and Doogat walked back from the artist's studio to the Kaleidicopia, the rest of the house members waited impatiently for their arrival. Particularly Podiddley of Brindlsi. Feeling furious with Tree for accusing him of stealing Janusin's rent money, the little Asilliwir paced back and forth in front of the hearth. He wanted to walk out on all of them, but he couldn't. Doogat prevented him. As long as he was Doogat's student, any situation that involved the Mayanabi Master was a potential learning experience for Po.

"Even this frigging house meeting," muttered the little thief under his breath.

Rowenaster came into the room from the kitchen. He had apparently decided against seconds of curry stew. Glancing at Podiddley, the professor pulled on his bifocals and returned to correcting mid-terms. Mab asked for hers. Rowenaster picked her exam off the top of the pile and handed it to the nineteen-year-old with a smile.

Mab looked at the grade. Her expression turned into astonishment. "This isn't a hundred percent. You said I aced it," she added accusingly.

The professor slipped his glasses lower on the bridge of his large nose. "Child, you *did* ace it. You only missed one question."

"Which?" she said angrily, skimming the six pages.

"Number forty-four."

"Hey," said Po interrupting with a get-even snigger, "that's *my* question."

Mab gave him a dubious look. "Your question?"

Rowenaster cleared his throat, hoping to avert the brewing argument between them. The professor was certain Po knew Mab had called the secret meeting to evict him. And Po, when angry, was not opposed to throwing a punch or two. Mab hadn't lived with Po long enough to be aware of this. Rowen decided to draw her fire. Smiling diplomatically, he said, "Uh—yes, Mab. I took one of Po's ideas and put it on the exam."

Mab's brown eyes blazed. "The only question *I* missed!"

Po grinned from ear to ear.

Rowenaster bit his lower lip. "Most everyone so far has missed it, Mab. It was a trick question. Really, quite unfair."

Mab stared at the Saämbolin professor. "Your landrace doesn't *do* things like that," she protested hotly. "You're predictable. That's why I study with you and the other Saämbolin."

Rowenaster pursed his lips, unsure if he'd just been complimented or insulted. He cleared his throat. "Well, Mab—the exam *was* on Greatkin Rimble. Perhaps you should've expected the unexpected."

Mab's reaction to Rowenaster's statement was peculiar. The young girl turned away from the professor, dropping the exam on the commons room rug and walked jerkily to the far side of the couch in front of the hearth. Without a further word, she picked up the comforter that rested there and pulled it over her shoulders. Timmer, who had been working on a musical score by candlelight, watched this with amazement.

"Somebody mind telling me what question forty-four was?"

Po answered her. "What is the *landdraw* of the Mayanabi Nomads."

"And?" continued Timmer, still looking at Mab.

"And," replied the professor, "most students write 'All.' That's because traditionally the Mayanabi are said to hail from all the landraces of Mnemlith. However, the correct answer is 'Unknown.'"

"Unknown?" asked Timmer skeptically. "How can their *landdraw* be unknown? That's like saying they don't have one. Or that they aren't born of Mnemlith or something."

"Nevertheless," said the professor. "According to Doogat, the correct answer is 'Unknown.' He says the Mayanabi were a Greatkin improvement."

Timmer regarded him with dismay. "Oh, no. Doogat's got *you* believing in the Greatkin, too? I'm disappointed in you, old man. What happened to good old academic skepticism? And tidy Saämbolin logic? No wonder Mab's upset. Better stop hanging around with Doogat, Professor. He's having a *bad* effect on you."

"Thanks for giving me your opinion," said Rowenaster drily.

"You're welcome," she replied, meaning it. Then feeling uncharacteristically generous toward Mab, Timmer asked, "Want some tea, love? It'll only take a second to boil some water."

Mab nodded dumbly, her eyes staring at the dancing flames in the hearth.

Timmer left the room for the kitchen. As she did so, Doogat, Barlimo, and Janusin arrived. Doogat broke off in mid-sentence, his attention immediately directed toward Mab. Frowning, he said nothing, taking a seat beside Podiddley who was now kneeling before the hearth turning logs.

"Been behaving yourself?" Doogat asked the thief.

"Some."

Doogat grunted, leaned against the couch, and closed his eyes.

Laughter exploded in the kitchen, followed by shrieks and giggles.

Janusin chuckled. "Tree's here. Timmer, too, by the sound of it." The Jinnjirri sculptor sat down in an overstuffed armchair, his dress draping beautifully in a soft puddle of magenta.

"Timmer's making tea for Baby Mab," Po said meanly.

"Why not for all of us?" asked Barlimo, hanging her many-colored shawl on a wooden peg in the front hall. "*I* could use some coddling, too."

"Good idea," replied Janusin, getting to his feet again. "Think I'll suggest it. Might relieve the bad mood in this room," he added, glancing at the huddled Piedmerri and the disgusted Asilliwir.

The swinging door swung shut after him. Moments later, more peals of hysteria issued from the Kaleidicopia's kitchen.

Doogat opened his eyes, his expression puzzled. Simultaneously, Barlimo got to her feet, instantly alert for impending Jinnjirri mischief. Doogat read the alarm in her face and said, "Perhaps you should go and see what—"

Too late.

The swinging door opened amidst giggles, and out pranced

Tree with a small orange pumpkin displayed on a tray like a kingly dessert. Surrounded by greens and gourds, everyone noticed that the top of the pumpkin had been cut like a jack o' lantern, the stem still on the lid.

Doogat's dark eyes narrowed. Something was *inside* the pumpkin. Something decidedly Jinnjirri—

Grinning like Trickster himself, Tree brought his gift straight to Mab. She looked up, her expression bewildered. Tree knelt down on one knee and motioned for the young girl to open the pumpkin. Mab did so hesitantly. She lifted the lid and froze. Her jaw dropped.

Inside was an upright cucumber crowned by a dollop of yogurt. At its base sat two tomatoes. Mab took one look at this obvious invitation and yelped. She attempted to throw the pumpkin away, but Tree and his lewd cohorts weren't through with the Piedmerri virgin. Tree grabbed the pumpkin out of Mab's scandalized hands and held it aloft like a prize. Announcing to the room, he said, "Okay everyone—pretend it's a proper autumn out." Then, winking at Janusin and Timmer, the three of them broke into song, Timmer's splendid soprano blending sweetly with Janusin's bass and Tree's tenor. Mab's face grew paler and paler with each word of the naughty ditty:

> When the weather's hot and sticky,
> That's no time to dip your dicky.
> Aye, but when the frost is on the pumpkin,
> *There's* a time for dicky dunkin'.

Chaos erupted in the room. Po and Rowenaster joined the "Invitational Trio" with helpless giggles. Barlimo, who was alternately horrified and utterly undone, hid her smile behind her hands. Her hair, of course, told the tale; it streaked with good-humored yellow and erotic lavender. Doogat jumped out of the way in time to miss being hit by the tray on Mab's lap as she threw it off. Mab ran out of the room. They heard Mab scramble upstairs. Presumably, she was fleeing to her second floor bedroom.

Doogat got to his feet hastily. Turning to Tree, he snapped, "You incomparable asshole!" Before Tree could reply, Doogat took off after Mab. He ran the flight of stairs with a nimbleness unusual in a man of sixty-two.

Tree shrugged. "Well, *I* needed a good giggle, even if Mab

didn't." Then, catching sight of Janusin and Barlimo's brilliant yellow hair, he started laughing all over again, his own hair following the lead of the other Jinnjirri in the room.

The next few minutes were spent in everyone going over the details of the previous scene. Po requested that "Dicky Dunkin'" be taught to all present. Tree gleefully complied with his request. The general mood of the group was so vastly improved by the time Doogat returned with Mab that the Mayanabi Master decided not to reprimand Tree further. Ushering the young Piedmerri into the room, he said, "Tree, Janusin, and Timmer—apologize."

"For *what*?" asked Timmer, wiping tears of humor off her cheek. "Mab was the best dupe I've ever seen."

Predictably, Mab began to bawl.

Timmer, who was really a kind-hearted soul, ran over to Mab and threw her arms around her reassuringly. "Mab," she protested. "Piedmerri are supposed to be *merry*, girl. What's become of your lovely *landdraw* nature?"

"Mab grew up on the northwest border of Jinnjirri, that's what!" retorted Doogat with supreme annoyance. "*In* the borderland."

The Jinnjirri in the room gaped, their smiles instantly fading.

Of all the borders surrounding the country of Jinnjirri, the northwest one was the most treacherous. Particularly to the psyche. Even the Jinnjirri born themselves had trouble with this border. They complained of spaciness and loss of ego direction when crossing from the Western Feyborne into Jinnjirri. The feelings could be pleasant, they said, as long as you didn't mind living without an internal—or external—reference point. Signs were posted along this "shift" to warn all non-Jinnjirri. As a result, only the travel-loving Asilliwir regularly crossed into this region. It was, said the Asilliwir, a natural high to them. Their horses, however, saw it differently and had to be specially drugged to make the journey in safety.

"Well, no wonder you're so afraid of everything, Mab," said Timmer gently. "You grew up not knowing which way was up—or down. It's a wonder you can cope at all." Timmer shook her head. "An earthy Piedmerri in a Jinnjirri 'shift.' What a nightmare."

Mab said nothing, her expression defiant.

Doogat, who was standing behind Mab, put his hands on her shoulders. "Be careful, Timmer. Mab's not nearly as weak as all that. She *did* survive, remember. Think of the strength that took, hmm?"

"Then, why does she cry all the time, Doogat?" asked Tree, perplexed.

"Same reason you look like a tree," replied the Mayanabi Master smoothly, his dark eyes boring into the Jinnjirri's shocked ones.

Janusin, who had always wondered about Tree's obsession, said, "This sounds interesting." But neither Doogat nor Tree would continue the conversation. Janusin sighed, crossing his arms over his powerful sculptor's chest, and retorted, "Well, can we at *least* have this blasted house meeting?"

As it was going on midnight, everyone agreed this was an excellent idea. Janusin and Doogat begged Timmer for caffeine. The blonde Dunnsung smiled and disappeared into the kitchen. Once there, she fetched tea and the personal mug belonging to each resident of the Kaleidicopia. For Doogat, she lent him one of her own. Ceramic, the mug was painted brilliant blue and decorated with gold dolphin-like creatures.

When honey and milk had been passed and tea stirred, Barlimo officially opened the Kaleidicopia's emergency house meeting. The Jinnjirri architect smiled, her hair turning an even-tempered green, and asked, "Any old business?"

It was clear from the expression on everyone's faces that the rent theft of two weeks ago was uppermost on their minds. People were careful not to look in Po's direction. However, the silent accusation was so palpable that the little Asilliwir started swearing under his breath. Doogat, who was sitting next to him again, tapped the contents of his Trickster pipe into the hearth, smiling at Po as he did so. "Needs a refill, don't you think?"

Po grunted and fell silent.

Barlimo looked relieved and asked for new business, calling on each member. She started the circle with herself. "Okay. Just the usual. A reminder to keep the front and back door locked. Tree, could you empty the basement garbage a little more regularly? With all the chemicals you use down there in the lab, I worry about fire safety. And as usual no one's been paying the papergirl. So, the *Daily Writ* is sending me hate mail. There are coppers on top of the icebox. Use them to pay the papergirl, please—not to tip happincabby drivers. All right?"

Heads nodded dutifully.

"Now for the good part," continued Barlimo. "Rents are

abysmal, and we're due for a Housing Commission inspection next week. If you can, give me the rent as soon as possible. Regarding the Housing Commission: I want this house spotless." The architect looked pointedly at Po. "That means I want to see spoons in the silverware drawer, Po. I want them out of your room."

"Is *that* where they all went to?" asked Mab. Po glared at her. She shrugged and closed her mouth.

"So get the house clean, folks. Otherwise, we may all find ourselves looking for new lodgings. And while I'm on it, *where* does the ad section of the *Writ* keep going? I pay for this paper, and I expect to read it when I come home from work. Clear?"

Heads nodded dutifully.

Professor Rowenaster was next. "Just two complaints. I'm not getting my messages. There's a box nailed to my door. If someone drops by, please let me know about it. I'm sorry I'm on the third floor, but that's how it is. Think of all the good exercise you'll get," he added, smiling. "My other complaint goes to Tree: can you keep your makeup gear in some other storage area besides the common front hall? It looks junky."

Tree sighed. "No problem, Rowen. I got fired tonight. By Janusin's darling," he added with no enthusiasm. The room groaned in sympathy. The hair color of the other Jinnjirri present turned a compassionate pale blue, even Janusin's. No one spoke. What was there to say? Most of the Kaleidicopions had expected Cobeth to fire Tree. Tree was Kaleidicopian and therefore a daily reminder to Cobeth of Cobeth's time spent at the house. Time Cobeth wanted to forget. Cobeth had a mean streak in his nature; he liked to get even. The residents of the K were a maverick family. When one person got hurt, all suffered. And Cobeth knew this. Tree took a deep breath. "Oh—guess it's me next. Um, I want off the pantry floor. Anybody else willing to do it? It's a bitch of a chore."

Mab raised her hand, nodding.

"Idiot," said Timmer, relieved that she didn't have to do it.

"Anything else, Tree?" asked Barlimo.

"Yes. The towels in the third floor bathroom—that's the one I use—are not, I repeat, *not* communal. I love you all within reason," he said to the seven people sitting around him. "However, using my towel is not within reason. And finally, I've got free passes to the new Merry Prickster Play. It's called

Rimble's Remedy. Stars your favorite Jinnjirri, Cobeth of Shift Shallows. Opens tomorrow night. See me if you want a pass."

"Count me out," said Janusin, his voice tired.

"What's the play about?" asked Timmer.

Rowenaster answered. "Religion. You'll love it."

Timmer gave the professor a withering smile and shut up.

"Jan?" said Barlimo. "Anything to say?"

The master sculptor shook his head, his hair turning a darker, more despondent blue. "Only that Room Five is now available. I'm taking most of Cobeth's house chores."

"Are you also running the Revel?" asked Barlimo.

Janusin nodded. "Oh, shit. That's right. The Trickster's Hallows." He took a deep breath. "It's our annual Rimble's Revel," he said to Mab who had never attended one. "Everyone comes as an aspect of Trickster. We try not to double up, so check around before you decide on your costume. If you need help with needle and thread, Tree is an accomplished tailor."

"Thanks for volunteering me, Janusin," said Tree with annoyance.

"You've got nothing but free time now," replied the sculptor.

"I have my classes!"

Professor Rowenaster started chuckling. "Did you study at *all* for my exam?"

Tree rolled his eyes, swore, and slumped in his chair.

Barlimo turned to Mab. "You're next, child."

Mab glanced nervously at Barlimo and then at Po. The little thief crossed his arms over his chest and stuck out his jaw. Mab blinked and decided to say nothing about her attempt to evict the Asilliwir. Barlimo had told her earlier that Timmer, Janusin, and Mab did not constitute a house quorum. So there was no point in taking a vote to oust Po. Cobeth's opinion—the fourth in the faction—didn't count now; he had moved out. Mab cleared her throat. "I've got just minor stuff."

The room immediately relaxed, Doogat and Barlimo in particular.

Mab smiled nervously and said, "I was wondering who was in charge of getting candles and flax oil for the house? I'm running low."

"Me," said the professor. "I can get a deal over at the University.

Mab nodded. "That's all, I guess."

"Great," said Barlimo. "Okay, Timmer. Let's have your list.

And try to keep it brief, will you? I want to see my pillow tonight."

Timmer was famous for long-winded, unasked for tutorials on The Proper Care of A House This Large. The blonde musician gave Barlimo an indignant scowl, quickly scanned the list she held in her hands, and pursed her lips. "Okay, the only thing that's simply got to be said is: DISHES!" she cried, glaring at Podiddley. "And don't you try to deny it, you little bugger. There's a dirty curry dish in the sink right now, and I know who it belongs to. You!"

Po yawned. "I was going to get it after the meeting, Timmer." He looked disdainfully at her. "You're so emotional."

Timmer jumped to her feet, her eyes blazing.

Before she could start berating Po, Doogat intervened.

"Timmertandi," he said authoritatively.

She paused in mid-sentence, turning to look at the Mayanabi.

"I think I can remedy the situation," Doogat continued, puffing on his meerschaum pipe in full view of Po. He smiled, the stem of the pipe held between his teeth firmly. "Po's going to live at my house for a little while. We'll call it Remedial Dishwashing."

Timmer's face blanched.

Po jumped to his feet. "I told you I'd smack your face if you said anything to him, Timmer!"

"I didn't!" she cried, taking refuge behind Doogat. "Tell him I didn't say anything to you," she begged the Mayanabi Master.

Doogat, who appeared to be enjoying her discomfort, regarded her innocently. "What're you talking about, Timmer?"

"For Presence-sake, Doogat!" she hissed as Po made a fist with his right hand. Before the Asilliwir could swing, however, Doogat reached out and grabbed the little thief by the shirt collar.

"Didn't Barlimo tell you how she felt about this kind of thing, Po?" Doogat shook the Asilliwir roughly. "Didn't she?"

Po, who had broken out in a sweat by now, muttered a meek, "Yes, Doogat. She did. She told me."

"And what did our good architect say, hmm?"

Po swallowed. "No violence in the house."

Doogat let go of his grip, and Po crumpled to the floor. Doogat surveyed him with approval and turned to Barlimo. "See," he said conversationally, "Po listens. You just have to know how to remind him."

Barlimo snorted. "I'll leave that to you, Doogat." Folding her hands in her lap, Barlimo looked down at Po and asked, "Did you have any business?"

Po shook his head, putting his face in his hands. He stared at the interlocking Asilliwir design on the rug beneath him, ignoring everybody.

"All right, then," said Barlimo happily, "I move this meeting be closed. We'll have another one just before the Trickster's Hallows. For guest lists and food particulars. Uh—let's say, in three weeks? Okay?"

Heads nodded dutifully.

Then people scrambled to their feet carrying mugs into the kitchen. In the street, the Great Library bells tolled one bell-morn. The entire group groaned, and everyone save Po and Doogat shuffled off to bed. Doogat waited for Po to get what he needed from his room—clothes, toilet articles, and Mayanabi texts—and ushered the little Asilliwir out of the Kaleidicopia.

As they walked down the front steps, Po asked, "How long do I have to stay with you, Master Doogat?"

"Until the House catches the real thief of Janusin's money."

Po stopped dead. "You knew? You knew I didn't do it?"

"Of course, I knew," muttered Doogat. "You're a Mayanabi first, Po. And a thief second."

The little Asilliwir smiled broadly. "Thanks, Doogs. Thanks for the confidence."

Doogat grunted and hailed a happincabby. As a pair of bay horses pulling a small covered carriage trotted toward them, Po asked, "So—how long do you think it'll be? Me staying at your place."

"That," said Doogat calmly, opening the carriage door for Po, "will depend on a great many things."

Part II:

SHIFTTIME

Mythmaker, Mythmaker—the Revel's begun,
Come speak the spell of Once Upon!
Let all things familiar be struck away,
The world's invited to a Prickster Play!

Chapter Twelve

IN PIEDMERRI, ON the morning following the Kaleidicopia's house meeting, Fasilla and Yafatah pulled away from the Asilliwir caravan camp, heading due east toward the land of Jinnjirri. Fasilla clucked to the pair of roan mares drawing their brightly painted wagon. Seeing a signpost just ahead, she said, "Read me the miles, child. Your eyes do be better than mine in this foggy dawn."

The fifteen-year-old girl did as she was bid. "One mile to the Jinnjirri *landdraw* border, Ma." Yafatah's glance fell to the wooden pointer hanging neatly below the crooked Jinnjirri one. She shook her head dazedly.

Fasilla caught the movement out of the corner of her eye. "Something wrong?"

"No," said Yafatah, pulling an orange blanket over her shoulders, "The sign for Speakinghast. It do remind me of something. That be all."

"A dream from last night?"

Yafatah, who was angry with her mother for taking her to Jinnjirri, refused to discuss it. Her mind, however, would not leave her alone. Finally, Yafatah looked back over her shoulder, unable to read the mileage for Speakinghast from this direction. Even so, the number remained in her memory: two hundred ninety-seven.

"How long would it take to get to Speakinghast?" asked Yafatah, hoping the question sounded idle.

"Depends," replied her mother, giving her a hard look. "Would you be travelling by horse—or by foot?"

Yafatah glared at her mother. "I doon't be planning to run away!"

"Who be saying you did?"

There was an awkward silence between them.

Fasilla reined the pair of roans to a stop. Yafatah huddled under the blanket farther, hating the fog, hating the early hour, and hating herself for having dreams that made people think she might be crazy. "Ma," she said more loudly than she had intended, "I *doon't* want to talk about it. I asked about Speakinghast because I do be curious. Because I havena' ever been there. All right?"

"No," replied her mother, trying to keep her temper. "It be *not* all right, Ya. You do be rude to me since breakfast, and I willna' have it. I realize, you do be sick. But you must try to be better to me, Ya." Fasilla's voice choked unexpectedly. "I love you, child. And—and you worry me."

Yafatah rolled her eyes under the blanket. "Then just leave me be, Ma. Doon't talk to me. Just drive."

Fasilla started to retort, then stopped herself. Her expression strained, she clucked again to the horses, heading for the worst Jinnjirri border of them all: the famous northwest shift—Mab's nightmare.

Yafatah shut her eyes under the blanket, her body rocking to the slow motion of the horses' gait. The wagon creaked as it rolled across muddy ruts and small potholes. The early morning fog swirled around them, and Yafatah shivered from the dampness. Shadowy forms from last night's sleep taunted her, their images remaining just out of reach. Except one. Trickster. Yafatah swore softly under her breath. Of course, she thought bitterly. Of course, *you* would be clear. You, stupid Greatkin Rimble. Yafatah bit her lower lip. It scared her that she was dreaming of Trickster. He was no good. No good at all. And it angered her that Rimble had appeared as old Jamilla in her dream. She loved Jammy. She would do almost anything for Jammy. Jammy was her friend. *Not* like Trickster.

"I would even go to Speakinghast for Jammy," she muttered.

Yafatah shrugged under her blanket. The thought of running away to a big city like Speakinghast appealed greatly to her right now. She could be anyone in such a place. No one in Speakinghast would know about her bad dreams, either. No one in Speakinghast would think she was sick. Or crazy. Yafatah sighed, her eyes downcast. Maybe if she had been born in a country like Saämbolin, her mother might understand her better. Maybe. And maybe not. This last was a singularly depressing thought, and Yafatah wiped a tear out of the corner of her eye.

"Why doon't you ever talk to me about me Pa?" she asked suddenly.

Fasilla stiffened. Without looking at her daughter, she said tersely, "Because there be nothing to talk about, Ya. You were carnival-begat. He was wearing a mask. It was dark."

"So, I was a mistake," Yafatah grumbled.

"Now, Ya—we do go over this many times. You were noo mistake. You do be an accident, but that doesna' mean I love you less. In Tammirring, they have a name for what you be: a Crossroads Child."

Yafatah raised her head. Her mother had never told her this. Genuinely curious, Yafatah asked her mother to explain further.

Fasilla shrugged. "I doon't speak Tammirring so well, but near as I can translate, it means you do be a gift from the Presence. *Because* you be carnival-begat. Protected, too, by the Greatkin."

"They doon't exist," scoffed Yafatah.

"They *do*. And mind your mouth lest one of them hears you."

"Oh, Ma," she muttered, her voice disappointed. "You do be so superstitious. Just like Cass. She thinks old Jamilla can give me the evil eye." Yafatah sighed. "Just because she be Mayanabi. And half-blind."

As this subject was a sore point between mother and daughter, Fasilla decided not to answer Yafatah. They would be at the door of the Jinnjirri healer in less than an hour. Let *her* handle Yafatah's strange allegiance to that old Mayanabi woman. Fasilla was certain Jamilla was at the root of Yafatah's illness. The Mayanabi were a crazy people, and some said their craziness was catching.

The horses suddenly stopped, their hindquarters quivering. They refused to walk farther. Fasilla gave the reins to her daughter and jumped off the caravan wagon. Going around to the back, the Asilliwir woman unhooked a leather feedbag. It was filled with oats and a potent mixture of wild baneberry. Baneberry was a tranquilizer; the horses would need it to get across the Jinnjirri *landdraw* border. She patted the roans' necks as she fed them. Fasilla, who was a skillful herbalist, watched their pupils. When she was satisfied that the drug had taken full effect, she returned the feedbag to the hook on the back of the red and blue wagon. She took her seat next to Yafatah once more and picked up the damp reins.

"This fog do add to the shift, doon't you think?" asked Fasilla conversationally.

"We doon't *have* to go to Jinnjirri, Ma," snapped Yafatah. "We could turn 'round, you know. Head to the Asilliwir desert for winter."

Fasilla slapped the reins on the rumps of the roans and urged them forward. She refused to argue with Yafatah about this one more time. They were going to Jinnjirri. And that was final.

As the horses crossed a narrow stretch of road, Yafatah's stomach lurched. She could feel the comforting *draw* of Piedmerri recede. Piedmerri was the home of Mnemlith's natural parents and caretakers. Famous for their skill at fostering—children, animals, or even plants—the Piedmerri were a race of ample laps and big families. The land itself was fertile and provided Mnemlith with most of its farm produce.

The land of Jinnjirri was fertile, too, but in a way wholly unlike gentle Piedmerri. In Jinnjirri, the fertility was of a raw, unbounded variety; in Jinnjirri, anything went. Status in Jinnjirri was not measured by a person's ability to provide an atmosphere that granted one the right to grow in an enclosed environment of emotional safety. In Jinnjirri, people were expected to reach their psychological edge and go beyond it. In Jinnjirri, status was based on originality verging on the eccentric. The more bizarre the relationship, project, or concept was, the greater acclaim the Jinnjirri accorded it. This was why only the dullest Jinnjirri—said the most eccentric Jinnjirri—would *ever* live in Speakinghast. Such persons were a disgrace to the *draw*, they added. Who but a bore could prosper in the confinement and structure of Saämbolin?

Yafatah regarded the lavender mist swirling ahead of the wagon with distaste. She forcibly relaxed her mind. The weirdness of the shift would be temporary, she told herself. Just a matter of a few disagreeable moments.

Unfortunately for Yafatah, things didn't quite turn out this way.
Rimble-Rimble.

Chapter Thirteen

AN EIGHTH OF a mile from where Yafatah and Fasilla prepared to cross the northwest Jinnjirri border, Kelandris of Suxonli forded a shallow forest river. Picking up her black skirts, she stepped lightly on the surface of protruding, moss-covered rocks. Halfway across she hesitated. The billowing mist of the Jinnjirri *landdraw* rose like a shimmering lavender wall not twenty feet ahead of her.

Kelandris shivered. She remembered crossing into Jinnjirri before, and she remembered disliking it. The shift had made her feel nauseous, and she had heard voices. She had also seen things—Tammirring fashion.

The landrace of Tammirring were Mnemlith's natural mystics. It was they who nurtured the spiritual psyche of the world. Psychics, seers, and prophets of all kinds abounded in this northern land. Being a people of extreme psychological sensitivity, the Tammirring rarely left the protection of their *draw*. The bustle and psychic smorgasbord of cities overwhelmed their acute inner senses, leaving a Tammirring feeling nervous and internally soiled. Even in their own country, the men and women of Tammirring wore veils to shield themselves from unwanted intrusions on their inner privacy. In this way, the Tammirring were similar to the hatted Jinnjirri. However, *unlike* the Jinnjirri, the Tammirring rarely involved themselves in politics or social reform. The Tammirring preferred the solitude of their own thoughts and inner promptings. Many claimed direct communication with the Presence. A few claimed to have actually seen a Greatkin. Kelandris was one of these latter. She claimed to have not only seen, but also to have spoken with the King of Deviance himself, Greatkin Rimble. He appeared for the first time, she said, soon after her eighth birthday. Rimble had remained her childhood companion. Then, at age sixteen, he had inexplicably abandoned her to the "justice of Suxonli"—just after she had danced for him and just after she had made love to a dark-eyed man professing to be Trickster's emissary. Kelandris shivered again, watching the lavender *landdraw* mist with dislike. The bright yellow of the leaves along Jinnjirri's border hurt her eyes. She regarded the color with the same hatred she reserved for the black robes she habitually wore. Yellow and black were Trickster's colors; they were The Wasp's Own. Kelandris scowled at the trees. Autumn was Trickster's glory. And her curse.

Kelandris glanced around herself furtively. Making sure she was completely alone, she raised her veil in an effort to see the mist more clearly. The late afternoon sun warmed her bronze-colored skin. The autumn wind caught several strands of her thick, black hair. The strands trailed over her broad shoulders, silky and glinting with blue highlights. Her hair was alive and full of motion. In contrast, Crazy Kel's pale, green eyes remained cool and devoid of passion. Only the acrimony of her perpetual sneer hinted at the furies this woman controlled. At thirty-three,

Kelandris was a woman aged before her time. Her lips were thin, her sex frozen. Black bangs blew into her icy, green eyes. Intent on watching the sideways motion of the lavender mist in front of her, Kelandris made no move to push the bangs out of her face. She stood alone, isolated—like a cold, stone statue at the entrance to a forgotten underworld. Neither ugly nor beautiful, Crazy Kel remained unfinished, her features as uncommitted as her passion. The woman in black frowned. She was trying to remember why she had left the Yellow Springs. Her lips twisted into an approximation of a smile. The girl, she thought. The Tammirring spy from Suxonli. The child who had seen something in the woods during the attack of the wild dogs. What had the child said in the darkness? What were her exact words?

He's gone.

Kelandris savored the words in her mind, wondering anew at their meaning. Abruptly, Kel's mood changed to anger. The child had seen with her inner senses what Kelandris could not! This puzzled Kelandris and simultaneously outraged her. Kel had been the Revel Queen—chosen by the Coins of Coincidence (also known as the Luck of the Trickster) to dance for Greatkin Rimble on the eve of his hallows. *She* was the one they had been waiting for; Kel was the prophesied *he*. She was the woman who could turn inside inside-out for Trickster. So who was this young Tammirring kitten? This rival vixen who would take her place? Crazy Kel's expression hardened, and she felt for her knife. This was a nervous gesture. Since yesterday, it had also become automatic.

The Jinnjirri mist swirled.

Kelandris considered crossing the river a little farther down, but decided against it. Moving south would bring her closer to the Tammirring girl. If she got too close, Kel was sure the Suxonli spy would pick up on her psychic nearness. Kel had already been hit once with a dart; she wouldn't give the child a chance to do it again.

"If it *was* a dart," Crazy Kel added to herself. She scratched at the small, angry scab in the middle of her forehead. This, too, was a nervous gesture. And like reaching for her knife, Crazy Kel was completely unaware of doing it. Blood from the torn scab wet the tips of her fingers. Crazy Kel frowned, staring at the crimson color.

She swallowed, feeling queer, all of her psychic senses on alert.

Something was going to happen, she thought uneasily. Something strange.

Kelandris flinched. The mist had left the bank and was swirling toward her legs. Jinnjirri *draw* was sneaky. Like the gender and hair color of its people, Jinnjirri *landdraw* was extremely mobile, able to change its location. Kelandris took a step backward and nearly lost her footing on the rocks. Making a hasty but ineffective gesture at the mist with her hands, she said, "Shoo. Go away."

The mist ignored her commands. Kelandris took another step backward and slipped into the cold river. The water reached to her knees. Kel ignored the shock of the cold and continued to back up. Her senses became confused, jammed up. Gasping, Kel wondered if she had inadvertently crossed from Piedmerri into the outermost border of shifting, unstable Jinnjirri. Panicking, Kel put her hands up to protect her face from the invading mist. As she did so, she caught sight of the blood on her fingertips again.

Blood Day Ritual—

Sound in her ears. A drone. Kelandris stumbled in the water and fled to the shore. The mist followed. Kel's robe, now soaked with river water, clung to her legs and made it difficult to move swiftly. Swearing, Crazy Kel scrambled up the bank, the sound of the drone increasing in her ears. She put her hands on her ears, biting her lower lip in a silent scream. *The drone. The sting. The blood. That night. In Suxonli—*

The Jinnjirri mist engulfed the woman in black.

Ah ya, RIMBLE! The Greatkin of Deviance. The Patron of Coincidence and the Impossible! Rescue when there's none! Disaster when the world least expects it! The Sting! The Wasp! Old Yellow Jacket—tonight he will be honored!

Kelandris staggered and fell to her knees. She rocked back and forth, her eyes shut, her hands clamped across her ears. The mist caressed her bloody forehead.

So sing it, ah ya, RIMBLE! Come, Trickster, come. Be yet again. But beware his back door ways, the thrall of his disrespect! Beware the color of his striped coat, the prick of his maddening sting! Change or be changed! Sing it, Yellow Jacket Yellow! The Wasp flies abroad tonight!

The mist slid down Kel's left hand, mixing with the blood on her fingers.

But where is Trickster's Common Ground? Where is this year's Revel Queen? Where is the she who dares to be he? *Why does she not greet her village chosen consort? He searches for the Wasp*

Queen and finds no one. He swears. He cannot find Trickster's Wild Kelandris.

In a nearby grove, the Wasp Queen smiles; she is making love with Trickster's Emissary. And her hands are bloody . . .

Yafatah squealed with dismay as she felt blood drip down the inside of her thigh. How could her bloodcycle have come so soon? Would she *never* get the rhythm of it? Surely, bloodcycles weren't this unpredictable? Or their flow this heavy? Rolling her eyes under her orange blanket, Yafatah was so put out with this messy turn of events that she failed to feel the first brush of the Jinnjirri *draw* as its mist tickled her shoulder. Her abdomen cramped. Shivering instinctively, Yafatah mumbled, "Why does the blood have to come right *now*?"

Crazy Kel stared at her hands, the lavender mist lacing them together with cruel stays from the past. Lavender turned to red in Kel's inner sight and dripped. Crazy Kel blinked in horror. Animal whimpers of fear rose in her throat. She rubbed her hands on her black—

—and yellow striped costume.

Crazy Kel pulled her veil over her face hastily.

"You do well to cover your face, missy," said Elderwoman Hennin. "Flout village law, if you wish. Break the Blood Day Rule. Dance if the blood comes to you on the eve of Trickster's Hallows. And see what happens. It matters little to me, but just remember this, missy: deviance has its consequences. Step outside village law, and you also step outside its protection." Elderwoman Hennin smiled here. "You can be sure of one thing about Trickster, missy. He'll offer you no protection of his own. That's not his way. He'll dance you and leave you."

"But Rimble's not like that," protested the young girl in the black and yellow costume. "He's a Greatkin. He's my friend."

Elderwoman Hennin met her eyes. "Trickster likes his dupes young. Know why? So he can make fools out of you. There's nothing nice about Rimble, missy. There's nothing the least bit nice about The Wasp."

Yafatah pointed dazedly at the Jinnjirri mist. She felt her mother reach for her hand as a gesture of comfort. The touch of her mother's hand hurt her heightened sense of touch, and Yafatah pulled away, huddling alone under her orange blanket. Images of the previous night's dreams presented themselves to the young Tammirring girl for the second time that morning. Yellow and black. Old Jamilla in yellow and black rags, motioning Yafatah to her side.

"Go to Speakinghast. Before it's too late."

"Too late for what, Jammy?" asked Yafatah, bewildered.

"For me to matter."

Yafatah blinked. "I doon't understand, Jammy."

"Fool," said the old Mayanabi woman softly. Then, she pulled back her raggedy cowl of yellow and black patches. She had pied eyes. Yafatah stared at the old woman's face.

"You be not me friend, Jammy! You be not me friend at all! You be Greatkin Rimble come to prank me!"

Yafatah's memory of this portion of her dream became so vivid that she began speaking the words out loud. Fasilla turned to her in alarm.

"Doon't get caught in the shift, child. Remember yourself!"

Fasilla's Tammirring-born daughter ignored her. Getting to her feet in the wagon, Yafatah wagged a finger at something Fasilla couldn't see and shouted, "I willna' do for you, Trickster! I willna' turn, and I willna' go to Speakinghast! Elderwoman Hennin be right. You be a wasp! And you do be pranking me with blood!"

Fasilla stared at Yafatah, her face pale. "Hennin?" she whispered.

Yafatah met her mother's eyes with fear. She blinked, feeling very disoriented. Where had all those thoughts come from? *She* knew no one named Elderwoman Hennin. Yafatah looked around herself frantically. She could sense someone else in the mist. Someone half-mad, someone choosing—

—*not to dance for Greatkin Rimble.*

Sixteen-year-old Kelandris stared at the blood on her hands. "The blood has come on Trickster's Eve," she whispered softly. "If I dance, I don't know what will happen. Something bad, say the Elders. But I am Rimble's chosen consort. And he is the Greatkin of Deviance. So, I must answer his call. I must be worthy of being his Revel Queen. I must not be afraid of the unexpected. Or the impossible. I must be Trickster's he," she whispered, her green eyes frightened. "But I don't know what that is. I don't know what that means." Kelandris swallowed. "Laws are made to help, not hinder. There must be a reason why the Elders say: No

Revel Queen shall turn for Trickster on the night of her first blood."

Yafatah frowned. "But this isna' my first blood. It do be me third." Yafatah looked at the Jinnjirri mist as it swirled around her thighs. "And Speakinghast be too far away. I canna go there alone. I should stay with me Ma—"

Crazy Kel blinked. "Stay with my mother?" She laughed bitterly. "Stay with the one who would not speak a single word in my defense at the Ritual of Akindo?" Crazy Kel's expression changed from perplexity to contempt. "Coward," she hissed at the voice in the mist. "You're not worthy to turn for Greatkin Rimble. Only women of courage are worthy. Only women of spirit. And such women do *not* stay home with their mothers."

"*I* have spirit," said Yafatah indignantly. "It be just that I love me Ma. And I be all she has."

"Excuses," muttered Kelandris. "Break the Blood Day Rule. It's the right of the Trickster's *he*!"

"But I'm the Crossroads Child," cried Yafatah. "I'm not the—"

Fasilla glanced sharply at her daughter. "Doon't forget yourself, Ya! This be shadows, Ya. This be not real. And it will pass, child. Let it go. Let it pass *over* you. Don't get caught—"

Yafatah clawed the air with her fingers.

Six hundred feet away, Crazy Kel clawed the air with her fingers. The identities of the two Tammirring merged, their psyches tangling. Crazy Kel sat up abruptly, her mind clear for the first time in sixteen years.

Yafatah stared wide-eyed at her mother. Then she announced, "I draw the Jinn-mist round about! That's my way to keep Trickster out!" Before Fasilla could wonder about her daughter's sudden drop of accent, Yafatah added in yet another voice, "Shifttime! Jinnaeon! End of the world! *Big* changes! *Big* doings!" Yafatah broke into wild peals of laughter.

Fasilla forced the roan mares into a trot. They splashed through the shallow river and up the bank into Jinnjirri. Fasilla urged the horses into a canter, glancing at her Tammirring child whenever she could afford to take her eyes off the dirt road. Yafatah was sitting on the edge of the seat, kicking the air with her feet like a small child. Yafatah caught her mother's worried eye and winked.

Fasilla said nothing, driving the mares northeast toward the house of the Jinnjirri healer. Without realizing that she was doing so, Fasilla now drove her daughter to the edge of sanity as well. This was a strange borderland of the psyche. Trickster territory. Unpredictable and fertile.

Yafatah shivered as the Jinnjirri *landdraw* pried away her Tammirring defenses and set her adrift in space and time. Single identity ceased to exist for Yafatah. Guideless, she felt as if she were drowning.

Yafatah's Trickster smile suddenly faded.

"Help," she whispered. "Help—"

Kelandris stood up slowly, feeling herself and yet not herself. She was not aware of Yafatah or Yafatah's distress directly. However, she did notice a queer sensation of having been psychically buttressed in some unexpected fashion. She tested the strength of it and found it worthy. She was just about to laugh for joy when she saw the flash of something black and yellow off to her left. Kelandris crossed her arms over her chest. She grunted under her veil.

"Don't expect me to welcome you with open arms, Rimble," she muttered at the little four-feet-seven Greatkin peeking at her from behind a nearby tree. "You're a stinking sonofabitch."

"Charming sentiments," he retorted. "And after all this time."

Kelandris scowled. "I should never have danced for you."

"But you did it *ever* so well," replied Trickster, his pied eyes glittering in the light of the early morning sun. "And I was so proud."

"You made me crazy," said Kelandris, looking around for a sizable stick or a good throwing stone.

Trickster watched her warily. "Don't blame *me* for what Suxonli did to you, kiddo."

"You abandoned me," she said calmly, grabbing a small boulder. She towered over Trickster by nearly two feet. "When I needed you most, too." Still calm, she added, "You're not a Face of the Presence. You're Its *ass*!" Kelandris lobbed the boulder at him. Her aim was so true that in order to get out of the way of it, Rimble had to dematerialize.

He rematerialized a few seconds later in the upper branches of a tree directly above Kelandris. Rimble looked down at her and said, "Well, we could do this all day. Or you could do something really useful—like make up for lost time."

"Me!" shouted Kelandris, her green eyes blazing under her veil. She grabbed the tree by its trunk and shook it. The trunk was narrow and supple, and she shook it with such vigor that she nearly managed to unseat Trickster.

He swore, scrambling for a better perch. "Mortals," he muttered under his breath. Then, looking down at Kelandris again, he said, "So?"

"So, I hate you," replied Kelandris, suddenly realizing that the psychic buttressing she felt was probably due to some trick of Rimble's. That meant it wouldn't last. That meant she would be crazy again. Anguished, Kel slammed the tree with her fist. Swearing at Rimble, she ran quickly away, her veil fluttering behind her. As she turned the corner, Trickster intercepted her. He jumped down from an outcrop of rock and prevented her passage.

"Get out of my way!" she cried.

"Kelanoorhin," said Rimble softly. This was Kel's name in Oldspeech, the language of the Greatkin. Rimble had taught Kel its meaning as a child: "she who blooms in the wild light." Kelandris had not heard the word spoken for sixteen years. Trickster had always used it as an endearment.

The woman in black hesitated, all her rage losing its direction. She cleared her throat, reaching under her veil and savagely scratching the bloody scab on her forehead. "What do you want?" she asked hoarsely.

"I want you to go to Speakinghast."

Kelandris snorted. "I'm Tammirring, Rimble. We don't do well in cities."

"I have a protected place for you. A safe house."

She shook her head, still refusing.

Trickster hadn't expected it to be easy to convince Kelandris to travel to Speakinghast. He decided to try his next approach: compassion and curiosity. If that didn't work, he'd go for revenge. That one was a sure motivator in Kel's case, and Rimble wished to avoid using it if possible. For one thing, Zendrak would be Kel's target. And Zendrak just wouldn't understand or appreciate it. Understandable, thought Trickster. No one likes being the target for revenge. Especially if you're not the party who's to blame for the problem in the first place. And Zendrak was utterly innocent regarding Kelandris of Suxonli. Yonneth? And Elderwoman Hennin? Well, that was a different matter altogether. Trickster would get to them in due time. The little Greatkin grinned. In due time.

Trickster picked up a few rocks and started juggling them effortlessly. "All sorts of legacies are passed from one generation to another," he said conversationally. "Why not a killing spiritual loneliness?"

"What do you mean?" she asked uneasily.

"Oh, you *know*. That bottomless pit you wake up with every morning? Call it soul ache." Rimble changed the direction of his juggling. "It's a feeling of being hungry for something that has no name. Can make a person real desperate inside. They'll do almost anything not to feel soul ache. Even go crazy," he added softly, his eyes meeting her hidden ones for a moment.

Kelandris stiffened. "I don't know what you're talking about."

"Then listen," said Rimble. At that very moment the stifled, terrified scream of a young girl travelled on the wind to meet them. Trickster grunted. "The future *can* scream, Kelandris. It's alive, you see. Just like that young girl. Fortunately for her, the child's mother is taking her to a healer. So that child's experience of soul ache will be short. Perhaps."

Kelandris said nothing for a moment. Then she asked. "You gave the Tammirring girl my madness?" she asked.

"You wouldn't let me in the front door, Kelandris. So I got creative."

The woman in black swore loudly. "You can't give that girl my madness, Rimble! I'm accustomed to it. I know why it happened. She won't understand. Her *body* won't understand. It's not her burden to bear. It's mine."

Rimble laughed harshly. "Are you saying you'll go to Speak-inghast for Yafatah's sake? That's her name, by the way. Yafatah. Means: opener of the door. Nice, don't you think?"

"What're you getting at, Rimble?"

"Only this: compassion becomes you, Kelandris, but we both know why you're following that child. Why you want her psyche left intact."

"Why?" Kelandris snapped.

Trickster smiled. "You suspect Yafatah knows things. Spiritual things. Sees things like you did once. Makes you itch, doesn't it? You wonder why you don't remember your dreams? Why you never see me anymore, hmmm? You're the shut door, kiddo. And Yafatah is your key."

Kelandris swallowed. "How long will Yafatah be mad?"

"You mean, how long will you be sane? Depends on you. Depends on if you go to Speakinghast or not."

Kelandris swore angrily. "What do you want me to do in Speakinghast?"

"Just turn."

"Like I did in Suxonli!" she exploded.

Trickster sniffed haughtily. "There's no reason to get sore about it."

"You tried to kill me!"

"Not me," said Trickster, his pied eyes turning hard. Then he added, "Sometimes you have to lose something in order to find it, Kelandris. Sometimes, you have to turn the inside inside-out. And enter through the exit. Sometimes, you have to turn contrarywise, Kelandris. Because nothing else will do."

"But why me!" she cried furiously.

"Because you're still my Revel Queen," said Trickster with unexpected affection in his voice. "Because you alone have tasted the poison of my sting and survived. Because you alone bore the full brunt of my touch at the Ritual of Akindo but were cheated of my true ecstasy."

Kelandris frowned, feeling confused. "I thought you said you weren't responsible for the Ritual of Akindo."

"The Ritual of Akindo was a potential."

"Of what?"

"Of cruelty."

There was a long pause.

Kelandris shut her eyes. She felt exhausted. She felt unsure of what Trickster was telling her. But it had always been like that. Even as a child, Kelandris had never been certain when Trickster was telling her something straight out or when he was simply hinting. The Ritual of Akindo was still too painful in her mind for her to want to dwell on it. She hoped in her heart that Trickster was *not* responsible for it. After all, he was a Greatkin. He was a Face of the Presence. Kelandris stared down at the ground. If Trickster *was* behind the Ritual of Akindo, she thought miserably, then that would mean Elderwoman Hennin had been right about the bandy-legged little Greatkin all along.

"There's nothing nice about a wasp," she muttered.

Trickster grunted. "Some wasps kill off certain kinds of parasites. The Univer'silsila wasp does that. Pretty generous, if you ask me. So—will you go?"

Kelandris shook her head. "No," she said firmly. "I won't."

Rimble stroked his black goatee. "Well, then you'll miss out."

Kelandris said nothing. She had no intention of falling for such an obvious ploy. Trickster was clearly wanting her to ask him to explain the meaning of his statement. Kelandris tapped her foot. "You're out of practice, Rimble."

Trickster shrugged. "I'd no idea we were having a contest here," he said disdainfully. "I was just trying to be helpful. Save you some revenge time. But if you're not interested—"

"Revenge against who?"

Trickster began picking lint off his black and yellow greatcoat. "That fellow." When Kelandris registered a blank, Trickster added, "Oh, you *know* the guy. Real tall with dark hair. Smells funny—"

"Zendrak!" she said, her heart starting to pound, her face paling.

"Was that his name?" asked Trickster idly. "Well, whatever. I just thought you'd like to tell him a thing or two. About *that* night. Uh—just before you danced for me?"

"You mean when I—"

"Yes, yes," said Trickster hastily, appearing not to want to discuss Zendrak and Kel's love-making on the eve of Trickster's Hallows. "That night," he repeated, and folded his hands primly in his lap.

Kel's eyes narrowed under her veil. "Zendrak's in Speaking-hast?"

"That's what I said, didn't I?"

Kelandris suddenly straightened. "Wait a minute, Rimble. You're acting like you don't know Zendrak. He said he was your emissary."

Trickster pursed his lips. "Well, well. Mortals *will* say the damnedest things." Rimble climbed up on a rock. "Just goes to show you can't believe everything you hear, hmm? And things did go *so* badly after he touched you."

Kelandris said nothing. She felt unexpectedly disappointed about Zendrak. She could hardly remember the few hours that she and he had spent together—the impact of it had been shattered by the Ritual of Akindo. Still, she was sure she recalled something special about that time. Something wild. Something powerful. Maybe even something good. Kelandris stared at the fall of a crimson leaf as it drifted lazily to the ground. Whatever had happened between herself and the man called Zendrak—she was sure it would never happen again. She was a convicted murderess now.

"*And* I'm Crazy Kel," she whispered.

"Yes," said Trickster unexpectedly.

Kelandris glowered at him.

Trickster shrugged. "It's not *my* fault. And neither will it be my fault if you *keep* being crazy. I've given you your way out. Your loophole."

"Speakinghast?"

"Take it or leave it."

Kelandris hesitated. Then without even a backward look, Kelandris of Suxonli turned northeast heading for the route that would take her around Jinnjirri and through the southernmost tip of Tammirring via the Eastern Feyborne Mountains. The trip would take her about two to three weeks depending on the weather in the mountains. By Trickster's estimation, Kelandris of Suxonli would arrive at the Kaleidicopia just in time for the "K's" annual Trickster's Hallows.

By then, Kelandris would also be quite mad again. And Zendrak's problem.

Trickster watched Kel disappear over the next rise. Doing a small pirouette, he rubbed his hands together and said, "Perfect!"

As it turned out, there were at least two people who didn't agree with this evaluation of Rimble's. The first person was Zendrak; the second was the Patron of Great Loves and Tender Trysts, Greatkin Phebene—Rimble's sentimental, rose-garlanded sister.

The Panthe'kinarok Interlogue

THEMYTH, THE GREATKIN of Civilization and Ancient Hospitality, eyed the place cards on the enormous round table sitting in the feasting hall at Eranossa. Sathmadd, the Greatkin of Organization, had invented the idea of place cards only that morning. Themyth leaned forward, slipping her wrinkled hand between delicate china and glassware to fetch the card resting directly to the left of her own place setting. She lifted it up and read the beautifully lettered script. The card said: Trickster.

Themyth grunted. Considering what Rimble had in mind for the mortals—a new game he called "topsy-turvy"—Themyth wondered if this was the best seating arrangement for her little brother.

Perhaps he should be put between Love and Imagination, she thought, rearranging five cards deftly. Themyth surveyed the new combination. Sathmadd on Themyth's right, Phebene on Themyth's left, and Rimble sandwiched between Phebene and Jinndaven. Much better, she decided and took a plum from the table's silver cornucopia.

"Ooh," she grunted, rubbing the small of her back gingerly, a strand of gray hair falling into her ancient face. Themyth wished Rimble had been a little less acrobatic in his love-making. Still, she mused with a naughty, pleased smile, Trickster's improvement had been most generous in both its size and effect. Themyth chuckled, instantly losing fifteen years off her apparent age. Two feet had been *quite* substantial—in more ways than one. She nibbled the soft, sweet fruit in her old hand.

Still grinning, Themyth rematerialized herself at her proper age. Regaining her stately composure, she unbuttoned the top of her fabulous, colorful coat of tales, feeling daring. And uncommonly randy. Called Eldest by the other Greatkin, Themyth's name meant "great story." It was she who chronicled all the histories of mortals and immortals alike. Her personal symbol was the blazing cave-hearth, and it was around the flame that Themyth's "memories" were most often shared.

Themyth's word was respected in all things. She alone held the honor of presiding over the great meet of her ragtag family, that once-an-age council they called the Panthe'kinarok—that Divine Potluck Feast wherein the fate of a world might be decided by the choosing of Bordeaux over Burgundy, and the outcome of a hundred-year war might be reached through someone spreading butter sloppily on a steaming dinner roll. Nothing was too small to "matter" in the Everywhen of the Presence.

Occasionally, however, the themes for the Age to Come were set into motion during the hours *before* the Panthe'kinarok. Under these circumstances, Themyth might be required to give counsel without benefit of long deliberation or sprawling family caucus. This was just the sort of situation that presented itself to Themyth now.

"Theeeemth!" cried the Greatkin of Love, running hurriedly toward the crone. "Oh, thank the Presence I found you!"

"What's wrong?"

Phebene was about to answer Themyth when her eyes fell on the newly arranged place cards. "Well, will you look at that? Maybe nothing."

The Greatkin of Civilization smiled.

Phebene straightened the garland of wild green roses on her head, saying, "See, I just talked to Sathmadd, and the old crab said she wouldn't put Trickster next to me. She didn't want to have to listen to 'the jokes' during dinner. 'The jokes,'" repeated the Greatkin of Love, rolling her eyes. "Maddi is such an eternal *prude*. I don't know how Rimble ever got her in bed last Panthe'kinarok."

"With difficulty," replied Themyth. "Believe me."

Their conversation was interrupted by a sleepy looking Greatkin of Imagination. Jinndaven walked toward his sisters slowly, his filmy robe of lavenders and mauves trailing gently behind him. He yawned as he reached them. His Primordial Face looked a little crumpled.

Phebene put her hands on her hips. "*Where* have you been!" she demanded. "I've been searching for you high and low! Sathmadd nearly caused a doomsday scenario," Phebene said, nodding at the large table behind them.

"What?" asked Jinndaven stifling a second yawn, "did she sit Trickster next to Mattermat and Troth?"

Mattermat and Troth were the Greatkin of All Things Made Physical and Death, respectively.

"Almost," replied Phebene. "Next to Mattermat and Themyth."

Themyth snorted. "Troth looks nothing like me. My wrinkles are better."

"Interesting," said Jinndaven trying to imagine Sathmadd's combination.

"Well, it certainly wouldn't have been fun!" retorted Phebene.

Themyth interrupted here. "It's all been taken care of, Jinn. Trickster will be sitting between Phebene and you."

All trace of Jinndaven's sleepiness vanished. "*Me!*" he cried, aghast. "That's a rotten idea. Stinks of Trickster, too. I object. Vigorously!"

"Why?" asked Themyth.

"I just spent the last two hours sleeping off Trickster's latest improvement. Experiment is more like it," he added with contempt. "The little rug-rat turned me inside inside-out. And I will not spend an entire nine course dinner seated next to His Short and Mighty!"

Phebene's reaction was unexpected; she dissolved in tears.

Themyth and Jinndaven both stared at the little puddle on the floor that was now the Patron of Great Loves and Tender Trysts. Neither of the two Greatkin knew what to say. Finally Themyth cleared her throat and mumbled, "She's such a sentimental lass. *Terribly* romantic, you know."

"Yes," said Jinndaven still looking at his liquified sister. He bent close to the puddle and whispered, "What if Maddi comes in this room, Phebes? Only Rimble has the right to change his Primor—" Jinndaven broke off unexpectedly, his expression alarmed. Trickster's *shift* was translating! To everyone! And everything!

Themyth waited for him to explain.

"He *shifted* me, Eldest. Rimble's got this crazy idea about transposing all Reality—us, too—into a higher pitch. Says it'll make us 'loose' for a while! Just look at Phebene!"

Themyth grunted. Jinndaven was such an alarmist. The crone squatted stiffly beside Phebene. "Phebes, it doesn't matter how much Jinndaven protests about the seating arrangements. Trickster belongs between you and the Greatkin of Imagination for this Panthe'kinarok. And that's my final decision."

Phebene instantly rematerialized as her lovely, radiant self. Throwing her arms around Themyth, Phebene said, "Good. That way there's hope."

"Hope for what?" asked Jinndaven dubiously. "Us?"

"No, you ten-foot narcissist. For those lovers. That's who I'm crying for. Kelandris and Zendrak."

"The names are familiar," said Jinndaven.

"Of course," replied Phebene indignantly. "Don't you remember that love story I started to tell you last millennium? We left off when Zendrak—"

Themyth interrupted here, her expression astounded and dismayed. "*Those* two are lovers?"

"Were," corrected Phebene. "But that's all going to change," she added, rubbing her hands together with pleasure. "True love to the rescue."

Themyth stared at Phebene. "You mean you really don't know?"

Phebene shrugged at Eldest, straightening her garland for the countless time. "Know *what*?"

Jinndaven rolled his eyes. "Why are there chills running down my back? Why do I have a bad feeling about this?"

The Greatkin of Civilization put her bony arm around the slender waist of the Greatkin of Love, and said, "Phebes, we need to talk."

Phebene narrowed her eyes. "Now, Eldest, you *know* how I am about unrequited love."

"Hates it," said Jinndaven nodding.

"It's more complicated than that—" began Themyth, scanning her long coat to see if she could find a tale to illustrate her point.

Phebene pulled away from Eldest, putting her hands on her hips. "I *want* a happy ending!"

"Would you settle for deviant?" asked Themyth, looking up.

"I will *not*! These two are mine, Themyth! Not Rimble's! He better stay clear, too! Otherwise, I'll suffocate him with roses! I'll plaster his face with valentines! I'll—" She broke off, searching for the worst possible punishment she could think of for Trickster. The Greatkin of Love smiled. "I'll stuff him to bursting with meaningful glances and cooing candlelit dinners for two. Eat romance, Rimble!" she cried, raising her fist. Then, before anyone could stop her, the Patron of Great Loves and Tender Trysts strode out of the feasting hall, her rainbow gown fluttering like battle banners.

Jinndaven looked at Eldest. "Was Trickster expecting this?"

Themyth bit her lower lip. "I don't think so."

Jinndaven stroked his chin. "Ah," he said thoughtfully. He imagined several possible outcomes. "Think Love can outsmart Deviance?"

Eldest shrugged, her expression also thoughtful. "Don't know."

Jinndaven grinned. "Well, I'd like to see her try."

Themyth picked up the hem of her long coat of tales and touched one or two of the brightly colored appliqués. She chuckled. "Me, too." She inclined her head. "I better go have that talk with Phebes. And you—" she said pointing a bony finger at the Greatkin of Imagination, "mum's the word. If Trickster finds out we're helping Phebene—"

"We!" cried Jinndaven.

"We," repeated Themyth firmly. "Just remember, dear fellow, you and Phebene are sitting next to Trickster for the Panthe'kinarok. That's nine courses, Jinn."

Jinndaven licked his lips, eyeing the table behind them. "We couldn't change the cards around again?"

"No, we couldn't," said Eldest.

Jinndaven rolled his eyes and began thinking of ways to help the Greatkin of Love outsmart Trickster.

Chapter Fourteen

FASILLA REINED HER roan mares to a stop just outside a small thatched cottage. The cottage was whitewashed, its shutters bright yellow. Rows of orange hollyhocks and royal blue irises fanned the short space between the windows and the dark, rich earth of the Jinnjirri healer's front lawn. Fasilla stared at the flowers in surprise. It was nearly autumn; these flowers were not only out of season, they weren't native to Jinnjirri. Fasilla shrugged. Well, anything could happen in the borderlands of a *draw* like Jinnjirri's. Especially if a Jinnjirri named Aunt lived on the premises. Fasilla pulled Yafatah to the side of the wagon. Jumping to the ground lightly, the Asilliwir woman coaxed Yafatah to do the same. The young girl did so hesitantly, her eyes half-closed, her face pale. As Yafatah joined her mother on Jinnjirri soil, the door to the cottage behind them opened abruptly.

"Hey," said a young man's voice. "Like—uh—are you expected or anything?"

Fasilla turned around. Before her stood an Asilliwir lad of about sixteen. His hair was short around the bottom of his neck, the top crowning his head with a mop of varied lengths and braids. He might be Asilliwir born, thought Fasilla drily, but this young punk had clearly adopted all things Jinnjirri. Especially his mishmash of brightly colored clothing—complete with tiny round mirrors and glass sequins. Fasilla stood closer to her daughter, encircling Yafatah's waist with her tanned arm.

"No," said Fasilla brusquely. "We doon't be expected. I be an old friend of Aunt's." She paused. "This be me daughter, Yafatah. She do be ill, so if we could be cutting the conversation? Be Aunt about or noo?"

The Asilliwir lad ignored Fasilla's question, peering at Yafatah. "Tammirring, huh?" He chuckled in disbelief. "Greatkin—you brought a Tammi through the Northwest Shift? Didn't you read the warning signs?"

"There do be none where we crossed!" snapped Fasilla, resenting the boy's suggestion that she might be an idiot. Yafatah had never had serious trouble with Jinnjirri *draw* in the past. Why should this time have been so different?

The boy eyed her with amusement. He bowed grandly to Fasilla and asked, "Whom may I say is calling at this preposterous hour?"

Fasilla's face colored. She had been so intent on getting Yafatah to Aunt, she had completely forgotten the time. Fasilla squinted at the newly rising sun.

"Five forty-five," said the boy with an insolent smile.

Fasilla lost her temper. "My name do be Fasilla of Ian Abbi. I was one of Aunt's closest schoolmates in Piedmerri. So watch your mouth!"

"Hey—like I could *care*," retorted the lad. "Seems everybody's related to Aunt one way or another. That's why she's Aunt. So—like why don't you just back off, okay?" he said huffily. "Try camping out here for a couple of hours. That way Aunt can get at least two hours of *sleep!*" he added with obvious contempt for Fasilla's thoughtlessness.

"Two hours of sleep? What—"

"Yeah. Two friggin' hours, lady. We've been having some trouble with the border weather. Aunt's been up all night trying to straighten it out. The flowers think it's spring, see. So do the trees. Ever heard a tree scream? Well, you will when Old Man Frost comes through here in about two weeks—with winter catching a free ride on his coattails." The lad grunted. "We got a name for warm days like these: Trickster Summer."

Fasilla glanced at Yafatah. Her dark-haired daughter had started shivering at the mention of Trickster's name. Fasilla touched Yafatah's cheek reassuringly. She turned back to the Asilliwir lad. "If you would be so kind as to wake Aunt, *I* will take the consequences of her displeasure."

"What displeasure?" boomed Aunt's voice out of the second floor dormer window. "Fas—you've aged! Get your ass in here and tell me why! Burni," she yelled at the Asilliwir, "take them to the kitchen. Put a brew on while you're at it. And make it black. I've got to prop my eyes open with *some*thing. Might as well be tea." The window slammed shut.

"Your name be Burni?" asked Fasilla as she and Yafatah walked in the front door to Aunt's cheery cottage.

"Yeah," he replied indifferently. "I used to be an arsonist."

Fasilla rolled her eyes, muttering, "Great." As she and Yafatah found seats in Aunt's tiny kitchen—lifting cut materials and dried herbs out of the way—Fasilla was careful to put Yafatah as far away from Burni as possible; she didn't want her only child coming under the influence of someone as dubious as a former arsonist. Aunt entered the kitchen a few moments later clothed in nothing but a striped cotton nightshirt.

Jinnjirri born, Aunt had long colorful hair that sprayed out of her head like a cascade of spiky rainbows. At thirty-six. Fasilla's exact age, Aunt was still a beautiful—if not exotic—woman. Or man. Currently, Aunt was a woman to please Fasilla. She remembered that her Asilliwir friend had been more than a little unnerved by an unexpected (but flattering) gender change on Aunt's part one lazy, hot summer between school terms in Piedmerri. Of course, there had been sexual implications in that change. Fasilla had been firm; she didn't want to introduce such complications into their three-year friendship. And that was final, said Fasilla, at the time.

Aunt studied the strain in Fasilla's posture and face. Fasilla had changed in the past twenty years since Herbalist School. Aunt wondered why, glancing at Yafatah. Aunt's eyes widened. Walking hurriedly to the girl's side, Aunt turned accusingly to Burni and Fasilla, saying:

"Why did no one tell me she had shift fever?"

Burni shrugged, pouring cups of hot cinnamon-spice tea for everyone.

"Shift fever may na' be all she has," said Fasilla slowly. "Otherwise, I would've given her baneberry and comfrey and let her sleep it off."

Aunt nodded her head, her hazel eyes peering into Yafatah's green ones. "I see what you mean. Let's bring her in here," she added, leading Yafatah into a small bedroom off of the kitchen. "Burni, you be nice to Fas while I examine the child."

"Doon't you want me with you?" asked Fasilla, getting to her feet. "I mean you might have questions. And it *do* be more complicated, Aunt. It do. Yafatah hasna' been sleeping well—"

Aunt shook her head, her thick mop of hair falling forward over Yafatah's slight shoulders. "Fas—you worry too much. You always have. Now sit and drink your tea like a good girl. And *let* me do my job, eh?"

"But—"

"Sit," repeated Aunt, shutting the bedroom door in Fasilla's face.

There was an awkward silence between Fasilla and Burni.

The boy shrugged. "She's quite good, you know. Especially with this kind of thing. Typical border born. *Very* opinionated." He grinned. "Opinions are 'bout the only things that *don't* shift around here."

Fasilla grunted. She'd forgotten how opinionated Aunt could be. Glancing at the pans and knickknacks hanging on the walls, she said, "Typical Aunt clutter. Just like our old dorm room together. She used to call me an Asilliwir simpleton." Fasilla laughed. "I couldna' find *any*thing in Aunt's mess. She could, though. Every time."

The bedroom door opened abruptly. Aunt ignored Fasilla's inquiring look and called to Burni, "Get me some of that fresh wheat juice in the icebox, will you? And a glass."

The door shut again.

Fasilla shrugged. Wheat juice was harmless enough. Strong and very green, but harmless. She wondered what Aunt wanted with it, watching Burni rummage in the cold storage of the literal icebox.

The boy looked over his shoulder at Fasilla, starting to laugh. "I can't find it—"

"Here—let me look," said Fasilla getting to her feet to help.

Several minutes elasped. The bedroom door opened again. Seeing the two Asilliwir with their heads stuck in the icebox, Aunt started swearing good naturedly at them both. Leaving Yafatah for the moment, then Jinnjirri pulled Fasilla and Burni away from the overflowing shelves. She reached in once, and pulled out a tall bottle of thick, green liquid.

"Asilliwir simpletons," muttered Aunt, grabbing a glass and disappearing into the bedroom once more.

Burni and Fasilla looked at each other. Chuckles soon followed.

Aunt, who was listening on the other side of the door, said, "Good. Can't work in a house full of worry." Putting the green tonic aside—it had already served its use—Aunt sat very still beside Yafatah. She brushed a strand of dark hair out of the child's damp face and added softly, "You just relax, child. I've got to get a second opinion. It'll just take a moment." Yafatah nodded and stared blearily at the wall.

Aunt closed her eyes. Her breathing slowed and deepened. A short while later, she smiled. There had been an answering tug on the other end of the psychic line; the Irreverent Old Doogat of Suf had received her message. He relayed that he needed a few minutes to consider the problem. Please keep the line open, he said, and he'd get back to her as soon as he could.

Aunt leaned back in her chair, waiting patiently for Doogat's long distance reply. This was a convenient method of communication, but it was only possible between Mayanabi of at least Sixth Rank and up. Aunt, like Doogat, was a Mayanabi Nomad. With hard work and application, Burni would become her student sometime in the next year. At present, the boy thought he was merely apprenticing to a master herbalist. He had no idea that Aunt was a Sixth Rank, Twenty-two Degree initiate of the infamous Order of the Mayanabi Nomads. Such rank was no small feat at Aunt's relatively tender age.

The Jinnjirri healer straightened in her chair; Doogat's reply was coming in now. Aunt's ready smile faded. She opened her hazel eyes slowly, her gaze falling on the young, dark-haired girl lying on the bed beside her. She studied Yafatah with bewilderment. The Tammirring smiled wanly at her. Aunt masked her present consternation with a cheery grin. She patted Yafatah's clammy hand and said, "Well now, child—seems you and your Ma have a bit of a journey ahead of you. Seems my 'second opinion' wants to see you for himself."

Yafatah struggled to speak. Her head felt as if it might split open from pain, and each word was an effort. "Where—do—he—be—liv—ing?"

Aunt leaned over and massaged Yafatah's tense neck, her hands warm and gentle. "Speakinghast, child. Doogat lives in Speakinghast."

Yafatah stiffened. Chaotic images of Trickster masquerading as Old Jamilla overwhelmed her mind, and she began to weep helplessly.

Chapter Fifteen

YAFATAH WAS TOO weak to fight Aunt's conviction that she should go to Speakinghast, but Fasilla wasn't. Fasilla listened to what the Jinnjirri healer said with an incredulous expression. She jumped to her feet in Aunt's tiny kitchen, her voice shrill.

"That do be near three hundred miles from here! And over fierce bad country, too! Yafatah do be *sick*, Aunt. What can you be thinking of?"

"Hush," said the Jinnjirri sternly. "Keep your voice down, Fas." The Jinnjirri inclined her head in the direction of the small bedroom in which Yafatah still lay. "The dose of drugs I gave your daughter was weak. I doubt she's asleep, yet. You don't want to frighten her, Fas."

Fasilla crossed her arms over her chest, staring out of the window at the brilliant Jinnjirri morning. The sky was deep blue and clear. A soft summer breeze rustled the orange and red autumn leaves on the trees standing near the cottage. Fasilla unbuttoned her yellow overtunic. Scowling, Fasilla wondered how long this "Trickster Summer" would last. She wiped sweat off her upper lip. Without looking at Aunt, she tried desperately to come up with a rebuttal to her friend's proposal.

"Taking Ya all the way to Speakinghast do be crazy, Aunt. It do be plain crazy." She shook her head. "I willna' take me daughter through the Eastern Feyborne. Not alone. It be one thing with a full Asilliwir caravan. It do be another alone. Look, if you canna help—we'll leave."

"To catch your clan-kin? They travel the opposite direction from where you must go," Aunt added, her voice clearly disapproving.

Fasilla spun on her old friend. "I *know* that! Didna' you hear me? I willna' take Yafatah through the mountains!"

"She'll be drugged, Fas. Just like she is now."

Fasilla shook her head, her eyes strangely haunted. "I canna do it."

Aunt frowned. Then, glancing out the window she watched Burni remove the harness from one of Fasilla's mares. Aunt had told him to give the roans a rubdown and fresh water to drink. Then Burni was to hobble the two horses and set them free to graze on Aunt's front lawn—making sure they stayed *out* of the hollyhocks and irises, of course. Aunt took a deep breath, thinking that Burni ought to be outdoors just long enough for her to get through this Feyborne thing with Fasilla. Turning her attention back to the Asilliwir woman sitting at her kitchen table, Aunt said, "Fas—I want you to be honest with me." She paused, putting a fresh pot of water on to boil for tea. "I want to know why you're afraid of the Feyborne."

Fasilla watched Aunt bend down to stoke the hot coals in the firebox of the kitchen's wood-burning stove. Fasilla shrugged. "There be noo person alive in all Mnemlith who hasna' got a healthy fear of them mountains. And you know that as well as I do, Aunt." She sipped the remains of her cinnamon-spice tea. "Them mountains be alive with things."

"What kind of things, Fas?" asked Aunt calmly.

"Greatkin," whispered the Asilliwir, her throat constricting.

Aunt inclined her head. "You've seen the Greatkin?" Unusual, she thought, for an Asilliwir born.

"Not 'the'—just one. I think."

"You don't know?"

Fasilla got to her feet and paced. "No, I *doon't* know. And I doon't want to talk about it, either."

Aunt met Fasilla's eyes sternly. "Exactly where was Yafatah born?"

There was a long silence.

"Suxonli. It be a tiny village in the Western Feyborne."

Aunt nodded. "I see. So you wintered in the Feyborne sixteen years ago. Unable to leave because you were pregnant with a Tammirring child."

Fasilla nodded. She stopped pacing, her shoulders sagging. "We were close before birth, Ya and I. And I saw things I shouldna' have seen."

"You mean, things you shouldn't have been *able* to see—as an Asilliwir?"

Fasilla nodded again, returning to her seat at the table. She put her head in her hands. "Ya was carnival-begat. It were not my intention to have a child at that time. Especially not a Tammi. We Asilliwir be a kin-loving race. And then Tammi—they do be so *cold*. So far away in their hearts. I do me best to love the child, but she be so different from me sometimes."

"Inward?" asked Aunt with a reassuring smile.

Fasilla nodded, tears streaming down her face. "I havena' said these things to anyone ever before. I doon't want people to think I do be a bad mother." She raised her head. "I love the child. I love the child fierce, Aunt."

"I believe you." Aunt paused. "But your love for Ya may not be enough."

Fasilla stared at her good friend. "What can you be meaning?"

Aunt took a deep breath, speaking slowly and emphatically. "Just this: Yafatah *is* a Crossroads Child. Carnival-begat, yes.

And carnival time is Greatkin Time. A literal crossroads of possibility—in this case, Rimble's."

At the mention of Trickster, Fasilla swore in Southern Asilliwir. Aunt, who was fluent in the language, smiled, scooping fresh tea into the pot. When Fasilla ran out of expletives, Aunt continued the conversation.

"Now most times, Fas, this just means the carnival-begat child is one having unusually strong gifts in some area. Maybe the child becomes a great artist. Or a great teacher. The direction will be determined by *landdraw*." Aunt poured steaming tea into Fasilla's cup. The scent of cinnamon sweetened the air. "Sometimes, though, something more comes through during a festival of the kind you attended."

"Something *more*?" Fasilla didn't like the sound of this.

"Yes. It's called a Gift of Spirit. It's a power. Needs training, too."

Fasilla's mouth went dry. "What *kind* of power."

"Depends on the Greatkin involved." She poured herself some tea. "Since it's Rimble, we'll have to assume Yafatah's Gift of Spirit has something to do with making change possible. Rimble-Rimble, you know."

Fasilla said nothing.

Aunt smiled. "How *you* ever ended up at a rowdy, wanton Rimble's Revel completely eludes me, though. 'Psychotropics' was *not* exactly your favorite class at school, as I recall." She waited for Fasilla to explain.

Fasilla swallowed. As school chums, they had argued well into the night over the proper and improper uses of mind-altering herbs and potions. Aunt's stance had been typically Jinnjirri: the less control the better. Fasilla shrugged. "I went on a dare." She smiled weakly. "I canna *ever* resist a good dare, you know. Gets me Asilliwir blood up."

Aunt chuckled. "Trickster seduced you with a dare. Interesting."

"Trickster had *nothing* to do with it! I didna' begat Yafatah with a Greatkin. I begat her with a Jinnjirri."

Aunt was taken aback. "My, the revel *did* change you." Her face briefly shifted to that of a man's and then returned to that of a woman's—making an obvious visual reference to her unrequited love affair with Fasilla some seventeen years ago on the salty fishing coast of western Piedmerri.

Fasilla crossed her arms over her chest indignantly. "I was

hardly myself at the revel, Aunt! I was under the influence! *Under the influence!*"

"Of Trickster?" she asked idly. "Or of the Jinnjirri?"

Fasilla's eyes blazed. "Of some foul hallucinogenic mixture! The villagers of Suxonli called it 'Rimble's Remedy.'"

Aunt's Jinnjirri hair turned a sickly chartreuse color. "Ah, yes. Three parts holovespa joyal jelly and one part powdered suxon mushroom. Their so-called 'secret recipe.' Sheer mind fire. Pretty and very toxic."

Fasilla licked her lips with distaste. "The color of your hair do be the way my stomach feels at the thought of the stuff." She shrugged. "Anyway, I conceived Yafatah under fierce weird circumstances."

"What did you *expect* from a Trickster's Hallows, Fas?" snorted Aunt. Then the healer added, "But you always were an innocent, weren't you? Perfect dupe." Aunt rubbed her eyes tiredly. "Look, Fas, this isn't going to be easy for you. None of it. Especially this next part. See, in certain terms—you *must* take Yafatah to Speakinghast. You must."

Fasilla regarded Aunt with suspicion and defiance.

Aunt gestured imploringly at Fasilla. "I can't do what needs doing for Yafatah. I also can't train her the way Doogat can—"

"*I* can train me own daughter!" retorted Fasilla angrily.

Aunt brought her fist down on the table. "No! No, you *can't*! This thing is much bigger than you, Fas! And it's not in your control!"

The Asilliwir herbalist laughed at the Jinnjirri. She started to get to her feet, but Aunt grabbed her arm and held her to her seat. Leaning close to Fasilla, Aunt said cooly, "Okay, Fas. Try this out. I'm not what I appear to be; I'm a Mayanabi Nomad." Aunt paused, letting the words sink in. "Yes. One of *them*. You see, you've stumbled into something *very* large."

Fasilla jerked her arm out of Aunt's grasp and slumped in her chair. "This—this canna be," she whispered, her eyes shocked. Her oldest friend in the world was a crazy religious person? Fasilla clenched her fists, wanting to scream. Nothing was as it was supposed to be. Nothing! Fasilla regarded Aunt with contempt and asked, "How long do you be this—Mayanabi?"

"Since childhood. I was born into it."

"And you never *told* me?" Fasilla snapped coldly. Her tone of voice and expression suggested that she perceived Aunt as the carrier of a fatal disease. A disease Aunt had exposed *her* to without her permission.

"Your prejudice—to use a euphemism—prevented me, Fas. I liked you. Even loved you." Aunt paused. "I thought you might end our friendship if you knew I was a Mayanabi Nomad."

There was a short pause.

Fasilla bit her lower lip. "I would have," she admitted, her face scarlet with conflicting emotions. She averted her eyes from Aunt's steady, dispassionate gaze. "I would have," she repeated in a whisper. Fasilla put her head in her hands and added forlornly, "Greatkin have *mercy* on me." She had just realized the far reaching effect of her religious prejudice.

Aunt grunted. "So, will you run out the door—or open your mind?"

Fasilla got up from the table, tears slipping down her cheeks. "Excuse me for a moment," she said hoarsely. "I—I need to check on Yafatah." Fasilla knew it was a weak excuse to get some time alone; she knew Aunt knew it, too. Fine, she thought numbly. "I—I do be right back. Promise."

Aunt nodded her head and reached for the loaf of bread on the table. Fasilla left the kitchen hastily and opened the bedroom door. Yafatah lay sound asleep on a blue summer quilt, her breathing regular, her face peaceful. Fasilla stood beside her child in silence, her expression bewildered and slightly scared. She caressed Yafatah's damp forehead. Fasilla's eyes brimmed with more tears. "I do be loving you, child. And if that do mean we must go to Speakinghast, then so be it. That be me commitment to you, Ya. That be me commitment to *you*."

Fasilla wiped away her tears with a handkerchief from her pocket. Blowing her nose softly, she left the room where her child slept, shutting the door to the tiny bedroom quietly behind her. She smiled wanly at Aunt when she returned to the kitchen.

Aunt, who was busy buttering a second piece of bread, met Fasilla's smile with a questioning glance. "So?" she asked.

"So, you do be Mayanabi. So what? I'll—I'll get used to it."

Aunt smiled broadly at her old friend and offered her the buttered bread. Fasilla accepted it with equanimity, reaching for the open jar of dark honey on the kitchen table. Relieved that the crisis was over, the two women made jokes while they ate. Then, pouring another round of tea, Aunt said, "You know, the things that happened in Suxonli sixteen years ago? They were a travesty.

A distortion of something potentially lovely—Remembrance."
She paused. "Do you know the real meaning of this word?"

Fasilla shook her head, her mouth full of brown bread, butter,
and dark honey. She swallowed quickly. "Only as an everyday
idea."

Aunt took a long draught of tea. "Then let me tell you a tale,"
she said matter-of-factly. "And in so doing, you may learn
something *useful* about the Mayanabi Nomads." Aunt leaned back
in her chair, half-closing her hazel eyes, her Jinnjirri hair turning
a milky opalescent as she entered the light trance of the storyteller.
"Since this tale concerns the Greatkin, we shall call it a Mythrrim,
a word which means Great Story. We shall call it the Mythrrim of
Remembrance." Aunt breathed deeply and began:

The Mythrrim of Remembrance

IT IS TRADITIONAL for us two-leggeds to think of ourselves as the
Firstborn Race of Mnemlith, but in truth—we aren't. Before we
came into existence, there were the Great Mythrrim Beasts of
Soaringsea. They were a wise, four-legged people enormous in
size and longevity. They were also marvelous to look at.

Winged, the Mythrrim were a wild mix of hyena, lion, and
giant falcon. They had brindle hides, large teeth, and rows of
horns down their backs. Their feathers were so brilliantly colored
that they would have made the Jinnjirri look dull by comparison.
But these beasts were not beautiful—unless terrifying things
please you. Mythrrim had dogteeth eight inches long, and their
eyes were large and protruding. They also liked their meals
fresh—freshly killed. The Mythrrim were carnivores, you see,
and they were peerless hunters. But let me not dwell on their grisly
side; instead, let me tell you of their laughter.

Like the lowly hyena, the Mythrrim could make a strange
chortling sound deep in their throats. It was the most infectious
laugh in the world—cacophonous and wild. And it travelled for
miles. So did their stories. The Mythrrim of Soaringsea were
wonderful conversationalists. They were also the greatest story-
tellers to have ever graced Mnemlith. We Mayanabi—we're a pale

imitation. You see, the *landdraw* of Soaringsea had gifted the Mythrrim with seven sets of vocal cords. They were born mimics. There wasn't a sound in the natural world that they couldn't imitate. And their memories? They spanned the centuries.

So, you ask, what happened to these fantastic beasts? Well, I can't tell you what became of them without telling you a bit about their means of birth. It involved the Greatkin: specifically, the Greatkin of Civilization and the Greatkin of the Impossible.

In the beginning, when the world was still young, Greatkin Themyth and Greatkin Rimble had a secret tryst. Since they had a wild and wooly time in bed, something wild and wooly was born from that union: the Mythrrim. As Theymth was Patron of the Hearth, she knew that the best and most important moments of mortal life were spent beside the blazing campfire. Or cave-hearth. Remember, this was a very primitive time. So Themyth not only taught the Mythrrim how to make fire but also how to speak. She had a reason for doing this; it was Themyth's desire that the Mythrrim be the teachers of the two-leggeds. Rimble thought this was an interesting idea and agreed to it.

So, for the first million or so years of two-legged existence, the Great Mythrrim Beasts of Soaringsea were our good-natured guides through triumph and tragedy. They gave unstintingly and unhesitatingly. And we took—in like fashion. As a people, we were ill-mannered and greedy. But we were also young. The Mythrrim forgave us our shortcomings. And when things got really bad for us—we were a pitifully vulnerable race—the Mythrrim regaled our hearts and spirits with heroic stories of our true parents: the Greatkin. In this sly way—a legacy of Trickster, no doubt—the Mythrrim *also* made sure that we remembered the Faces of the Presence—the Shining Ones of Eranossa and of Neath.

In time, these talks around the cave fire became an integral part of our lives—and of our society. We attached special meaning to the stories and the comraderie shared at these gatherings. And we gave these meets a name; we called them *kinhearths*. Well, all went smoothly for a great many years—thousands, in fact. The Mythrrim kept their covenant with us, and we kept kinhearth with them. Some centuries later, however, we began to become a little lax in our attendance at the kinhearth. Our survival as a race was assured by this time. And so our interest in matters of kinship and spirit strayed. We were no longer dependent on each other for protection, you see. Travel and exploration captured our attention.

The cave fires still burned brightly through the night, but we did not come. After a while, we forgot that there had ever *been* any kinhearths at all. We lost our understanding of who we were and who we might become. Gradually, we even lost our understanding of history and eventually came to believe that we were the most important and only beings alive. Well, the Mythrrim got together one year and decided that our disinterest in kinhearth was a bad thing.

So the Mythrrim started over again with us. Fortunately, the Mythrrim were a long-lived people. Thus, they knew something of patience. And kindness. Taught by kindness, we learned of kindness. And thus the world was once again a good place in which to be alive. But this golden age didn't last. We did it again; we forgot the stories of the Greatkin. In so doing, we cut ourselves off from our divine inheritance. And again, we were faced with the challenge of our age empty-handed. We had no myths to guide us, no heroes and heroines to emulate. We had only ourselves to turn to, but *we* at this point were in a state of extensive befuddlement. And alienation. So we were of little help to ourselves. We whimpered a lot, I think.

Anyway, the Mythrrim called another meeting. They talked long into the night about us two-leggeds. They decided we were a sweet species but perhaps not overly bright. There was some dissension about this conclusion. Being a fair people, the Mythrrim investigated the situation further. In the upcoming centuries, they kept a watchful eye on our forgetfulness. In due time, the Mythrrim were able to understand its cause. Much to their surprise, these great beasts determined that we two-leggeds were not so much forgetful as intoxicated.

Furthermore, it seemed we were neither an inattentive nor retarded people. In fact, it appeared we had learned the most important thing of all; we had learned to love the Presence with all our hearts. Just as the Mythrrim and Greatkin did. We had one minor failing, however. We kept extending this love to include all creation. We were so entranced and delighted by the works of the Great Artist that we forgot about meeting the Great Artist Itself. And kinhearths had been a way to meet this One. Face-to-face, as it were.

Now, the world was very large. And it was filled with an endless array of wonders. So, there we'd be—attentive one moment and sensually drunk off our asses the next. Overwhelmed by stimulation. Giddy with emotion and the sheer invigoration of being incarnate. When a people is in such a state for several thousand years, it becomes forgetful. They Mythrrim understood this. And they did not fault us for our weakness or our love. *They* were mortal like ourselves. And they in their adolescence had responded in much the same way. However, the average lifespan of a Mythrrim was three thousand years. We didn't have time like that on our side. So the Mythrrim decided we needed some help. But what kind? After long deliberation, the Mythrrim went to the Parent of All Remedies: Greatkin Rimble.

Rimble conferred with Themyth. Together they concluded that we *did* need help. But, said Rimble, the help should come from our own kind. The dilemma we faced was ours and ours alone. We must mature as a race, he added. We must fall down and learn to pick ourselves up. Themyth agreed, but less whole-heartedly. She wasn't at *all* sure we could manage on our own. Neither were the Mythrrim. Trickster listened to their doubts. Then, he laughed, saying:

"I didn't say I'd mar*ooo*n them, folks. I just said they should grow up. Don't worry. They'll have guides. Two-legged guides culled from all the *landdraws* of the world. And we'll train 'em special like, so they don't forget the names of my brothers and sisters. Including my own, of course."

The Mythrrim were dubious. We had a predilection, they said, for forgetfulness. We had a penchant, they said, for intoxication.

"No problem," said Rimble. "We'll just find us some teetotaler types. No finger-wagging temperance boobs, mind you. Just some people with a disinterest in drunkenness. Folks who'd rather talk to the Artist than spend hours in a gallery of the Artist's works." Rimble pulled on his goatee, thinking. "Okay," he said, rubbing his hands together with excitement. "We'll even give these people their own special name. We'll call them—uh—yes. The Mayanabi. The Friends of Illusion."

"*Friends* of Illusion?" asked Themyth. "How about 'Masters of' or even 'Breakers of'?"

"Rubbish," said Rimble hotly. "Illusion has its place! It's not some spiritual *disease*, you know. It's very classy scenery. And as it comes from the Presence, it should be given just honor!"

Themyth decided Rimble had a point. So did the Mythrrim. In this way were the Mayanabi "born." They were Rimble's wonder children; a kind of everyrace with a high degree of spiritual curiosity and sobriety. The Mythrrim trained them, teaching them the Great Stories—the myths of all the ages and all the peoples of

Mnemlith. Then the Mythrrim retired to Soaringsea where some say they remain to this day. As the ocean currents around this archipelago make it impossible to land there with safety, we have had no contact with these great beasts for millennia. Only the Mayanabi keep their memory alive. Most *draws* say they never existed. The Mayanabi know differently.

Anyway, after the Mythrrim left us, the Mayanabi Nomads set about the business at hand: Remembrance. Soon no portion of the world was left untouched by the storytelling of this group. Certain areas of Mnemlith were entrusted with the memory of a particular Greatkin. Suxonli was given the Remembrance of Rimble. Now called the Trickster's Hallows.

Each Remembrance—each festival ritual—was very potent. Typical of the teaching of the Mythrrim themselves, a properly done Remembrance did more than simply entertain. It changed people. It literally altered the inner psyches of those listening to the recitation. The ritual, you see, was simply an outer working of the power or influence of the particular Greatkin being honored. In a very real sense, a properly done Remembrance causes a kind of spiritual quickening. It prepares people for the experience of kinhearth—for direct contact with the Presence.

Rimble—being a curious fellow—watched the doings of the Mayanabi with great interest. Then he made an improvement. He devised a backup system. After all, he said, there was nothing to prevent two-leggeds from becoming deaf to the Mayanabi. Furthermore, there was nothing to prevent the Mayanabi from becoming deaf to each other. So, Rimble caused a little fluctuation in two-legged genetic coding. He inserted a small transposable element deep in the biology of our race. This element would cease being "silent" only if triggered by an external stimulus—a certain wasp venom. Not to be confused with the current so-called "Rimble's Remedy" of Suxonli. The venom would be given by a carrier or emissary at a particular moment to nine carefully selected people—the emissary being included in this nine. The selection of these individuals would be based on the person's tolerance for ambiguity, multiplicity, and general contrariness. At least one of each *draw* would be represented by Rimble's Contrarywise. Nine was the minimum number needed to sustain the "shock" of Rimble's fail-safe. They would not appear, however, unless the world at large was in some kind of dire spiritual straits. The Nine would be under Rimble's direct guidance and protection. At least, this was the idea. No one counted on Suxonli's stupidity, however. No one believed for a moment that Suxonli would reject Trickster's *he*.

The *he* was a girlchild of great spiritual sensitivity and capability, and was the responsibility of Suxonli to not only recognize this girl but also to train her. If they failed to do this, disaster would strike when the girl reached puberty and danced for Trickster at his Festival of Remembrance. Basically, Rimble's power would enter the Revel Queen, and if she didn't know how to release it into the *draw* of Tammirring, she would be psychically cooked. So would the other people in the ritual. The girl, you see, would be Trickster's literal common grounding for the psychic charge. If she succeeded in sustaining the charge, then Rimble's Nine would come together at a certain time in a certain place and "keep kinhearth" for the world. Kind of a booster shot for the Mayanabi. An infusion of renewal. However, if the Tammirring girl failed to discharge the psychic potential of Rimble, then the Nine would lack the grounding needed to generate fresh kinhearth and so would fail in their purpose. Sixteen years ago a tragedy occurred in Suxonli, one that you witnessed, Fas—so I don't need to describe it to you.

But Suxonli's tragedy is the least of the bad news.

If the Greatkin were to cease to matter to us, we would literally cease to matter—quite literally. Kinhearth, you see, is the stuff of *landdraw*. It is what forms the geological matrix of Mnemlith. It literally holds the earth together. The Mythrrim, despite their great adoration of the Presence, would not be able to offset the situation. They would not be able to counter the effects of *akindo*—the opposite of kinhearth. In this way, our forgetfulness would cause our world to end. The weave of the world would literally pull apart, and there would be no one present who could reweave it into a new design. Or pattern of consequence. Pray that we come to our senses. Pray that Trickster's *he* does the same. Prey that she remembers who she is, Fas, and soon, for she is Trickster's turning point. I tell you, all the dreams of all the years depend on it. This is the Jinnaeon, the prophesied whitewater of time. Now we change. Or we *are* changed. Period.

Aunt ended the story here. She stretched slowly, rubbing her eyes. She looked over at Fasilla. The Asilliwir herbalist was sitting in her chair, her knees under her chin. Her face was very, very pale. Aunt touched her friend's arm gently. Fasilla jumped.

Then, seeing Aunt, she said, "Them fools in Suxonli. They didna' train the girl."

"I know."

There was a long silence.

Fasilla cleared her throat. "And me Ya do be mixed up in this, yes?"

"Yes."

"How?"

"I'm not sure," said Aunt reaching for the remains of her cold tea. "Doogat says she may be one of Rimble's infamous loopholes. A fail-safe fail-safe."

Fasilla nodded. She was silent for a few moments, then glancing in the direction of Yafatah's room, Fasilla said calmly, "We go today, Aunt. Soon as me horses have rested. We go east to Speakinghast. You'll come with us, of course?"

"*Me*?" said Aunt with surprise. She started to say more but was cut short by a strange rumbling sound. Eyes widening, Aunt grabbed breakable knickknacks off the walls of her cottage, yelling at Fasilla to protect Yafatah from falling objects in the tiny bedroom. Fasilla crossed the shaking floor with difficulty, her heart in her throat. So this was a "shifttime," she thought—the Jinnjirri equivalent to an earthquake. She ducked a shelf of books as it came crashing to the floor right in front of her. Fasilla swore, deciding she much preferred the sandstorms of her native Asilliwir than this sliding and shaking of Jinnjirri. You could see a sandstorm coming in the desert, and you could take precautions. But when the earth *itself* moved, where was one to go? Fasilla threw open the bedroom door. Drugged, Yafatah was still sleeping comfortably. Gathering her daughter into her arms, Fasilla started to return to the kitchen with Yafatah. As she neared the thick doorjamb of the small bedroom, Aunt cried out:

"Stay exactly where you are, Fas. Doorways are good during a shift." Aunt grinned. "Like I said, change or be changed."

A few moments later, Fasilla heard Aunt swear. She followed the Jinnjirri's irritated gaze. Fasilla's terrified, hobbled mares were making for Aunt's hollyhocks—with Burni in hot pursuit.

"Welcome to shifttime," grumbled Aunt. "Rimble-Rimble."

Fasilla met Aunt's eyes. "You'll come with us to Speakinghast? Say you will." Glancing at the broken knickknacks on the floor, Fasilla added, "I haven't the courage to go alone. Not after this."

There was a long pause.

Aunt rolled her eyes, muttering, "Well, well, Doogat. Or shall

I call you Zendrak? We'll meet again. Let's hope it's under better circumstances."

Sixteen years ago, Zendrak of Soaringsea had brought Kelandris to Aunt and entrusted the healing of her savaged mind and body to this capable Jinnjirri healer. Kelandris had been a terrible patient, trying to commit suicide whenever Aunt relaxed. It had been a long ordeal. However, Aunt was a Mayanabi and Zendrak was her commanding elder, so the Jinnjirri had stuck with it.

And so Kelandris had lived.

Chapter Sixteen

AS THE EARTHQUAKE in the northwest border of Jinnjirri reached its height, Mab woke with a start at the Kaleidicopia. Her long years spent in the shifting *landdraw* of Jinnjirri had heightened her sensitivity to its earthquake activity whether she lived there or not. This was a childhood legacy that Mab wished to forget. Mab grabbed the sides of her single bed out of habit, looking fearfully around her room for evidence of fallen objects. Seeing none, the Piedmerri sank back into her pillows, her breathing ragged.

"You don't live there anymore," Mab told herself firmly. "It's over with Jinnjirri. It's over. And whatever's going on there right now—it can't touch you. You're in Saämbolin." Mab swallowed, closing her eyes thankfully. "Saämbolin," she repeated, a trace of a smile on her lips.

Suddenly, a passionate argument exploded on the stair landing just outside her room. It was Timmer and Tree; Timmer sounded furious about something. Mab pulled the brown blanket on her bed over her ears. This, too, reminded her of her life, in Jinnjirri. Moody silences and tempers. Mab's fingers clenched the bed so hard that her knuckles turned white. Nothing in Mab's life had been stable. Not her family life, not her friends, and not the land. She tried to tell herself she had been stupid to move into the Kaleidicopia, but she knew better. With all her heart, Mab wished she could live in an orderly Saämbolin household, but she knew from experience that it would never work.

"I'm just too weird," she whispered. "You don't grow up in a

Jinn artist's colony and *not* come out weird." Mab scowled. "So I end up living at this house. Because I understand it. I don't *like* it," she yelled in Timmertandi's general direction, "but I *do* understand it!"

Voices out in the hall reached a fevered crescendo. Rolling her eyes, Mab got out of bed and stumbled blearily to the door of room two. She poked her head into the second floor hall. Scowling at both Timmer and Tree, the Piedmerri asked crabbily, "Do you have to do this *now*? And do you have to do it right outside my room?" She peered out the windows on the second floor landing. "I bet it's not even seven bell-morn yet."

"It's not," said an equally crabby voice. Janusin lounged next to the open door of room six, his violet nightshirt crumpled, his hair dark blue with pronounced streaks of red. He looked as if he had hardly slept at all. The sculptor yawned and added, "So what's this about? Now that you've drawn an audience."

Timmer, who was dressed smartly in pastels and soft cottons, put her hands on her hips. Her long blonde hair tumbled backward over her slender shoulders. "It's about that scum-bum Podiddley. Not *only* did he leave his curry dish in the sink last night—some influence that Doogat is!—Po left all the spoons of the house in his bedroom. And then he locked it! Po could be gone for weeks. There's no telling *what* might flourish in his pigsty."

"Great gobs of mold probably," muttered Mab.

Janusin eyed Timmer and Tree with a baleful look. "You woke me up on account of *dishes*? That blasted house meeting went until one bell-morn!"

"Oh, Jan—who're you trying to kid?" snapped Timmer. "My room is right across the hall from yours. You bawled most of the night."

Janusin's hair shot with brilliant red.

"Shit," muttered Tree, "now we've got fireworks for sure."

Before Janusin and Timmer could make a real go of it, however, they were interrupted by a remarkably fresh looking Rowenaster. Ignoring the color of Janusin's hair, he beamed merrily at the disgruntled Kaleidicopians as he joined them from the third floor. Doffing his feathered academic hat at Timmer and Tree, the Professor asked, "What's this? An early morning second floor landing party?"

Tree swore. "*Some*body wipe that frigging smile off his face, will you? It's too hard to take at this hour."

Rowenaster chuckled. "'This hour' is the one at which I

normally rise, Tree. Perhaps you'd like to accompany me to the Great Library. I could introduce you to a new concept: studying."

"That's it!" snapped Tree. "I'm leaving! And Timmer, I don't care *who* cleans up Po's room for the house inspection. You want to make it my job—fine! Meanwhile, I'm going *out* for breakfast!" Tree started down the stairs then wheeled around, his eyes meeting Mab's hopefully. "Want to come, too? I'll wait."

Timmer snorted. "Smitten," she muttered. She stormed into room three and slammed the door.

Mab swallowed, feeling very much on the spot. "Uh—"

"Oh, forget it!" said Tree and disappeared down the stairs to the first floor of the Kaleidicopia.

Mab stared at the floor. Janusin muttered four-letter words under his breath and retreated to his room. This left the professor and Mab standing in the hall in silence.

Rowenaster cleared his throat. "Charming place, don't you think? Probably makes you want to live here forever."

Mab shrugged. "Rent's cheap."

Rowenaster nodded. "Did you sleep well? Short as it was," he added with a patient smile.

Mab shrugged. "Sort of. Until the shift in Jinnjirri woke me."

"What shift?"

Mab sighed deeply. "Curse of the *draw*. Mine, I mean. We Pieds are real close to the land. Sometimes we know things at a distance. It's like a twitching of the skin. I can't explain it." She paused. "Just something I learned. Mostly, I just wish it would go away. I don't live in Jinnjirri anymore. And I'd rather forget I ever did."

"You don't miss your folks?"

Mab shrugged. "Only a Saämbolin would think to ask that. Miss them? They're too busy with their artistic lives for me to miss them. I was always underfoot. Oh, and *very* dull. I didn't know how to party, they said. I was too serious. Too intense. Dull."

Rowenaster chuckled. "One just can't win, can one? Over at the University, I'm perceived as something of a libertine because I choose to live in this house. The registrar is convinced I have orgies every weekend."

Mab didn't smile. "Well, they did—at my house."

There was an awkward silence between them.

Mab shrugged, then ducked inside her bedroom, shutting the door softly behind her. Professor Rowenaster stood in the empty hallway in silence, his expression troubled.

• • •

On the far side of town, deep in the heart of the labyrinthine Asilliwir Quarter of Speakinghast, the wooden sign for Doogat's Pipe and Tobacco Bazaar creaked in the warm breeze. At the back of the shop, Po "slaved" over a sink of dirty dishes while Doogat entertained him by reading Po a tediously dry Mayanabi text on the "Art of Personality and Gradual Self-Effacement."

"Nearly done?" asked Doogat cheerily, knowing full well that Po wasn't.

"I was about to ask you the same thing," muttered the little thief.

Doogat put the text down, his expression disapproving.

Po caught it out of the corner of his eye and whirled around. "Now don't start on me, Doogs. I've been minding my mouth and manners ever since I got to this dump—place—last night. And I'm worn out with the effort."

Doogat raised an eyebrow. He looked singularly unsympathetic. "Keep washing," he said and picked up the Mayanabi text.

Po swore under his breath. He scrubbed a particularly greasy pan in silence. Then he asked, "So when do I get to test for Eighth Rank?"

Doogat grunted, refusing to answer him.

There were nine ranks in total in the Order of the Mayanabi Nomad, and thirty-three degrees in each rank. Zero Degree, Ninth Rank was the starting point for any new initiate. Conversely, First Rank, Thirty-third Degree was the greatest mastery a Mayanabi Nomad could achieve. As far as everyone knew—Aunt included—there had never been a First Rank Master; the normal lifespan of two-legged mortals simply didn't allow for the time needed to learn that much.

"Oh, come on, Doogat," insisted Po. "Nobody's a Ninth Rank forever. Have a heart."

"And indulge your vanity?" retorted Doogat. "I don't think so."

Po rolled his eyes, banging the pot around in the sink. There was a sudden tinkle of breaking glass. Po froze, staring into the soapy water. He was *certain* there were no breakables in the rinse sink. He heard Doogat get to his feet behind him. Starting to sweat, Po reached gingerly into the water. "Shit," he muttered, his hand still hidden by suds.

"Well, pull it out and let's see the damage," said Doogat disgustedly.

Po hesitated. "Now Doogat—I swear there was *nothing* in this sink. Nothing that could break. I checked. Really, I did—"

"Greatkin alive, Po—just pull it out."

So Po did. He blanched. He held the delicate hand-blown stem of Doogat's favorite and *only* red crystal glass. Po swallowed. "Uh—Doogs—I didn't put this in here. You've *got* to believe me."

"I do," muttered the Mayanabi Master. Doogat reached into the rinse water and retrieved the red bowl of the glass. It was etched in magnificent goldleaf. Doogat pursed his lips. He shook his head, saying:

"You miserable little—"

Po stepped backward, flinging his wet hands to both sides of his face in an effort to protect his ears from Doogat's hefty punch. Doogat regarded him with surprise and said, "I wasn't referring to you, Po. I was referring to Greatkin Rimble."

Po frowned, completely befuddled. "Oh. Good. I think."

Doogat continued to stare at the broken crystal, his expression slowly changing from thoughtfulness to horror.

Thinking Doogat was exaggerating his reaction for his benefit, Po rolled his eyes, saying, "Doogs—it's *only* a glass."

Doogat raised his head sharply, his black eyes boring into Po's. "Remember when I boxed your ear last night at the house meeting?"

Po took another step backward.

"Do you?" shouted the Mayanabi.

"Yes, Doogat. Yes, I remember. Very well."

"Well, consider your ear boxed. Then for now."

"Now? Why now? What did I miss?"

Doogat threw his dark blue riding cape over his shoulders. "A glass is *never* just a glass. *Nothing* is ever as it seems. You got that?" He met Po's eyes evenly.

"Uh—sure, Doogs. Uh—where are you going?"

"Out," replied Doogat. Then, without a word of farewell or explanation, Doogat left the little tobacco shop, slamming the door after him.

Po followed his trail into the front of the shop, the scent of rich tobacco leaves tickling his nose. Meerschaum pipes of every description hung on the far wall under glass. Jars of dried herbs and potpourri rested in neat rows on a long table. Mosaic tiles decorated the slanting archways of the small store. Po shrugged. It was almost time to open the shop for business.

Catching a glimpse of Doogat disappearing down a crowded street, Po shook his head and muttered, "There's no predicting a Mayanabi Master. Especially one who smokes a meerschaum Trickster pipe."

Chapter Seventeen

DOOGAT'S TRANSFORMATION INTO Zendrak took place in a matter of moments. It occurred under the cloaking dark of Doogat's blue cape and cowl. As "Doogat" reached a small, private promontory overlooking the vast horizon of Lake Edu, something shimmered there and faded. And again. Finally, called from Neath by Trickster's Emissary, Further materialized in three-dimensional form. The mare stood at a proud eighteen hands, her blue-black coat exactly matching the sheen of Zendrak's raven hair. The last of Doogat's friendly wrinkles and crowsfeet vanished. The wisdom of sixty-two years was replaced with the lean intelligence of Zendrak's apparent forty-five. The eyes, however, remained the same: cold, reflective, and black like obsidian.

This man's eyes—as well as his shape-changing ability—were both the result of his *landdraw*. Born on the "big island" in the Soaringsea archipelago, Zendrak had inherited the volcanic characteristics of this northern *draw*. The "big island," also called Feralisle, not only turned the inside inside-out on a regular basis with lava and ash but it also wandered freely—popping up at unexpected locations, occasionally at odd intervals or "inbetween" times. Feralisle was just that: wild.

Zendrak's body imitated Feralisle's structural mobility with precision, throwing off "skins" like the ash of its volcanic counterpart. Zendrak's body had the peculiar ability to completely renew itself with matter. What was molten on Feralisle became a process of molting on Zendrak's person. As a consequence, Zendrak's concept of self included a natural multiplicity of identity. And soul ache.

As far as Zendrak knew, he *was* the two-legged landrace of Feralisle. This knowledge produced a gnawing loneliness of soul that threatened to overwhelm him on bad days. For like Kelandris, he was a kind of involuntary *akindo*. Made kinless by *draw*, Zendrak was a biological freak. He was a sport of nature. He was also the result of one of Trickster's improvements; Zendrak was the progeny of Rimble's recent love affair with Themyth. However, Zendrak was only three-quarters Greatkin. The final quarter was that of a Mythrrim Beast—and therefore quite mortal.

Zendrak mounted Further easily, stowing his blue cape in his saddlebag and retrieving his dark green one. He sighed. Today was definitely turning out to be one of his bad days. First that hasty message from Aunt about the Tammirring child this morning at dawn. And now this: some kind of cryptic request from Rimble to meet with him immediately. The subject matter was apparently Kelandris; after all, Crazy Kel was slightly cracked. And so was the glass. Sounded like a fairly equivalent description of Kelandris to him. Zendrak swore softly as he whispered his destination to Further: southeastern Saämbolin in the foothills of the Bago-Bago Mountains at an old standing-stone site. What made this particular site interesting, thought Zendrak grabbing a handful of Further's black mane, was that it had once been dedicated to Greatkin Phebene.

"Hardly Rimble's usual fare," he muttered to himself, squeezing the sides of the mare's body with his long legs.

Further began to run in place. Gritting his teeth against the cold shock to come as Further and he entered the Everywhen, Zendrak urged the mare into a dead run. She complied. When Further reached the extreme of her speed, both horse and rider shimmered. And were gone.

For Further, time was not fixed. Time could be "jumped" by travelling through a series of Trickster's loopholes: literal constellations of coincidence. To a Power of the Fertile Dark, cause and effect—like distance—were not facts; they were working illusions. As far as the mare was concerned, the past, present, and future were concepts and therefore as interchangeable or discardable as cards in a cut deck. For a denizen of Neath—a portion of the Everwhen of the Presence—time occurred simultaneously. Further nickered softly, signalling Zendrak to prepare for her "jump." Freeing his left hand from the entanglement of her mane, Zendrak caught a line of time and tugged. A gate of coincidence opened. There was a wild whooshing sound, and they entered the Everywhen.

A moment later, horse and rider galloped into the open plains of southeastern Saämbolin. A muted, rolling mountain range loomed in the near distance: the Bago-Bago. This range, like the snowy Feyborne, marked a natural dividing line between *landdraws*—that of lawful Saämbolin and musical Dunnsung. One of the best loved rites involving Phebene was a contest between musicians to see if they could make the mountains sing. They almost always succeeded. But then, thought Zendrak wearily, this is a much milder *draw*. Not like remote Tammirring.

Zendrak's thoughts turned to Kelandris. He recalled Rimble saying he intended to nudge Yafatah to Speakinghast—but the sly bastard had not mentioned how or why. Zendrak suspected Trickster had entangled the two Tammirring women in some fashion; Rimble had been searching for years for the means to breach Kel's formidable psychic fortress of rage and fear. Zendrak's eyes softened with sorrow.

"You crazy, lovely woman," he whispered.

Zendrak tried to put Kelandris from his mind. Her strong face lingered, however, tormenting him not with guilt, but with a profound sense of regret. He had long ago ceased feeling guilty for his role in Kel's tragedy; there was no point to it. Like Kelandris, Zendrak of Soaringsea had been royally duped.

The scenario in Suxonli Village had been "improved" from the start. Trickster had meddled with Kel's bloodcycle just enough so that sixteen years ago, it arrived for the first time very late in Kel's adolescence: at the age of seventeen on the eve of Trickster's Hallows. And on that night, in those mountains, the scent of her blood had drawn Zendrak to her. His had been a Mythrrim response, instinctual and animal. Even now, Zendrak felt a trace of this four-legged lust. Groaning softly, Zendrak buried his face in Further's mane and salty horse smell.

Images rose unbidden. Sweat and smiles. Regret stung Zendrak again. He knew that the Kelandris he had once loved—that trusting, passionate, seventeen-year-old—was gone forever. Suxonli had broken her mind with its barbaric Ritual of Akindo. *Enough* memories, thought Zendrak angrily. He guided the blue-black mare into a grove of deciduous trees and signalled her to slow. Further did so, hardly puffing from the brief eighteen-hundred-mile journey. The sun now stood directly overhead; a bare five hours had elapsed in real time. For Zendrak and Further, the trip had lasted but minutes.

Further slowed to cross a leaf-strewn stream. She dipped her nose in the cold mountain water, drinking long and deep. Then she raised her head abruptly, her ears twitching backward and forward, her senses alert. Water dripped from her muzzle. Snorting, she continued drinking. Zendrak looked around himself. Trickster was here somewhere—of that he was sure. He decided to wait until the bandy-legged little Greatkin deigned to join him. Several minutes passed. Further raised her head again, her gaze fixed on something tall moving through the trees to their right. Zendrak peered into the dappled forest. If that was Trickster, he had grown about two feet. Zendrak shrugged. Why not? Changing form was Trickster's prerogative. All the same, it made Zendrak uneasy. He wondered if Rimble had done something so diabolical this time that the little Greatkin feared Zendrak's anger and fist—hence the increase in size? Zendrak dismounted from Further, his green boots disappearing briefly into the icy water at his feet. He told Further to remain close. The mare butted him with her wet nose and continued drinking. Zendrak left the mountain stream, heading for the shrouded figure standing in the forest.

"Greetings, Trickster's Emissary and son," said a melodious voice.

Zendrak said nothing, his expression wary. The figure in front of him *looked* like Greatkin Phebene. Sounded like her, too, he thought. Trickster had really outdone himself this time. Zendrak put his arms over his chest, waiting to see what the little Greatkin wanted.

Phebene smiled, removing her rainbow cowl from her radiant face. "So suspicious, Zendrak?"

"What now, Rimble?" asked Zendrak with irritation. "You called. I've come. Let's get on with this, shall we? I'm not interested in your pranks today. Especially if this concerns Kelandris—"

"Oh, it does," said the tall Greatkin. She laughed merrily. "Come, my beleagured friend," she said extending him her hand.

"Where?" asked Zendrak, staying put.

"To the clearing up ahead. To my memory stone—my mnemlith. I've spread a picnic for us. You missed breakfast, did you not?"

Zendrak made a brushing off gesture with his hands. "You go ahead. I'll follow, Rimble."

Phebene sighed sadly. "Zendrak—we're going to have to do something about this lack of trust."

Zendrak rolled his eyes. "You're not amusing, Rimble. You're really not. If I'm mistrustful, I have and have *had* good reason to be."

"Wise thinking when dealing with the Greatkin of Deviance. However, your attitude becomes foolish when speaking with the Greatkin of Love."

Zendrak snorted. "I'm not falling for it, Rimble."

Phebene shrugged. "Follow me anyway," she said calmly, her soft voice taking on more authority. "And that's an order, Emissary."

Zendrak swore under his breath and did as he was told. Greatkin Phebene and Zendrak emerged some moments later in a lovely clearing ringed by trees covered in oranges and golds. In the center of the clearing stood a single, moss-covered standing stone. It was as the Greatkin had said—the memory-stone dedicated to the Remembrance of Phebene. A linen tablecloth covered with a wonderful array of gourmet dishes rested on the ground directly in front of the mnemlith. A spray of wild, green roses crowned the center of the picnic.

Seeing the roses, Zendrak muttered, "Very authentic."

"Thank you," said Phebene graciously. Then she took a seat on a round rainbow cushion, offering the other one to Zendrak.

Zendrak grumbled and sat down.

Phebene made light-hearted small talk for the next half an hour, plying Zendrak with the most wonderful assortment of foods imaginable (Jinndaven had helped with this). After a while, Zendrak began to wonder if maybe this wasn't the Greatkin of Great Loves and Tender Trysts after all. An unsettling thought at best, he decided. Trickster's Emissary had little knowledge and little dealing with the Greatkin of Love.

Phebene poured Zendrak another glass of black currant wine. Its taste was sweet but not cloying. As she replenished her own glass, she said, "So tell me about soulmates, Zendrak. Tell me about mating for life."

Zendrak scowled. This was a very personal topic to him. And he would not discuss it with Phebene unless he knew it *was* Phebene. Trickster would only use the information to his advantage; he would never respect it. Zendrak shrugged, saying, "There's not much to tell. I am Mythrrim—we mate for life."

Phebene pursed her lips. "You identify more with your mortal self than with your Greatkin inheritance?"

Zendrak downed the remains of his wine. "When your father is the Greatkin of Deviance, it makes it easy to identify with *anything* but him."

"And Themyth—who is your mother? What of her?"

"I've never met her."

Phebene shook her head. "Nonsense, Zendrak. Every time you tell a Mythrrim, you're meeting the Greatkin of Civilization. Every time. Besides, it was Themyth who took the mortal form of Mythrrim to carry you. So, in a very real way, you do identify with the Greatkin in you."

"What's your point?" he asked grumpily, accepting more wine from Phebene.

"I want you to consider the following: what if there were a Greatkin who didn't know it was a Greatkin? What if *you* had grown up without all the training you received from the Mythrrim Beasts of Soaringsea and the Mayanabi Nomads? What do you think that would have been like?"

"Dangerous for everyone concerned. Especially for the Greatkin himself."

"Herself," corrected Phebene.

Zendrak frowned. "What are you saying?"

"I'm saying, Zendrak," said Phebene touching his cheek, "that Kelandris is your sister."

Chapter Eighteen

MANY MILES FROM where Zendrak and Phebene spoke, the noonday bell ringer of the Great Library of Speakinghast fingered the ropes of the large, copper bells hanging in the wooden campanile. Like a reed bending in the wind, the young Dunnsung woman pulled down slowly. Copper clappers hit and resounded: Lunch.

The carved doors to the University of Speakinghast swung wide. Gossiping students poured into the congested streets of the busy city. All of Mnemlith's two-legged landraces were generously represented in this scholarly group: the clannish Asilliwir; the aristocratic Saämbolin; the passionate Jinnjirri; the musical Dunnsung; the veiled Tammirring; and finally, the land-loving Piedmerri.

As this student population swelled the sidewalks and cobblestone byways, well trained horses wheeled to avoid collisions. The riders shouted at the oblivious academics, their travelling cloaks billowing in the warm autumn wind. Alert shepherds ordered their dogs to protect young lambs from this noon crush while harlequin geese honked. Tammirring seers offered to read runes or bestow amulets for a price. Asilliwir merchants shouted prices of their luxury items and herbal cure-alls while Saämbolin bookbinders exhibited their craft. Hatted Jinnjirri entrepreneurs sold roasted chestnuts on the street corners. Dunnsung bakers, dusted with the flour of their expertise, sang the wonders of their wares to tempted passersby—rows of custard tarts and chocolate filled pastries adding a sweet scent to the potpourri of existent smells. Piedmerri farmers watched for students attempting to pilfer their blush-apples and sweet pommins, swatting young, scholarly hands when they could catch them.

Now the lace and velvet faculty of the University pressed forward. Professor Rowenaster was among their number. The seventy-year-old Saämbolin edged out of the doors of the main classroom building with difficulty. He rolled his eyes, wishing he hadn't agreed to meet Barlimo for lunch at this hour. Thirty minutes earlier or later would have avoided this chaos. Pushed from behind, two Saämbolin students fell against the professor. Seeing that it was Rowenaster—chair of the prestigious Myth and Religious Antiquities Department of the University and Archive Curator for the locked stacks and "permission-only" reference materials of the Great Library—the hapless students blanched. No one escaped the University of Speakinghast without taking Rowenaster's celebrated Greatkin Survey course. No one graduated without passing it, either. Worse, the Professor had a well known memory for facts and faces. It was a gift of his *draw*. Mumbling profuse apologies, the students backed up.

Rowenaster frowned at them. "Your names?"

"Names, sir?"

Rowenaster eyed them reprovingly over the rims of his silver bifocals. "Yes, names. Though your parents seem to have neglected instructing you in manners, I assume they were gracious enough to give you names?"

"Dirkenfar and Crossi, sir."

"First term?"

They nodded uncomfortably.

The professor smiled. "Good. See you in six weeks." He pointed at the ceiling. "Fifth floor, Room 99. Be prepared." Rowenaster bowed his head slightly and walked down the steps of the main building. He was chuckling.

Rowenaster turned left on Great Library Boulevard. As prearranged, he found Barlimo lounging next to a small marble fountain in one of Speakinghast's numerous parks. This particular fountain was of a young woman bending over pouring water. As the professor approached, Barlimo patted the rump of the lovely statue and said, "This has got to be my all-time favorite work of Janusin's."

Rowenaster chuckled. "Because he used your shapely behind for a model?"

Barlimo grinned, her eyes twinkling. "So, professor. Where to?" She gestured in several directions. "Myself, I feel like something cheery."

"Cheery food. Well, that sounds like a request for Dunnsung cuisine to me. We're sure to be seranaded at this time of day— probably with a full complement of lotaris, drums, and flutes." He paused. "In fact," he said, turning east toward the Dunnsung Quarter, "isn't Timmertandi playing at that little place down on Ronpol Street? Might be fun to surprise her."

"I don't know, Rowen," muttered Barlimo. "She sees enough of us as it is at the house. Maybe we should try somewhere else."

"You just don't like jazz and folk in one mix."

Barlimo scowled at him.

"Oh, come on," he said, taking her by the arm. "Who knows? It might be cheery. Just the thing to brighten your mood," he added, nodding at a strand of escaped blue hair.

Swearing, Barlimo tucked the telltale strand back under her lemon scarf. Today, Barlimo was dressed in several light layers of varying shades of yellow and aqua. As usual, she carried her multicolored wool shawl over her shoulder. Shrugging at a turning weathervane, she commented, "I *want* it to be fall."

Pulling out a monogrammed handkerchief and wiping his brow, Rowen pointed at his academic velvets and muttered, "Don't we all."

The Saämbolin and the Jinnjirri walked slowly toward the large marble archway spanning the entrance to the Dunnsung Quarter of Speakinghast. As they approached it, the sound of street musicians singing a four-part harmony met their ears. Around the next corner, another Dunnsung ensemble played for coppers. Accompanied by a tin whistle and a gourd drum, two members of this six-person troupe stepped forward and began doing a lively folk dance. It involved swift hip shimmying and complicated hand movements reminiscent of the kind of "sacred signing" done at

Dunnsung Remembrances. One of the dancers had bells attached to his ankles, and the other—a woman as blonde as Timmer—wore a wonderful set of green veils. They danced so wonderfully with each other that Barlimo and Rowenaster felt obliged to leave them a handful of silivrain—Saämbolin silver tender worth five times a copper.

As the two housemates walked away, Barlimo muttered, "I can tell this is going to be an expensive lunch."

"Nonsense," said Rowenaster, bowing gallantly as they neared a small restaurant called The Piper's Inn. "I'm treating, Barl. And there'll be *no* discussion about it," he added firmly as Barlimo started to protest.

"Yes, professor," muttered Barlimo drily. "Whatever you say, professor."

Rowenaster gave her a withering smile and propelled her toward the open door of the small eatery. A blond host met them in the open hallway. "Two?" he asked. When Barlimo nodded, the Dunnsung led them to a cozy corner table. It had a good view of the Lake Edu shoreline and of the brilliant orange foliage that graced it.

"Lovely," said Rowenaster, glancing at the teal-blue waves. "Couldn't have a nicer view," he added to Barlimo. "See? Cheery."

The host handed Rowen and Barlimo two beautifully scripted menus. Pointing to a chalkboard on a nearby pillar, he said, "That's the special of the day. We're featuring fresh laska fish sauteed in garlic, butter, and mild Piedmerri herbs. I recommend it," he added with a smile.

"I'll keep that in mind," said Rowenaster, his stomach rumbling softly.

The Dunnsung glanced toward center stage. "We'll also be offering you a musical treat shortly. One of the city's finest jazz and folk quintet ensembles will play for your listening pleasure. The group is called 'Core.' Please—feel free to sing along or dance. We Dunnsung think music and laughter help digest our food," he added looking hard at the elegant Saämbolin professor.

Rowen patted Barlimo's hand. "*Try* not to be a stuffy Jinn today, dear."

Barlimo scowled. "Jinnjirri are never stuffy and you know it."

The host grinned. "Enjoy your lunch," he said and left.

Barlimo looked over at the professor. "One of the city's finest?" she asked, seeing Timmertandi's music in a different light. Her only encounter with Timmer's music to date had been several wee-hour rows with the Dunnsung musician over whether rent included practicing at odd hours in the studio. Barlimo—and the rest of the house—didn't think so. Timmer had accepted their verdict grudgingly. Barlimo hoped Timmer wouldn't be thrown off by seeing Rowenaster and herself here. Barlimo genuinely liked the Dunnsung; she just didn't like being kept awake by the endless repetition of Timmer's half-learned musical pieces. Furthermore, the lotari wasn't her favorite instrument in the world. It was stringed and made a reverberating drone. Still, Timmer had a strong, pure soprano. Barlimo settled into her chair, hoping for the best.

After Rowenaster and Barlimo had made their food selections—Rowen choosing the special and Barlimo choosing a fresh water bouillabaisse—the two housemates began discussing the issue uppermost in Barlimo's mind: the Saämbolin Housing Commission's continued harassment of the Jinnjirri residents of the city in general and of Barlimo in particular. Barlimo took a drink of water and asked, "Did you get a chance to speak to Master Curator Sirrefene this morning?"

Rowenaster shook his head. "I had classes, and she had meetings. However, both she and her husband are attending The Merry Prickster play tonight. So I'll ply them with theater peanuts and see if I can't extract a promise out of Gadorian himself."

"What kind of promise?"

"That he lay off the Jinnjirri. I'll point out to him that there are many academics on the Hill who are partial to the creative thinking of the Jinnjirri. Such partiality could hurt his re-election."

"Really?"

"I doubt it," said Rowenaster drily, "but Guildmaster Gadorian doesn't need to know that."

Barlimo rubbed her eyes. "I'm surprised Gadorian even listens to you, Rowen. Considering where you live."

"But that's exactly my point," said the professor. "And my advantage. I live *in* the Jinnjirri Quarter. Therefore—as far as the Guildmaster knows—I've my Saämbolin ear to the ground. I hear things, he thinks, that no one else does." Rowen grinned. "Of course, I *do* hear things no one else does, but that's because there's no place in all of Speakinghast quite like our beloved Kaleidicopia. Speaking of which, you missed a beauty of fight this morning on the second floor landing. Timmer and Tree."

Barlimo grunted. "No, I didn't. I had the misfortune to be grilling some toast over the coals in the kitchen hearth when Tree grumbled in, grabbed some fruit from the cold storage, and slammed the back door. He's really quite smitten with Mab, isn't he?"

"That's what Timmer says, too."

"Personally," said Barlimo breaking off a piece of bread from the dark, round loaf in the center of their wooden table, "I don't see what Tree sees in the child. And I mean child. Mab's nineteen going on twelve."

Rowenaster handed Barlimo the dish with a fresh slab of sweet butter in it, saying, "I think there may be good reason for that, Barl."

Barlimo took the dish, waiting for him to continue.

Rowenaster steepled his fingers. "I think Mab may be a little emotionally—uh—backward. Frozen." He paused. "It was something she said this morning about her home life in Jinnjirri. It may be that Mab never had the chance to grow past the age of twelve." Rowenaster shrugged. "What Tree finds attractive in this—well, I can't imagine it, either."

Barlimo's eyes softened unexpectedly. "I see," she said. "A wooden boy and a snowflake girl. One is stiff and the other frozen. Makes a wild kind of sense." She paused. "I'll tell you something that doesn't though—Gadorian going to see Cobeth's play. It's all Jinnjirri."

Rowenaster raised his gray eyebrows. "Oh, is it *Cobeth's* play now?"

"That's the word at the house. Even Tree says so."

Rowenaster muttered something under his breath. Then he said, "The Master Curator doesn't share her husband's dislike of Jinnjirri."

"I wonder why that is?"

Rowenaster cleared his throat, looked around himself, and whispered, "Sirrey had an affair with one of your *draw*. They only made love once, but apparently Sirrefene has never forgotten it."

"That bad?"

"That *good*."

Barlimo buttered her bread. "Oh. That could explain a lot of things."

"Yes, it could," agreed Rowenaster. "Sirrey and Gad were newly engaged at the time."

There was a long silence.

Barlimo sighed. "I hate it when street politics are decided by private bedroom entanglements."

Rowenaster shrugged. "You should see the dirty laundry on the Hill. It makes Sirrey's indiscretion look noble."

Their conversation was suddenly curtailed by a lot of fanfare and shuffling around taking place in the center of the restaurant. The serving lad reached Rowen and Barlimo's table with their salads just as the quintet began tuning up their instruments. Turning his chair around so he could have a better view of Timmer, Rowenaster smiled at Barlimo and said, "Now remember, Barl. If you *don't* like Timmer's music—lie at dinner tonight, all right? I don't want indigestion before the play." Muttering to himself, he added, "Presence only knows what *Cobeth's* going to do to my stomach."

Timmer introduced herself and the other members of the quintet. Then, without further delay, she broke into a bawdy Asilliwir ditty that bufooned the Saämbolin. The Dunnsung roared with laughter as did the Asilliwir. Barlimo's hair turned bright yellow with delight. Leaning toward the professor—who was looking decidedly disgruntled—Barlimo said, "*Very* cheery."

Timmer continued with a series of swiftly paced pieces then ended the first set with a moody melody from Tammirring. The drone of the lotari filled the room with a strange yearning, as if each note were reaching for the next but never quite touching—like lovers parted. As the wild applause died down, Timmer caught sight of Rowenaster and Barlimo. Surprised at first, her expression speedily changed to naughty. Whispering hurriedly to the fellow playing the horn, she returned to center stage and said, "Before we break, there's one more song I'd like to play for you. I just learned it last night." Timmer winked at her two housemates. "It's called 'Dicky Dunkin'."

Rowenaster hid behind his napkin.

Barlimo put her head in her hands, muttering, "Tree—you're finally famous."

Chapter Nineteen

TREE SAT IN the special effects and makeup studio of The Merry Prickster's playhouse. He was taking a momentary break from packing up all his belongings. At present, he held a crumpled playbill in his hand, his spiky hair a mottled red-black. Tree had returned to the playhouse an hour ago to retrieve the last of his special effects paraphernalia—particularly his flash pots and powders. Hearing someone come clattering down the stairs to the playhouse laboratory, he looked up, glowering.

Rhu of Nerjii burst into the room. She was the stage manager for tonight's production of *Rimble's Remedy*. Seeing Tree's expression and furious shade of hair, she took a step backward. She held up the playbill in her hand, her voice tentative. "Uh—you saw it?"

Tree grunted. "It's what I didn't see, Rhu. So I'm fired— okay—but I still think I deserve *some* credit for all the work I've done." Tree threw the playbill to the ground. "My name is conspicuously missing, Rhu. I hope this wasn't your idea."

Rhu's Jinnjirri hair turned pink with embarrassment. "Good Greatkin, Tree—you know I wouldn't do something like that to you! We're friends. Once lovers. Come on. You know me better than *that*."

Tree pursed his lips. "I thought I did. But to tell you the truth, Rhu, I'm not sure of anyone's true feelings toward me here. Cobeth's pretty fucking charismatic. And I've noticed you two spending a lot of time together."

Rhu's hair turned flaming red. "So that makes *me* part of some kind of conspiracy? You got fired! Why can't you accept it with good grace?"

Tree stood up. "I would, Rhu—if I'd been given the reasons for my firing. After two years, you'd think the Pricksters would have *that* much loyalty." He threw some cast iron pots in the leather bag beside him. "You know—without my effects this show would be little more than top-heavy, preachy doggerel. And don't you deny it!" he snapped as Rhu started to do just that. The two

Jinnjirri glared at each other. Tree shook his head, adding, "Why *was* I fired, Rhu? Or don't you know?"

"Cobeth doesn't discuss all his decisions with me."

"Translation: you don't know."

Rhu ran her fingers through her hair and switched gender.

Tree put his hands on his hips. "Oh—we're getting tough now?"

"What?" asked Rhu.

"Your apple's showing, sir," said Tree touching Rhu's throat.

Rhu's face and hair both turned pink this time. Wagging a finger, Rhu switched back to being a woman. "You make me so angry, Tree, that I can't even remember what I'm doing!"

"Or who you are?" asked Tree idly.

"What in Neath does *that* mean?"

Tree slung his leather bag over his shoulder. "A word of advice, dearie. Cobeth's a cruel lover. We have one very drawn and quartered sculptor back at the house—"

"Yeah," retorted Rhu. "I know all about him. He's a slow sop."

Tree met her eyes evenly. "Janusin's a very gentle man, Rhu. You'd bloom in his company. Cobeth did."

"Not the way I heard it."

Tree snorted. "I'm the oldest member of the house—besides Barl—so I have a little perspective on Janusin and Cobeth. I was there the whole time. Believe me—Janusin catalyzed Cobeth's talent."

Rhu's eyes narrowed. "Cobeth has plenty of talent of his own, Tree! What's the matter with you? Jealous of him?"

Tree's expression turned unexpectedly sad. "Not at all, Rhu. I wouldn't want Cobeth's kind of talent. I'm quite satisfied with my own—such as it is."

"You *are* jealous."

Tree shook his head. "Of a bloodsucker? Don't make me laugh, Rhu."

"A *bloodsucker*!"

Tree walked toward the door of the laboratory and opened it. Looking back over his shoulder, Tree added, "Yeah. Cobeth of Shift Shallows can't *do* anything with his own talent, so he takes talent from everyone else, hoping their dedication and love of art will direct his own. When it doesn't, Cobeth leaves his victim drained of ideas. And nerve. Then he goes off in search of his next patsy. Better watch out, Rhu. I think you're next."

"I'm a stage manager, Tree. Not an actor like Cobeth. That's hardly the same catagory."

"Just the same, Rhu—Cobeth will take you and leave you. It's called envy, dear girl. And envy has many faces."

Rhu tried one last time to convince Tree that he was wrong about Cobeth. "Tree—you *are* jealous. Not that I blame you. Cobeth's good at anything he touches. But I think this—uh—attitude is beneath you. I'm sure that if you work hard enough, you'll be as famous as Cobeth's going to be with this play. And when that day happens, Tree, I'll be there cheering you on."

Tree grunted. "If Cobeth leaves you your vocal cords."

Rhu's hair blackened with fury. "Get out! You *and* your bad feelings!"

Tree smiled thinly. "Gladly, m'lady. Gladly." Tree walked out of the laboratory, up the stairs into the main foyer of the playhouse, and through the large front doors of the two storey building. He shielded his eyes from the golden sunshine of late afternoon. In the Saämbolin Quarter, bells told the time: five bell-eve. Tree scowled. Three hours until showtime at the playhouse. He couldn't decide if he wanted to attend the opening night of *Rimble's Remedy* or not. He knew Mab was planning to go—along with Barl, Timmer, and Rowen. The professor would sit with his academic cronies, of course, up in the box seats. Tree sighed. Must be nice to have that kind of silivrain, he thought tiredly. Then a gloomier thought occurred to him. He wondered how Rowenaster was going to take this play of Cobeth's. Tree bit his lower lip. Cobeth may have left Tree's name off the playbill, but he hadn't treated Rowenaster in this fashion. In fact, Cobeth had given the professor so many acknowledgments that it was almost embarrassing.

Tree took a deep breath. "I don't know, Rowen. By this evening's end, you may wish we could exchange places. I wouldn't want to be known as the 'guiding inspiration' for *Rimble's Remedy*. I wouldn't want that at all."

Professor Rowenaster and Barlimo stopped by the Great Library on their way home from eating at The Piper's Inn and an afternoon of shopping for the house. Rowenaster had picked up a fresh supply of tapers and flax oil, and Barlimo had replenished the supply of spices and dried fruits for the "K's" well stocked pantry.

"This'll only take a moment," said the professor as they

approached the front desk of the closed stacks in the basement of the Great Library. Smiling at the Saämbolin Guildguard sitting at the desk, Rowenaster reached inside the drawstring purse he kept hidden in his velvet pocket. He pulled out a collection of Saämbolin passes, searching for his "permission only" card that would permit him to pick up several texts in the locked archives. He frowned. The card appeared to be missing. "That's odd," he muttered to Barlimo. "I haven't used it in a week. I've been so busy with exams that I haven't had time to get down here."

"Maybe it's back at the house. Or in your office at the University," said Barlimo.

"Maybe so," said Rowen going through the cards a third time. "Well, no matter." He smiled at.the Guildguard. "Noolie, could you let me in? I've just got a quick pickup to do. Barlimo will wait out here."

Noolie, who had known Rowenaster for the past thirty-four years, shook his head. "Sorry, professor. You know the rules. No card. No admittance."

Rowenaster stared at the old man. "For Presence sake, Noolie—can't you make an exception to the rule? I *am* the curator."

Noolie shook his head. "Nope. You'll have to get a pass from Sirrefene."

Rowenaster put his hands on the desk. "The Master Curator is gone for the day, Noolie."

The white-haired Guildguard shrugged. "I can't help that, Professor Rowenaster. Come back tomorrow. We're almost closing anyway."

Rowenaster swore. Then, reining his temper, he said, "*You* could go back there and pick up the texts for me—and I could stay out here at the desk. There's nothing in the rules that says the Archive Curator is forbidden to guard the desk."

"You sure?" asked Noolie.

Rowen peered over his bifocals at the guard. "*I* wrote the rules, Noolie!"

Barlimo rolled her eyes. "You Saämbolin! If we Jinjirri were running this place, Rowen and I'd be halfway home by now!"

The Saämbolin Guildguard eyed her distastefully. "With all due respect—if you Jinnjirri were running this place, we wouldn't have a book left in the entire six storey building. Your people don't train the intellect the way we do. Probably can't. It's not *your* fault you're such an emotional *draw*." Noolie smiled, his posture proud and patronizing.

Barlimo's hair turned a steaming red-orange under her scarf.

Rowenaster cleared his throat. "So, how about it, Noolie? Will you pick up these books from the Trickster Archives?" He handed the guard a slip of paper with three titles on it. All of them had to do with Suxonli. When Barlimo commented on this, the professor added, "Thought I'd brush up on a few things before the play tonight."

Noolie regarded Rowenaster warily. "I *suppose* I could go back there. Just this once." He looked at Barlimo. "We Saämbolin aren't in the habit of making exceptions to *our* rules."

The Jinnjirri architect said nothing.

The Guildguard got to his feet slowly, removing a large key ring from the inside of his desk. He stumped over to the enormous wrought iron gates in front of them all and opened them. Giving Rowenaster a putout grunt, he locked them and disappeared into the rows and rows of bookcases that lined the room beyond.

Of all the goods exchanged in Speakinghast, none equalled the value of the books in this closed storage area. Stealing from the Archives was tantamount to raiding the treasure trove of a monarch—these books being the crown jewels. In general, no self-respecting thief could resist the challenge of breaching Archive security; book theft from here accorded status and privilege to this underclass of the city. Black market prices for rare manuscripts and texts from the Archives fetched hefty fortunes in ransoms—ransoms that the academics on the Hill were more than willing to pay. Rowenaster had doubled security in the past year as there had been at least two successful breakins in the last six months. Before this time, there had been six thousand three hundred and forty-nine attempts during the thirty-seven years that Rowen had acted as Archive Curator. Attempts were fine with Rowenaster; they could be thrown out of court. Successful thefts on the other hand, could not. Furthermore, a successful theft these days would make a thief miserably intimate with a harsh system of justice known on the street as "Gadorian's Revenge." A series of graduated punishments, "Gadorian's Revenge" was the result of a humiliating library internship that the Guildmaster had endured during adolescence. There had been no less than twelve successful breakins during the one summer he worked in this capacity. Furious that the existent laws for book theft were so lenient, Gadorian concocted the following—never dreaming that one day he would be able to implement his "program for redress":

First offenders were to be publicly humiliated by flogging. Then fed and housed by the Saämbolin Guild for a period "not to exceed ten years," thieves would work off their moral debt to society through indentured service to the City of Speakinghast. Translated, this group got stuck doing general street sewage collection and public privy cleanup. Second offenders were not so fortunate. Branded on the forehead with the searing imprint of the Seal of the Great Library—a wild Mythrrim Beast rising from flames grasping six scrolls in its taloned feet—second offenders were banished from Speakinghast. Family and friends could visit outside the city limits. The converse, however, was not true. Guards posted at the city's five gates enforced this with inspections and a complicated system of passes. Third offenders or persons disregarding banishment lost both hands to the fall of the bloody ax. So far, no one had gone the whole route. This pleased Rowenaster. In the professor's opinion, "Gadorian's Revenge" was barbaric and ought to be outlawed. Especially since the system of punishments had been the fantasy of an angry youth and not of a wise man.

Barlimo nudged the professor. "Think Noolie's napping back there? He's been gone an awfully long time."

Rowenaster was just about to ask one of the other Saämbolin Guildguards to go fetch Noolie when the old man reappeared, his expression annoyed. Rowenaster frowned. "Where are the texts?"

"Suppose you tell me!" retorted Noolie. "I ain't got time for Trickster silliness, professor. I take my job very seriously. And if you've got any other fool errands you're thinking about—save them."

"What *are* you talking about?" asked Rowenaster indignantly.

"I'm talking about there not *being* no section with these numbers!"

Rowenaster stared at Noolie. "No section? Of course, there's a section. It's all my personal research on Greatkin Rimble."

"Ain't there," repeated Noolie stubbornly. "And don't think you're going back there to check, neither. You need a card, professor, and that's my final word on the matter." Noolie glared at Rowen, his hand reaching for the short sword at his side.

Rowenaster rolled his eyes and swore, "All right, Noolie. But I'll be back here first thing tomorrow morning, and if I find that there *is* a section on Greatkin Rimble in there—I'll have your mouth washed out with soap for your insolence to me today. I'll also see that you're suspended for the next week."

Noolie crossed his arms over his chest. "There ain't no section."

"Oh, yes there is!" snapped Rowenaster. Picking up his candles and flax oil, he strode angrily out of the basement of the Great Library.

Barlimo followed the professor in silence, her hair turning thoughtful indigo under her scarf. Why was it that things like this always happened when Greatkin Rimble's name got mentioned? The Guardsman Noolie was probably a very nice person, underneath all his prejudice, she thought. But put Trickster in the middle of it, and Noolie doesn't even give Rowenaster the time of day—much less the respect he so obviously deserves as Archive Curator alone. She mentioned her thoughts to the professor as he hailed a happincabby to take them back to the Kaleidicopia.

Rowenaster took off his glasses and rubbed his eyes tiredly. "If Rimble's the reason for this mess, then just *think* what we've got to look forward to tonight. The Prickster play—my, that name sounds ominous suddenly—is all about Rimble. At this rate, Barl, I wonder if I shall survive *Rimble's Remedy*?"

Barlimo sighed, thinking about the true purpose of the Kaleidicopia and said, "I wonder if any of us shall."

By the evening's end, Mabinhil Of Matterwise would be asking the very same question. . . .

Chapter Twenty

THE SPEAKINGHAST PLAY-GOING crowd poured into the Jinnjirri playhouse slowly. With the exception of a small group of Saämbolin university students (all of whom were seeking extra credit in Rowenaster's Greatkin Survey course), the professor himself, Guildmaster Gadorian, Master Curator Sirrefene, and the three residents of the Kaleidicopia entering now, the audience was comprised of an unhatted, neighborhood Jinnjirri membership. Mab's eyes remained wary as she followed Barlimo and Timmer to their seats in the third row. Mab hadn't mingled in the company of this many Jinnjirri since living in the northwest border of Jinnjirri itself. And had it not been for her interest in Cobeth, Mab doubted that she would have come at all. With her nearly one hundred percent grade average in Rowen's class, she was hardly in need of any extra credit. Mab watched the Jinnjirri parade past her in a festival of shimmering color, costume, and gently shifting gender.

Timmer sighed happily. "Gorgeous, aren't they?" she said to Mab. "Finding myself in bed with a Jinnjirri is my all-time favorite fantasy." Suddenly realizing whom she was speaking to—"the Piedmerri Virgin"—Timmer put her hand to her mouth and mumbled an apology. "I forget you don't think about such things. Much less with a Jinnjirri," she added. "Must've been so weird growing up where you did."

Mab shrugged and said nothing. She preferred to forget the northwest border of Jinnjirri. To pretend it didn't exist. Cobeth, on the other hand . . .

Mab felt strangely drawn to the man. Mab had arrived at the "K" during Cobeth's final month at the house. Since Mab was new and unprejudiced toward him, Cobeth had treated her with an indifference bordering on kindness. Janusin's anger toward Cobeth had made her feel pity for Cobeth. In short, Mab was Cobeth's secret champion. Mab fingered the playbill in her hands, her eyes sad. She knew it was stupid to feel something for the Jinnjirri sculptor-turned-actor. To begin with, Cobeth was indeed Jinnjirri, and Mab had promised herself firmly after leaving the Jinn borderlands that she'd never *ever* have anything to do with a Jinnjirri on an intimate basis. Living with the Jinn was one thing, bedding them was quite another. And secondly, Cobeth was such as attractive sort of fellow that Mab was sure he could pick and choose his girlfriends from the best Speakinghast had to offer. She was quite sure a man of Cobeth's genius would never see anything of value in a dumpy, nineteen-year-old Piedmerri virgin. Mab sighed. Still, Tree liked her. And the artists in her mother's entourage had shown their sexual interest in Mab on more than one occasion. Mab winced at the memory and crossed her legs under her forest green tunic.

Timmer reached in front of Mab and tugged Barlimo on the sleeve. "Where's Rowen?" she whispered to the Jinnjirri architect.

Barlimo, who was dressed in a fabulous cobalt blue and magenta robe covered in rhinestones and feathers, removed her plumed hat and said, "Sitting with Gadorian and Sirrefene."

"*They're* coming to this?" asked Timmer in an impressed voice. "That's quite a debut for old Cobeth. Quite a debut." She sank back in her chair. "I should be so honored," she added wistfully.

Barlimo grunted. "Gadorian and Sirrefene aren't here for Cobeth. They're here for political reasons. Election time," she added nodding at the well-to-do Jinnjirri sitting up in the box seats of the theater.

Timmer nodded. "Well—what*ever* the reason—I think it's a good thing the Guildmaster and Curator are here. For Rowen's moral support. When Tree and I were doing the dinner dishes tonight, Tree said Cobeth's really gone around the bend with his interpretation of Greatkin Rimble's carnival in Suxonli. Says Rowen's going to hit the rafters."

"Why?" asked Barlimo with interest.

Timmer shrugged. "Tree says Cobeth didn't do his homework. Says the play is actually just a soapbox for Cobeth's latest personal quest."

"Quest or conquest?" said Barlimo rudely.

The musician and the architect burst into laughter.

Mab, who had been listening to this conversation with growing annoyance, interrupted them angrily. "*Why* is everyone at the 'K' so hard on poor Cobeth? Janusin does nothing but put him down for being a lousy student; Tree swears Cobeth can't act; and both of you sit here judging the play and the performance before ever having seen it!"

Timmer raised an eyebrow. "Hmm. Me thinks I detect a little interest in Cobeth here."

Mab glanced at the Dunnsung, her face turning scarlet.

"I hope not," muttered Barlimo.

Timmer tapped her chin thoughtfully. "Well, well. And I thought I was going to have to go to the opening night cast party all by my lonesome. You *will* join me, won't you?"

"Timmer—" began Barlimo in alarm.

But Timmer was feeling angry with Mab for defending Cobeth, so she would not stop. Furthermore, she was weary of Mab's push-and-pull attitude about the Jinnjirri in general. One sure way to cure it, she thought, was to take this fool girl to an all-out Jinnjirri party. Sex and drugs and anything else you could imagine. Timmer patted Mab on the arm, saying, "Loosen up. Life's too short to spend it cowering in a corner. Besides, Cobeth will be there. In all his glory," she added drily.

"I don't know, Timmer," said Mab cautiously. "I grew up in the middle of that kind of party."

Timmer rolled her eyes. "Do you honestly think you're the only one who's ever had trouble in their lives? Shake it off, Mab."

The little Piedmerri shook her head. "No—I—I don't think this is what I want to do, Timmer."

Timmer grunted with disgust, then seeing a couple of Jinnjirri friends, she waved wildly and got up to talk to them. Relieved that Timmer was no longer badgering Mab into going to the cast party, Barlimo smiled at the Piedmerri and said, "So how do you like living at the 'K'?"

"Oh, it's all right. I kind of wish it were a little more private." She shrugged. "But I've only been at the House three months. Maybe I'll get used to it. Having my personal life be of interest to all of you, I mean." Mab smiled as diplomatically as she could.

Barlimo chuckled. "What a *nice* way of putting it, Mab. Listen, girl, you have the right to tell anyone at anytime in that house to butt out. And in no uncertain terms, either. That's why all the bedrooms have locks on them—to insure that you can and will be left alone."

"Does it work?" asked Mab dubiously. "Telling people to butt out?"

Barlimo said nothing for a few moments. "Well, okay—let's be honest. Locks on doors—or on hearts—only work minimally at a place like the Kaleidicopia. Don't get me wrong. No one will come bursting into your room without your permission. Despite outward appearances, we're a pretty civilized lot. However," she continued, "in the *long* run, it's impossible to keep secrets when you're rubbing elbows with six to eight people on a daily basis. The Kaleidicopia is a kind of two-legged hothouse. Spend some time in the domed gardens on the third floor and you'll see what I mean. They're even warm in winter. Which is what *we* should be."

"Our tempers or our skins?" asked Mab wryly, recalling the argument Tree and Timmer had about Po's dishes this morning.

Barlimo nodded. "Tempers will do for starters. Passionate feelings let us know we're alive," said Barlimo. "Especially we Jinnjirri. And sometimes, Mab, the people who come to the 'K' can't feel anymore. Life's knocked them down too many times, or they got badly scarred once and they couldn't find the courage to try again."

Doogat's words at the previous night's house meeting echoed unexpectedly in Mab's mind. What had the Mayanabi said? Something like, *"All that Trickster wants from you right now is that you try again."* Mab touched the strand of hair that Doogat had pulled out of her face. She stared at the playbill in her lap, thinking about what Barlimo had said about passion—that it was a good thing. A kind of thaw maybe. Mab pressed her lips together, wanting to go to the Jinnjirri cast party after all. She wanted to feel what she felt toward Cobeth—she wanted to feel it with all her heart and soul. Mab took a deep breath. What if her "passion" landed her in bed with him? She let the breath out slowly. "Then, so be it," she whispered.

Timmer returned to her seat at this point. The undaunted Dunnsung nudged Mab's arm. "So did you reconsider about the party?" To Timmer's surprise, Mab smiled at her.

Out of Barlimo's hearing, Mab said, "I've decided I'd like to come."

The musician laughed, looking about herself at the Jinnjirri. "Oh believe me, Mab—we'd *all* like to do that!"

Chapter Twenty-One

UP IN THE box seats of the playhouse, Master Curator Sirrefene turned to Professor Rowenaster and asked, "So how's your survey course going? Have you flunked half the class?"

"Not yet," replied Rowenaster, his gray eyes twinkling.

"But he will," retorted Guildmaster Gadorian, pulling out a handful of theater nuts and offering some to Sirrefene and Rowenaster.

Unlike his wife, Guildmaster Gadorian was a corpulent fellow of short stature and many chins. By contrast, Sirrefene was lithe and physically animated. Both of them wore white velvet tonight, the brightness of the color startling against their dark brown Saämbolin skin. Both officials were in their mid-forties. Sirrefene shook her head at the peanuts.

"I don't want to spoil my appetite, Gad. Remember, we've still got the opening night party to attend."

Gadorian shrugged, popping more nuts in his mouth. "Theater groups are notoriously impoverished. What food they'll have will be on loan." He glanced over at the professor. "Are you going?"

"I wasn't invited," said Rowenaster, munching nuts.

Sirrefene pulled her gold-rimmed glasses off her nose. "You

weren't invited? After all you did for the Pricksters? Why you practically wrote the play!"

Rowenaster pursed his lips. "Rumor has it that the original script suffered severe alterations in the past two weeks." He patted the playbill in his old hand. "Nonetheless, I see I have been generously provided with a quarter page of acknowledgments." He sounded skeptical.

"They're probably meant to placate you," muttered Sirrefene.

"Then Cobeth's a bigger fool than I think he is, Sirrey. He lived with me for five years at the Kaleidicopia—he ought to know better."

"Thinks you're senile," said Gadorian. "Most *draws* do when we Saäms reach your age, Rowen."

"Too bad Cobeth never took my class," said the professor cooly.

Gadorian poured Rowen another handful of peanuts. "Speaking of the Kaleidicopia—I don't know why you do it, my friend. Surely with your salary you could afford to live alone."

Rowenaster met Gadorian's eyes evenly. "We've been through this many times, Gad. And as always, I say the following to you: I don't *want* to live alone; I like the diversity of *draws* at the 'K'; and I continually learn there—day and night. Remembering his promise to Barlimo to get the Saämbolin Housing Commission off her back, he said, "You should drop by sometime—and not in an official capacity. You might find that we aren't the rogue's gallery that you so fondly imagine us to be while you sit far above us in your ivied, administrative towers."

Sirrefene grinned. "Watch out, Gad—Rowen's up to something."

"I am indeed," replied the professor. "And so are you, Gadorian. The answer to your unspoken question is: yes, I intend to keep living at 'that house' on Wise Whatsit Avenue. So you better rethink any Housing Commission coups that involve the 'K.' It could look very bad for you on the Hill, Gad." He paused. "This being an election year and all."

"I see," said the Guildmaster, his expression far from pleased.

Rowenaster ignored Gadorian's bad humor, and turning to Sirrefene, he said, "Master Janusin's almost finished with his statue of Greatkin Rimble. You know," he added, glancing in Gadorian's direction, "the one the Library Museum commissioned? Sirrey's new project, isn't it?"

Gadorian scowled. "What're you getting at, professor?"

"Me? I'm just making polite conversation," he said, giving the Guildmaster a broad smile. Continuing to speak to Sirrefene now, he said, "For a while there, none of us at the house were sure if Jan would make the museum deadline. He's had some bad luck in love recently." He winked at Gadorian. "And we all know what jolts of that nature can do to an artist at work. Of course, being evicted from one's own home would be even more traumatic than a lovers' quarrel. Might stop the creative process altogether. What do you think, Gad?"

Gadorian said nothing for a few moments, his expression disgruntled. Finally, he muttered, "The Guild paid a hefty sum for that statue. Indeed, for the whole 'Panthe'kinarok Series.' "

"Yes, it did," agreed the professor. "And the studio in back of the 'K' is *such* a nice place to work."

There was a short, thoughtful silence between the three Saämbolin. "Oh look, Gad," said Sirrefene unexpectedly. "There go the house lights."

Outside in the street, bells rang the quarter hour; the show was fifteen minutes late starting.

Gadorian rolled his eyes. "Jinnjirri," he muttered.

Below the box seats, the red velvet curtain of the stage moved sideways. A shrouded figure in a zigzag-black and yellow cape and cowl stepped out, his yellow boots noiseless on the stage floor. The figure raised his arms. As the room quieted and oil lamps were extinguished, Cobeth addressed the audience, his voice calm and authoritative:

"For all you good folk who're regular supporters of our playhouse, we have a surprise for you. This theater season, The Merry Pricksters are going to be doing something a little different. A little daring." He paused dramatically. "We live in a time of alienation and spiritual decay. How many of you know all the names of the Greatkin? Until I started working on this play, I didn't." Cobeth glanced in the direction of the box seats. "Not all of us are lucky enough to endure"—he mimed the buffoon—"I mean, *take* the good professor's survey course." The room clapped its appreciation for Rowenaster. Cobeth chuckled. "After all—we shifty types can't always get into the celebrated University of this *fair* city."

The audience hissed and booed at the box seats above them.

Master Curator Sirrefene turned to her husband, her voice terse and unamused, "You know who *that* was meant for, don't you?"

"You and me, dearie. You and me."

Rowenaster said nothing, his expression strained.

Cobeth continued his monologue. "Well, good friends—The Merry Pricksters are coming to your untutored rescue. As you know, this troupe has been famous in the past for its bawdy humor and gentle political satire—hence our name. We propose something a little more radical now. We propose an out-and-out confrontation with the soul ache of our age. We call on the power of Greatkin Rimble to 'remedy' our situation."

The gels on the oil lamps in the theater changed from yellow to an eerie blue. Cobeth removed his cowl and cape, handing it to someone standing in the wings. Cobeth walked to center stage. He was wearing a full face mask of hand-woven, dyed materials. One side of the face was striped with diagonals of yellow and black. The other side was a caricature of a young female fool's face. It was studded with shining bits of black mirror. The rest of Cobeth's costume was a mismatched mix of yellow coattails, striped harlequin pants, and a leather dildo hanging over his own genitals. The dildo was a foot and a half in length and resembled a gorged wineskin more than a functional penis. Cobeth raised his arms, again—the gesture one of summoning and supplication. Then Cobeth spoke the following, his voice filling the playhouse with the power of the priest speaking directly to Goddess, God, and Trickster:

> Hail, O Thief, of the black-eyed night,
> Aid me now with slippery tongue
> To tell the tale sweetly and beguile them all,
> And hide the meaning in the rushes.
>
> Sting now, sting the despair!
> Bring the world's soul ache to air,
> And while away my mortal hours
> With the salt-humored hiss of your Art.
>
> Hero-heroine quicken once more,
> For civilization falters
> And markets her lifeblood on altars
> Of dead-ending devotions.
>
> Holy Heretic return now
> To speak your truth with a clean whistle

And a wise-rhythmed breath,
Come inspire me and say of sacred joy!

Trickster true, many taled, and sane,
Come love this telling to life.
Greatkin Rimble of the Thousand Names:
I will speak for you again.

The reactions of the people who knew Cobeth well were predictably mixed.

Down in the third row of the main house, Timmer reached over Mab to tug Barlimo's magenta sleeve again. "Rowen wasn't kidding when he said this play was about religion. And where did Cobeth ever learn to write like that?" Timmer sounded impressed.

Mab smiled triumphantly to herself—one for you, Cobeth, she thought.

Barlimo stroked her chin. "It's not his," said Barlimo.

"What?" asked Timmer and Mab together.

The architect shrugged. "I've no proof. But I'll wager you both a lot of silivrain that that poem was written by someone else."

Mab rolled her eyes.

Up in the box seats, Sirrefene regarded Rowenaster with surprise. "What do you mean, you don't think The Merry Pricksters wrote that invocation? If they didn't write it, and you didn't write it—who did?"

Rowenaster steepled his fingers. "Don't know, Sirrey. But I'd like to meet him. Or her."

Chapter Twenty-Two

"KELANDRIS CAN'T POSSIBLY be my sister," said Zendrak cautiously, his black eyes never leaving the face of the Greatkin sitting in front of him. He met Phebene's smile with suspicion, still certain that the Greatkin replenishing his empty glass of black currant wine was *not* the Patron of Great Loves and Tender Trysts, but was actually Trickster himself beautifully disguised as rainbow-robed Phebene. "To begin with, Rimble—the arithmetic is wrong. Need I remind you? I'm five hundred and twenty-seven years old. Kelandris of Suxonli is a mere thirty-three."

Greatkin Phebene laughed merrily. "You're not using your imagination, Zendrak. Themyth and Rimble made love in the Everywhen. Thus, it was a simple 'matter' for them to deposit you and Kelandris in different times and *draws*. Perhaps the drink has gone to your head, my friend."

Zendrak frowned, looking at the crystal glass he held in his hand. Come to think of it—he *was* feeling rather intoxicated. Unduly so for a Mayanabi Nomad, too. Zendrak held the glass up to the candlelight, trying to see the color of the wine. The sun had long since gone down, and although Zendrak had the nagging sense that he was supposed to be somewhere other than where he now was, he made no move to leave. Zendrak sniffed the contents of his glass. "What have you done to me, Rimble?"

Phebene smiled, ignoring his question. She offered Trickster's Emissary a slice of chocolate cake from the picnic hamper. The piece was large and covered with a thick fudge-like frosting. It was a chocolate lover's delight.

Zendrak shook his head, pushing the cake away. "I don't like sweets," he mumbled, trying to get to his feet. Too drunk to stand, Zendrak quickly sat down again, holding his head in his hands. He felt giddy and disoriented. He peered at the night. What *time* was it? Zendrak blinked. Meeting Phebene's sympathetic gaze, he muttered, "What were we just talking about?"

"Your dislike of sweets," replied Phebene. "Which *must* change."

"It must?"

"Trickster's orders," she lied. "We think your disposition needs a little improoooving, shall we say?" Phebene winked at Zendrak and offered him the cake again.

Zendrak took the plate from her hand gingerly. He assumed that when Rimble said "we" he was referring to his Multiple Primordial Face. It never occurred to him that Greatkin Phebene might be the genuine article, *or* that she might be one of a conspiracy of three—herself, Jinndaven, and Themyth. Had Zendrak known, he would've refused to participate. As much as he complained about Rimble, Zendrak still honored the foppish little Greatkin—and, in fact, loved him.

"Take this cake, for example," continued Phebene. "It was just an ordinary chocolate confection until your good buddy, Rimble, spit cherries into the batter. Complete with saliva. Right in front of Jinndaven, too."

Zendrak winced. "And I thought Podiddley was disgusting."

Phebene nibbled on the piece of cake on her plate. "On the contrary. I think it was an improvement." She sighed. "Jinndaven, poor dear, has yet to be convinced of this. You see the cake was his dessert contribution to the Panthe'kinarok feast. He's calling it 'Utter Chocolate Decadence.'" She motioned for Zendrak to try a bite himself.

Thinking that Rimble was ordering him to do so, he complied. To Zendrak's surprise, the cake was delicious. Particularly the frosting. He took another bite, smiling at Phebene.

Phebene nodded. "It's a certain ecstasy, you see," she said softly.

"A certain ecstasy?"

Phebene reached over and touched his forehead. Zendrak yawned sleepily. Phebene blew on his face, saying, "Love always is."

Zendrak blinked. "What did you say?"

Phebene cleared a place for Zendrak to lie down. Pulling a comforter out of her seemingly bottomless picnic basket, she draped it over Zendrak's broad shoulders. It was made of gossamer rainbows. As Zendrak closed his eyes, Phebene whispered, "A friendly piece of advice. Beware the boy who expects his just desserts. He's ravenous, Zendrak."

Zendrak nodded, drifting into a sweet sleep. Meanwhile, Cobeth's play in Speakinghast ended with a triumphant curtain call.

Rimble's play, however, had barely begun.

And one of his leading Nine had just missed his cue. . . .

Chapter Twenty-Three

THE ENTIRE THEATER was empty now save for one seat up in the balcony. Professor Rowenaster sat in silence, his fingers steepled, his gaze distant. Only moments before, he had sent Gadorian and Sirrefene off to find a late night snack without him. Cobeth's play had so enraged both Saämbolin officials that neither Sirrefene nor Gadorian had felt like attending the opening night cast party of *Rimble's Remedy*. Cobeth had continued to make indirect slurs against the Saämbolin Guild throughout the play, and the predominantly Jinnjirri audience had cheered him on. Rowenaster grunted; he hoped Cobeth's political attacks would not jeopardize the Kaleidicopia. It would be just like the scrawny sculptor-turned-actor to try to make trouble for the Kaleidicopia by irritating Gadorian. A kind of parting shot at Janusin. Cobeth was fully cognizant of the artistic deadline Janusin faced with the Great Library Museum; Janusin had used Cobeth's face as his model for the sculpture of Greatkin Rimble.

"And a very great pity *that* is," remarked the professor, preparing in his mind what he intended to say to Cobeth about the play *and* about the tiny postscript on the playbill's last page. Rowenaster reread the words: "*Rimble's Remedy* is the first in a new collection of plays written by Cobeth of Shift Shallows entitled *The Panthe'kinarok Series*." Rowenaster shook his head, his contempt for Cobeth bristling anew. It was hard to believe that even Cobeth could sink so low as to steal the name of Janusin's commissioned work for Master Curator Sirrefene. Rowenaster got slowly to his feet, muttering, "What *are* you playing at, Cobeth?"

Staring at the empty stage below him, the professor decided to go find out. As Rowenaster descended the stairs to the main seating area of the playhouse, he swore at Cobeth softly for acknowledging him as the "guiding inspiration" for the play. *Four* of Rowenaster's academic colleagues—all of them Jinnjirri and none of them particularly prejudiced against the Saämbolin—had confronted Rowen during the play's intermission, each of them complaining about the poor scholarship evident in the writing of the script and questioning *his* involvement in the project. At the time, Rowenaster had made excuses for Cobeth's sloppiness. But now, he thought coldly as he strode purposefully toward the backstage door of the playhouse, it's time to have a little discussion with my ex-housemate. Ducking through the door, Rowenaster removed his maroon travelling cloak. He folded it over his right arm. A small clump of mud from the hem fell to the dirty floor. Despite the Saämbolin's great age, Rowenaster had ridden by horse to the theater district of Speakinghast. The professor was seventy but spry.

Rowenaster knocked loudly on Cobeth's well marked dressing room door. A few Jinnjirri stagehands moved props and costumes off the stage behind him. Fearing that Cobeth might have already left for the opening night party, Rowenaster knocked again.

The door flew open. "I *said* come in!" cried Cobeth with exasperation, his Trickster costume half-on and his makeup half-off. When the actor saw who it was, he added with hypocritical gallantry, "Do, do, *do*, come in, professor." He bowed.

"Thank you," said Rowenaster cooly. He was used to Cobeth's fluctuations of mood and his caustic humor; he had spent the last five years living in the same house with the fellow.

Cobeth returned to his makeup table and continued swabbing his neck and arms with a Piedmerri cold cream. "What can I do for you?"

"I have a request."

"Which is?"

"Next time you decide to bastardize a religious rite," said the professor calmly, "leave my name out of it."

Cobeth raised his eyes to meet Rowen's in the mirror. "Bastardize? Don't you think that's a little strong, old man?"

The professor chuckled quietly. "I'm a deeply religious man. Did you know that, Cobeth? No? Well, I am. I began teaching my Greatkin survey course forty-five years ago because I loved the Presence—not because I needed to make a good living as a Saämbolin academic. You see, I really believe there *is* a Presence, Cobeth. And, therefore, a Greatkin Rimble. Furthermore, when I was but a youngster of ten, my Saämbolin parents took me to see Rimble's Remembrance in Suxonli. My parents were scholars themselves. Suxonli was a field trip, one I was privileged to join. And while there, Cobeth, I understood something."

Cobeth turned around to face the professor, his smile skeptical. "And what was that, professor? Even if I don't ask," he added silkily, "you're bound to tell me anyway. You're *so* fond of lecturing."

Rowenaster pursed his lips, wishing very hard that he were Master Doogat. In Rowen's opinion, Cobeth was sorely in need of the Mayanabi's famous "Podiddley Punch." The professor took a deep breath and decided to keep to the point. "I learned this, Cobeth: the Trickster's Hallows of Suxonli Village is not a dead religious ritual, its origins lost in antiquity. *Rimble's Remedy*, as you call it, is nothing less than a literal passion play—Greatkin for mortal and mortal for Greatkin. Done right, the ritual can produce a certain ecstasy of spirit. Done right," he repeated for emphasis.

Cobeth folded his hands on his knee. "Oh—I see. You're

implying I didn't do the rite 'right.'" He smiled at Rowenaster icily. "And you're Speakinghast's resident expert on Rimble. So I'm told." He leaned forward. "Do you know what an expert *is*, professor? An expert is someone who knows more and more about less and less. You're an academic, Rowen. Proud of your 'field trip' to Suxonli." Cobeth started laughing. "You can't tell me a thing about Suxonli that I don't already know. You see, Rowen—I grew up in that village."

"I don't believe you."

"Then that's your foolishness," said Cobeth tapping the Trickster mask beside him with his fingers. "I even had another name there: Yonneth."

Rowenaster said nothing, his expression unconvinced.

"All right," said Cobeth amiably. "Let's assume you don't like me, professor. Let's assume that the entire house has taken sides with Janusin against me—often happens when a relationship breaks up. Especially a Jinnjirri one. We're such a passionate people, we tend to cause others to feel their own emotions as strongly as we feel ours—"

"I don't see what this has to do with anything," said Rowenaster, yawning impolitely. And obviously.

"Well—it's like this, professor. I think you were so busy disliking me through the play that you missed the point of *Rimble's Remedy*."

Rowenaster said nothing, his eyes angry.

"I shall now *tell* you the point," continued Cobeth cooly. "I shall spell it out for you, old man. See if you can catch it." The actor picked up the Trickster mask. "There's a time coming. A wild time, a Trickster time. No broken people will survive it. Only those who become whole through the sting of holovespa will know what to do when this time comes. Only those who can stand the sting of the 'whole wasp' will survive the chaos of Trickster's *shifttime*. They will be called Contrarywise, and they alone will hear the hiss-whisper of Greatkin Rimble. And do his bidding."

Rowenaster frowned. Was it his imagination, or was Cobeth lapsing into some kind of singsong trance state? He sounded almost Tammirring. Was it possible that Cobeth had been telling the truth about where he had grown up? The professor crossed his arms over his chest. Something about Cobeth's manner was definitely Tammirring. It looked very strange on a Jinnjirri born. And very wrong.

Cobeth continued his monologue with increasing fervor. "The

Contrarywise will gather in every city, in every town, and in every village. They will answer Rimble's call to revolution. They will be Merry Pricksters all—prancing and dancing and goosing the politicians. Beware the flashing of their smiles, the brilliance of their eyes—for they will have looked upon the Shining Face of Greatkin Rimble and found the ecstasy that has no words. They will have incorporated the Wasp's Sacrament into their very bodies—and soared!"

Rowenaster cleared his throat uncomfortably. This was the kind of talk that had made Gadorian start swearing during the play. The Guildmaster had been sure that Cobeth and his merry band were plotting civil unrest and possibly political overthrow of the existing structure—namely him.

Cobeth's hair turned milky white, his eyes glittering with a feverish fanaticism. "Now do you get it, professor? Now do you get the big picture? The whole vision—from the Whole Wasp?" He pointed at the bloated leather dildo sitting on the chair next to him. "Think it's empty? If you do, you're wrong. It's filled with holovespa. And you know where I'm taking it, professor? To the cast party. I'm going to intiate some people. I'm going to create me some Contrarywise."

Rowenaster smiled thinly, thankful that neither Sirrefene nor Gadorian would be attending this Jinnjirri farce. "And I suppose you'll be 'initiating' people in Rimble's name?"

"But of course," replied Cobeth. "I certainly wouldn't do it in my own. That would be egotistical."

Rowenaster met his eyes squarely. "I'm glad you're so *clear* about what credit should go to whom, Cobeth. In light of this, I'm sure you intend to write Janusin a full apology for the mistake on the last page of the playbill. You know—the one where you appropriated Janusin's series title? I'm sure you'll want to draft that letter right now, Cobeth. You wouldn't want Janusin to lose any sleep over your mistake."

Cobeth crossed his arms over his chest and smiled innocently. "What mistake, Rowen? I don't recall there being *any* mistake at all."

Chapter Twenty-Four

TIMMER AND MAB hurried along the crowded streets in the theater district of the Jinnjirri Quarter. Timmer felt conspicuously out of place, being of a non-Jinnjirri *landdraw*. For Mab's part, she wished Timmer would slow her brisk stride. Piedmerri were notoriously short in the leg and ample of weight, and Timmer's pace was more than Mab could presently handle. Worse yet and unknown to Timmer, young Mab lacked an accurate sense of direction. The northwest Jinnjirri border had scuttled it. In such a shifting region, the four cardinal points lost their value. Fine for Jinn, but devastating for a Piedmerri. Losing sight of Timmer for the countless time, Mab swore softly. Then the swing of Timmer's striking pale blonde hair caught her eye, and Mab turned to follow. When Mab finally caught up to the musician, she said, "Where *is* the opening night party?"

"At Rhu's house. This street dead-ends in a cul-de-sac at the bottom of the hill." She pointed. "See where all those happincabbies are? That gothic two storey is Rhu's place."

Mab squinted into the darkness, just able to make out the softly glowing coach lights of the well appointed carriages. She slowed, her eyes widening. "Will you look at this mist pouring in? And at this time of year, too." She shook her head in amazement. "Must be on account of it being so warm. Land meeting water."

Timmer nodded. "Lake Effect."

In Speakinghast, anything and everything could be reduced to one cause—Lake Edu. If it was forty below—not uncommon in this part of the world during winter—with a wind chill of minus sixty, the residents of Speakinghast blamed it on the large lake due east of the city. If they woke with sinus headaches and a bad case of the grumps—this was the fault of the lake's changing pressure systems. Of course, colic, oil that smoked too much, and burnt food were also the result of the "Effect." In this city, one might even hear:

"Not tonight, dear—the tide's out."

Timmer watched the mist sweep down the street in front of her.

She seemed to lose her previous self-consciousness regarding her *draw*. Doing a small, dancing turn, Timmer breathed deeply of the scent of fresh water lake—raw with a slightly fishy smell. The Dunnsung lifted her gray shawl above her head, making the hand-dyed material ripple like a gossamer veil in the gentle Trickster Summer breeze. She looked like a will o' the wisp, her footsteps silent, her pale hair damp from the caress of the mist. Mab regarded Timmer with fascination, wishing she could get her round Piedmerri body to move as gracefully as Timmer's.

The Dunnsung waited for Mab to catch up. When Mab did, Timmer remarked, "I adore nights like these. They make me think of Jinnjirri, and what it must be like in that fabled land. Soft and shimmery and—"

"Weird," said Mab bluntly. She was getting very tired of Timmer's constant romanticizing about Jinnjirri. Likewise, Timmer was becoming increasingly irritated with Mab's narrow cynicism—it ruined the fantasy.

Timmer scowled and said nothing further. She decided to dump Mab as soon as they got to the party. After all, thought Timmer, Mab grew up in Jinnjirri, so *surely* she could handle a simple Jinn cast party on her own. Timmer pulled her shawl across her chest angrily.

Mab turned to Timmer as they approached the gabled house at the end of Renegade Road. "Do you think Barlimo believed that story about you and me grabbing a late night snack on the way back to the 'K'? I mean, do you think she'll put it together that I went to the party after all?"

Timmer glared at Mab. "What if she does? You're a big girl, Mab. You reached your majority three years ago. That hardly makes you in need of a chaperone."

Mab nodded, wincing at the tone of Timmer's voice. She appreciated the older girl's confidence in her ability to handle her own affairs, but Mab didn't want to get to the party and find herself abandoned, either. She also knew that Barlimo's concern for her well-being had been genuine. Somehow, she wished Timmer hadn't lied about their destination to the Jinnjirri architect. Not that she needed someone to rescue her or anything dumb like that. The Merry Prickster party was just that—a fun, theatrical party. Furthermore, it wasn't *in* Jinnjirri, so the land would stay put. Mab smiled. A Jinn party in Saämbolin might be enjoyable. Mab walked resolutely up the front steps to Rhu's communal household. She stepped aside for two elegantly garbed Jinnjirri women who were both crossdressed as men. Their hair sprayed out of the top of their heads, falling in different lengths to their shoulders. One smoked a small briar pipe. The other carried a hooded bird with a brilliant display of tail feathers on her crooked right arm. The two women walked past Mab in stately procession, their voices deep, their smiles sensual. Mab watched them disappear into the crowd inside, nodding her head. These Jinn were not like the ones at the Kaleidicopia. These Jinn resembled the kind of people who had raised her—artists of a particular flavor: iconoclastic, flamboyantly decadent, and sexually "on stage."

Timmer stared at the sheer number of people passing through the open front door. She had attended many Jinnjirri parties in the past, but never one hosted by The Merry Pricksters. She wondered if the troupe had an unusually good reputation as party-givers or something; the turnout here was astounding. Eyeing some of the exotic costumes surrounding herself and Mab, Timmer nudged the Piedmerri and said, "You might find some ideas for the Kaleidicopia's Trickster's Hallows. Even *feels* like a carnival here tonight."

Mab nodded slowly. "It does a bit," she said more nervously than she wished. "Do you think there'll be intoxicants?"

"You're asking me?" asked Timmer in surprise. "I thought you knew all about this kind of party."

Mab shrugged. "I lived in the country. This is a city—a Saämbolin city. I understand the Guild regularly raids the homes of drug smugglers. Or users. I just wouldn't want to get caught in something like that. I don't do drugs. I never have—"

Timmer put her hands on her hips. "Surely you don't expect me to believe *that*, Mab. You grew up in Jinnjirri. The Jinn are notorious for their experimentation with 'shifting' states of mind. I'm told their tolerance is *draw* inherited."

Mab took a deep breath. "Yes—that's true, Timmer." Mab's voice took on an edge. "But *I* am not Jinnjirri. *I* am Piedmerri. And we like our sex *and* our thinking stable."

"Remind me not to go to Piedmerri," groused Timmer. Catching sight of several Jinnjirri fondling each other in the corner of the commons room as she and Mab entered, Timmer smiled with relief. "Now this is more like it." She sniffed the air. The smell of Royal Sabbanac floated out of a back bedroom toward the two women. It was a mild hallucinogenic, its scent acrid and ropy. An Asilliwir incense masked the full odor of this home-grown

Jinnjirri weed. Timmer smiled dreamily and added, "I think it's time I lost my virginity."

Mab stared at Timmer in surprise.

"My *Jinnjirri* virginity," Timmer amended hastily. "You're quite right, Mab—I dumped my Dunnsung one long ago. In the back of an Asilliwir wagon, if I recall correctly. I was drunk at the time—the Asilliwir make a murderous resinous wine called retzin. It's pure rotgut." She grinned. "Anyway, he had a beard. The moon was out, and we were young and lusty—".

Mab rolled her eyes. "You're only twenty-three, Timmer. You make it sound as if you're a grandmother."

Timmer scowled at Mab. Pointing a slender finger in the Piedmerri's round, cherubic face, Timmer retorted, "You know what your problem is? You're a literalist. You have no sense of the romantic. No sense of mood. It's a good thing you aren't an artist. You'd put clay feet on everything you created!"

Mab's eyes brimmed with tears. "We're an earthy people, Timmer. I'm—I'm sorry—if I don't—if I'm not—"

Timmer swore, feeling guilty for having made Mab cry. "Oh, forget it, Mab. It's not important. Let's get something to eat," she continued, ushering the little Piedmerri to the sumptuous spread of food on the central feasting table.

Accented with flowers, the dishes were a varied mix of hot casseroles in cast iron pots, vegetable and meat stews, cheese pastries, tossed salads, and roasted potatoes in butter. On a separate groaning board to their right stood pies, cheeses, and liquored fruits. Jinnjirri servants dressed in white and black served Piedmerri champagne in silver goblets. Timmer grabbed two goblets and offered one to Mab. Mab took it gingerly. Seeing this, Timmer decided it was time to part company with Mab. The Dunnsung had come to the party to play with the natives. As far as Timmer was concerned, Mab was a Piedmerri prude. And no prude was going to spoil her fun tonight!

So without a word of explanation, Timmer said, "See ya." Then she wheeled away from Mab heading for one of the smoke-filled back rooms, certain that Mab would never follow her. And Timmer was right.

Mab watched her go, her face scarlet with embarrassment. She liked Timmer. And she wanted Timmer to like her. Mab took a sip of the bubbling drink in her silver goblet, feeling depressed. No matter where she went—she never belonged. She was even an outsider at the Kaleidicopia. And now Timmer was angry with her for being so stolid. Mab wished she were Jinnjirri. She wished she could just let go for once—

A Jinnjirri in a state of half dress interrupted Mab languidly at this point. He smiled at the Piedmerri and changed gender. "Which do you prefer?" asked the randy Jinn, her breasts swelling under Mab's very nose. The Piedmerri swallowed. "So it's men?" continued the Jinnjirri, immediately accommodating Mab by switching back to being a man. The Jinn smiled seductively. "My specialty is virgins."

Mab turned scarlet and downed her Piedmerri champagne.

The Jinnjirri chuckled, leaning indolently against the feasting table. "I can always tell a virgin. I can smell them." He leaned toward Mab and sniffed. "Mmm—Piedmerri wholesome. Mother's milk and soft muscle. You're the kind of young woman I like to get lost in."

Mab took a step backward. Trying to remember what had possessed her to attend this party in the first place, Mab realized she was very alone here. Very. Maybe she should leave. Now. Mab ignored further comments from her would-be deflowerer and set her goblet down on the table. She turned toward the front door and came to a complete standstill as she saw a familiar face enter the front door.

It was Cobeth.

Dressed in an overtunic of geometric black and yellow, Cobeth swept into the house, his trailing scarf looped artistically around his neck, his makeup perfect. Cobeth accepted a round of spontaneous applause with modesty and returned the hugs and congratulations of his well-wishers with impish smiles. The charisma of the man was so strong, it was like an independent presence. Mab reconsidered her decision to leave.

"I can at least tell him I think he did a good job," Mab muttered to herself. "It's more than anyone else from the 'K' will do." She nodded. "And after that, I'll go home."

Mab approached Cobeth shyly. The Jinnjirri actor saw her almost immediately. His expression at first startled, then thoughtful, Cobeth gently disengaged himself from his crowd of admirers. He walked toward Mab, Jinnjirri whispering to each other as he did so. Mab twisted a strand of her hair nervously. She felt as if *she* were suddenly on stage now. It was as if Cobeth's magnetism extended beyond him to include her, too. Mab flushed with the attention.

"You're the *last* person I expected to see here, Mab," said the actor amiably as he joined her at the feasting table. "Did you come alone?"

Mab shook her head. "Timmer's in the back somewhere."

Cobeth nodded, helping himself to some food. He picked out four kinds of vegetables, some mild cheese, and a generous helping of roasted potatoes. "I've stopped eating meat," he explained. "Came out of a meditation I was doing. Makes me a better channel."

"Channel?" This was a Tammirring term. She wondered how Cobeth meant it.

The actor took a bite of potato, chewing with vigor. "Yeah. A channel for Trickster. I get stuff from him all the time now. Even see him on occasion," he added matter-of-factly.

"But you're a Jinnjirri. I thought only Tammirring—"

Cobeth made a rude gesture of dismissal with his hand. "We've got to break out of this single *draw* crap. We've got to start thinking in terms of multiple identity." Stuffing another potato in his mouth, he added, "Rimble—I'm starved. I haven't eaten since lunch. You?"

"I had dinner at the house."

"Of course. Well, Mab—you must have dessert then." He pointed at a coconut-custard confection on top of the groaning board. "That's fresh Saämbolin Silk Pie. Rhu baked it this morning. Tops even Barlimo's good cooking." He smiled. "I'm very partial to sweets." Then he added coyly, "Of *all* kinds."

Mab blushed, catching the obvious sexual reference in Cobeth's last statement. She helped herself to a piece of Saämbolin Silk and changed the subject, saying, "Your play—it was very good."

"You liked it?" asked Cobeth, appearing both surprised and genuinely delighted by Mab's compliment.

Mab struggled to speak, her mouth full of the sweet, rich pie. "Oh, yes. It was wonderful. I'd like to see it again," she gushed. "You can really act, Cobeth. I think you made the right decision— getting out of sculpting, I mean. You've really found yourself."

Cobeth smiled broadly. "I'm amazed you think so. I figured you hated my guts as much as everyone else back at the 'K.' Well, well," he said touching her cheek, "you've suddenly become quite interesting, Mab."

"I have?"

Cobeth nodded. "I would've paired you with Greatkin Phebene—you know, light, love, and syrup. But here you are. At *this* party." Cobeth cast his eyes around the room. "A very

debauched, very depraved crew. But ever so loyal to Trickster—
and to me. Rimble-Rimble," added Cobeth, turning his attention
back to Mab. His eyes danced with a strange wildness. "Deviance
can be fun—oh, yes indeed."

Mab said nothing.

Cobeth peered at the little Piedmerri. "Did I say something
wrong?"

Mab shook her head.

"Yes, I did—I can feel your discomfort. What's wrong, Mab?"

Mab glared at the actor. Talking to Cobeth was like talking to
a blasted Tammirring. What was he—a mind reader? A sensitive?
Mab sighed. "I—uh—it's just where I grew up, that's all. I'm just
not very fond of deviance. And I don't think it's always fun."

"*Sure* it is," said Cobeth.

"No—uh—no, it's not." Mab set her pie hastily on the table.
She had already been through one discussion like this with
Timmer, and she didn't want a repeat performance with Cobeth.
Mab backed away from the actor.

"Where you going?" asked Cobeth, his expression puzzled.

"Uh—home." She headed toward the front door.

Cobeth put down his plate of food. He caught up with Mab, his
boyish face apologetic. "Mab—I didn't mean to offend you.
Please. Stay."

Mab shook her head, tears spilling down her cheeks. "You—
you don't really mean that."

"Sure I do," replied Cobeth warmly. He slid his arm around
Mab's waist, propelling her firmly toward the stairs leading to the
closed off bedrooms on the next floor of the house. Mab was so
much in need of even a *scrap* of reassurance from someone that
she allowed Cobeth to guide her up the stairs. She was tired of
being friendless and alone. Cobeth was a familiar face—they had
lived together at the Kaleidicopia. That made him more than an
acquaintance, she thought. Or a stranger.

When they reached the top of the stairs, Cobeth said, "Come
on."

"Where?"

"To my room."

"You're living here?" she asked in surprise.

He nodded. "There's a whole bunch of us. Rhu and me share a
bed." He paused, seeing the confused disappointment on the little
Piedmerri's face. "What's this?" he asked, brushing a strand of
hair out of her tearful eyes. "Why, Mab—how dear. I had no idea

you felt that way about me." He kissed her forehead jauntily. "Well, you're in luck, my love. Rhu and I have a very loose arrangement—true Jinnjirri style."

"What do you mean?" asked Mab cautiously.

"I mean, child—I'm available."

Then, without permitting Mab to question him further, Cobeth herded her into his bedroom. Seeing the double bed, silk sheets, and tastefully placed mirrors on the ceiling, Mab panicked. Cobeth closed the door behind her before she could flee. He gave her a teasing smile, his waifish charm irresistible. "Mab, Mab—you've got to take chances. Trickster is the Patron of All Exceptions. And sometimes you have to make an exception to your own rule. That is, *if* you want to grow." He lifted Mab's chin with his hand. His face was inches from her own.

Mab breathed shallowly, her lips parting. Cobeth's Jinnjirri sexuality was so powerful now that Mab felt her body respond to the seduction despite the warnings of her heart and mind. Cobeth kissed her neck, sending shivers down her back. Frightened by the intensity of her feelings for Cobeth—emotional and physical—Mab started to pull out of his arms.

"Mab, it's all right."

She hesitated, her eyes searching the utter innocence of his gaze.

Cobeth stroked her lips with his finger. "You've been touched by deviance before—haven't you, Mab? Touched deeply by Trickster. Introduced to the Fertile Dark before you were ready." He kissed her mouth. "But now you're ready, Mab."

Mab caught her breath, her eyes bright and yielding.

Cobeth pulled her gently toward the bed. "You're one of the special ones, Mab. I know." He smiled. "Trickster tells me so. He tells me you're one of his Contrarywise. But you're uninitiated, Mab. And that must be remedied. So come to me, my darling—in his name. Let me bring you home."

As Mab sank into the pillows on the large double bed, Cobeth buried his handsome face in her full breasts. Raising his head and smiling at her, he began untying her blouse. Mab shut her eyes, her face flushed.

"Is this really happening?" she whispered.

Cobeth breathed the good scent of her skin and sweaty arousal deep into his lungs. He seemed to be revivified by it. Leaning close to her ear, he whispered, "Welcome, Mab. Welcome to

Greatkin Rimble's ecstasy." Then Cobeth reached under the pillow to his left.

Mab felt the movement and opened her eyes. She stared.

Cobeth was holding the wineskin dildo from *Rimble's Remedy*. Laughing oddly, he squirted some of its contents into his mouth. Before Mab could ask him what he was doing, the Jinnjirri actor kissed her with his tongue. Mab groaned, her entire body responding to the overwhelming push of Cobeth's potent, Jinnjirri pheromones. Her mouth opened. Cobeth never hesitated. Lifting the leather stinger of "the whole wasp," he shot an ample dose of holovespa into the back of Mab's throat.

The little Piedmerri swallowed before she could stop herself.

Chapter Twenty-Five

RIMBLE FINALLY FOUND Zendrak—drunk out of his mind—under a spreading oak tree at the foot of the Bago-Bago Mountains in southeastern Saämbolin. When Trickster tried to rouse his Emissary, Zendrak muttered sweet nothings and pulled Phebene's rainbow comforter over his head. This was *not* what Rimble expected. The little Greatkin fingered the comforter thoughtfully. Then, smelling the scent of black currant wine and Utter Chocolate Decadence on Zendrak's breath, Rimble started swearing at the Patron of Great Loves and Tender Trysts.

"You can't feed mortals from our table, Phebes!" he cried at the sky and earth. "It's too rich for the poor sods!" Then, spitting into his hands, Rimble grabbed Zendrak by the tunic collar and threw him roughly to a sitting position against the oak tree. Zendrak shook his head groggily. Before he could even open his eyes, Rimble punched him soundly in the stomach. Zendrak promptly lost the remains of his picnic with Love.

Unfortunately, he managed to keep his colossal hangover.

Zendrak leaned backward against the tree, wiping the vomit off his lips with the back of his hand, his eyes rolled upward in his head, his expression pained. "Don't talk to me, Rimble," he whispered. "Just don't talk—"

"I most certainly *will*!" yelled the annoyed little Greatkin.

Zendrak tried to bury his ears in Phebene's comforter. Rimble ripped it out of his hands and tossed it behind him into a thicket of bushes. "Rimble—" groaned Zendrak, "—have a heart."

Trickster snorted. "Look at you, Zen-boy. You sound like a whining school kid. 'Have a heart,'" he added in derisive mimicry of Zendrak's earlier plea. "You're pathetic." Trickster crossed his arms over his chest. "I think I should disown you."

"Disown me?" asked Zendrak wincing from the sound of his own voice.

"You're a disgrace to the family. *Kelandris* would never succumb to the wine and food of Love. Never." Trickster wagged a finger in Zendrak's bleary eyes. "And don't pretend Phebes didn't tell you who Kel was, either. It would be just like her to spoil my surprise—in the name of Truth, you know. Truth is terribly 'in' with the group at Eranossa this year." Trickster paced back and forth, grumping as he walked. "See—that's the thing about Eranossa. It's the home of the Bright Ones—we're talking light not brains, mind you—and Neath's the home of the Dark Ones. They're obvious, we're subtle. And like I keep trying to tell those Eranossa dimwits, you can't go around exposing everything to the full blast of the noonday sun. *Some* things have to incubate a while. Not that I have anything against Truth—"

Zendrak belched rudely.

Rimble ignored the editorial comment and continued his monologue. "—not that I have anything against Truth. It's just that some truths have to become known gradual-like. And you finding out that Kel's your twin is *one* of them. I don't want the two of you joining forces too soon, see. If you weren't so obssessed with this soulmate thing—"

Zendrak forced his eyes open all the way. "I am *not* obssessed—"

"You certainly are!" snapped Trickster. "It's all you ever think about." He made a frame with his hands in the air. "Kel and the Lost Chance." He rolled his eyes. "Idiot."

The light of the rising moon made Zendrak's eyes glitter coldly. "Phebene was quite sympathetic, Rimble. *She* understood what it's like to be part Mythrrim—and alone."

"You don't *need* Phebene!" yelled the little Greatkin, losing his temper with Zendrak entirely. "I'm the Greatkin of Coincidence and the Impossible! I'm hope when there's none to be had! Do you think I'll give you only *one* opportunity with Kelandris of Suxonli? Do you?"

Zendrak shrugged, his expression skeptical.

Rimble pulled at his black goatee. "Even now, Kel makes her way to you, Zendrak. She is *on* your trail—hunting you with a vengeance."

"So Phebene tells me," muttered Zendrak, crossing his arms over his chest. "Nice of you to make Kelandris think *I* was the reason everything went sour in Suxonli. Nice of you to confuse me in her mind with that soul-sucker Yonneth." Zendrak spat on the ground in front of Trickster. "I've got a good mind to quit being your Emissary."

Trickster raised one of his black eyebrows. "I see. Well, whatever you want." He shrugged. "You're easily replaced."

"By whom?" asked Zendrak indignantly.

"Yonneth. Cobeth. The name doesn't matter." Seeing Zendrak's consternation and disbelief, Rimble smiled. "He's just begging to work for me, you know. In fact, he's quite convinced he already is."

Zendrak's eyes narrowed. "And is he?"

Trickster refused to answer, his pied eyes cool.

Chapter Twenty-Six

WHEN ROWENASTER ARRIVED back at the Kaleidicopia after speaking with Cobeth, he found Barlimo and Tree cleaning up the filth that was in Po's room. Barlimo had removed her play-going clothes and now wore an old smock and apron. Likewise, Tree had abandoned his "autumn regalia." The green-haired Jinnjirri stood naked from the chest up, his lower half covered by a pair of patched trousers. Po's room was on the first floor of the House. So when the professor opened the front door of the 'K,' he heard the following:

"I've found another one. That makes seventeen total, Barl."

"Seventeen what?" yelled Rowenaster as he removed his maroon travelling cloak in the front hall. Hanging it on a peg, he joined the Jinnjirri.

"Spoons," replied Barlimo, lugging an enormous bag of garbage out of Podiddley's room. Pausing to smile at the professor, she added, "Those Asilliwir and their damned tea. When Po comes back, I'm going to make him buy his *own* tea service."

"*If* he comes back," corrected Tree.

Rowenaster chuckled. "Wishful thinking, wouldn't you say?"

Barlimo scowled at the Jinnjirri and the Saämbolin. "Po *will* be back, fellows. You can count on it."

"Why?" asked Tree, making a mournful gesture that included the entirety of Podiddley's pig pen—better known in the house as "Room O." Rowenaster walked closer, trying not to breathe. Like Tree, he had never seen the inside of Podiddley's lodgings.

The professor's eyes widened.

Po's room was littered with dirty clothes, the mass of them literally reaching a height of calf deep. Mugs with souring milk added a unique, foul, pungence to the existent mustiness of month-old unwashed underwear. The window was open, but even that did little to alleviate the odors here.

"Incense," said the professor. "Does anyone have any?"

"Janusin probably does. But he's out at some pub drowning his sorrows," said Tree. "His hair was so blue, it frosted."

Barlimo met Rowen's inquiring glance. "I told Jan about Cobeth stealing the 'Panthe'kinarok Series' title. He was none too happy about it."

"I can imagine," muttered Rowenaster. Picking up a couple of books with broken spines, the Saämbolin professor added, "I don't suppose anyone's come across my library card, have they?"

Barlimo shook her head. "That was the first thing I looked for, Rowen. No sign of it."

Rowenaster sighed. "Blast. That just means I have to spend *all* of tomorrow morning riding the infamous 'Saämbolin-Paper-Go-Round.' Better known as the Bureaucratic Bunglebush."

Tree smiled sympathetically. "You'd think the Saäm would be nicer to their own kind than they are to us mere rabble," he added to Barlimo.

The Jinnjirri architect snorted. "As was so *clearly* pointed out to me this afternoon at the Great Library, Tree—the Saäm don't make such exceptions."

"What a tedious lot," remarked Tree. "No offense intended, professor," he added with a quick smile.

Rowenaster chuckled good naturedly. "Believe me—*I* think they're pretty tedious, too. That's why I live here with you Jinnjirri dullards."

This brought laughter from both Tree and Barlimo.

Rowenaster went into the kitchen and rummaged in the cold storage for a piece of fruit. Finding a pommin, he smiled with delight. Like young Yafatah, pommins were the professor's favorite luxury fruit. "Who else is home?" he asked returning to the dauntless Jinnjirri duo in Room O.

"Nobody but us fools," said Tree, carrying out a soup bowl covered with a fine layer of gray-green mold.

"Timmer and Mab stopped to get something to eat on the way back from Cobeth's play," said Barlimo. "They were going to the same place where you and I had lunch today, Rowen. Timmer said she could get meals there for cheap since she was playing for the restaurant."

Rowenaster shook his head. "Can't be that place, Barl. The Piper's Inn serves lunch only. They must've said something else."

"Very possibly," agreed Barlimo, starting to strip Po's bed. "There were a lot of people talking around us. It was very hard to hear."

"What did you think of *Rimble's Remedy*?" asked Tree, passing Rowen as he returned to Room O, sponge and pail of suds in hand. "Were you utterly embarrassed by all those acknowledgments on the playbill?"

Rowenaster gave the green-haired Jinnjirri a disgruntled scowl. "I would've preferred that Cobeth had given most of them to you, Tree. I'm surprised your friend Rhu didn't make Cobeth put in a good word for you. She was listed as being the editor for the playbill."

"I think," said Tree, knocking spider webs out of the upper corners of Po's room, "that The Merry Pricksters as a whole have been 'won over,' shall we say? Especially Rhu. The cast party is at her house, tonight. Rumor has it that Cobeth and she are lovers—and *don't* tell Janusin I said that, okay? Cobeth's hurt him too much already. Add something like this, and I'm not sure Janusin will finish that blasted Trickster statue in time for the Museum's deadline."

Barlimo sneezed as a cloud of dust settled around her head. Taking out a handkerchief, she mumbled, "I sound like Timmer."

Rowenaster looked at Barlimo strangely. Then out of the blue he said, "You're *sure* Timmer went out to eat?"

Barlimo shrugged. "That's what she said she was going to do. Although at the time, I did think it was odd. Before the play, she had been talking about going to the opening night cast party. She had even tried to get Mab to tag along with her. I guess Mab must've talked Timmer out of it entirely. Timmer and Mab were laughing together during intermission."

Rowenaster peeled the pommin in his hand, his expression uneasy.

Finding an unused bag of penis sheaths under Po's pillow, Barlimo chuckled and said, "Oh, Po—do dream on."

Catching sight of the condoms, Tree wrinkled his nose. "Can you imagine bedding Po? In *this* mess?"

Rowenaster bit into the sweet, orange meat of the pommin. He chewed slowly, his face a frown.

Barlimo looked up. "Isn't that pommin any good? I just bought the batch yesterday. The Asilliwir trader *swore* they were fresh."

Rowenaster met her eyes. "There are drugs at the cast party, Barl. And not the usual variety." He paused. It was a well known fact at the 'K' that Timmer had more than a passing interest in drugs. "I wonder," continued the professor, "if Timmer knew there would be drugs at Rhu's? You keep a very clean household here, Barl. Would Timmer be likely to want you to know she was going to a party of this nature?"

Tree stopped cleaning.

Barlimo's good-humored hair paled. The Jinnjirri ran to fetch her wool shawl from the peg in the front hall, muttering, "Damn, Timmer!"

Tree joined her, his face stricken. "I'm coming with you."

"We don't know that Mab's there," said Barlimo as calmly as she could manage. Her hair betrayed her, however; it turned a mottled, worried gray.

Tree touched a strand of it. "Yes, we do."

Chapter Twenty-Seven

THE HOLOVEPSA MAB had ingested came on in fifteen minutes. During the wait, Cobeth had regaled Mab with first-hand stories of the Rimble's Revels he had attended in Suxonli. Feeling no ill effects from the holovespa at this point, Mab had listened with genuine interest. Cobeth, who had spent years at his sister's knee—specifically Kel's—now spoke of the coming Jinnaeon. Using Kel's native Tammirring understanding of the Greatkin as his own, Cobeth reinterpreted his sister's vision of Rimble's *Shifttime*. The inspiration belonged to Kelandris, but the words were Cobeth's:

"It's time, Mab. It's time to sing with a new voice. It's time to dance a new dance." Cobeth fondled Mab's belly, placing his hand on top of her womb. "It's time to dream a new dream for the world. Choose, Mab. Choose the color of your fate."

Mab frowned at Cobeth, unsure of what he meant.

The Jinnjirri actor laughed. Turning over on his back, he began singing a lively little tune. Written by Kelandris, it was now a Suxonli drinking song:

> When the Wasp's ascendant in the northern sky,
> As above, so below—patterns go awry!
> So choose, choose, choose
> The color of your fate,
> Make it Yellow Jacket yellow
> Rimble's at the gate!
>
> Sing it—ah ya, *Rimble*,
> As we turn contrary-round,
> Be nimble boy, be nimble girl
> While we shake the foundations down!
> While we shake the foundations down!

Cobeth finished the tune and grinned. "We're going to tear this city apart, Mab. And rebuild it. From the foundation up." He kissed her on the mouth. "You can help, Mab. You can help spread the good news of the sacrament," said Cobeth glancing at the dildo on the floor. "*You* can give initiation." He spoke softly. "This is such important work, my darling. Would you turn down the chance for *real* purpose in your life? There's a whole new order of things a-borning. Join us, Mab. Join Rimble's Own, and we'll give birth to a new way of thinking and being."

Mab swallowed, tears unexpectedly coming to her eyes. Something ancient stirred in her *draw*—a distant memory, a gentle call. Unknown to Mab, Cobeth addressed the genuine Contrarywise potency in herself—addressed and irritated the potency into premature wakefulness. Psychic pressure intensified. Mab stared at the dildo on the floor, feeling disoriented.

"That aphrodisiac in the wineskin? It's very—uh—strong."
Mab coughed hoarsely. The room had suddenly taken on a
larger-than-life reality, and she wasn't sure she liked it. Mab
raised her eyes, looking at herself in the mirrors above her in the
ceiling. She watched her half-clothed body change proportions.
Then her face shifted.

"Wh—what?" she whispered. *"Wh-what?"* Memories of Jinnjirri changing gender that frightened her as a child flooded her
mind. Mab's pulse raced. She began to sweat. She sat up abruptly,
her skin pale. Making weak fists with her hands, Mab whimpered.
"This is no aphrodisiac! This is a—"

Cobeth grinned at Mab, sinking back into the pillows. He made
faces at the mirror above him, giggling wildly. "It's great, isn't
it?"

Mab's breathing became very shallow. "Make it stop, Cobeth!
Please," she begged, her voice becoming shrill with panic.

Cobeth stopped playing with himself in the mirror, turning his
head to look at Mab. "Don't be ridiculous, girl. You can't stop
holovespa once it's got started. That would be like trying to stop
a horse who's just been let out of the racing gate. Crazy—and it
can't be done. So relax. Sit back and enjoy the show," he said, his
attention returning to the mirror above them. "This is only the
beginning," he added with a shiver of eager anticipation.

Mab staggered to her feet, clasping her hands to her head. "I
can't do this, Cobeth. I can't, I can't, I can't—"

Giving her a bored look, Cobeth got to his feet nimbly.
Grabbing Mab by the arm, he dragged her into the bathroom. "Get
in there," he said, pointing to the empty showerstall. Mab did as
she was bid, wondering if she would ever survive this—
wondering, in fact, if she were still breathing. What if she forgot
how? Mab consulted Cobeth on this point.

The Jinnjirri rolled his eyes. "You Piedmerri," he grumbled,
turning on the hot and cold water simultaneously. "I hope
Trickster doesn't call many of your *landdraw*. You Pieds really
know how to spoil a good time." Then, without a backward look,
Cobeth left Mab standing alone in the shower at Rhu's house.
Grabbing the leather dildo from the play, he went downstairs to
share his good time with a more appreciative audience.

Upstairs, Mab fell to her knees under the running water.
Clutching her head in her hands, she began to rock. The shower
drenched the skirt she still wore. It also drowned her terrified
sobs.

Barlimo and Tree rode in a happincabby to Rhu's house. Sticking her head out of the slowly moving coach, Barlimo yelled at the driver:

"Can't you go any faster?"

"Too much traffic, ma'am," he yelled back. "There's a lot of people out tonight. And a mist besides."

Barlimo sat back in her seat heavily, her hair turning a darker shade of gray. Sitting opposite her, Tree watched Barlimo's hair change color in silence. Then, looking out the window, Tree stared at nothing, his feelings tangled. There was only one thing he was certain of: if Cobeth or anyone at that party had harmed Mab in any way, Tree would personally thrash the crap out of them. He made a fist unconsciously, his jaw clenching. Barlimo interrupted Tree's thoughts:

"There really *is* a lot of traffic out there." She peered into the gently moving mist. "And most of them seem to be mounted Saämbolin Guildguard. I wonder why that is."

Tree stiffened. "How close are we to Renegade Road?"

"We've just turned on to it," replied Barlimo. She paused. "Are you thinking what I'm thinking?"

Tree nodded. "A Saämbolin raid on a Jinnjirri party?"

Barlimo grunted, running her hands raggedly through her hair. After considering their options, Barlimo said, "All right. I'll tell you what I think we should do."

Tree leaned forward, his eyes on hers.

"I figure it this way. If it *is* a raid—then, we've probably got only the slightest headstart on the Guildguard. When they arrive, the party will scatter—the Guildguard picking up as many Jinn as they can. We've got to have found Mab and Timmer before that point." Barlimo touched Tree's furious red hair. "That means, my friend, that we can't waste time beating Cobeth—or anybody else—into the ground. Do you understand? And do you agree?"

Tree remained motionless, his eyes smoldering.

Barlimo waved her hand in front of his face. "Tree, are you listening to me? We've got big trouble on our hands. If you or anyone else from the Kaleidicopia gets caught by the Saämbolin Guildguard on the premises of a *drug* raid—the house is finished. Gadorian is just itching to throw the book at us. Rowen said Gadorian and Sirrefene's response to Cobeth's play was negative. All we need now is for either the Guildmaster or the Master Curator to find out that Cobeth's a former Kaleidicopian."

Barlimo smiled at the Jinnjirri sitting opposite her in the carriage. "I'm sure Cobeth'll show up at our Trickster's Hallows, Tree. You can beat the piss out of him then. I'll even help."

"Maybe the Saämbolin will do it for us tonight," Tree muttered.

Barlimo laughed sardonically. "Have you *ever* known Cobeth to get caught doing something he shouldn't? He's the master manipulator. You can be sure Cobeth will have an escape route out of Rhu's house. And I bet he smuggles all of The Merry Pricksters along with him. How many are there now, anyway? With you gone, I mean?"

"Nine."

Barlimo stared at Tree.

"Something wrong with that?" he asked.

"No. No—nothing's wrong with it. It's probably just a coincidence," she added with a shrug. Just the same, a chill went up her spine.

Tree smiled without enthusiasm. "Rimble-Rimble."

Barlimo said nothing, wondering where Zendrak was tonight.

Coming out of the back room briefly where she had been smoking Royal Sabbanac and nibbling on the ear of a Jinnjirri woman, Timmer noticed Cobeth's presence—and Mab's absence. After making a few hasty inquiries, Timmer learned that Mab had last been seen going up the stairs with Cobeth—the actor's arm around her waist. Much to Timmer's horror, she also learned what Cobeth liked to do upstairs. Besides make love, he liked to initiate people into some arcane religion through the ingestion of holovespa. And no, Cobeth did not use small dosages of the drug. He believed—they said—in going for the jugular of the Presence. The more intense the trip, the more valid the religious experience. Timmer swore. Mab might be a pain in the ass—but she wasn't deserving of *this*. Taking the stairs two at a time, Timmer ran toward Rhu's room. She found the door ajar. Hearing the sound of weeping coming from the bathroom, Timmer winced.

"That's *got* to be old tear-ducts Mab," she murmured and walked hastily toward the bathroom. As she reached the open door, Timmer heard the sound of a man's voice. "*Now* what?" she added, entering the steamy room slowly.

Timmer's jaw dropped.

"Doogat!" cried the Dunnsung. "What in the world are you doing here?"

The Mayanabi Master flinched. "Not so loud, Timmer—please. I've got a terrible headache." Turning his attention back to Mab, Doogat coaxed the trembling nineteen-year-old out of the showerstall. Mab stared at Timmer stupidly while Doogat threw a dry towel around her bare breasts and shoulders. Timmer crept closer to Mab.

Looking at the Piedmerri's dilated pupils, Timmer said, "Is she going to be all right?"

Doogat grunted. "Should be. Mab's had quite a scare though—haven't you, old girl?" he asked Mab amiably, wrapping a second towel over Mab's dripping brown hair.

Mab didn't answer.

Timmer swallowed. "I feel awful about this, Doogs. It's all my fault that Mab's even here at this party. I talked her into it."

Doogat shrugged. "It hasn't been a good night all the way around, Timmer. Take what blame is yours in this matter, but please—leave the rest of it. The negligence isn't all yours to shoulder." He sighed sadly.

Timmer looked away, feeling embarrassed about her earlier impatience with Mab. It had probably been an act of courage for the Piedmerri to come to this party at all. An act of courage that Timmer knew she'd never understand from the outside. The blonde musician took a deep breath. Bringing her attention back to Doogat and the shivering young woman next to him, Timmer said, "So—uh—what can I do to help?"

Doogat smiled at Timmer and told her to fetch a bathrobe of Cobeth's from the next room. "If the Jinnjirri wants it back, he can come and get it at the Kaleidicopia. Leave him a note to that effect, will you, Timmer? I'll finish drying Mab in here."

Timmer did as she was told. A few moments later, Doogat heard a soft cry of surprise from the next room. Craning his head around the corner of the bathroom, he called, "Is everything all right in there?"

Timmer reappeared, a purple bathrobe draped over her shoulder and an envelope in her hand. Timmer's face was pale. "You're not going to believe what this is," she said hoarsely. "You're just *not* going to believe it."

Doogat took the bathrobe and put Mab into it. Then, meeting Timmer's expectant gaze, the Mayanabi Master said, "Janusin's rent money?"

Timmer's mouth opened. "*How* did you know?"

Doogat smiled, picking Mab up in his arms. "There are

different kinds of thieves in the world, Timmer. Cobeth's one kind. And Po?"

Timmer's face turned scarlet. "I guess I owe Po an apology."

"I guess you do," agreed Doogat, his dark eyes twinkling.

Timmer held up the lavender envelope. Its wax seal was broken. "I saw it while rummaging for a pencil on Cobeth's desk. Money's all here. Every cent." She swore. "Cobeth's really got it in for Janusin. The 'K,' too, apparently. *Now* we know what was behind Rowen's overdue playbill kudos. They were a half a page of pure guilt. Or mockery. Rowen's library card is in here."

Doogat encouraged Mab to relax against his chest. Then, his expression curious, he said, "What library card?"

Timmer reached into the envelope and pulled out a tattered piece of paper. "Rowen was grousing about it over dinner at the Kaleidicopia. I wasn't paying much attention."

On the word "attention," Doogat suddenly stiffened. Listening intently for a few moments, he turned to Timmer and asked, "Is there a back way out of this house?"

Timmer nodded. "Yeah—I was out on the porch earlier. Why?"

Doogat walked swiftly out of the room, clasping Mab firmly in his arms. "Come on!" he yelled at the Dunnsung. "Quickly, Timmer, quickly!"

Muttering under her breath about the weird ways of the Mayanabi, Timmer followed Doogat out of Rhu's house without further delay. As she exited out the back—the Saämbolin Guild-guard entered from the front. The night was cool, the mist eerie. Timmer's eyes widened with surprise. Before her stood Tree. Glancing at the happincabby to his left, she observed Barlimo motioning the driver to wait. "I don't believe it," Timmer mumbled, and felt grateful for this coincidence.

Barlimo walked quickly toward Doogat. As she reached him, she touched Mab's wan, sleepy face with a kind hand. Raising her eyes to meet those of Trickster's Emissary, Barlimo whispered drily, "I thought you were supposed to prevent this kind of thing."

Doogat replied in Zendrak's voice, his tone equally as dry, "I was."

"Wonderful."

He shrugged, his head still throbbing with a hangover.

Part III:

RECOGNITION CEREMONY

By the venomous sting of his Chaos Thumb,
Trickster pricks nine, one by one,
His circle of genius for the turn to come;
Back pocket people for that rainy day
When the weave of the world pulls away.

—OLD SUXONLI SAYING

Chapter Twenty-Eight

COME AUTUMN IN Speakinghast when mornings were clear and brisk, the copper bells of the Great Library rang the sleep from the city with plangent thunder. Soon horse-drawn carts creaked and jolted down wide avenues of brown cobblestone. Asilliwir spice wagons, fragrant with exotic miles, censed the air with mysterious perfumes that tantalized: woody cinnamon, musk, and rare green patchou bark; pungent clove, orange molly, and wild titchiba balm. Here were scents to clear the mind and pleasure the tongue.

"And all for a most reeeasonable price," cried Asilliwir hawkers, twirling their moustaches and grinning.

This brought chaffing laughter from the other Speakinghast merchants who huddled around small campfires, ceramic mugs of hot, black teas clasped in their gloved hands. Well known for their "creative pricing," Asilliwir scalping and bargain buys predominated here. This was a haggler's heaven. Called the Asilliwir Open Air Market, people of all *draws* flocked to the painted caravan wagons and clan-run stalls.

Despite the lingering Trickster Summer, the air was chill at this early hour. Men and women wrapped themselves snugly in bright, woolen blankets. They recounted local gossip as they sipped their steaming brews. A few newly arrived traders added long distance scandal and humor to the talk. Merchants of all *draws* exchanged monies for Saämbolin Guildtender. Called silivrain by the Saäm, the minted coins were referred to as "silies" by everyone else.

Farmers from the outskirts of the city haggled in rough dialects with early risers, their tables covered with a rich harvest of fall fruits and vegetables. Fishwives slapped their pre-dawn catches on crushed blocks of ice, gutting them deftly with shiny knives. The wool dyers called to one another and waved. Their hands were permanently stained with vegetable dyes, their brilliant clothes likewise. Sleepy students on the way to early morning classes at the University of Speakinghast picked their way across the crowded marketplace. They eyed freshly baked Piedmerri breads and sweet rolls as they decided what to purchase for a quick breakfast.

The city was alive with bustle and color. And as Speakinghast entered its first hour of business, it remained unaware that a tall figure in black had just outsmarted the city's convoluted Saämbolin pass system by stowing away inside a large hay wagon. While the Piedmerri farmer driving the wagon turned left down a busy street, the stowaway jumped free. She brushed pieces of hay off her veil and robe. Straightening, she whispered a rhyme to herself and joined the slowly moving crowds at the Asilliwir Market.

Yes, Kelandris was crazy again.

Following Rimble's suggestion that Zendrak and not Yonneth was the true villain in the Suxonli tragedy, Kel had driven herself into a mental corner of uncertainty. What Kel remembered about Zendrak at the Hallows was sweet. What she remembered of her beloved brother, Yonneth, was strange and distorted. Kel's fear that Trickster was deliberately trying to confuse her—for his own purposes—had only made the muddle worse. The psychic scarring left from the Ritual of Akindo prevented Kelandris from trusting her own perceptions—or memories. Thus, within days of leaving the northwest border of Jinnjirri, Kelandris had imagined and reimagined the events in Suxonli so many times and in so many different forms that she no longer knew which events had actually occurred and which had not. By the morning of the fourth day, Kel remembered Zendrak as the one who had poured a toxic dose of holovespa down her throat. And Yonneth? He was still Kel's best loved brother and the man to whom she had willingly given her maidenhead.

Despite Kel's waking confusion, her dreams at night remained honest. Most of them revolved around the question of incest with Zendrak—which Kel could not understand—or accept. As Kel's internal strain increased, she answered her dreams by saying that Rimble was the Patron of Deviance, and anything—even incest—was possible at his revel. Rimble was the great taboo breaker. Nothing was too sacred, too established, or too dangerous to be challenged by Trickster. Still, Kel's village indoctrination contradicted Rimble's direct bloodline in herself. So upon waking, Kel lapsed into rhyme, unable to reconcile the laws of civilization with the challenge of deviance.

Trickster thought this was just fine.

Like Zendrak, Kelandris was three-quarters Greatkin and one

quarter mortal Mythrrim. But as Aunt had pointed out to Fasilla, *un*like Zendrak, Kelandris had not received the formal training necessary to control her formidable capacity to act as mortal grounding for the Remembrance of Rimble. Fragmented as she now was into several personalities, Kelandris remained difficult but relatively harmless. Unified into one self, Kelandris wielded enough power to not only "shake the foundations down" of Speakinghast, but of civilization itself. Unified, Kel might also become aware of Yonneth's whereabouts. As a Mythrrim, she would hunt and kill him for his outright abandonment of her during the improvised "trial" preceding the Ritual of Akindo. Kel had expected familial loyalty from her favorite brother and received strange shrugs and silences. In many ways, this had cut Kelandris more deeply than the brutal community flogging that had followed the trial.

The extremity of Kel's reaction to Yonneth's betrayal of her was unusual for a Tammirring and typical of a Mythrrim. As a rule, the Tammi preferred little involvement in the affairs of one another—particularly the Tammi in Suxonli. Remote as the snowy mountain peaks that surrounded the tiny village, the people of Suxonli perceived emotional intimacy as an undesirable obstacle in their quest for mystical union with the Greatkin and the Presence. Kel's Mythrrim heritage, however, disturbed the serenity and indifference of her Tammirring *draw*. For a Mythrrim, kinship was forever. Like soulmating, kinship required nothing less than one hundred percent commitment, involvement, and affection. Yonneth, who was Jinnjirri born and therefore as isolated by his art as the Tammi were by the divine, had no idea that Kel considered his acts against her as an emotional treason worthy of confrontation and a merciless death.

Trickster thought this was *not* fine.

To begin with, Yonneth had his uses—ones Rimble planned to exploit in the Greater Scheme of Things. Trickster needed an Emissary and a Hallows *he*, but he also needed a Cosmic Dupe. Currently, Yonneth was well on his way to winning this plum role. Furthermore—and perhaps more importantly—Trickster knew Kelandris was not yet ready to face Yonneth. As a child, Kel had truly loved her youngest brother. To this day, a portion of Kelandris believed Yonneth had not intended to abandon her at the trial. After all, he had been a mere fifteen years old at the time of the Ritual of Akindo. If Kelandris were confronted with the true disloyalty of Yonneth's character, Trickster feared Kelandris might lose the thin thread of fluctuating sanity she still possessed.

In the hopes of preserving Kel's life, Trickster decided to throw Kelandris off Yonneth's trail entirely by sending her directly into the arms of the one man in the whole world who could understand her, love her, and—Presence willing—turn her rage. To Rimble's credit, the little Greatkin had made these plans well before Phebene had stuck her sweet nose into his business. In fact, it had been Trickster's intention from the start to buy Kelandris the time she needed to heal from the fiasco in Suxonli—specifically in Zendrak's company. Deviance would get Kelandris to Zendrak one way, and love would get her there in quite another. Although Trickster would never have admitted it to Phebene, he supposed that one way was not necessarily better than the other—so long as you got to where you needed to be.

In Kel's case, this meant Doogat's house. However, without a guide to bring her there, Trickster doubted that Kelandris—in her multiple state of mind—would ever find the tiny tobacco shop. It lay at the heart of the labyrinthine Asilliwir Bazaar—a busy, permanent maze of awnings, arches, and businesses. Had Kelandris been sane, Trickster would've taken her there himself. Insane, Kelandris could neither see nor hear the little Greatkin. Thus Trickster was forced to improvise. Enter Podiddley . . .

In a park across the street from where Kelandris now walked, Po cupped water from an artesian well to his mouth. Splashing some of it in his bleary eyes, he cursed Doogat—and then Mab. For the past three weeks, the Piedmerri girl had been living with Po at Doogat's place. To date, Mab had not slept uninterrupted by nightmares since the now infamous Jinnjirri party at Rhu's house. Every night—no exceptions—Mab would wake with a panicked cry, her young body drenched with sweat. The images of her dreams changed, but the underlying feeling remained constant: she was alone in circumstances that were out of her control. Doogat said Mab's reaction to the unhinging effects of the holovespa drug was a normal one for a Piedmerri born. Doogat also promised that it would pass in another week.

"Just in time for the Kaleidicopia's Trickster's Hallows," Po muttered without enthusiasm. For reasons that Doogat refused to explain to him, Doogat was adamant that both he and Mab should attend this masked carnival at the house. Po's own participation seemed logical to him—with any luck he would be living again at the 'K' in a matter of days. As a house member, Po was entitled to attend house affairs. "But in Mab's case?" he said with bewilderment. "Seems idiotic so soon after Rhu's." Po yawned.

The little thief leaned idly against the stone cistern behind him. Yellow leaves drifted to the ground from the trees above, covering the crimson leather of his beaten, muddy boots. This morning, Po had dressed in his favorite raggedy-man garb. A patchwork of loosely hanging materials hung sloppily over the loose fit of his red harem pants. Po wore a fiery gem in the lobe of his right ear, and a floppy, knit hat covered his receding hairline. Po had a stringy beard and moustache, both bearing the tale of his recent breakfast: sweet bun powdered with white sugar and cinnamon. The drink from the well had dislodged but not removed the crumbs. At thirty-eight years of age, Po cut a paunchy figure— soft and apparently harmless.

Stepping off the mossy stairs that led up to the old well, Po sauntered into the early morning crowds. As he walked, the nonchalance of his previous posturing faded, replaced now by a taut, alert readiness. This was Po the pickpocket—a professional beginning his "day at the office." Drawing shamelessly on the tracking skills he had acquired through his long years of study as a Mayanabi Nomad, Po decided to take a closer look at something interesting moving down the far side of the street.

Po grinned. A veiled Tammirring in black was an uncommon sight in Speakinghast. Only widows wore black and only then in the villages. If this woman were village bred, she was probably ignorant of city street smarts. Po twirled the tip of his limp moustache, his blue eyes twinkling. He congratulated himself on the easiness of the mark in front of him and wondered where the Tammi pigeon wore her purse. Humming softly, Po decided to find out. Jumping cracks and potholes in the street, Podiddley of Brindlsi merrily ran to mug one of Rimble's Contrarywise Nine— and Trickster's own daughter.

Using the crush of the marketplace crowd to his advantage, Po bumped into Kelandris. In the midst of regaining his balance, Po "fanned" Kel—felt her pockets—proffering heartfelt apologies. His exploration had been successful; Kelandris carried something that felt like a purse in the left pocket of her black robe.

Kelandris, who had permitted no one to touch her—sexually or otherwise—since the beating in Suxonli, swore at Po and ordered him out of her way. As had been her habit for the past sixteen years, Kelandris spoke in verse. Podiddley listened to her uneasily. Perhaps this black pigeon was mad. He calculated Kel's height, guessing accurately that she stood at a formidable six-feet-four. Better make this quick, he decided. Po continued to offer Kel his apologies. He did it so infuriatingly well that Kelandris never felt Podiddley slip his right hand into her robe pocket. He filched the contents and turned to walk away. Then he froze. Had he heard what he thought he had heard?

Kelandris repeated herself softly, laughing all the while:

"Little man, I'm your bane. Little man, I bring you pain. How cheap is life when quartered by a knife?"

Podiddley swallowed. Turning around slowly, all of his Mayanabi and streetwise senses alert, Po smiled cooly at Crazy Kel. Po carried an Asilliwir akatikki in his belt, but judging by the deft way Kelandris played with the knife in her hand, he doubted he'd get it to his mouth in time. Still, he decided to try. Feigning alarm at something unseen approaching Kelandris from behind, Po pulled his akatikki free. Kelandris bought Po's distraction briefly. She started to look over her shoulder. Changing her mind, however, she whirled on Po, her knife already sailing toward her intended target. Kelandris, like Po, was capable of split-second action; her survival on more than one occasion had depended on it.

Po yelped with surprise, his right hand now bloody. The loaded akatikki fell to his feet. Taking instant advantage of Po's disbelief, Kelandris moved on the little thief. She crushed the akatikki with the heel of her black boot, retrieved her knife from Po's torn flesh and punched him soundly in the solar plexus. As Po gasped for air and doubled over in pain, Kelandris calmly slipped her right hand inside Po's left pocket and plucked *his* purse—unaware that Po carried something of hers in his right pocket. Podiddley, for his part, never felt the theft. His entire attention was focused on the powerful left-handed grip that Crazy Kel had on his raggedy-man tunic. Kelandris yanked Po toward her dark veils. Standing nearly a foot and a half taller than the little Asilliwir, Kelandris literally lifted Po into the air.

Laughing again, Kel said, "The blood's clean, but the knife is not. Let flesh turn green with stinky rot!"

Without further ceremony, Kelandris threw Podiddley against the wall of a nearby house. She whirled away from him, her black veil fluttering wildly in the sudden autumn breeze. Podiddley sank to his knees, his heart pounding. He cradled his right hand painfully, trying to gauge the extent of the damage. Bone showed through the bloody pulp. Swearing, Podiddley decided the damage was beyond his ability to dress. Especially if the knife had been dipped in poison or anything equally as bad. Po staggered to his feet, his solar plexus in almost as much distress as his bloody hand. Turning west on Khutub Street, Po took his hurts to the best healer he knew: the Irreverent Old Doogat of Suf.

Two blocks away, Crazy Kel let out a cry of surprised rage. She had just discovered the loss of her purse. Wheeling around, Kelandris doubled back the way she had just come. She arrived at the wall where she had left Podiddley to find him gone. Swearing, Kelandris lifted her veil partially and smelled the ground where Podiddley had squatted in pain. Using the keen senses of her Mythrrim heritage, Kelandris picked up the scent of not only Po's freshly spilled blood but also of his unmistakably bad personal hygiene. Moving swiftly, Crazy Kel caught sight of Po just as he opened the front door to Doogat's Pipe and Tobacco Bazaar. Po let himself in with difficulty. Kelandris hesitated, then ducked into a nearby alley to wait for Po to reemerge from the little Asilliwir shop.

Sudden movement caught her eye; a bright autumn leaf drifted lazily down the street toward her. The leaf pirouetted nine times, then without warning, it lifted high into the air and blew across an adjacent cobblestone avenue. Kelandris watched the leaf as it disappeared around the corner. The woman in black shivered unconsciously.

Chapter Twenty-Nine

DOOGAT HUNG A "Temporarily Closed" sign in the window of his pipe and tobacco shop. While he went to get his green medicine bag, Po fidgeted. Doogat could be a ruthless physician, his cures equal in severity to the occasional harshness he employed as a Mayanabi Master. Po swallowed. There was this certain jar full of *the* nastiest antiseptic—

Po's eyes widened as Doogat returned to the back of the shop; Doogat was carrying a clear jar filled with liquid that looked black. Po got to his feet, his face paling. "Is that what I think it is?"

Doogat started laughing. "You big coward—"

"Now, Doogs—now put that *down*!" cried Po, starting to edge around the small table in Doogat's kitchen. Doogat uncorked the bottle, his amused eyes as dark as the antiseptic he held. Po squealed and made a beeline for the back door. Doogat neatly intercepted him, and, grabbing his arm, doused the knife wound generously. Po howled with pain, tears streaming from his eyes. Pulling away from Doogat—who let him go—Po cursed Doogat, Doogat's family (whoever they were), the Mayanabi, and every Greatkin he could think of.

Doogat recorked the bottle. "Feel better?"

"NO!" bellowed the little thief.

Doogat rolled his eyes and put on a pot for tea. "Sit down," he said, pointing to an empty chair. "I'll make you something comforting now."

"You wouldn't know how," Po retorted.

Doogat decided to change the subject. Self-pity never helped anyone heal. Glancing again at the gaping hole in Po's hand, Doogat nodded imperceptibly. Po would need stitches. The Mayanabi reached for a blue jar over his wood-burning stove. He unscrewed the lid and smelled the medicinal mixture of herbs inside. They were fresh enough to use. Grabbing a small handful, Doogat put some in the strainer he'd need for Po's mug. Closing the blue jar, Doogat set it back on the shelf.

"What're you doing?" asked the little Asilliwir, his expression suspicious. He had been watching Doogat's movements out of the corner of his eye.

"Making you some baneberry tea."

"That's a tranquilizer, Doogat. Why do I need a tranquilizer?" Po sounded extremely nervous.

"I have to clean up your hand, Po."

Po scowled and said nothing. There was no point in contradicting Doogat. Po was certain that if he fought Doogat, Doogat would win. He always did, it seemed. Po reached for a piece of fruit on a platter in the middle of the kitchen table. Doogat slapped his good hand gently, shaking his head.

"You want to feel the stitches? No? Then, drink baneberry on an empty stomach."

Po swore and slumped in his chair. Suddenly remembering that he had a stolen purse in his pocket, he pulled it out and set it in front of him. He hoped there were a lot of silies in it—or the Tammirring equivalent. This morning's "easy mark" had probably taken him off the streets for at least a week. Po opened Kel's black drawstring pouch. Reaching inside, he froze. Feeling the contents again, he let out a small cry of frustration. He pulled his hand out, holding a string of black glass beads.

"Shit," he said.

The sudden clatter of breaking ceramic startled the little thief. Doogat was never clumsy. Po turned to look at his Mayanabi Master in surprise. Doogat was staring at the black beads in Po's hand.

"Where did you get those?" asked Doogat, his voice a whisper.

Po put the beads on the table. "My day's take. Why?"

Doogat walked slowly over to where Po sat. He picked up the beads, his hand trembling. "I lost a set like these once. A long time ago. I thought they were gone forever."

"You sure these are yours?" asked Po, fascinated by Doogat's reaction. He had never seen Doogat lose emotional control over anything. "*Could* they be yours?"

Doogat peered at one of the beads. Po got up to see what the Mayanabi was doing. Doogat showed him the tiny markings on each of the glass pieces. Pointing to the entire string of beads, Doogat said, "In the commonlang of your people, Po—these would be called runes. My people have a different name for them—we call them Kindrasul."

Po said nothing, hoping Doogat would continue. This was the first time Po had ever heard Doogat mention his *draw*. Po, who was Asilliwir and clannish by nature, had a strong interest in all things genealogical. Proud of his own family lineage, the little thief had often wished that Doogat would let him trace his. It was Po's opinion that Doogat spent too much time alone. He also felt that Doogat's strictness as a Mayanabi teacher was the result of Doogat's lack of experience with a large, close family. Po was certain that Doogat was an only child—not spoiled, mind you, but certainly isolated.

Doogat fingered the single bead in his hand, reading the markings by touch. He smiled. Turning to Po, he said quietly, "These are mine. They have my door on them."

"Door?"

Doogat frowned, thinking of a suitable translation for the concept of a Mythrric "door of remembrance." He set the beads down on the table and went to fetch Po's medicinal tea, still turning the problem over in his mind. As he poured boiling water into the strainer over Po's mug, Doogat said, "A door is a place of entry—and exit. It's a threshold of exchange. A place of meeting. Every mind has such a place in it. Every mind can open and shut. When my people work with the Kindrasul they open themselves to certain kinds of information—messages. But they can only do this by using their own personal—uh—access code. Their own door." Doogat handed Po the mug full of baneberry. "The glass in a string of Kindrasul is alive. Psychically sensitive. It can be impressed with the—uh—feeling tone of the person whose beads they are. This particular string will only open for me." Doogat paused. "Drink up, Po. I can't keep the shop closed all day."

Po drank the bitter tea reluctantly.

Doogat poured himself a regular cup of black tea then joined the little thief at the table. Picking up the beads once more, Doogat shook his head. "Rimble-Rimble. I've no idea where I even lost these. What did the person look like—the one you stole from?"

Po shrugged. "Never saw her face."

Doogat sniffed the glass beads idly, not expecting to recognize the scent of the woman who had previously owned the beads. Doogat froze. Momentarily forgetting that Po was in the room with him, Doogat reacted to Kel's body scent like a cat that has just discovered a female of its own kind in heat. Doogat, who was fighting hard not to turn into Zendrak, let loose with a mournful wail.

Podiddley was so startled by the animal-like behavior of his Mayanabi Master that he pushed back from the table, upsetting his own chair. He landed in a painful heap on the stone floor of the little tobacco shop. Exposed nerves and bruised bone screamed at him, and Po swore in agony. Cradling his hurt hand, Po leaned against the wall, his face breaking into a sweat. Doogat knelt beside him hastily.

"You all right?" asked the older man.

Po sucked in his breath and whispered, "I was about to ask you that."

As the bells in the Great Library campanile rang ten bell-morn, Fasilla, Aunt, and Yafatah drove through the west gate of Speakinghast. Handing Yafatah the forged pass Aunt had made for them, Fasilla said, "Doon't lose that, child. We'll need it again should them Saäms stop us for anything. They have strict curfews in this town. And strict laws. Here—put it in me travelling pack."

Yafatah nodded and did as she was told. The young Tammirring girl had all but recovered from her bout with "*landdraw* fever." On the morning of the fourth day when crossing out of Jinnjirri and into southern Saämbolin, Yafatah had suddenly regained her mental composure—and Kelandris had lost hers. Shaken and disoriented, Yafatah had cried for hours. She had felt a sadness and a loneliness that she could not understand or forget. Despite the queerness of her shared rapport with Kelandris, in an odd way Yafatah had valued it. She had never known another Tammirring, and the psychic intimacy she had experienced with Kel had shown her what being among her own *draw* might be like. Ever since that morning, Yafatah had hoped to meet up with travelling Tammirring. So far, she had been disappointed. It seemed that the Tammirring kept to themselves—and to their northern native land. Yafatah sighed, scanning the crowds in front of her for veiled women and men. Suddenly, Yafatah broke into a smile.

"There be Tammi here," she whispered softly, pointing to a group of slowly moving university students. Their colorful veils fluttered with the animation of their conversation. "Look, Ma—me own kind."

Fasilla, who had been feeling that Yafatah was growing stranger and stranger by the day, responded curtly. "There they be, Ya. And there they stay. We havena' come to this city so you can socialize. We must see the Master Doogat. When that be done, we'll go home to Asilliwir."

Yafatah's face fell. She turned away from her mother and refused to speak to her for the rest of the drive to Doogat's. Fasilla put up with this only barely. At the moment, Fasilla felt annoyed with everyone—especially her good friend, Aunt. Some days ago, Fasilla had wanted to turn back at the pass through the Feyborne Mountains. Just as she had reined her roans to a stop, Aunt glared at her in obvious disapproval. So Fasilla had continued driving her wagon toward Speakinghast. Fasilla sighed wearily. Wending her way down the crowded Asilliwir Quarter streets, she felt quite certain that this whole trip had been a terrific waste of time. Besides, Yafatah was well now. Or mostly well. The child didn't need to see the man named Doogat. At least, that was the way Fasilla saw it.

"Doon't you *want* to go home?" Fasilla asked her daughter suddenly.

Yafatah shrugged, her young mind stimulated by the bustle and enormity of the cultural capital surrounding them. At the moment the city seemed like an oasis. Here she could learn of other *draws*, make Tammi friends, eat strange foods. *And* ride in a Saämbolin happincabby, she thought, watching one trot past. A tear of yearning slipped down Yafatah's cheek. Without answering her mother, the Tammirring girl pulled her red veil down over her face and black hair. She wanted to stay in this city. She wanted to make it her home.

After several wrong turns, and several stops for directions, Fasilla, Yafatah, and Aunt arrived at Doogat's Pipe and Tobacco Bazaar. Bringing the roans to a standstill, Fasilla handed the reins to Aunt and hopped to the ground. The Asilliwir woman read the "Temporarily Closed" sign in the window and swore. Rubbing her neck tiredly, she decided to take the wagon to the nearest caravan park. Once camped, the three travellers would be free to scout out the public baths in this section of town. Fasilla smiled. First things *first*, she decided, stepping off the front porch to the little tobacco shop. Climbing back on the wagon, Fasilla said, to both Aunt and Yafatah, "It do be closed right now. I·doon't want to wait. Shall we find a place to camp? We do be fierce dirty—what say you to a hot bath, child?"

Yafatah nodded mutely.

Aunt frowned, staring at Doogat's shuttered shop. Her Mayan-abi senses told her he was in there. They also told her that Doogat did not wish to be disturbed. *Later*, she thought at him silently. *One of us will return later. Fine*, came the answering reply.

As the Asilliwir wagon drove away, Kelandris stepped out in the street. She watched Fasilla's wagon disappear around the corner, her expression wary and angry. Scowling under her veil, Crazy Kel returned to her hiding place. If the Asilliwir thief didn't come out of the shop soon, she might have to go in after him. He had her pretty thing. He had her special, pretty thing. And she wanted it back.

Tree was the next to arrive at Doogat's. He had come to visit Mab. Carrying a bouquet of fresh flowers in his hand, he opened the back door of Doogat's kitchen. He was surprised to find both Po and Doogat inside. He wondered why no one was tending the shop. Then Tree saw Po's wounded hand.

Eyeing the sewing needle and roll of bandages on the kitchen table, Tree muttered, "Maybe I should come back later."

"Nonsense," said Po gaily. he was feeling very good and very relaxed thanks to the baneberry tea. The little Asilliwir beamed at the Jinnjirri and offered him a ringside seat.

Tree declined it, starting up the stairs that led to Mab's room.

As Tree put his hand on the banister, Doogat asked, "Did you happen to see anyone in black hanging around out there?"

Tree shook his head. "Should I have?"

Po broke into peals of laughter. Patting Doogat on the back with his good hand, the thief winked at Tree and said, "Doogs thinks there's a ghost from his past haunting the place. Thinks she means to do him in, too. Can you imagine that?" continued Po. "Doogat's never taken by surprise." Po giggled. "Would be fun to see it happen. Just once," he added hastily as Doogat picked up the jar of black antiseptic again.

Tree inclined his head at the stairs. "Mab up?"

"Don't think so," replied Po. Then, seeing the flowers in Tree's hand, he added, "Now isn't that sweet. Flowers for the Piedmerri Virgin. Course nobody believes *that* anymore. Cobeth— "

"I do!" snapped Tree.

Po shrugged. "Cobeth makes his moves pretty fast—"

Doogat intervened at this point. "Shut, up, Po." Then, without warning the little Asilliwir, he poured more antiseptic on Po's knife wound. Po's shrieks of dismay sent Tree running up the stairs three steps at a time.

Tree had been coming to visit Mab faithfully ever since the party at Rhu's, bringing her little gifts and news from the house. For the past three weeks, Tree had worked hard to convince the little Piedmerri that all Jinnjirri weren't bad. This had been Doogat's idea. Tree wasn't sure if he was succeeding or not. Furthermore, in the past two days, Tree had noticed something disturbing in the Piedmerri's general mood. Tree wasn't altogether sure what it was that disturbed him. Mostly, Mab just seemed empty in some way. Empty and yearning to be filled up. But by what? Tree shook his head as he approached Mab's closed door. Tree hoped holovespa wasn't addictive. It never occurred to the Jinnjirri that Cobeth might be.

Tree knocked softly. "Mab? You up?"

"Come in," said a dull voice.

Tree opened the door, thrusting the flowers in front of him. When Mab didn't respond with exclamations or thanks, Tree poked his head into her room. The windows were shut, the drapes drawn. The heavy, oriental tapestries hanging on the walls made the room seem smaller. Almost claustrophobic today, thought Tree uneasily. Mab sat on the corner of her single bed, her shoulders hunched, her expression distant.

"You okay?" asked Tree, coming into the room and squatting beside Mab.

Mab said nothing.

Tree's green hair turned a little gray. "Mab?" He touched her cheek gently. She responded by turning away from him. Tree licked his lips worriedly. He had never seen Mab so depressed. Tree sat down beside the Piedmerri, laying the flowers in his lap. "Did you have bad dreams?"

Mab nodded.

Tree took a deep breath. "About Cobeth?"

Mab nodded. "He raped me."

Remembering Po's jabs, Tree took Mab literally, his voice horrified. "He did? At the party?"

Mab finally looked at Tree. She shook her head. "Not at Rhu's. In my dream." She laughed, the sound of it brittle. "But maybe psychic rape counts as much as physical?" Her eyes looked to him for confirmation.

Tree shrugged. He had never heard of a psychic rape. "Don't know. You could ask a Tammi," he added lamely.

Mab shook her head. Then, crawling toward the wall next to her bed, Mab left Tree where he was. Picking up her pillow, Mab stuffed it across her belly and sat in a hunched position. A silent tear fell down her cheek, her eyes staring at nothing.

It scared Tree to see Mab like this. She didn't look altogether sane. He decided to go and fetch Doogat. Leaving the flowers he had brought for Mab on the bed, Tree hurriedly left the room. Tree reached the downstairs just as Doogat was finishing bandaging Po's stitched hand. Doogat looked up as Tree walked into the kitchen.

"What's wrong?" asked Doogat immediately.

Tree gestured helplessly. "Mab's so sad. She's sitting curled up in a little ball on her bed. And she'll hardly talk to me."

Doogat frowned. Then, telling Po to open the shop and handle the till, Doogat followed Tree upstairs. The Mayanabi Master opened the door to Mab's room slowly. Mab hadn't moved from her spot against the wall. Doogat motioned for Tree to come in and shut the door. Tree did so. Doogat got on the bed with Mab while Tree watched. Mab gave no sign of recognition to Doogat, her eyes unblinking. Doogat grunted. Reaching for Mab, he pulled her away from the wall toward him. Mab didn't fight him. Holding Mab in his arms, he began speaking to her softly about the good things in the world. He told her about kindness and hope. As he continued, Mab began to shake. Doogat smoothed her hair. This tiny gesture of caring undid Mab completely. Sobbing, she buried her face in Doogat's chest, begging Doogat to keep Cobeth away from her.

Tree stared, taken aback by the wrenching sound of her weeping. Tree had cried once like that. Tree shivered, not wanting to recall the circumstances that had produced this much pain in him. Tree turned away, forcing his mood to change, forcing his frosted hair to shift to green.

"Cobeth can't hurt you now, Mab," said Doogat gently.

"He can!" she cried. "I can't keep him out at night. There's a door open somewhere. There's a place—"

Doogat shut his eyes, searching Mab's psyche to see if what she was saying was true. His Mayanabi senses scanned her emotional body. Doogat grunted softly. There *was* a small place, a small back door where someone could slip in against Mab's will. Doogat poured some of his understanding of goodness into her wounded psyche. As Mab's fragile emotions steadied, her body relaxed in Doogat's arms, the fear leaving her eyes.

"That's better, hmm?" asked Doogat with a smile.

Mab nodded, her breathing becoming more regular.

"Good." Putting his left hand on the back of her neck, Doogat asked, "Do you trust me, Mab?"

She nodded.

"All right," said the Mayanabi Master. "I'm going to put you to sleep now, Mab—without herbs. Do you think you might let me do this?"

Mab smiled and shut her eyes. Before she had taken the next breath, Mab was sound asleep. Doogat removed his hand from the back of her neck. Lowering Mab to the bed, he pulled a blanket over her body. Tree's jaw dropped. He had never seen anyone put someone to sleep like that—or so swiftly.

"What—what did you *do*?"

Doogat smiled. "It's an old Mayanabi trick."

Tree pressed him for more information, but Doogat simply smiled. Gesturing toward the door, Doogat indicated that he wanted Tree to come downstairs with him.

Outside in the street, Kelandris watched people come and go from Doogat's shop. Her hand clenched; she wanted her black beads. Now. She could see Po from where she stood in the alley. She felt relieved that he was still inside—she had begun to wonder. Just as Kel had decided to find out if the shop had a back door, Po had removed the sign from the window and opened the shop for business again. Now the only problem was the matter of ambushing Po while customers stood at the counter. Kelandris crossed her arms over her chest, feeling uneasy about the prospect. Kelandris disliked small, enclosed spaces. They made her feel panicky. Sometimes, she would break out in a sweat and remember things she didn't want to remember—especially in a crowd. Kelandris continued to watch the steady give and take of Doogat's clientele as she considered the logistics of staging a successful mugging. The more she looked at the size of the tiny tobacco store, the more she felt reluctant to enter it. Kelandris swore. She wanted her pretty thing back. She wanted it back real bad. Without it, Kel knew she would have those incest dreams about Zendrak again. They had stopped as soon as she had found the string of Kindrasul when she had crossed the Feyborne Mountains on her way to Speakinghast.

For one hundred and eighteen years, Zendrak's Kindrasul had lain hidden in a rocky cleft of one of the mountain's steep crags. Trickster's Emissary had dropped it accidently when he had returned from the Everywhen on the back of Further—right into a particularly violent wind and lightning storm. The noise had been so deafening and the wind so strong that Zendrak had neither heard nor felt the loss of his glass beads. Kelandris had nearly missed seeing the beads in the cleft. But just as she walked past, her knife fell out of her sleeve. The knife had never done this before, and, in fact, due to the snug fit of the sleeve, Kelandris had thought the knife was impossible to lose. Frowning, she had leaned over to pick it up and been distracted by the glint of something black and shiny off to her right. Forgetting her knife for the moment, she pulled the string of Kindrasul free from the dirt and loose rock. Smiling, Kelandris had attributed her good fortune to having the luck of the Trickster that day.

Actually, Kel owed her thanks to Phebene.

As soon as the Mayanabi master had closed the door to Mab's room, Doogat offered Tree some bread and honey in the kitchen. Tree accepted, eyeing the fresh brown loaf and golden honey hungrily. Doogat put a slab of sweet butter on the table and handed Tree a knife. As Doogat brewed more tea, he asked Tree what news he had from the Kaleidicopia.

"Mostly bad, I'm afraid," said Tree, cutting off a large slice of bread. "You know, if I didn't know better, I'd say that Cobeth had it in for everyone at the house. I was thinking about it on my way over here this morning. I mean, when you look at it—Cobeth's hurt every single house member. Some of them twice over. Like Rowen."

Doogat grunted. "I can't believe no one has proven Cobeth stole Rowen's Trickster materials from the Great Library, I would've thought it easy—considering he had Rowen's library card in his possession on the night of Rhu's party. Surely, you've got probable cause to search Cobeth's lodgings. Even the Saämbolin would agree to that."

Tree shrugged. "Yeah, Doogs—but you forget. No one at the house wants the Saämbolin Guildguard to know any of us were there on that particular night." Tree spread honey on his bread. "How Cobeth managed to come out smelling like a frigging rose, I'll never understand. Timmer says there were all sorts of drugs in Cobeth's desk. He must've dumped them down the garderobe—or had the biggest hangover ever known."

Doogat smiled. "Cobeth *is* clever."

"Yeah. The sonofabitch. I just wish he'd get caught once."

"Maybe he will," said Doogat idly.

Tree sighed. "I know Timmer would like that. After this morning, she's ready to kill Cobeth with her bare hands."

Doogat poured cups of black currant tea. Ever since his picnic with Phebene, he had developed a liking for this particular flavor. The rich, fruity smell sweetened the air. "So," said Doogat quietly. "What's Cobeth done to Timmer?"

Tree chewed his mouthful of bread and honey. Swallowing, he said, "Oh—just broken up her musical quintet. Nothing major, you understand. Just Timmer's livelihood."

Doogat narrowed his eyes. "Explain."

Tree shrugged. "Seems Cobeth has a need for a theatrical orchestra now. And he's handpicking the members himself. As far as I know, Cobeth hates folk music. You should've seen the stinks he raised against Timmer when the Dunnsung would practice out in the studio."

"So you think he's intentionally breaking up her band—to punish her?"

Tree sighed, rubbing his eyes with his free hand. "I've no idea, Doogat. But Cobeth fired me from The Merry Pricksters for no better reason than that." Tree bit off another bite of bread. Chewing thoughtfully, Tree added, "Neath—I don't know, Doogs. Maybe Cobeth's still taking it out on Janusin. And we're just catching the fallout from the fireworks."

"Maybe," said Doogat quietly.

At that moment, Po came bursting into the kitchen. Pointing to the windows in the front of the shop, he exclaimed, "She's out there, Doogat! The one who had the beads! The woman in black is out in the street!"

Doogat jumped to his feet, ordering Tree to hail a happincabby. "Have it brought around back. Po you come help me with Mab. Then all three of you return to the Kaleidicopia. Remain there, please. Tell Barlimo what has happened. Tell her the ninth has arrived. She'll understand."

In a few moments, Doogat had completely cleared the little shop of customers, visitors, and residents. Doogat put the sign that read "Temporarily Closed" back in the window. Changing his blue robe for green, Doogat's features swiftly turned into Zendrak's.

Then, taking a deep breath, Zendrak let Kelandris see him.

Chapter Thirty

KELANDRIS STARED AT the familiar face looking at her through the window of the tobacco shop. Her body stiffened, her skin breaking out in an ice-cold sweat. She knew that face. She had seen that face a thousand times in her dreams. Kelandris raised her hand timidly as if to reach for Zendrak's raven-black hair. The shock of seeing Zendrak so close to her momentarily cleared Kel's mind of confusion and rage.

"Oh, my dearest love—" she whispered.

Then Trickster's recent sabotage set in. Certain that Zendrak was the one who had betrayed her in Suxonli, Kel's open hand tightened into a fist. Letting out a cry of fury, Kelandris pulled her knife and ran up the stairs. Zendrak opened the door for her. Kelandris entered cautiously. Zendrak saw the knife and backed up, his stance ready, his expression unreadable. Kelandris smiled cruelly under her veil. Sniffing the smell of fresh tobacco mixtures, Kelandris quickly scanned the size of the little store. She noted the hanging beads separating the shop from the kitchen in the back and the stairs leading to the second floor of Doogat's residence. Wondering where the little Asilliwir thief was, Kel circled Zendrak slowly. Zendrak made no move to stop her, watching Kelandris intently. The tension between them was extreme. Zendrak's heart pounded, every sense alert. The question was *when* Kel would attack him—not if. Kelandris chuckled. Zendrak flinched. Her laugh was the laugh of a madwoman. And yet it was controlled. Zendrak swallowed, aware perhaps for the first time of how extremely dangerous Kelandris was to him. He was mortal; he *could* be killed. And so could she.

Without warning, Kelandris moved on him.

Thrusting from underneath with her knife, Kelandris aimed for Zendrak's abdomen. Zendrak responded instantly. Bringing his right hand in close to his body, he slammed it against Kel's left wrist and knocked the weapon wide of its target. Surprised by the speed and accuracy of Zendrak's block but not bested, Kelandris maintained her hold on the knife. Seeing this, Zendrak continued a full twist to the right, grabbing Kel's weapon hand. They faced the same direction now, her chest against his back. Kelandris seized the chance to crush Zendrak's windpipe with her free arm. As she tightened against his neck, Zendrak elbowed Kelandris viciously in the solar plexus. Kel automatically folded against Zendrak's broad back. Zendrak pulled her trapped left arm forward and brought her knuckles down hard across his knee. Prepared to break Kel's arm if she refused to relinquish the knife, he slammed her hand against his knee a second and third time. Finally, the pain caused Kel's fingers to open. The knife clattered to the floor. Before Kelandris could regain her balance, Zendrak dropped her over his hip. Kel hit the floor soundly, landing on her back. Momentarily dazed, she made no move to get up. Zendrak took advantage of Kel's brief immobilization and applied a variation of the Mayanabi trick he had used on Mab.

Straddling Kelandris, Zendrak put a knee on each arm and reached for the back of Kel's neck with both hands. As soon as he made contact with her skin, Kel's body entered a state of light paralysis. Kelandris swore, her eyes rolling upward under her veil. She fought to remain conscious. Zendrak shifted his weight, simultaneously freeing her arms and deepening the psychological rapport between them. Kel's body relaxed despite her overwhelming desire to throttle the man leaning over her. Unable to move an inch—much less make a decent fist—Kelandris fought Zendrak for mental autonomy. And succeeded. Taken aback by the weight and discipline of Kel's will, Zendrak redoubled his efforts to disarm Kelandris psychically as well as physically. He pressed her for surrender and pressed her hard.

Kelandris sucked in her breath, hating Zendrak. Attacking him with the full brunt of the rage she felt for Yonneth, Kelandris managed to break the mental hold Zendrak had on her. Screaming at Zendrak to stop touching her, she struggled to free her head from his hands. Zendrak maintained contact, his body sweating, his concentration fierce. Terrified by the merciless gaze in Zendrak's dark eyes, Kel raked his cheek with the sharp fingernails of her left hand. She drew blood. Zendrak winced but said nothing. Kelandris extended her fingers then curved them like the claws of the Mythrrim she was. She raised her hand to swipe at Zendrak again, a low growl rumbling deep in her throat. Zendrak answered in kind, snapping at the air in front of her veiled face. Startled, Kelandris stared at him, her heart pounding.

Mythrrim faced Mythrrim in silence.

Zendrak shifted his weight, the collar of his green tunic pulling slightly to the side. Kel's breath caught. Something black and shiny hung around his neck. Kelandris reached tentatively for Zendrak's obsidian beads. Zendrak released his physical hold on Kel's neck and smacked her hand away from the Kindrasul. Kel tried again. Zendrak growled at her, his dark eyes hooded and angry. Kelandris started to attack him, arching her back. Zendrak slapped her face, knocking her against the floor. Kelandris shook her head dazedly. Now she spoke, her voice desperate and pleading.

"My pretty thing. Give it!"

Noting with interest that Kelandris had momentarily dropped her habitual rhyme of sixteen years, Zendrak said evenly, "*My* pretty thing."

Kel's voice became more anxious. "Give it. Give it back. If you love, give it back."

Zendrak frowned, momentarily startled by Kel's inclusion of the word love in their conversation. He noted she had said, "If you love, give it back." Not, "If you love *me*." The first statement was typical of Greatkin Phebene, the second of Trickster. Cautiously, Zendrak asked, "Would you like some tea?" He wondered how much baneberry he'd need to use in order to knock her out.

Kelandris shook her head. "Not me. T is for thee but not for me. Phebene sez: tea for two, cakes and kin—odds are great, Rimble won't win."

Zendrak said nothing for a moment, reassessing the situation. If

Phebene were speaking through Kelandris at present, she might be telling him to disarm Kel through something other than dirty tricks. Quite a challenge. He turned back to the veiled woman lying below him on the floor. Changing his tactics, Zendrak pulled the Kindrasul free from his neck, watching Kel's left hand clench and unclench with greed. Holding the obsidian beads just out of her reach, Zendrak said, "On the other hand, I can see how much *my* pretty thing means to you. And you've already taken such good care of it, yes?"

"Yes. Keeps bad dreams away. Give," she added, trying to grab the black glass beads from his grasp.

Zendrak held the Kindrasul above his head. "I'll give the beads to you, Kelandris. But only on one condition—that you stop fighting me right now. If you don't, I'll hide my pretty thing where you'll never find it."

Kelandris snarled at him under her veil. She made a move to sit up. Zendrak knocked her flat, a terrible growl building in his throat. He meant business. Flexing his fingers in full view of Kelandris, Zendrak let her see the length of his own talon-nails. Kel hesitated then grabbed for the beads again. Zendrak let loose with a fearsome roar, all seven sets of his Mythrrim vocal cords vibrating. Ceramic and glass jars in the back of the shop shook. A few shattered. Kelandris reacted with blind panic and swiped at Zendrak's open neck. As before, she drew blood. This time, Zendrak decided to retaliate. Throwing Kel backward, he shredded her veil. Kelandris howled, putting her hands in front of her face. Zendrak punched her soundly in her unprotected diaphragm. Kelandris groaned, trying desperately to turn her belly away from him. Zendrak prevented her, forcing her to concede dominance to him. Animal to animal, Kelandris understood. Swearing and sobbing, she begged him for the Kindrasul. It was as if she were pleading for his mercy.

Zendrak listened to her in silence, trying to asses the true level of Kel's sincerity. After all, like himself, Kelandris was Trickster's own child. Deciding that her tears were genuine, Zendrak gripped the Kindrasul tightly in his hand and flooded the string of beads with the comprehension and compassion of his five hundred years of life. Then he handed them to Kelandris.

With a small cry of relief, the woman in black clasped the Kindrasul to her heart. She was so elated by the return of "her pretty thing" that she never felt Zendrak slide his hands around the back of her neck again. Kel shut her eyes, drinking in the emotional warmth of the beads she held. As the true depth of Zendrak's affection filled her body with the sounding of Zendrak's own emotional feeling-tone, Trickster's Emissary quickly sneaked in the back door of Kel's injured mind. Once there, Zendrak pressed Kelandris for the memory of a certain forest glen on the outskirts of Suxonli Village. And the love they had made there.

Kelandris opened her eyes, her expression startled through her torn veil. Realizing that Zendrak had breached her psychic defenses, she blasted him with the raw power of her fury. Zendrak stood his ground. Kel's attack failed. The loving power with which Zendrak had invested the Kindrasul had opened Kel's heart briefly. Zendrak only needed a psychic toehold to successfully scale Kel's rage. Now he had one. Kelandris whimpered in distress. She twisted and untwisted the beads in her hand anxiously, her eyes focused on the brown rafters in the ceiling of the tobacco shop. She felt Zendrak's continued, steady intrusion into the darkest memories of her life. Kel gritted her teeth.

Zendrak picked his way carefully through her psyche. Kelandris tensed. Zendrak could feel Kel's terror of Suxonli's judgement against her through his fingers. Coaxing Kelandris to match the steady rhythm of his breathing, Trickster's Emissary reminded Trickster's *he* of all that had preceded the actual revel in Suxonli.

Kelandris strained against Zendrak's gentle hands as he probed her neck muscles for a deeper, more personal entry point into her hopelessness. Thorns of Kel's despair cut him. He ignored their pull. He had found what he was looking for: Kel's memory of her love for him. As he edged toward the memory, preparing to make Kel conscious of it again, he noticed Kel's grip on the Kindrasul tighten.

Without warning, a moving wall of fear slammed into Zendrak's heart. Cursing Kel for fighting him, Zendrak struggled to maintain his sense of direction in Kel's emotional labyrinth. Pain stung him from all sides.

No matter what Zendrak tried, Kel's fear remained unyielding.

Taking a deep breath, Zendrak lowered his head briefly, frustration and exhaustion evident in his dark eyes. He cursed Trickster. And again. He did not want to force Kelandris to open to him. Nor did he wish to cram his superior mental training down her throat. Her independence was precious to him as was her formidable fighting spirit. He loved her for her faults as much as for her strengths. Zendrak's dark eyes swam unexpectedly with tears. He needed a way to regain her trust. The memory of the joy they had shared in a forest glen in Suxonli was the only certain ground that he personally held with Kelandris. And it looked like Yonneth had stolen even that. The cruelty of this enraged Zendrak.

Feeling at a loss, Zendrak hesitated. There *had* to be another way through Kel's fear other than by sheer force of will. Zendrak ran through his entire repertoire of tricks, deciding that if he found no other solution than force, he would stop where he was; he would press Kelandris no farther. No matter *what* Trickster said about it. Zendrak bit his lip very well aware of what would happen if he failed with Kelandris here. Very simply put: the world as he knew it would come to an end. Kelandris was a member of Rimble's ennead, his Nine. Without her, the other eight were powerless. Kel was the ground wire for the psychic charge of the turning ceremony which the Nine would dance in Speakinghast in a few days time. If the Nine did not turn, civilization would falter. There would be no evolutionary leap; Trickster's silent genes would remain silent. And the Greatkin would cease to "matter."

Zendrak swallowed. The temptation to overcome Kel's fear by aggression was tempting. He could've done it as soon as she walked into the little tobacco shop, knife in hand. His was a trained mind, hers was not. Zendrak rolled his eyes. He didn't want the world to end any more than Trickster did. Was the integrity of Kel's psyche worth such a price? Zendrak's hands trembled on the back of Kel's neck. The threat of extinction frightened him. Struggling against his own panic, Zendrak reminded himself sternly that *he* was not Trickster. It was not his responsibility to save or doom the world. He was merely Trickster's Emissary—and a very mortal, fallible one at that. He raised his dark eyes, meeting Kel's scared green ones. Seeing the fear and helplessness in her eyes, his heart broke.

"I can't do it," he whispered. "I can't get through to her. Rimble—you hear me? I can't do it. Find yourself another Emissary."

Zendrak started to pull his hands away from Kel's neck, but was stopped when Trickster's *he* grabbed his arms and held them close to her body. Zendrak opened his eyes in surprise to find Kelandris staring sternly at him. Greatkin faced Greatkin. Kel's green eyes glittered cooly. Still gripping the Kindrasul in her left hand, she draped the string of beads over both of Zendrak's exposed forearms. Zendrak said nothing, trying to understand the meaning of her action. Suddenly Kel's expression changed. The power of her Greatkin bloodline was replaced by a strange mortal vulnerability. Kel's hold on the Kindrasul intensified. She resembled a drowning person, the beads her lifeline. A lifeline—

A smile broke over Zendrak's face slowly. Keeping one hand on the back of Kel's neck, he reached for the Kindrasul. Resting his palm over Kel's fingers, Zendrak dropped his defenses against Kelandris, using the black glass beads from Soaringsea as a universal translator of the ancient trust they shared as Mythrrim. Like a mneumonic cipher, the Kindrasul allowed Zendrak to communicate with Kelandris at a purely non-verbal level. As love often did, thought Zendrak with chagrin. He swore at himself for being so slow-witted. The way through Kel's fear had literally been under his fingertips. Courtesy of Phebene.

Zendrak laughed with relief. Kelandris met his eyes shyly, her madness temporarily at bay. A trace of a smile touched her full lips. Zendrak regarded her with undisguised affection. Kelandris looked away abruptly. She felt blinded by the radiance of what she saw in Zendrak's face. After so many years of deprivation, Zendrak's love seared her heart like a blast of light from the noonday sun. Gathering her courage, Kelandris tried to meet his gaze once more, but she found she couldn't. Tears wet her cheeks.

Zendrak watched Kelandris in silence, his expression patient. He had waited sixteen years for this day; he could wait a little longer. Zendrak fingered the Kindrasul thoughtfully. Kelandris must have sensed his personal, emotional "door" on the glass when she had first found them and smelled his psychic scent on them as clearly as Zendrak had smelled hers this morning. It was the nature of obsidian from Soaringsea to retain such an impression, regardless of time elapsed. The intense *draw* from the volcanoes of these northern isles marked everything with an indelible clarity of emotion. Like the igneous rock that spewed out of Soaringsea's lava cones, emotions rose in a Mythrrim from the innermost depths of its being: straight from the core. To a Mythrrim, the emotions of two-legged society seemed muddled and lacking in the crystalline purity of the black glass Zendrak and Kelandris now held in their hands. Zendrak's eyes softened as he looked at Kelandris with renewed respect. A Mythrrim could starve to death on the emotional diet of most two-leggeds. It was a wonder that Kelandris had not. Zendrak took a deep breath and refrained from his desire to take Kelandris in his arms and simply hold her. Although Zendrak was certain that every cell in Kel's body ached for the company and kinship only a Mythrrim could offer her, he also recognized that Kelandris was only temporarily sane. When they let go of the Kindrasul, Kel would be faced with a choice: sanity or madness. Still, thought Zendrak, there *was* something he could do to help Kelandris. If she would permit him to do so, he could clear away some of the rubble of her two-legged life in Suxonli.

Zendrak eased himself off Kel's body. Kneeling beside her now, one hand on her neck and the other still clasping the Kindrasul under Kel's fingers, he drew from his Mayanabi training and reached inside her mind again. Kelandris stiffened, her eyes wary. Zendrak smiled at Kelandris reassuringly, flooding the Kindrasul with peace. Kelandris remained tense, but she did not fight Zendrak as she had done before. Zendrak modulated his breath to match her own and touched Kel's psyche with the skill of the Mayanabi Master that he was.

Carefully, cautiously, Zendrak weakened the last of Kel's two-legged ties—what few were left her after the Ritual of Akindo—and strengthened her Mythrrim ones. This was a dangerous psychic surgery, especially if Kelandris refused his help later on—choosing madness over sanity—thereby isolating herself from not only her societal roots but her animal ones as well. *Very* dangerous, he thought, continuing with the process. Forcing himself to ignore the nervous twinge of his stomach, Zendrak impressed Kel's mind with the wisdom of Mythrrim laws of kinship. Such laws were more ancient and more gracious than any the two-leggeds had yet evolved.

Zendrak cut deeper, and Kelandris began to feel very lightheaded. Zendrak spoke quietly to Kel, telling her Mythrrim stories of the Greatkin and the Presence. Kel's body slowly relaxed. Zendrak freed her psyche further. By leaving Kelandris only her Mythrrim heritage to consult, Zendrak hoped to sidestep the laws of Suxonli. If he could literally undercut the potency and legitimacy of Suxonli's Blood Day Rule in Kel's mind, he might be able to minimize Yonneth's damage. Also, by offering Kelandris a taste of ancient Mythrrim loyalty, Zendrak hoped to expose Yonneth's "brotherly love" for the sham that it actually was. Zendrak frowned. Sundering Kelandris from her Tammirring culture would make her utterly dependent on him for a while. After all, other than Kelandris, he was the only Mythrrim walking around in two-legged form at present. Zendrak swallowed. He knew he could handle it. But could she? What if Kelandris perceived such dependence as a threat to her survival? Risky, he thought, considering Kel's current mental instability. Still, Kelandris *was* his sister—and the child of two Greatkin. Furthermore, she was just plain willful, defiant, and dogged. In short, utterly creative and contrary. Good often came from such traits. He took a deep breath. But so did bad.

There was no guarantee this psychic surgery would work. The entire operation rested on the folly of a calculated risk. Worse, the calculated risk banked on a trust engendered by a dimly recalled past love. Zendrak rolled his eyes, preparing to commit himself to Love's Keeping.

Zendrak watched Kelandris play with the Kindrasul nervously. Her movements were jerky and her green eyes only marginally lucid. *Here goes*, he thought without enthusiasm. Then, pressing his fingers into the back of Kel's neck, Zendrak eased the last thread of two-legged morality away from her heart and soul. Closing his eyes, he poured a hundred thousand years of Mythrrim civilization into Kel's psyche. Kelandris shuddered. She started to fight Zendrak but stopped when he triggered her memory of a certain forest glen in Suxonli. Kelandris blinked, her expression disoriented.

Time rolled backwards. . . .

Chapter Thirty-One

COSTUMES AND TORCHLIGHT! Shrieks and laughing fury!

The season was late autumn. Kelandris was seventeen, and the place was Suxonli. This evening, as had been the custom for centuries, the villagers of this small mountain community celebrated the Trickster's Hallows. They called it Rimble's Revel. This was Carnivale and Mardi Gras. This was Trickster's Treat. And an ancient Remembrance.

So sing it: ah ya, *Rimble!* Come, Trickster, come! Be yet again! But beware his back door ways, the thrall of his disrespect! Beware the color of his striped coat, the prick of his maddening sting! Sing it, Yellow-Jacket Yellow! The Wasp flies abroad tonight!

Tonight villagers donned masks and honored all unknowns. They must. Tonight the costumed beggar at the door or the nodding hag at the hearth might be Trickster himself come to merry-prank you. Tonight anything could happen. And while the rest of the world prepared for sleep, all Suxonli stirred. Witness a streaming, screaming time!

Doors slammed as two hundred villagers swarmed from their mountain homes, the children leading. This was an instinctive exodus, choreographed by the generational hive-mind of Revels past. Here was a clarion call sounded by history and answered in full by the dancing, prancing men and women of Suxonli. Here gathered the Wasp Queen's hive, each member *Rimblessah*—Trickster blessed and Trickster drunk with wild abandon.

The curious and the hedonistic travelled for miles around to join in the ecstatic revelry of Suxonli's wild festival. Strangers smiled at each other under homemade masks of terror. All were eagerly included in the rapacious clowning of this host village. No one was safe from Trickster's Touch tonight. And that was the way everyone wanted it—particularly young Kelandris. Dressed as a hermaphrodite, Kel wore Rimble's yellow and black. Tonight she'd lose her maidenhead to a costumed villager—like every Wasp Queen had done before her. If she conceived, the crops would flourish in the following year. If she didn't, no one would begrudge her a good time. Tonight was sorrow's banishment and joy's release.

Voices! Louder!

Change or be changed!

Dance high, dance hard with the shriekers in the street!

Sporting exaggerated breasts, a striped penis sheath standing erect between her legs, Kelandris led the Hive into the village square. Lips buzzed, children laughed. Now the five elderly members of the village council processed. Advancing slowly toward this year's Revel Queen, they carried a large straw wasp on their shoulders. Kelandris pointed to the effigy. She laughed maniacally—as per ritual instruction. Then the Wasp Queen chanted, her young voice piercing the crowd's clamor:

> Bugaboo you, you old Stingaroo!
> Sing Rimsah, ya Rimble,
> Nothing's taboo!

On cue, the crowd erupted into giggles and wild hilarity. Tonight Trickster was theirs. Pulled from the Fertile Dark into the revel torchlight, Greatkin Rimble was no longer a thing of terror or reverence. Tonight Trickster was ripped off his Greatkin pedestal, and his form made disposable. He was the Changeable One. Tonight Trickster would perish in the village flames. But set free, his spirit would enter every woman, man, and child. The villagers each wore a masked version of the Great Fool's face, both claiming and buffooning him. Theirs was a serious silliness.

The Wasp Queen lifted a torch high and set fire to the idol of Rimble. And for a brief moment of glory, Trickster's gossamer wings fanned the air with light in the harvest scarecrow-wind. And now the children came. They played a pinching tag game called Trickster's Touch. They were Rimble's little stings.

Singing the rhyme, chanting the rhyme, and again!

Grabbing hands, the village boys and girls snake-spiralled through the adults, shrieking and stomping their feet. They goosed every onlooker, village born or not, and chortled:

"Rimble-Rimble!"

The older villagers joined in. The snake-spiral swelled in size and speed. The line of masked and costumed bodies undulated like the wave of a wild electrical current. Then the village gave voice. They screamed. This was the signal for departure from the village. As the snake-spiral slowed, the villagers broke hands. Grabbing torches, all Suxonli scampered up the steep mountain path known as the Long Revel Trail. Spooking out the darkness, the torches lit the night with a will-o'-the-wisp beauty that wove a garland of flickering jewels along the black earth shoulders of the Western Feyborne.

Kelandris—as per ritual instruction—cut away from the crowd. Heading to a secluded glen, the Wasp Queen waited for the Coins of Coincidence to choose her Trickster lover for the evening. The selection would occur in the center of the old circle of standing-stones high at the upper end of the Long Revel Trail. Selection of the Queen's lover could take hours, reaching a frenzy of drumming and chanting. Such frenzy was necessary. Anyone wanting to embody the King of Deviance—becoming as fertile as Trickster himself during the Rite of Coupling with Rimble's Revel Queen—could only enter the stone circle of ancient monoliths if he heard Trickster call his name. Once called, each man underwent a literal trial by fire.

He danced barefoot on a bed of living, steaming, red-hot coals. Those who danced and were *not* called were burnt. But those who heard Trickster's voice whisper their names, danced long and wildly. Finally, one dancer was chosen from this corps. He was chosen by "chance" through the single fall of the copper Coins of Coincidence. Then, amidst great hooting and joyous hissing, the night's King of Deviance went in search of his Queen. They would couple in privacy, and, on cues known only to themselves, the godstruck pair would return to the community. The Revel Queen would dance her newfound fertility and womanhood into the ground. She would act as the hub in a great turning wheel. It was an awesome sight, this turning. And a high honor.

Tonight's Queen slipped through the woods silently, her yellow boots muffled by pine needles that covered the path. She reached the glen, breathless. Nervous and excited about the sexual initiation to come, she pulled off her mask, wiping the sweat off her face. Then she heard the sound of a horse approaching. Rolling her eyes, Kelandris thought perhaps one of the village outsiders had misunderstood the ritual instructions and, seeing the Wasp Queen leave the crowd, had decided to follow her through the woods. Kelandris put her hands on her hips, prepared to redirect the intruder sternly.

The sound of the approaching horse stopped. Kelandris listened intently for a moment. Nothing. Deciding that the rider must have returned to the main trail, Kelandris pulled out a tortoise shell comb and feathered her long blue-black hair away from her high cheekbones and wide brow. It was a self-conscious gesture, purely adolescent. Kelandris stopped her primping, listening to the steady drone of drums in the distance. She glanced at the lone torch near her feet. It cast moving shadows on the trees. Kelandris swallowed. Sitting in the comparative dark as she was, Kelandris suddenly felt edgy about her lover-to-be. What if Trickster picked a real loser, she thought uneasily. Or worse—what if Trickster went for out-and-out deviance, selecting one of her brothers to be her mate? Kel put her comb away and got to her feet. She began to pace. What if Trickster picked Yonneth? After that incident in the blizzard last year, she thought uncomfortably, she wouldn't want Yonneth to even *think* about bedding her—much actually do it. She reviewed the incident with distaste.

Eight months ago, their mother had sent Kel and Yonneth to fetch more firewood for winter. On their way home, they were overtaken by a snowstorm. Scrambling for their lives, Kelandris had directed their team of horses to an old shepherd's shack in the area. Yonneth and she found it without mishap. Entering the hut, Kelandris immediately began cleaning the ashes out of the fireplace. Yonneth went for a supply of wood in the back of their wagon. Making sure the horses were secure and protected from the storm, he returned to the hut, his mood lousy, his Jinnjirri hair gray-blue.

Kelandris smiled at his ill-humor. She had two other brothers—Garr and Tommo—both of them Tammirring born. Kelandris felt closer in spirit to her Jinnjirri brother, however. Her mother said it was because they were both adopted. Kel knew better. Yonneth—"her Yonneth" as she affectionately called him—was special. He was different. He was smart. He was also an artist. Talent like Yonneth's set him apart from the Suxonli community. Kelandris identified with his isolation. She felt truly kindred with Yonneth. His loneliness was hers. So she thought.

Making a fire now, Kelandris watched Yonneth play idly with some twigs of kindling, making stick houses and crushing them softly under his fist. Kelandris, who had a good sense of humor in those days, chuckled.

"Oh, come on, Yonn," she said gaily, "it's not so bad up here. I've food in my pack, and there's blankets in the cupboard. We'll be warm and cozy in no time." She grinned. "Buck up, sweetie. We're having an adventure."

"I don't *want* an adventure," snapped Yonneth, his Jinnjirri hair streaking with a vexed shade of red.

"Well," said Kelandris with a sigh, "can't be helped, brother mine. Nature *does* these things sometimes. Rimble-Rimble."

Yonneth scowled at his older sister. "Don't let's start on *him*, okay? It's bad enough being stuck in a blizzard, much less have to talk about him."

Kelandris rolled her eyes. "Presence alive, Yonneth—are you *still* sore about me being Queen at next Hallows? I mean, it's not like you were excluded from the Coin Toss on purpose. Suxonli law is very clear, Yonn: only Tammirring maidens can play the Queen."

"It's a stupid law," he muttered, his Jinnjirri body changing gender as he spoke. Yonneth now resembled a skinny fifteen-year-old girl.

Kelandris shrugged, her good humor starting to ebb. "It's an ancient law," she corrected. "Look—there's nothing you can do about it. We Tammi are the natural mystics, and you Jinn are the natural artists."

Yonneth crossed her arms over her chest. "Trickster's got to be *crazy* to have you dance for him. You're as lawful as a Saämbolin."

"What's that supposed to mean?" Kel demanded angrily.

"It means, sister dear, that you haven't got a deviant bone in your whole frigging body!" Yonn glared at Kel, then changed back to being male.

"I do, too!"

Yonneth smiled at Kel derisively. "Yeah? Then how come you refuse to carry the holovespa in your Queen's dildo? Every Wasp Queen for the past nine years has given out the remedy. *Every* Queen. The village is *up* for a good time, Kel. Looks to me like you plan to spoil it!"

Kelandris opened her travelling pack and pulled out a wad of beef jerky. "We don't need holovespa to soar," she said quietly. "You watch—I'll make you high without it. You just watch me dance—"

Yonneth made a rude noise with his lips. Taking a piece of jerky, he bit into it angrily. "Kel—I hate to tell you this, but you're nothing special. And when you dance, nothing's going to happen. Maybe we'll get a little dizzy. That's all." He bit off another mouthful of jerky. "Face it, Kel—the ritual's dead. And holovespa puts life back into it."

Kel's green eyes glittered with frustration. "You don't know what you're talking about!"

"Oh, and I suppose you do?"

Kel's eyes filled with tears. She was certain Yonneth was in error, but she couldn't explain how she knew it. It was a gut feeling, deep and implacable. "Shit," she muttered.

"Well, *that's* an improvement. Obscenity becomes you," he added, fluttering his eyes at her. "Rimble-Rimble."

Kelandris bit her lower lip, feeling angrier and angrier. Finally, she asked, "Just what *is* it you need to feel at the hallows, Yonn?"

"Decadent. Sexy. Overwhelmed by Trickster."

Kelandris frowned. "Overwhelmed? In what way?"

Yonneth stretched out in front of the fire, lying only a few inches from Kelandris. "I want to be entered by Trickster completely. I want to be forced to surrender. To submit."

Kelandris regarded her brother uneasily. This was a side to Yonneth she had never seen. And she wasn't sure she liked it. Kel swallowed. "You sound like you want to be raped. Is that what you think the Divine does?"

Yonneth shrugged, his hand touching Kel's knee. "Might be fun for starters—"

Kelandris got to her feet instantly, every Greatkin sensibility in her outraged. "What's the matter with you, Yonneth? Where's your heart—?"

Yonneth started laughing. Wagging a finger at Kel, he said, "See? What did I tell you? No deviance." He shrugged at his sister. "So you don't like rape. How about incest? Besides," he said standing up and patting the bulge in his trousers, "I'm not your blood brother. So there's no harm."

Kelandris backed up, picking up her travelling pack. She couldn't believe Yonneth was acting like this. "You goddamn stay away from me! You hear?"

The Jinnjirri continued to taunt her. "Who knows, Kel—maybe Trickster will pick *me* for your lover at the Hallows. I mean— Rimble-Rimble, right? And there wouldn't be a thing you could do about it, either. Unless you plan on breaking some of your precious Suxonli laws."

"Shut up, Yonneth!" Kel yelled at him. As she spoke, she thrust her hand deep in the front pocket of her travelling pack. Her fingers closed on the knife hilt she found there. One more step, she thought. Tears brimmed in her eyes. One more step—

Yonneth laughed at Kel's discomfort. Apparently losing interest, he went to fetch a blanket from the cupboard. Kelandris watched him with hooded eyes, her hand still gripping the hidden knife. But Yonneth never made another sexual reference that night. Or at any other time. In fact, Yonneth had brought up the subject and dropped it so quickly that Kelandris had since wondered if maybe she had imagined the whole thing. Perhaps misinterpreted Yonneth's motivation? After all, brothers were brothers, and even Garr and Tommo had teased her on more than one occasion until she had cried.

Kelandris played idly with the strings of her Revel Queen mask, continuing to listen to the drumming in the distance. Her shoulders sagged briefly. With all her heart, she wished Yonneth had not said those things about Trickster maybe choosing him to be her consort for the night. The thought made her feel physically ill. Kelandris fingered the small throwing knife she had tucked in the bra of her harlequin costume. She hoped it wouldn't come to this. She fervently hoped not. She stopped pacing, trying to calm herself. Telling herself that her present mood was neither inviting nor loving, Kelandris forced herself to think pleasant thoughts about Trickster.

She failed miserably.

Kelandris swore at herself and then at Yonneth. Kicking at a stone—and stubbing her toe—Kelandris knelt on the ground and began to cry. Wishing that she were anywhere other than where she was, Kel begged Rimble not to send Yonneth to her tonight. Wiping her eyes jerkily, she whispered, "Let me *be* the Revel Queen. If you send me someone horrible, I'll never trust you again, Rimble. Never." Kelandris blinked back more tears. Suddenly realizing just how damaging Yonneth's idle comments had really been, Kelandris panicked. What if Trickster took offense at her distrust of him? What if Greatkin Rimble was testing the heart of his Revel Queen. Kel put her hand over her mouth, utterly ashamed. She bowed her head. Taking several deep breaths, Kelandris raised her hands slowly in honest supplication to the Presence, the One who directed Rimble. Lifting her tear-streaked face, she shut her eyes and whispered a prayer she had written only that afternoon.

It was at this moment that Zendrak stepped silently into the clearing.

Unaware of his presence, Kel opened her hands like petals of a flower, her voice low and intimate. She sounded as though she were speaking to her oldest and dearest friend:

> No major miracles please,
> Unless you want to tease me.
> Walk with me,
> Walk in me.
> Let my body be your road, your carriage.
> Let my womb be yours,
> Filled with the wonder of your unknown.
> Hold my heart close to your own
> Let it beat in time to your divine noise,
> So that your sound may,
> Like a tuning fork—*hummm*
> And send me deeper into your embrace.
>
> Breathe me.
> Let me be lost in you,
> So that I may truly be found.

And let me praise you like a moon-eyed calf,
Drunk on night silver and gambolling joy.
Silly.
Let me be silly in your presence,
So that you might laugh
And in so doing, teach me your best jokes.
And when I die,
Kiss me passionately,
So that I might wake in death
And see your radiant face.

Kelandris opened her eyes, feeling queerly comforted. She got slowly to her feet. Hearing the rustle of clothing behind her, she turned around. A tall man in green stood in front of her. He gazed at her in silence, his expression thoughtful. Heart pounding, Kel took in every detail of his arresting face.

Blue-black hair that brushed back like raven wings, high cheekbones, and olive skin. Full lips. A nose that was hooked—like a great bird's beak. The man's dark eyes reflected her face in the torchlight. Like the black glass of a scrying mirror, she decided. Kel figeted under the man's steady regard. She felt pierced. As if her thoughts were no longer private.

Kelandris licked her lips nervously. "Who are you?" she whispered.

"I am Trickster's Emissary."

A chill skittered up Kel's spine. And she didn't know why. Still hearing the drumming in the distance, she asked, "Uh—did the Coins of Coincidence—"

Zendrak chuckled. Walking toward Kel slowly, he said, "No, dear heart. I'm not part of your village ritual. I'm part of something else. Something a bit larger. But just the same, Rimble sends you his greetings."

"He does?" she asked, taking a step backward.

Zendrak stopped where he was, opening his arms to her, his eyes kind. Then his strong physical scent swept toward her on the autumn breeze. Mythrrim to Mythrrim, she was undone. Zendrak's personal body odor intoxicated Kel's senses like a heady high. Her pulse raced. Gasping, the Revel Queen touched her chest unconsciously, aware of a pulling sensation in her heart. Pulling or sliding or aching—she wasn't sure which.

Still holding his hands open to her, Zendrak gestured gently for Kel to come to him.

Kelandris shook her head. "You don't understand. There's this ritual going on tonight. And I'm supposed to make love with—I mean—I—" Kel clapped her hand over her mouth in embarrassment. The man in front of her was a total stranger. And Kel doubted very much that it was wise to discuss such matters with someone from the outside—particularly someone who hadn't even come for the Hallows. Kelandris blushed furiously. "Excuse me," she said as calmly as she could manage. "You'll have to go now. I'm—uh—waiting for someone."

Zendrak inclined his head toward the chanting of the villagers at the end of the Long Revel Trail. "Oh, they'll be at it for at least an hour yet." He smiled. "Rimble says so."

"Rimble says—" Kel broke off in mid-sentence. "Who *are* you?"

The man in green removed his long travelling cloak. He smiled at her, "My name is Zendrak." Laying the cloak on the ground, he added, "I stand in for Rimble sometimes."

More interested in what the man was doing than in what he was saying, Kel's eyes widened. Was he making a *bed*? "Didn't you hear me?" she asked anxiously. "You have to go now. I'm waiting for—"

"Me," said Zendrak quietly.

There was a short silence while Kel deliberated the truth of this. Zendrak raised an eyebrow. "Perhaps you prefer someone else?"

Remembering Yonneth, Kel swallowed. "Well—uh—no. You're—just fine."

Zendrak smiled. Lifting Kel's chin gently with his hand, he kissed her lightly, his warm tongue playing over her half-open lips.

Kelandris thought she was going to die on the spot. From bliss. The last of her reservations about the rightness or wrongness of loving Zendrak folded. Zendrak's breath brushed her face. Kelandris groaned softly. Zendrak's personal animal scent—sweet, musky, and inviting—teased her senses. Delightfully drunk now, Kel could hardly see straight. Zendrak kissed her again, this time more thoroughly. Kel tried to match his five hundred years of passion, but her inexperience made her slightly clumsy. His eyes twinkling with amusement, Zendrak convinced Kel to come up for air. Then he taught her how to kiss him.

Happily for all concerned, Kelandris proved to a quick study. Touching Kel's breasts for the first time, Zendrak stiffened abruptly. Kelandris had a razor-sharp knife hidden in her bra. Eyeing Kel ruefully, Zendrak pulled the knife free and dropped it on the ground. Zendrak chuckled. Then he said, "Trickster told me you'd be fierce. He wasn't kidding. Tell me," he asked, "do you often make love in full armor?"

Rolling her eyes, Kelandris picked up the knife and threw it expertly into a sapling. "There," she muttered. "You've disarmed me."

"And you're vexed," said Zendrak, his voice sober. "You've misunderstood. I enjoy a woman who fights her own battles. And shows her spirit openly." He stroked Kel's cheek with gentle fingers. "Spirited women are the very best kind. And they're also the hardest to come by."

Kelandris wrinkled her nose in disagreement. "Oh—Tammirring makes my kind everyday. It's in the *draw*."

Zendrak laughed good-naturedly. "Believe me, Kelandris of Suxonli, the world has never seen one such as *you* before." Taking in the whole of her hermaphroditic costume, Zendrak bent to loosen the leather dildo from her striped belt. Holding the erect penis sheath by its engorged stem, Zendrak winked at Kelandris. "I don't think you'll be needing this for a bit. I've a very generous nature." Patting the lower portion of his green robe, Zendrak added, "And I'm happy to share."

Kelandris started to smile then hesitated. The color drained out of her face as her seventeen-year-old virginity got the best of her. "*How* generous?" she asked hoarsely, all of Yonneth's taunts coming to mind. Tales of pain and blood. Kel started to tremble. "My brother—" She broke off, tears in her eyes.

Zendrak studied the fear in her face. He dropped the leather ritual dildo to the ground and pulled Kelandris to him, enfolding her pounding heart in his arms. He kissed her lovingly then said, "Brothers can be cruel sometimes, Kel. You must refuse such violence."

"I do," she said adamantly, glancing at her knife stuck in the sapling.

Zendrak followed her gaze. "Weapons are ineffective against psychic violence, Kel. Only spirit can overcome this kind of attack. Spirit, courage, and refusal."

Kelandris listened closely to Zendrak's words. They made her feel strong inside. Strong, relieved, and hopeful. She smiled tentatively at the man in green. "Okay," she said. Kel shrugged shyly, her face scarlet. "Let's—uh—share."

Zendrak chuckled. "Okay."

The boyishness and innocent glee of Zendrak's ready smile undid Kelandris utterly. Abandoning her fear of Zendrak's male differentness from herself, she allowed Zendrak to remove her costumed codpiece. Kel's eyes widened as she felt Zendrak's fingers explore the confines of her costume—and release her from it. Then, giving Kelandris a reassuring smile, the man in green kissed the tuft of dark hair between her legs. To him, she was a Mythrrim and she was "in season," which meant desirable.

Kelandris felt a twinge in her abdomen.

Zendrak raised his eyes to meet hers. "The blood comes now."

"The blood?" asked Kelandris, unsure of what he meant. Then, feeling the wash of something wet issuing from her vagina, she yelped. Her menses had arrived for the first time. Kelandris regarded the blood dripping slowly down the inside of her thigh with horror. "It *can't* come now!" she cried. "The Blood Day Rule! I'm the Queen! The village expects me to dance!" Kel covered her mouth, her eyes desperate. "They'll be so angry if I don't dance." Tears brimmed in her eyes. "And so angry if I do."

"Rimble-Rimble," said Zendrak, his tone matter-of-fact.

Kelandris regarded him wildly. "What should I *do*?"

Zendrak kissed her belly. "Make love."

"Yes, but—"

"And then decide," he added calmly. "Hmm?"

Kelandris shut her eyes, feeling anguished by her internal conflict. Zendrak got to his feet. Mythrrim to Mythrrim, Kel's first blood sounded a passion in both their bodies that neither could restrain. Kelandris groaned, buckling. Zendrak lowered her to his cloak. Slowly, inexorably, he convinced Kel's body of the rightness of their mating. This was animal-talk. Kelandris opened her legs, inviting the spreading reach of Zendrak's fingers inside her. He stretched her and aroused her. Then, Zendrak entered her.

Greatkin to Greatkin, their bodies fit together like a living socket and plug, the current of raw sexual potency streaming from one to the other and back again. Surprised, Kelandris immediately clamped down on her energy. But it was like trying to hold back an enormous waterfall. Power surged and threatened to overwhelm her if she didn't let go. Zendrak pressed his hand against the area between Kel's ovaries.

"Just breathe," he told her quietly.

Kelandris tried to do so but ended up panting instead.

Zendrak cupped one of his hands around the back of Kel's skull and slipped the other into the curve of the lower portion of her spine. The effect was immediately calming. It felt to Kel as if he were absorbing unclaimed current directly into his hands, thereby steadying the wild fluctuations of psychic energy in her body.

"Follow me," he said calmly and began to slowly rock his penis back and forth inside her vagina. In no time, the power began to build again. This time, Zendrak took control of it, allowing Kel only as much as she could safely accommodate. Kelandris groaned, arching her back. The pressure building inside her body made her feel dizzy and almost nauseous. Losing the rhythm between them, she squirmed under Zendrak.

"I can't do this. I can't—"

"Yes, you can, Kel," replied Zendrak, kissing her firmly, thrusting his tongue deep inside her mouth. Kelandris hesitated then met his passion with her own. Lights danced before her shut eyes. She felt her body finally relax into Zendrak's full embrace. Now something shifted between them. Something controlled, something electric, and something wildly fertile. Zendrak pulled back from Kel for a moment. He studied the dazed expression in her face then said, "You're doing fine."

Kelandris frowned helplessly. "But *what* am I doing?"

"Becoming the *he*. Becoming a divine potential. The line to your womb is open now—thanks to your blood. Through you, Suxonli Village will come face-to-face with the Presence. And all will be changed."

Kelandris hadn't the faintest idea what he was talking about. She shuddered, surrendering briefly to the steady pulsing of power streaming out of her hands, legs, and crown. She blinked. Heart pounding, she stared hard at Zendrak.

"What—what?"

"Let it happen, Kel. Become both."

Kelandris shook her head dazedly. She felt terribly strange—as if her body were literally changing shape. Or sex, she thought. Like a Jinnjirri. She felt for her breasts. They were still there. Utterly confused, she couldn't get rid of the sensation that she might be female and male simultaneously.

Zendrak kissed her forehead. "Don't fight it, Kel. It's what you were born to do." Then Zendrak whispered Trickster's rhyme:

> Will you turn the inside inside-out,
> And be sanely mad with me?

Will you master the smallest steps of my turnabout,
And come to my ecstasy?

Kel's world suddenly doubled, and she saw Zendrak's face
from both a male and female perspective. It was as if all the
concepts of gender she had ever held paradoxically collapsed and
expanded inside her mind at the exact same moment. She was no
longer male *or* female. She was a peculiar intermarriage of both.
And yet her physical body remained female. Had she always been
like this? Kel put the question to Zendrak.

Trickster's Emissary nodded. "The visible rests on the invisible. Always." He stroked Kel's cheek. "In this way, my maleness
rests on my femaleness. In a manner of speaking, you could say
I am Trickster's *she*." Zendrak smiled, massaging Kel's abdomen
deeply. "However," he whispered, "I'll never embody it the way
that you do, for I cannot menstruate. I don't turn the inside
inside-out."

Kelandris swallowed. She had never seen a woman's bloodcycle in quite this way before. Then an idea occurred to her. "But
the Jinnjirri can—"

Zendrak shook his head. "The Revel Queen is Tammirring for
a reason, Kelandris. The *landdraw* of this region makes your
people's minds elastic. A Jinnjirri turning into a *he* would
mentally burn up. The power of the *he* can only be grounded by
the internal *draw* of a native Tammirring."

Kelandris played with the dark hair on Zendrak's chest. "Oh."

Zendrak kissed her nose. "You could *dance* for Trickster
anywhere, I suppose. But I think it would be easiest in Tammirring. Especially in Suxonli. Here you and the land understand
each other on an intuitive level. Here your seasons are its seasons.
Here," he said moving his hips again, "you're at home."

Kelandris gasped, passion building between them once more.
This time, Kel allowed herself to feel the *he* surge through her
psyche. Using Zendrak's energy to stabilize herself, she opened to
the complete bisexuality of Greatkin Rimble. It was a wild glory.

And Trickster's Emissary and Trickster's *he* reveled in it.

Chapter Thirty-Two

SOMEONE POUNDED LOUDLY on the front door to Doogat's tobacco shop. Jolted out of their shared trance and their remembered lovemaking, Zendrak and Kelandris opened their eyes groggily. Forcing himself to focus on the outside world again, Zendrak stared at the vexed face glaring at him through the window. It was an Asilliwir woman of about thirty-five years of age. Still holding Kel's neck with one hand and the Kindrasul with the other, Zendrak debated what to do while the Asilliwir woman continued to sledgehammer the door. He needed to make sure the transfer of two-legged apperception of reality to four-legged was complete in Kel's mind. Feeling the woman in black suddenly stiffen against him, Zendrak swore softly. Clearly, the beating on the door was frightening Kelandris. Now the muffled voice of the Asilliwir reached him:

"You there in green! Doon't pretend I canna see you! Open up!"

The unusual accent of the woman broke Zendrak's concentration with Kel. Zendrak squinted in the direction of the clamoring Asilliwir. Abruptly Aunt's mental Mayanabi message returned to him in full: "Need second opinion on 'shift fever' victim. Girl, aged fifteen, a Tammi. Name: Yafatah. Begat during Rimble's Remembrance in Suxonli. Father Jinnjirri, but unknown to either mother or child. Mother's name is Fasilla. Personal friend of mine. Born in southern Asilliwir. Physical symptoms to follow . . ."

"Shit," said Zendrak angrily. This was Fasilla again and as before her timing couldn't be worse. He bit his lower lip, caught between his duty to Rimble—who wanted Yafatah in Speakinghast—and his caring for Kelandris.

Zendrak let go of Kel's neck and placed both of his hands over the Kindrasul. Impressing the black glass beads with his heart's deepest longing for Kelandris, he leaned close to her face and whispered, "Wait here, Kel. I'll only be gone a moment."

Kelandris said nothing, her green eyes bewildered.

Zendrak left Kel's side and hurried to the front of the tobacco shop. He flung open the door, blocking the Asilliwir woman's entry with his great height and broad build. "Yes?" he said curtly.

"I be Fasilla of Ian Abbi. Be you Doogat of Suf?"

"Doogat's out for the afternoon." Zendrak pointed to the sign in the window. "Shop's closed. Come back tonight. Say—seven bell-eve?"

"But—"

Zendrak shook his head, closing the door firmly in Fasilla's face. He turned around hoping to find Kelandris still lying on the floor. She was not. Zendrak cursed raggedly. Neither Kelandris nor the Kindrasol were to be found anywhere. Zendrak tore through the scarlet beads that divided the tobacco shop from the kitchen. The door leading outside to the store's back alley stood open. Zendrak stepped into the narrow cobblestone byway. He looked in either direction for some sign of the woman in black. The street was empty. Calling Trickster every four-letter name he could think of, Zendrak ran his hand through his dark hair with frustration. Deciding to track Kelandris via the pull of the Kindrasul on his heart, he opened his mind to receive emotional impressions from the black glass beads of Soaringsea. Without warning, Zendrak slammed into a gleeful wall of psychic static.

Opening his eyes in surprise, Zendrak muttered, *"What?"*

"First things first, Zen-boy," said a familiar voice.

Zendrak spun around. "Rimble!"

Trickster grinned. "In the flesh, so to speak. Meet Old Jamilla."

Zendrak put his hands on his hips, regarding Trickster with grudging admiration. The little Greatkin was no longer four-feet-seven, but a whopping five-feet-three. Dressed in a tattering of rags, Rimble currently appeared as a pied-eyed, toothless old woman. Zendrak smiled sourly. "You've grown."

"That's what happens when I matter to mortals." Trickster batted her eyes coquettishly. "And believe me, Zen-boy, I matter *ooo*dles to Yafatah."

"Yeah? Well, Kelandris of Suxonli happens to matter *ooo*dles to me, Rimble." Zendrak crossed his arms over his chest, glaring at his father. "Where is she? Where is Kel?"

"Wandering."

"That's not an answer, Rimble."

Trickster shrugged. Then, before Zendrak could open his mouth, Rimble wagged a disapproving finger in Zendrak's face.

"And don't even *think* of asking Phebene for help. I've had about all I can stomach of that lollipop loony. She's a sugar-coated, meddling, tinsel-tot."

Zendrak chuckled derisively. "Poor Rimble. *Such* a sad story—sharing the stage with Phebene. Perhaps you just can't manage to swallow all that you dish out at the Panthe'kinarok? Of course, we mortals have been gagging on your meddling for centuries—not that you'd care."

Trickster's pied eyes narrowed. "What an ass you are today."

"Like father, like son."

"With one difference, Zen-boy. *I* don't get duped by Love."

At that moment, several Saämbolin students walked past the two Greatkin. One of them laughed merrily, her eyes kind. Grabbing the hand of the boy closest to her, she tweaked his nose saying, "I'm on to you, sweetie. You kick and scream whenever I mention love. But I know better. You've got a yen for tenderness a mile wide. You're a closet romantic, my friend, and I'm just the one to open your door." Then, glancing in Trickster's direction, the girl added firmly, "So help me, Phebene."

Catching sight of Trickster's scarlet face, Zendrak started laughing. Speaking softly to the Greatkin next to him, Zendrak said, "Point in Tinsel-Tot's favor. She's talking to you, Dad. Direct."

"All lies," protested Trickster indignantly.

Hearing Rimble's comment, the Saämbolin girl looked over her shoulder at the old woman clothed in rags. Beaming broadly, she called, "Smile, grandmother. Nothing can stop true love—not even Trickster himself."

"That does it!" retorted Rimble. Without warning, the Greatkin began spitting expertly at the Saämbolin students. Wiping Rimble's phlegm off their fine velvets, the students complained fastidiously and walked away.

"Just *wait* until I return to Eranossa, Phebes," muttered Trickster. Before Zendrak could retort, Rimble materialized a blue robe out of thin air. It was Doogat's size. Rimble handed it to Zendrak. "You better change."

Zendrak shook his head. "Sorry. I'm busy. I've a lunatic to find."

"Like I said, Zen-boy— first things first. You've an overdue appointment with a young Tammirring girl named Yafatah. Come along," she added, extending her arm to Zendrak.

Zendrak refused it, his expression furious. "If you think I'm going to leave Kelandris 'to wander,' you're sadly mistaken, Rimble."

Trickster smiled cooly. "That's why I'm here."

"Why?"

"To make *sure* you attend to first things first."

Chapter Thirty-Three

STAYING BEHIND AT the caravan camp in the Asilliwir Quarter of Speakinghast while her mother went to check on the availability of Doogat, Yafatah walked slowly back to the red and blue wagon belonging to her mother. She carried a heavy pail of water, the warm water sloshing to and fro as she made her way across the heavily populated caravan park. Before she had left for Doogat's, Fasilla had suggested that Yafatah wash some clothes while the noonday sun still shone high overhead. Yafatah was now doing so. Aunt, for her part, had gone to fetch bread and fruit for snacks, leaving Yafatah alone in the safety of the caravan camp. Borrowing a chunk of gray soap from a neighboring campsite of Asilliwir merchants carrying spices and bolts of bright cloth, Yafatah carefully set the pail of water on the back stairs of the red and blue wagon. She went inside to fetch a pile of her dirtiest laundry.

As she pulled a wooden trunk from under her cot, Yafatah sighed. She wished her mother would let her go exploring in Speakinghast. They had passed any number of marvelous stalls and shops on their way to the caravan park. It seemed silly to be surrounded by paradise and not be permitted to smell the flowers of its gardens. Yafatah scowled. She considered taking a walk despite her mother's admonishments to the contrary. Yafatah stopped sorting her laundry. She figured she had at least a half hour before either Aunt or Fasilla returned. A half hour was plenty of time to see the city sights. Yeah, she thought, grabbing a red traveling cape. Smiling, Yafatah escaped.

The fifteen-year-old had not gone more than a block when she heard someone call her name. Turning away from a particularly delectable looking pastry shop in front of her—rows of cream and fruit filled goodies teeming in the window—Yafatah stared at an old woman in patchwork rags waving to her from across the busy street. Yafatah's eyes widened in disbelief.

"Jammy!" she cried in delight.

As the young girl ran to meet Trickster, "Old Jamilla" turned to the man dressed in blue beside her and said, "At least *somebody* loves me."

Doogat rolled his black eyes.

Trickster opened her arms wide to receive Yafatah, saying, "Well, well, kiddo—what a surprise to see you here. I thought Tammirring didn't like these big cities. No headaches or fear of the crowds?"

Yafatah shook her head happily, throwing her arms around Jamilla and giving her a ferocious hug. "I do be so glad to see you, Jammy. I looked for you in Piedmerri, but I couldna' find you. There do be queer things—" Yafatah broke off, suddenly suspicious of the man in blue.

Trickster smiled at Yafatah. "He's all right. He's with me. In fact, my sweet, *this* is Doogat."

Doogat, who was still thinking about Kelandris, gave Yafatah a perfunctory bow, his dark eyes distant. The young girl eyed him skeptically. Then she pursed her lips and remarked, "You ought to spend more time in your shop, Master Doogat. You do be making me ma fierce mad with them hours you keep."

"My sincere apologies," said Doogat, his tone slightly sarcastic.

Yafatah nodded briskly. Turning her attention back to Trickster, she said, "Oh, Jammy—I didna' have anyone to talk to. And me blood came early, and we went into Jinnjirri where I got sick. On account of the shift and all. And then—oh, Jammy—and *then*, this weird willy thing happened." Glancing at Doogat briefly, Yafatah tossed her head. "I got tangled with another Tammi. Her name was Kel, and she was fierce crazy. But really, Jammy, she didna' scare me overmuch."

"Why not?" asked Doogat, taking an interest in Yafatah's story for the first time.

"Because, Master Doogat—she were a true Tammi," replied Yafatah, her face reverent. "She be like a starry night that goes on forever. She be vast and deep. And ever so dark. But this dark do be a good kind. Like the hidden places inside the oldest mountains. That Kel, see—she touches the heavens but walks the earthy world. She stands between, knowing both." Yafatah nodded with enthusiasm. "And I shall never be the same again."

Trickster squeezed Yafatah's shoulder. "Mystery is a power of the Fertile Dark. And you have met it well, kiddo."

Doogat said nothing, his heart made unexpectedly heavy by Yafatah's description of her contact with Kel's mind. He turned away from Old Jamilla and Yafatah, stuffing his hands into the pockets of his blue robe. Scanning the bustling street again for a tall woman in black, he sighed painfully. Somewhere out there, a mystery walked. A mystery that he longed to love with all his heart. And soul.

Holding the Kindrasul tightly in her hand as she entered the Saämbolin Quarter of the city, Crazy Kel muttered wildly to no one. Turning east, she headed for the park grounds of the Great Library of Speakinghast. Kel had seen the tall hedge of the library's central garden from a distance and without knowing why, she felt a need to see it up close. Avoiding several tour groups, she crept closer to the iron gate at the entrance to the twenty-five-foot hedge. A sign in six *landdraw* languages hung over the gate, announcing the time of the next tour. Kelandris read the Tammir-ring translation. Her eyes turned thoughtful under her shredded veil. She read the translation again, this time out loud:

" 'Welcome to the Great Maze of Speakinghast. The only one of its kind in the world, the Great Maze is famous for the complexity of its unique spiral design and for the twenty-foot statue of a fabled Mythrrim Beast in its very center. The Library wishes to caution you against entering the Great Maze without a guide. We take no responsibility for you if you choose to disregard this warning. It *is* possible to get lost here—for days. Tours are conducted at one, three, and five bell-eve. An admission price of twenty-five coppers is payable to your guide. Thank you for your cooperation. *Master Curator Sirrefene.*' "

Kelandris, in natural contrary style, ignored the warning completely and entered the spiral labyrinth of boxwood hedges. The sweet scent of the shrubbery delighted her at first, then, after an hour of walking, it became slightly sinister and oppressive. Kelandris sat down on a marble bench to rest. The bells of the city tolled twelve noon, the ones in the Great Library thundering loudly above her. Startled, Kelandris got to her feet and took the first path that opened before her. She ran blindly yelling at unseen accusers.

As Rimble's Luck would have it, Kel stumbled upon one of two tracks in the whole maze that led directly to the winged statue in its middle. The Power of Coincidence, it seemed, worked for Trickster's daughter as easily as it did for Trickster's son. Or perhaps the black glass beads in Kel's hand called to the black glass statue ahead, and the statue answered in *draw*. Whatever the reason, Kelandris found her way to the Mythrrim Beast in impossible record time. She slowed as she caught sight of the squatting, twenty-foot, female legend.

Recognition Ceremony.

Voices sounded in Kel's mind. Voices that had lived a hundred thousand years, speaking still in generational memory of the Mythrrim Beasts of Soaringsea. Voices and the storyteller's gestures. Whispers and the long sigh of heaven. Such was the power of the Great Ones who spoke through Mythrrim; such was the power of the Greatkin, the beloved of the Presence. And now the Eldest came to Kelandris. The woman in black struggled to hear the murmur of Greatkin Themyth, the mother of Mythrrim. Kelandris reached for the black statue in front of her, her voice strangling in strange whimpering sounds. She was an animal calling to her kin. The statue remained silent, its glistening black eyes open and lifeless. Again, Kelandris called. The statue made no response. Weeping, Kelandris pawed at it wildly. Her fingers slid off the glass. She kicked at the statue, hurting only herself. Rocking back and forth, her fists balled into her stomach, Kel's voice assumed the cry of a hunting bird in distress. She gave a series of soft, high pitched screeches. Then, exhausted, Kel crawled under the folded wing of the obsidian Mythrrim and fell into a sorrowing sleep.

Rimble-Rimble. At the east entrance, Rowenaster prepared to take his survey class on an unofficial excursion into the spiral labyrinth. A few of his Jinnjirri students tittered nervously as Rowenaster counted heads. Tree, who happened to be present for this particular field trip and was wishing he weren't, decided to have some fun with his fellow Jinn. Naturally paranoid of all things Saämbolin, the Jinn were uneasy to begin with in this enclosed space. Smiling wickedly, Tree announced, "Did you know this is where the city takes its dissidents? Loses them in this place, forever and ever."

At least half the students fell silent, their eyes casting about for some discreet means of escape. The professor took stock of the situation. Watching the Jinnjirri students separate hastily from the rest of the *draws*, Rowenaster gave Tree a withering smile.

"Thanks."

Tree grinned. "You're welcome, roomie."

Rowenaster pursed his lips. "Speaking of the 'K'—I'm thinking we ought to reshuffle the house chores soon. How'd you like to be recommended for garderobes and other stinky things?"

Tree rolled his eyes. "Okay, okay. I get the message: shut up."

"Such an excellent pupil," said Rowen, continuing to count heads.

"Hey, professor," said another student presently. She had just read the warning hanging over the iron gate, and, being a lawful Saämbolin, she felt uneasy about walking out of schedule into a place where one could get lost "for days." Rowenaster had a reputation for being a careful teacher, but, on rare occasions, Professor Rowenaster had been known to do the absolutely unexpected. Such unpredictability in one of her own *draw* made this first-term student very uncomfortable. "Professor," she called again.

Rowenaster broke off his count for the second time and said, "What is it, Torri?"

"Are you *sure* you know your way through this maze?"

Tree came to Rowen's rescue. "Presence alive, girl—he's only been taking field trips in here for the past twenty years."

Torri swallowed. "Oh," she said, her face scarlet.

When the professor had gone back to counting heads for the final time, one of the other equally uneasy Saämbolin nudged Torri. Then he winked, pulling out a large ball of brilliant orange yarn.

Tying the end to a bar of the iron gate, he said, "I'm with you, Torri. Ain't nobody getting me in there with *that* crazy old coot. Ever noticed how many weird things happen around Professor Rowenaster? It's almost like he's got Trickster sitting in his back pocket or something. And he's so friendly with the Jinn—kind of makes you wonder," he added, his tone of voice implying a sexual reference. "The registrar says he *lives* with shifts."

Torri watched the fellow double knot the yarn to the gate, her expression relieved. "Well," she said amiably, "Trickster *is* the professor's graduate area of special emphasis."

"So queer for a Saäm."

"Very," she agreed, and fell in line with the rest of the students.

Admonishing the members of his class not to lag behind or go off on their own inside the spiral, the professor led ninety first-term pupils into the Great Maze of Speakinghast. This was only a fourth of the actual class roster. Tree joined Rowenaster at the head of the group.

Recalling his previous conversation with the professor, Tree said, "When *is* the next house meeting, anyway? I mean, we *are* having a Hallows, aren't we?"

"Janusin's picking up the invitations for the party today. So yes, we're definitely having one. Regarding the next house meeting, I thought I saw a note in the kitchen this morning asking for people's schedules. Barlimo muttered something to me over her breakfast tea about wanting us all to convene tomorrow night."

"Tomorrow!" cried Tree. "But Mab's only just *returned*! She's hardly in a state to handle a fucking house meeting, Rowen! She's so depressed, I'm worried she might try something serious! You know—like killing herself." Tree stuffed his hands in his colorful fall garb. "If Barlimo hadn't insisted that I go on this field trip with you, I'd be home right now watching over her."

"No doubt, Tree," replied the professor drily. "And to no avail. Too much caring can be as damaging as too little."

"I'm *in love* with Mab," replied Tree.

"That's no excuse."

"No excuse? No excuse for *what*, Rowen?"

"To hurt Mab."

Tree crossed his arms over his chest. "Oh, what do you know? The last person *you* were ever in love with is probably so old by now, they've taken up permanent residence at the Great Library Museum!"

Rowenaster glanced at the Jinnjirri's streaking red hair. "Temper's showing, dear."

They walked in silence until they reached the last turn of the spiral that opened into the central courtyard. Rowenaster stopped the group and motioned for them to move closer to him. Torri and the Saämbolin carrying the ball of orange thread hung back. Rowenaster gestured for them to join the rest of them. Torri did so. The Saämbolin hesitated; he had just come to the end of his ball of yarn and had not had time to tie it off yet. He smiled stupidly at the professor, his hands behind his back.

Rowenaster peered over his bifocals at the student. "What seems to be the problem, Widdero?"

"Problem? No problem here, sir."

Rowenaster rolled his eyes and pushed through the group to reach the dissembling fellow. The professor stopped in front of

Widdero and snapped his fingers impatiently. "All right—let's have it."

"Have what, sir?"

"The yarn, the string, the bread crumbs—whatever it is you've brought along to help you find your way back. Like Tree said, boy, I've been doing this a long time."

Widdero showed Rowenaster the end of the ball of yarn. "I just ran out of length."

"That's not all you've done," replied the professor cooly.

Widdero swallowed hard. "Sir?"

"You've also hung yourself with it, Widdero."

"Sir?"

"You heard me. You get no credit for this field trip. I ought to flunk you for missing the point of the whole class. Instead, I'll send you home."

The Saämbolin student stared at Rowenaster.

"Now!" snapped the professor, pointing in the direction from which they had all just come. Widdero backed up, then realizing that Rowenaster had no intention of giving him an explanation, he cursed the professor loudly. Turning away, Widdero followed the orange thread in his shaking hand. He disappeared around the corner.

Widdero's curses woke the woman in black who lay sleeping under the obsidian wing of the Great Mythrrim Beast of Soaringsea. Raising her head, Crazy Kel listened to the sound of an old man's voice speaking to an invisible audience in the corridor to her right. She herself also remained unseen, her black robe further obscuring her under the shadow of the black glass.

Rowenaster regarded his students cooly, daring anyone to question his judgment or authority. No one did—not even Tree. The professor nodded at the eighty-nine stunned faces standing in front of him.

"Sit down. I have something I want to say to all of you."

People sat, their robes rustling, their mouths closed.

"You may think my conduct toward Widdero to be harsh. Well, it's not." Rowen paused. "I can see by your dubious expressions that you don't agree. All right," he said, cupping his hands behind his back like a sea captain beginning his morning constitutional on deck, "I'll explain my thinking to you. First off, Widdero's refusal to trust the unknown is typical of my *draw*. We like our mazes solved before we start. And my friends, that simply won't do in these changing times."

The professor began to pace, excited by a subject that was particularly near and dear to his heart. Rowen's long maroon robe slapped gently against his spindly seventy-year-old legs as his Saämbolin teacherly passion overcame him. Stopping suddenly, Rowenaster glared at the group and said:

"You take this class because it's required. I teach this class because I love it. Every morning, I bring the best of myself to this group in the wild hope of making one or two of you aware of the greater powers at work in our lives right now. Why? Because we two-leggeds are at our childhood's end. And it's time we put away our balls of yarn—and arrogance. This is Jinnaeon. Shifttime— the time of World Renewal. And hope." Rowen paused. "We may either welcome or resist these forces, but we may not stop them. We can change—or be changed. Your friend, Widdero, has just had a mild taste of what is in store for all of us. Do you wish to be shattered or transformed? Think about it."

Tree, who was sitting in the front row, stared at Rowen in disbelief. The old professor sounded like a street corner doom and gloomer. *Or* Doogat, mused Tree thoughtfully, noting how much Rowen's teaching methods had changed in recent months. Where the Saämbolin had once been polite and precise, he was now hard-hitting and hasty. Was the professor responding to some unseen deadline or something? Tree stiffened. Maybe the old man was *dying*, and no one knew it. Tree inclined his head, studying the movements of Rowenaster. The Jinnjirri shrugged in disagreement with himself. The professor looked as hale and spry as he always did. So, thought Tree, something else must be bothering Rowenaster of Speakinghast. But what?

"Now the majority of you here saw a certain play several weeks ago," continued Rowen. "It was called *Rimble's Remedy*. We discussed it at some length in class, and we concluded what, Torri?"

The young Saämbolin girl turned scarlet, trying to recall the substance of that long conversation. She had been doodling in her notebook at the time, thinking about her pitiful lovelife. Torri swallowed hard. "Uh—I know we talked about the Prophetic Vision. Of the Tammirring, I mean."

"Correct," said Rowenaster warmly.

Torri smiled, assuming she was now off the hook.

"And?"

"And?" she faltered.

Rowenaster put his hands on his hips, speaking to the group at large. "And I read a poem to you. It was one I had found etched into a wall in an old cave outside Suxonli Village. Anybody remember it? No? All right, then, I'll repeat it to you." Rowenaster paused, removing his bifocals from the bridge of his large nose. Regarding the group sternly, he said:

> By the venomous sting of his Chaos Thumb,
> Trickster pricks nine, one by one,
> His circle of genius for the turn to come;
> Back Pocket People for that rainy day
> When the weave of the world pulls away.

On the other side of the hedge, Kelandris leaned forward, her torn veil fluttering with the sharp intake of her breath.

Rowenaster eyed his students with a mixture of impatience and resignation. "Okay—so why am I reminding you of this poem? And what does a poem from a little known village in southern Tammirring have to do with me chastising one of my 'best students?' " He paused. "Plenty."

Tree cleared his throat. "Professor," he whispered, "are you—are you okay? I mean—"

Rowenaster snorted at the Jinnjirri. "As I was saying—there *is* a connection between the two. That connection," he continued forcefully, "is Mystery. And Mystery cannot be approached by the mind's cleverness. Try it, and Mystery will smite you with outrage."

Kelandris fingered her shredded veil thoughtfully, her talons hidden.

"We pride ourselves on our modernity—cool, capable. In control. But for how long? Every day we're confronted by the inexplicable." Rowen paused. "I'm referring in part, of course, to the impossible statue standing on the other side of this hedge. *No one knows how it got here. Yet it exists.*"

Kelandris crawled between the front paws of the obsidian statue and began grooming herself with teeth and tongue.

"Now," said the professor suddenly squatting in front of the group and studying each of their uneasy faces in turn, "the Suxonli poem is a mystery, too. It's very old. Its author remains unknown. Nevertheless, we do know this: the poem is a prophecy. A prophecy *for our time*," he said in a low, emphatic voice. "Do you know what this means, children? Do you understand what we—your generation and mine—collectively face? Can you imagine what it will be like *if* the weave of the world pulls away without the help of Trickster? Without the control of the Nine?"

No one said a word.

During the intervening silence, something clicked in Kel's mind. The Nine. The Nine were important. The signal. Trickster would send out a signal to gather in one place. Nine would leave the hive; nine would fly to Speakinghast. But who were these nine? And, then she knew. Kel remained motionless staring at Rowenaster's face.

"Goosebumps?" continued the professor. "Then you begin to know the potency of Mystery."

"It's just a poem," retorted Torri. "Written by Tammi *for* Tammi. That makes the prophecy their problem—not ours, professor."

Rowenaster said nothing, cleaning the lenses of his bifocals with a monogrammed silk handkerchief. "That's exactly my point, Torri." He set his silver glasses back on the bridge of his dark nose. "You—*all* of you—should've known about this prophecy before now. It was your birthright," he added giving the three Tammirring in the group a look of consternation. "Nor should I have been the one to bring it to your attention." Rowenaster shrugged. "Each *draw* has a responsibility to uphold in the greater scheme of things. As a Saämbolin, mine is to teach what I know. The Dunnsung are here to remind us of the harmonies in the universal language of music and dance. The Piedmerri provide nurturance—be they farmers or parents. The Asilliwir keep cultures alive by the exchange of news and goods from one border of the continent to the next. The Jinnjirri must create—pursuing self-expression regardless of exterior conditions. And the Tammirring? Theirs is perhaps the most awesome responsibility of all. The Tammi are the caretakers of our collective soul. It is they who listen to the winds of the universe and translate the sigh into direction for all of us." Rowenaster paused. "Now this is the point: if one *landdraw* sickens, we *all* sicken. And that play—*Rimble's Remedy*—is a shocking indication of a growing spiritual malaise—one that started in Tammirring at least sixty years ago. It has now spread to the Jinnjirri. I put it to you that the Saämbolin will be the next to be so infected. *Our* problem, you see."

Tree stared at Rowenaster anxiously, listening to the angry comments of the Saämbolin students sitting near him. He considered moving into the company of his own *draw*. If Rowenaster was going to foment a minor civil riot on the grounds of the Great Library of Speakinghast, he wanted to be among his own kind when tempers flared. Then, deciding not to call attention to himself by standing up, Tree put his head in his hands, muttering, "I don't believe this. I just don't *believe* this."

Rowenaster continued to speak from his unchallenged soapbox. "Why do you think there's so much unrest in this city? Why do you Jinnjirri think Guildmaster Gadorian is cracking down on your quarter? Because he's afraid. There are far more Jinn in Speakinghast than Tammi. Let's face it—the Tammi are loners. But you, Jinn—you organize, you take sides, you reveal yourselves through your art. Although he doesn't know it, Gadorian senses a growing Tammi and Jinn despair. This can produce instability. Civil unrest in a city." Rowen glanced at Tree.

Tree bit his lower lip, thinking about the atmosphere of decadence at the playhouse where the Merry Pricksters performed. He wondered if he had inadvertently contributed to it in some way. He had always been somewhat of an artistic dilettante. Commitment, he mused grimly, had never been one of his strong points. Neither in artistic mediums nor in personal relationships. Tree winced, thinking about Mab. She needed stability right now. Did he have any to give her? He hoped so.

"So Guildmaster Gadorian reacts," continued the professor, "albeit blindly for the most part. Still, the Guildmaster wields a great deal of power in Speakinghast, so, blind or not, the effects of his reaction are strongly felt. Particularly by the Jinnjirri—who are our society's scapegoats at present. It's all quite unnecessary. But nothing can be done, you see, until we recognize what we're dealing with—namely change on a massive scale. And explosive spiritual turnabout. Meanwhile, the Jinnjirri suffer."

"And that's *our* fault?" asked Torri indignantly, referring to the Saämbolin students who were present in the group. The majority of them were younger than twenty years of age. "I mean *we* did not create this world—or its prejudices, professor. If anyone's responsible for the problems of the Jinnjirri, I'd say it was *your* generation of *landdraw*."

The Saämbolin sitting near Tree passed whispers back and forth.

"Torri—you're not listening. I'm not blaming any one *draw* for our present predicament. I'm not even pointing the finger at the Tammirring. You're thinking only in terms of yourself. This is not a question of *draw* against *draw*—at least, I hope not. We're talking about a collective whole here. We're talking about a situation that affects all Mnemlith at once."

Torri gave him a superior look and said, "What has *that* to do with me? I mean, I get up in the morning, I go to school, I come home. In short, professor, I live my life as responsibly as I can manage. And I don't appreciate being told that I'm not only responsible for myself—but for the attitudes of my whole fucking *draw*! Much less the entire *world*!"

Rowenaster shrugged cooly. "So?"

Torri's eyes blazed. "*So* I take this class because I have to—not because I *want* to. And *you* shouldn't abuse your privilege as a teach at our great university by trapping students in this boxwood maze, *forcing* them to listen to your anarchistic opinions because they can't leave without running the risk of getting lost 'for days'!"

Tree stroked his chin. Torri had a point. He regarded the professor steadily, curious to see what the old man would do with it. Rowenaster surprised Tree; he chuckled.

"Torri, change is *already* upon us. It's no longer something we can avoid—it simply *is*. The Presence is not a static thing. It needs to grow as you and I do. And when the Presence grows, we're affected. These are great times when the Powers of Neath are loosed—like the wasp's poison in the poem."

"And that's another thing," snapped Torri hotly. "You're obsessed with Greatkin Rimble. Just because Old Yellow Jacket was *your* area of emphasis, that doesn't mean he's *ours*! I mean, Rimble's not even *real*!"

Rowenaster got to his feet, beginning to pace again. Everyone watched in silence. As he walked, the woman in black on the other side of the hedge played idly with Zendrak's Kindrasul. She fingered each of the marked beads haltingly, reading the inscriptions on the black glass through the tingling in her thumb and forefinger. Shadowy images formed in her mind. Kelandris blinked, her expression surprised.

Rowenaster stopped pacing. Turning to face the mutinous but captive class in front of him, he asked, "How many of you believe in the Presence?"

Thirty-six out of a possible eighty-nine raised their hands slowly.

"And how many believe in the Faces of the Presence? I'm talking about the Greatkin, of course—*including* the Wasp," he added drily to Torri.

Half of the hands raised stayed up. Tree's was one of them.

"I see," said Rowenaster, his shoulders sagging.

Torri interrupted here. "Tell me, professor—was it your intention to convert us into believers through this class?"

Rowenaster shook his head. "No. Nothing that simple."

A few of the more sympathetic students tittered.

"Then, what *was* your intention, Rowen?" asked Tree unexpectedly.

Rowenaster smiled sadly at him. "I was hoping to expose you to Mystery. I was hoping to bring you into contact with something larger than yourselves. I was hoping to move you to wonder." The professor paused, looking toward the direction in which he had sent the chastened Widdero. "Perhaps I should send you *all* home. Clearly, no one has entered the Great Maze this afternoon free of their everyday 'strings.'"

"You make this field trip sound like an initiation rite!" Torri protested.

"Do I? Well," said Rowen thoughtfully, "maybe it is."

"You're also creating mystery where there isn't any," Torri continued.

"Perhaps—perhaps not. I certainly didn't create the mystery standing on the other side of this hedge. Obsidian is not natural to our *draw*, Torri. A solid block of cut glass. We 'moderns' can't duplicate it. Think of that."

Tree did, and it gave him chills.

At that moment, Kelandris squawked like a bird.

The woman in black stared wildly at the glass bead held between her thumb and forefinger. She had just found Zendrak's Mythrrim perspective on the events in Suxonli sixteen years ago. Voices. Images. Kelandris shook her head, her green eyes dazed. Here was the *whole* story.

Kel's animal exclamation surprised and perplexed Rowenaster. He turned around. He walked cautiously toward the central chamber of the spiral, his students scrambling to their feet and following him in curious silence. Jaws dropped at the sight of the twenty-foot winged statue. As Rowen's class assembled behind him, Kelandris stood up, the feet and chest of the Mythrrim Beast framing her tall body.

Rowenaster frowned, his expression bewildered.

Themyth's daughter bowed to the group, saying, "Welcome, O my kin. Gather round, and you shall hear a Mythrrim of old made new in the telling of this time and place. Come, come—don't be afraid. I speak for us all."

Rowen's class hesitated, waiting to see the professor's reaction.

Tree nudged Rowen. "That's *her*," he whispered.

"Who?"

"The woman that scared Doogat. Po drew me a picture of her."
Tree paused. "She's crazy as a loon, Rowen. What do you think
we should do?"

"Humor her," said the old man and proceeded to sit down.

The rest of the class followed suit—all except Tree. Seeing
that he was the only one standing, the Jinnjirri squatted beside
the professor and asked, "Are you *nuts*? Po says she's got a
knife—"

"Yes," replied Rowen cooly. "And there's something odd in all
this."

"What's *that* supposed to mean?" asked Tree, wondering if
Rowenaster was addling right in front of him.

"It means, sit down and shut up!" replied Rowen in a low,
urgent voice.

Tree snorted but did as he was told.

Kelandris smiled beatifically at them all. Then, clearing her
throat, she proclaimed, "We shall call this Mythrrim by its proper
name. Now listen and attend."

Chapter Thirty-Four

THE TURN OF TRICKSTER'S DAUGHTER

In the winter, in the dead of winter
In the mountains, in the snowy mountains
In a warm cave, in a warm, wet cave,
Civilization gave birth

To Trickster's maverick daughter.

She was the bloom of Story,
She was the flowering of earth,
She was the wild seed of Heaven.
In a warm cave, in a warm, wet cave,
No one hailed the impossible birth

Of Trickster's dark-haired daughter.

In Suxonli for seventeen years,
The Wild Kelandris slept
In waiting silence for seventeen years,
Wild Kelandris kept covenant
With the cave, with the warm, wet cave:

She was Trickster's dormant daughter.

Until one sacred eve when Greatkin power readied,
Until one sacred eve when Greatkin power called
A stranger to touch her blessed loins and heart
In a forest bed, when Greatkin power made
Her warm cave wet with fertile blood

And roused Trickster's randy daughter.

But while the Wasp Queen coupled with her mate,
A boy cheated at the King's testing fire.
While the Wasp Queen loved her chosen mate,
Yonneth inflamed himself with deviant desire.
Soaring drunk on Rimble's Remedy—
Yonneth lusted for Trickster's lovely daughter.

His penis cruel from thoughts of raping,
Yonneth hunted the wood for the Wild Kelandris' flower.
While his sister's dewy bloom was sweet lovemaking
With the velvet touch of dark-eyed night,
Yonneth hunted, he hunted the wild, wet wood

For the rosy petals of Trickster's smiling daughter.

But deviance itself foiled Yonneth's brutal desire:
While the Queen learned kindness from the giving green,
Yonneth stumbled under spell of the holovespa liar
And railed against the power of unrequited dreams.
Weeping, he wandered lost in phantasmagoric mire

Far from the blush of Trickster's blossoming daughter.

Now the Queen rose from her forest bridal bed,
Now the Queen danced to the droning village drum,
Now the Queen turned to the rise of her own ecstasy,
Spinning alone, spinning free, the Queen soared
On the passionate wings of her Greatkin female-*he*.

All hail, Trickster's hermaphroditic daughter.

Calling the Hive, she summoned Suxonli's mind,
Pricking herself, she summoned eight more in kind.
This was the nest for the shock of the new,
The fate of the many rested on these few.
Here was a Tammirring revel, not a Jinnjirri one
Here was an ecstasy to which Yonneth could not come.

So Yonneth was angry with Trickster's Daughter.

Someone will pay, the Jinnjirri said
Someone will come to my raping bed.
So Yonneth took foul pleasure behind a silent tree
From a young girl dazed on Rimble's Remedy,
Yonneth forced Fasilla to his brutal bed.
He smiled as her screams drowned out the repeating call
Of Trickster's turning daughter.

The Queen spun faster, the dance blurred round the fire!
Hive mind united; suddenly rage and rape were the
Queen's own mire
The Queen's mind fell through Yonneth's shifting maw.
Shock! Shock entered the Queen, shock entered the *draw*!
Power surged and streamed, power screamed and
Faltered . . .

Inside Trickster's disoriented daughter.

Stumbling, the *he* lost control of Rimble's line;
Eight were too few to ground Yonneth's rage
T'was a bad beginning for Rimble's first nine.
As the minds of his circle began to cook and burn,
All Suxonli was swept into the searing rogue turn

Of Trickster's injured daughter.

Flesh blackened as eight innocents fell dead,
What power was this? Why was the Queen still alive?
Then a boy emerged from the autumn wood

Bearing the wrong answer for the questioning Hive:
With glee, he threw bloody underwear at the masked face

Of Trickster's menstruating daughter.

Outraged, the meanest Elder of all proclaimed:
   "You have broken the Blood Day Rule,
   Suxonli's daughter has broken village law,
   Like a child, you played with maverick power,
   Like a child, you tampered with Tammirring *draw*.
   You knew the rule,
   You knew the law.
   Like an adult, you shall be punished
   For all Suxonli's sake."

Then, they bound Trickster's taboo daughter.

The ropes charred, they fell away
In unspeakable sympathy, the ropes would not stay.
The spirit, hands, or heart
Of Suxonli's Wild Kelandris,
The ropes would not take part in Suxonli's rejection

Of Trickster's Greatkin daughter.

Now Kelandris spoke her mind:
   "You took a drug as you drummed the fire,
   You swallowed yellow holovespa liar.
   Weak, O my people, weak is this Hive—
   Were you stronger of will, eight might be still alive!
   Suxonli is Tammirring's disgrace,
   You have averted your eyes from Trickster's Face.
   You are lazy and soft, O village mine,
   Yet, stand ready to assault
   The only one soaring at the ancient fire
   Without the straw wings of holovespa liar!"

So said Trickster's defiant daughter.

The Hive swarmed, the Hive hissed
Against the insolence of Kelandris.
The sting of a whip cut open her back

As each conscience lashed out
With the cruel whine and cruel crack
Of Suxonli's village law.

Beware you wasp-tongued Daughters!

Sick with the toxin of repeated stings,
Kelandris wept, searching the night
For her green-robed King.
He answered by mind, appalled at her pain,
Returning through time while the murderous Hive
Gave Kelandris the very drug she decried

To silence Trickster's truthful daughter.

Begging Trickster to allow her to die,
Kelandris fell to the ground, barely alive.
Now something shimmered in blue and black,
Thundering hoofbeats of the Green King come back.
He knelt by his mate, he beat away the Hive

And protected Trickster's savaged daughter.

The Hive pressed forward.
Smelling the drug on their breaths,
Zendrak spat and cursed the spot.
Unafraid of masks and revel, torchlight,
He stared into their eyes,
And promised the *draw* of Suxonli would rot
For the crime commited against Kelandris tonight,

Such was his love for Trickster's only daughter.

Touching her battered body with a lover's care
the King lifted the Queen to the back of his mare,
Riding in silence, they left Tammirring.
Now Zendrak crossed the border shift and wilds,
Listening to the Queen's frantic whimpering—
He realized she would lose their unborn child.

Zendrak wept for Trickster's sad daughter.

His beloved entered a private world of pain

For sixteen years at the Yellow Springs,
His love made the dark journey of the insane.
Under the watchful eye of a certain Aunt
By the water, by the iron medicine water,

Zendrak left Trickster's mad daughter.

The journey was long, and longer still,
Healed of body but not of heart,
Crazy Kel refused the daylight of sunlit climes,
Preferring the dark gray of her shadow rhymes
Instead of her Green King's summer thaw:

Such was the despair of Trickster's wounded daughter.

There would be no renewal for any *draw*,
No common ground of change,
No life-giving fertility
From the woman in mourning black;
Such was the supposed sterility

Of Trickster's *akindo* daughter.

Like father, like daughter,
She's contrary but not always wise,
And she'll continue to masterfully block
The schemes of the one with pied eyes.
Unless Rimble turns her heart—there'll be no dance

Of remembrance by Trickster's ice-queen daughter.

Meanwhile, the Green King waits for the new bloom,
Meanwhile, the Green King warms the winter soul
Of Trickster's frozen ground
Like patient time knowing spring will come again,
Zendrak collects a new circle of more seasoned kin

For Trickster's winterbloom daughter.

Staring very hard at the mesmerized faces of both Rowenaster
and Tree, Kelandris broke off suddenly. Then she whispered,

"And you shall be outcast one and all if you heed the heresy of Trickster's wild call."

Eyes locked between the three in silent, astounded recognition of their naturally occurring deviant nature. Kelandris swallowed hard, covering her mouth with a bewildered hand. Then, shaking her head violently, Kelandris muttered sharp cries of denial. Before Rowenaster or Tree could say anything, the woman in black climbed out from under the obsidian legs of the Mythrrim statue and fled down the path that had brought her into the Great Maze of Speakinghast.

Torri broke the stunned silence. "Hey, professor—*that* was a good one! You really had me going there for a while. I mean, on our way in here I was thinking maybe you'd gone stark raving or something." She and the rest of Rowen's class grinned with renewed appreciation for the professor's off-beat teaching methods. "And *all* the time, you had this wild actress waiting to speak poetry to us—Mythrrim style. Hey, and *now* I see why Widdero had to go. He was going to spoil everything, wasn't he? I mean, what if we'd decided to leave in a huff or something? That ball of yarn—well, we could've found our way out with that." Torri beamed at Rowen. "Pretty amazing piece of street theater, professor. *Wait* till I tell Widdero how he nearly messed everything up. He'll stop being sore right then and there. He'll be amazed—and sorry he missed the fun. Wow, professor," she added breathlessly. "You're *brilliant*."

Rowenaster blinked, then, realizing that Torri was expecting him to answer her, he smiled woodenly. Feeling suspended between some ancient place and the present, Rowen muttered, "Thank you."

Chapter Thirty-Five

NEITHER TREE NOR Rowenaster spoke much on their way out of the spiral labyrinth. Excusing himself from the professor's company, Tree headed for the comforting walls of the Kaleidicopia. He arrived in time to see Janusin open the door to Doogat, Trickster disguised as Old Jamilla, and a young Tammirring girl. Tree stopped where he was, wondering if Doogat would talk to him about the woman in black who had spoken poetry in the maze. Tree licked his lips, desperately wanting some answers. He felt light-headed and very nervous about something. He knew the woman in black was responsible for some of it, but he didn't understand why or how. He ran his fingers through his frosted Jinnjirri hair, his hand shaking. Tree decided to enter the K.

Seeing the color of Tree's hair, Doogat walked toward Tree, his expression thoughtful. When he reached the Jinnjirri, he said, "What happened to you?"

Tree shrugged. "That woman—the one at your place this morning?"

Doogat stiffened. "Yes?" he asked intently.

"Well, she's—she's very strange, isn't she?"

Doogat pursed his lips. "Where did you see her?"

"In the Great Maze. Rowen took his class in there. Field trip." Tree cleared his throat uncomfortably. "That woman was in there. Under the Mythrrim statue. She—she started talking. Uh—speaking. Kind of formal like. In verse." Tree shook his head, tears coming to his eyes without warning. He fought for emotional control. "She told such a sad story. I can't get it out of my mind. Doogat—I'm—so scared. I don't know what's going on," he whispered, his voice catching. "Please—I want it to *stop*."

Doogat grunted, gratified to learn that Kelandris had spoken as a Mythrrim. It meant his operation of psychic release on her had been successful. Turning his attention back to the trembling Jinnjirri before him, he said, "Where is the woman in black now?"

Tree shrugged. "She stared very hard at Rowen and me at the end of it all. I guess she didn't like what she saw because she started cursing Greatkin Rimble and this fellow in the poem. Zen—something."

Doogat winced. "Go on," he said unhappily.

Tree nodded. "Then she ran away. And this stupid Saämbolin girl started jabbering at Rowen. Something about him being a brilliant teacher. It was real hard to even understand what the girl was saying. I felt like I was two people at once—a student on a field trip and someone I didn't know. I *knew* things, Doogat. Weird things."

"And you felt older than your years?" asked Doogat calmly.

Tree started sobbing in earnest now. He nodded his head several times, unable to speak. Doogat regarded him with compassion and pulled the twenty-one-year-old to his chest. He held him close while Tree bawled.

Hearing the sound of Tree's crying, Janusin poked his head out of the kitchen. Seeing the terrified frost of Tree's hair, the sculptor walked toward Doogat hastily. When he reached the two men, Janusin said, "Sweet Presence, Tree—what *happened*?"

Doogat handed Tree a green handkerchief from inside his pocket. Frowning at the telltale color, he handed it to Tree and wondered if Trickster had planted a green handkerchief in his change of clothes for a reason. On the other hand, he thought, Tree's favorite color was green. Perhaps "Old Jamilla" had known Tree would show up at the house—*with* the information he needed about Kel's well-being. Rimble-Rimble.

"Tree's all right," said Doogat quietly to Janusin. "Or he will be in a bit. Nothing that a cup of Barlimo's black brew won't fix," he added. "Shall we?" Doogat asked, pointing Tree toward the Kaleidicopia's swinging kitchen door.

"Good idea," said Tree when he'd caught his breath.

Tree's calm was short-lived, however.

While Janusin poured steaming cups of Barlimo's favorite dark tea, Doogat made introductions. Hearing the name "Yafatah of *Suxonli*," Tree shrieked. His hair lost all pretense of balance, pale green shifting to stark white. Janusin stared at Tree, toothless Old Jamilla, and Doogat.

"An explanation would be nice," said the sculptor to the Mayanabi Master, his expression bewildered.

"*I'll* say," said Tree warmly. "A nice, cozy explana—"

Old Jamilla smiled at this point. Tousling Tree's hair, she interrupted gleefully, saying, "Too many explanations make you stiff, boyo—like wood."

Tree jerked his head away from Trickster, his eyes angry.

Doogat gave Trickster a look of disapproval—which Trickster ignored—and answered Janusin by saying, "Seems Tree and Rowen spent part of the day with someone else from Suxonli. Kelandris. The same woman who knifed Po."

Old Jamilla inclined her head, her expression sly. Doogat watched to see what Trickster was going to do. When the old crone continued to drink her tea complacently, Doogat wondered if maybe he had misread the look on Trickster's face. Perhaps Trickster wasn't *always* up to something.

Janusin put his hands on his hips. "Seems everybody in this

house has met up with this woman in black—except me! Even Mab's aware of her. Did I miss something?"

"*I* haven't met her," retorted Timmer from the floor of the commons room. The Dunnsung was busy transposing music on a sheet of brilliant white paper. Humming a few bars to herself and making inky notes with a feather pen, she yelled, "Maybe this Tammirring Terror is Po's soulmate in disguise. Knifing Po was just her way of getting close. Tammi fashion."

Yafatah, who had been listening in silence until now, left the group and walked into Timmer's view. "She do be no terror," said the girl. "She do be a very sad lady. And I'll thank you not to slur me *draw*," added Yafatah indignantly.

"Excuse *me*," replied Timmer in her haughtiest voice. "And just who are you, anyway?"

"Me name be Yafatah. Master Doogat says I will be living here—with me ma, of course."

"*Live* here!" said Timmer, spoiling the notation she was making. Swearing first at her own clumsiness and then at Doogat's meddling, Timmer got to her feet. She brandished her feather pen like a sword and stormed into the kitchen. "I *demand* a house meeting. Everyone's here except Rowen, and Barlimo. That's a quorum. And you," she said pointing the wet pen at Doogat, "will be first on my shit-list!"

"I beg your pardon?" said Doogat cooly.

Timmer advanced on the Mayanabi Master, her eyes blazing. "You don't live in this house, Doogat—*we* do! You're Po's teacher, and that's as far as your influence goes here at the 'K.' We accept new members by vote—our vote—and nobody's voted on this little Tammi brat! Or her mother! Do I make myself clear?"

"Perfectly," said Doogat.

Trickster started laughing. His mouth was toothless, his guffaws loud, and his pied-eyes wild. Everything about Trickster was an exaggeration, even his humor.

Doogat took a deep breath. "Perhaps this would be a good time to tell them, Jammy," he said to the amused Greatkin.

"Tell us what?" asked Po, entering the kitchen. He had been listening to Timmer's tirade from inside his first floor bedroom. He thought Timmer had done an admirable job of taking Doogat down. Smiling, the little Asilliwir took a seat at the kitchen table. Yafatah, who had returned to the kitchen, was standing behind Po's chair. She sniffed the air uncomfortably.

"Doon't you bathe?" she asked.

Po shrugged. "I'm Asilliwir. We're used to going for long periods of unwash. Caravan life," he added grandly, expecting Yafatah to know nothing about any of it.

Yafatah snorted. "I be kin to Clan Abbiri. We do be one of the oldest caravans in all Asilliwir. And *we* wash!"

Po's face turned as scarlet as his dirty tunic.

All of Po's housemates burst out laughing.

Timmer regarded Yafatah with grudging interest. "Well, maybe I was too hasty," she admitted. Then the Dunnsung added, "But can she pay her rent, Doogat?"

The Mayanabi took a deep breath. "It doesn't matter if she can or not, Timmer—"

"It certainly does," retorted Janusin.

Doogat regarded the sculptor kindly. "No, it doesn't." Doogat waited to see if anyone else wished to contradict him. Everyone remained silent. Everyone except Old Jamilla. Picking up one of the invitations to the Kaleidicopia's Trickster's Hallows that lay in a neat stack in the center of the kitchen table, Trickster began humming an odd little tune. It got on the nerves of everyone present with the single exception of Yafatah. Janusin grabbed the invitation out of Trickster's gnarled hand, slapping the beautifully calligraphied paper back on top of the pile. Trickster immediately reached for it again. Janusin moved the pile.

"Stop snooping," said the sculptor with irritation.

Trickster beamed at him. "It's my nature."

"Well—curb it, will you?" snapped Janusin. The invitations were his contribution to the Hallows. They had been expensive, and he didn't want unnecessary fingerprints all over them. The sculptor crossed his powerful arms over his chest, glaring at the short little crone.

Doogat cleared his throat loudly. "Mind if I steal back center stage?" he asked Trickster. "I mean, I *was* saying something of importance here."

Trickster batted her eyes at Doogat. "*Do* continue."

Doogat gave Trickster a weary look and turned to Timmer. "Yafatah doesn't need to pay rent. She and her mother will be here as my guests."

Timmer wagged a finger at Doogat. "You can't *have* guests, Doogat. Only house members can have guests. You act like you *own* the 'K'!" she added with disgust.

"I do."

There was a stunned silence. At that moment Barlimo walked

into the kitchen, a bag of groceries in her arms. Heads turned immediately to Barlimo. Everyone present begged her to refute Doogat's statement. The Jinnjirri shrugged. "Sorry, loves. It's true. The Kaleidicopia belongs to Doogat. I'm simply the architect." Chuckling at their disappointed faces, Barlimo added, "Oh, come on, my friends. Did you really think I ran this place out of my own pocket? The Kaleidicopia takes up half a city block—in the nicest section of the Jinnjirri Quarter. Even an architect's salary needs supplementing under conditions like these. And Doogat's been that supplement. So before any of you go pulling any *more* long faces, those of you behind in rent can *thank* him for his charity of heart."

Nobody said anything.

"Such a well mannered lot," remarked Old Jamilla drily.

"Yeah," said Doogat. "They remind me of you."

Old Jamilla made a rude sound with her lips and stared distantly out of the kitchen window. Then she said, "Rowen's on his way back."

"I don't see anything," said Barlimo, craning her neck to put herself in Old Jamilla's line of vision.

"Perhaps I was mistaken," said Trickster, turning to look at the closed kitchen door. "Everyone here is so uncommonly contrary, it's difficult to tell you apart."

Now Mab walked slowly into the kitchen. Her slippered feet made no noise on the tile floor. She was wearing a pink bathrobe and looked sleepy. Tree regarded her worriedly. Mab smiled and patted his hand. "I'm much better than I was," she whispered. "Started feeling more myself about two hours ago. Around noon."

Tree frowned, a strange thought popping into his mind. Noon was just about the time that Rowen's class had entered the labyrinth of the Great Maze. Well, that was ridiculous—connecting the two events.

The front door of the house opened and slammed shut. As predicted, the professor had returned home. Seeing strange capes hanging on the pegs in the hallway, Rowen headed for the kitchen, his expression dour. He was more than a little relieved to see Doogat.

"I have to talk to you," said Rowen in a low voice that only Doogat could hear. "I witnessed something *very* strange this afternoon."

"After dinner, Rowen," said Doogat. "I think this is a house meeting."

Rowenaster scanned all the faces. "So it is," he said grumpily. "I should've known I'd get no peace of mind *here*. And all I've been thinking about for the past hour is a hot tub for these poor bones." He sighed mournfully.

Timmer rolled her eyes. "He's trying to get out of the house meeting."

"Please?" asked Rowen, pouring on his old-man waifish charm.

"Take a vote," announced Timmer. Then, turning to Doogat, she added nastily, "Or don't we get to vote anymore, *Master* Doogat?"

Doogat shrugged. "Go ahead and vote."

So they did, and Rowenaster was given permission to bathe unanimously.

As the old man stumped out of the room, Yafatah said, "What be his name?"

Barlimo clucked her tongue at herself. "Heavens, child—I forgot you hadn't been introduced. We'll do the honors at dinner. That's at eight sharp," she added to Yafatah and Old Jamilla.

"Can't stay—though thank you very much for the invitation," said Trickster smiling at Barlimo. Then, making an unexpected departure, Trickster bowed to Doogat, and left via the back door.

No one noticed that the invitations to the Hallows also left with the pied-eyed crone. She had stolen them during the testy vote over Rowen's attendance at the house meeting. Whistling between her gums, Trickster saluted a pair of particularly lovely looking autumn trees. The leaves rustled as the wind gusted suddenly. Now laughing with maniacal glee, Trickster threw Janusin's careful invitations into the air—literally scattering them to the four winds. Papers fluttered far and wide as Trickster personally selected those who'd attend the Hallows at the 'K.' Then Trickster began to turn. The clothes of Old Jamilla blurred and fell to the ground. They were empty. Down the street, a whirlwind of leaves pirouetted. Now they blew high into the air, joining the dance of black and yellow invitations as they drifted to each guest on Trickster's elite list.

One invitation dropped so suddenly out of nowhere that it scared a bay gelding pulling a happincabby as he clopped rapidly through the city streets. The bay reacted by shying, nearly upsetting the happincabby. As it was, the gelding's Saämbolin driver had to scramble to stay on the carriage. When the driver had recovered the reins, he noticed one of the wheels of the happincabby was loose. He pulled his horses to a stop. The Jinnjirri passenger inside the cab stuck his head out.

"What's the problem?"

The driver hopped to the ground, flinging Trickster's invitation through the open window. "Somebody's litter scared my horse," he muttered as he jumped off the cabby and investigated the wheel.

The Jinnjirri inside read the invitation carefully. He reread the invitation twice more, feeling more and more agitated as he did so. He knew this feeling. It was an aching in the heart. It was a calling that demanded an answer sooner or later. He had felt it once in Suxonli—sixteen years ago when his sister was turning for the Hive as Rimble's Revel Queen. He had been too drugged out on holovespa and too high on the adrenaline rush of rape to respond that time. But this time, he thought, a slow, smug smile spreading over his lips, *this* time he'd be there. Oh, yes indeed.

Cobeth folded Trickster's invitation neatly and put it in his pocket.

Chapter Thirty-Six

FASILLA LOST HER temper with Aunt. If the Jinnjirri healer wasn't going to help her find Yafatah, then she had no more time to waste talking to her. Fasilla got up from her bed inside the red and blue caravan wagon and started for the door. Aunt started swearing at her, the Jinnjirri's long hair turning four shades of crimson. Fasilla turned around, her eyes furious and hurt.

"Aunt—we do be friends for many years. Doon't let's spoil it. I must go and find me child. This do be a fierce large city. There do be all kinds of people here. Some of them be good. And some of them be bad."

"Yes," agreed Aunt getting to her feet. "But why do you *automatically* assume your very careful, very smart daughter is going to run into the bad ones? Trust the child, Fas. You can't keep her tied to you like some kind of animal. She must be free to explore. She must be free to make mistakes—"

"*No!*" cried Fasilla, her expression wild. "No, Aunt. She

doon't have to be free to make mistakes! You do be very wrong! Very!"

Aunt's eyes narrowed. "What's wrong, Fas?" she asked, her voice suddenly calm as she dropped into a healer's light trance. Her hair shifted to obvious opalescent white.

"Doon't you be trying to doctor me, Aunt. I be in no mood for all your Mayanabi tricks," Fasilla added, all her previous prejudice returning. "You doon't have a child of your own—"

"I have Burni," snapped Aunt. "And any number of other children who come to learn from me. Giving birth to a child is a wonderful thing to do, Fas—"

Fasilla started laughing at Aunt, her expression bitter. "Yes, when the child is expected. Or wanted." Fasilla's voice caught. "It took me months to want Yafatah. Months. She doesn't know this and I don't ever want her to find out. You understand?"

Aunt hesitated. "Do I need to remind you how sensitive Yafatah is? She's a Tammi, Fas. You can't hide things like this from a Tammi."

Fasilla started to retort then slumped against the wall. Tears slipped down her cheeks as she cried without sound. Aunt considered holding Fasilla in her arms, but decided against it. She suspected Fasilla was very close to telling her about the night in Suxonli. Such memories had to find their own way to the surface. All Aunt could do was be there when Fasilla gasped for air. Aunt sat on the bed again, trying to give Fasilla both physical and psychic room in which to speak freely. She wished Doogat had told her sooner about Fasilla's rape. Until three weeks ago, she had not known of Fasilla's participation in the Trickster's Hallows at Suxonli. Aunt watched Fasilla cry, her expression compassionate. What a terrible night that was, she thought, remembering the condition of Kelandris when Aunt had arrived at the Springs to take care of her wounds. Aunt grimaced.

Fasilla wiped the tears off her face with the sleeve of her yellow tunic. Looking at Aunt sideways, she said, "I hate the Tammi, Aunt. I hate them." She swallowed. "I—I know that do sound fierce bad. Like you said, Yafatah be Tammirring born." She paused, flinching from her feelings, her back flat against the wall, her eyes shut tight. "You see—something happ—happened the night I—" she broke off, unable to say the word "conceived." She shook her head, her breathing ragged. "It be hard to love a child given in rape. And Ya was such a child."

Aunt said nothing, her expression sad.

Fasilla swallowed. "I did love Ya in time, of course. After I left Suxonli." She paused. "The villagers didna' agree that I had been raped, you see. One of the elders—her name was Hennin—told me over and over that I'd come to the Hallows of me own free will. So there be noo one to blame but meself. After all, Rimble be the Greatkin of Deviance and deviance, she said, isna tame. If Trickster saw fit to have his way with me, then it do be an honor," added Fasilla in a dull, pained voice.

"Elder Hennin said *that*?" asked Aunt with dismay.

Fasilla shut her eyes, rocking on her knees. "Over and over, Aunt. Seemed like every day." Fasilla clenched her fists. "I wanted to leave that cursed place—that Suxonli. But I couldna' do so."

"Why?" asked Aunt.

Fasilla's shoulders sagged. "Every time I started to cross them wretched Feyborne Mountains, I began to bleed. I didna' wish to kill the child—"

"You were trying to cross the border?"

Fasilla opened her eyes abruptly. "Of course not, Aunt. I told you, I didna' wish ill on the child. The rape be not her fault." Fasilla's voice was weary. "I tried to cross them Feyborne just to get free of *Suxonli*. Not Tammirring. But the *draw* wouldna' let me leave, Aunt. I swear it. The *draw* of Suxonli wouldna' let me leave."

Aunt frowned. She had never heard of such a thing. The Jinnjirri healer rubbed the back of her neck wondering if Fasilla had her facts straight. A rape on a hallucinogenic drug would have been a very traumatic, very terrifying thing. Aunt cleared her throat and said gently, "The villagers gave you no help after the revel? No healing?"

Fasilla laughed coldly. "They were too busy nursing their own wounds to be bothered with *mine*, Aunt. Besides, I wasna' Suxonli born. I be an Asilliwir outsider." Fasilla spat against the far wall. "Me clan? We wouldna' do such a thing to a person—be they outsiders or noo. We do be civilized, we Asilliwir. Not like them foul Tammi." Fasilla took a deep breath. "What healing I got, Aunt, I got from me own people—nine months after the revel."

"You left after Ya's birth?"

Fasilla nodded. "And I willna return there—ever. 'Tis a cursed, wretched place."

Aunt regarded Fasilla steadily. "And if Ya wishes to see her *draw*?"

Fasilla swallowed, her eyes downcast. "Then she will journey there alone. I willna' return to Suxonli."

Aunt nodded. "So you keep Ya away from her own kind. You make her Asilliwir so she won't hear the call of her Tammi *draw*. What love is this?"

Fasilla's eyes filled with tears again. She covered her face with her hands, unable to look at Aunt. "I canna' go there, Aunt," she whispered. "Presence forgive me—but I canna'."

Aunt got off the bed. She squatted beside Fasilla, stroking the younger woman's fine, brown hair. "I agree with you, Fas. You cannot return to Suxonli. But, my dearest friend, Yafatah may have to go there someday. None of us truly understands what a Crossroads Child is. In order for Ya to find out, she may have to go where you cannot follow."

"No!" cried Fasilla with sudden despair. "Doon't say this thing to me, Aunt! Doon't say this thing!"

Aunt pried Fasilla's hands away from her eyes. "Look at me, Fas." The Asilliwir met Aunt's even gaze with fury. Aunt nodded, saying, "I think my words come as no surprise to you. You carried this child, Fas."

"I doon't understand what you're talking about," she said angrily.

Aunt pulled a strand of hair away from Fasilla's lips. "I think you do. I think you knew there was something queer about Yafatah before she was born. You're not a stupid woman, Fas. I went to school with you, remember. You've got a good mind. You can put odd things together and see the sense in them."

Fasilla's face paled. "Shut up, Aunt. Just shut up."

Aunt ignored Fasilla's discomfort. "That night in Suxonli was also queer—"

"*Queer?*" shouted Fasilla with rage. "Be *that* what you call a rape?"

Aunt swallowed, her hands sweating, her expression hard. "You weren't the only one who was hurt that night, Fas. As you well know."

There was a stunned silence.

Fasilla started to get to her feet. Aunt grabbed her arm and held Fasilla to her previous kneeling position. Fasilla's eyes blazed. "Doon't *touch* me," she said in a low, dangerous voice. "You willna' make less of my pain. You willna' do what them Suxonli did to me. You willna say it was Rimble's will—"

Aunt slapped Fasilla, yelling, *"It wasn't Rimble's will!"*

Fasilla blinked, her cheek scarlet where Aunt had struck her. The fight suddenly went out of her. Fasilla gazed distantly at Aunt. "In Suxonli, they say the Presence do be a Trickster."

"Well, they're wrong!" snapped Aunt, the Mayanabi in her disgusted.

Fasilla said nothing, her expression disoriented. Then she muttered, "But Rimble do be a Face of the Presence, and even we Asilliwir call this Greatkin by roguish names."

Aunt took a deep breath. She moved toward Fasilla, sitting with her, her back against the wall of the wagon. Aunt stared at the wooden ceiling above her, choosing her words carefully. She glanced sideways at Fasilla and said, "Do you remember what you were like when you were five years old?"

Fasilla nodded.

"And when you were twelve?"

"Yes—so?"

"How about when you were sixteen? Do you remember what you thought, what you wore?"

Fasilla frowned. "Where do you be taking this?"

"Are you a five, twelve, or sixteen-year-old."

"Of course not, Aunt. I do be thirty-six."

"But you were all those ages once, weren't you. And at each one of them, you thought that was all you were. But at thirty-six, you can see that you're actually much, much more. You're every 'face' you've ever had. Every age you've ever been. The Presence is like that, Fas. It's a composite of all times, moods, and expressions of Itself. To say that the Presence is a Trickster is as stupid as saying *you* are nothing more than a five-year-old. You are that five-year-old, but you're also every age before and after. You wouldn't want to limit yourself by using a child's mind to solve adult problems, would you?"

Fasilla stared at Aunt. "But Greatkin Rimble doon't be five, Aunt."

"Of course not. However, Suxonli's idea of him is. Trickster, like any of the other Greatkin, is more than what he appears to be. Although you can't see the other Greatkin when you look at Rimble, his reality, in fact, rests on the entirety of the Presence. Uh—like my Jinnjirri femaleness rests on my maleness," she explained briefly switching gender. "Just because you can't see my breasts right now—that doesn't mean they're not there, Fas." To demonstrate the point, Aunt became a woman again. "If you think of me as *only* a man or *only* a woman, you miss the bigger picture. Likewise, if you think of the Presence as having but one face, then you understand the Presence with the mind of a five-year-old. That's why Trickster *is* Trickster, Fas. He's there to remind us that the Presence has many faces. That's why he's changeable. But changeable doesn't mean evil, Fas. It doesn't mean cruel. It doesn't mean deceit. Those are *our* constructions. That's what we do when we become afraid of change. We say it's Rimble's will when it's really our own. Rimble didn't rape you—Yonneth did. If Yonneth had answered the call of Kelandris—if *Suxonli* had answered the call of Kelandris—there would've been joy. Not violence. Deny Trickster, and you deny your own need to change. Suxonli denied Trickster that night. In so doing, they denied the Trickster in each of them. And in you, since you were there."

"What do you be meaning?" asked Fasilla slowly.

Aunt smiled at her friend. "Look at you, Fas. You're as angry with Suxonli now as you were all those years ago. In school, you were an easy going and merry soul. Suxonli froze you, Fas. Like it did to young Kelandris. You haven't been able to leave the trauma behind. You go over it daily, I wager—not that I blame you. Presence alive, woman—I'm not sure I could've borne the child of a rape. I'm not sure at all. Much less love her—as you clearly do."

A tear slipped down Fasilla's cheek. "I do love Ya," she whispered.

"I know," replied Aunt gently. "And you must let her change. You must give to her what Suxonli stole from you. And if you can't, you must let others do it in your stead. People die inside when they aren't allowed to change."

Fasilla swallowed. "You think I do be killing Ya's spirit?"

Aunt nodded. "I do. And that's not love, Fas. That's fear. Yours."

Fasilla sagged against the wall. "I doon't know how to be different."

Aunt took a deep breath. "You must try, my friend."

"Or?"

"Or Doogat has asked me to take you back with me to Jinnjirri."

Fasilla stiffened. "Without Ya?"

"Without Ya."

Fasilla's face paled.

Aunt got to her feet, offering Fasilla a hand up. "Come on."

"Where?" asked the Asilliwir, standing up without Aunt's help.

"To the Jinnjirri Quarter of Speakinghast. To a three storey monstrosity called the Kaleidicopia Boarding House."

Chapter Thirty-Seven

As THE TIME neared eight bell-eve, the commotion in the Kaleidicopia's large kitchen subsided. House members and guests filed into the dining room, each carrying a contribution for the table. Conversation was lively between everyone save Yafatah and her mother. The young Tammirring girl felt annoyed with her mother's continued anger over her brief exploration of the city shops and bustling streets. As Fasilla launched into yet another well meant litany of possible dangers, Yafatah slammed the platter of bread on the dining room table and stormed out of the house. She ignored her mother's sharp commands to return "this instant" and sat on the front porch of the Kaleidicopia, her mood sullen.

Yafatah heard the door open and close behind her softly. She stiffened, expecting to hear her mother's voice. She was very surprised to hear Barlimo's instead. She looked up as the fifty-year-old Jinnjirri plunked down beside her on the steps. Yafatah shrugged, saying, "I doon't be hungry, so doon't be asking me to come back to the table with you."

Barlimo grunted. "Then nobody gets to eat."

"Why?"

Barlimo shrugged. "I like to say grace, and I don't say grace until everyone's seated and silent at the table. Personally, I'm starved—so I'd appreciate it if you got over the sulks as soon as possible." The Jinnjirri smiled cheerily at the Tammirring.

Yafatah frowned. "I doon't be sulking."

"Oh. Well, maybe you Tammis call it something else. Where I come from, when a person goes off on their own feeling sorry for themselves—not to mention misunderstood—we Jinn call it sulking. Especially if it's aimed at making one person uncomfortable. And you've done that royally. Your mother's sitting in there crying."

Yafatah shrugged. "I doon't know what she be doing *that* for."

"You scared her, Ya—that's all."

Yafatah sighed, staring at a passing happincabby. "I doon't understand why she be so scared of everything, Barl. I mean, she wouldna' have come to the city if Aunt hadna' ridden with us. I like Aunt—Aunt's not scared." She paused. "I know I should be kind to me ma. But mostly I feel fierce angry with her these days. All I wanted to do was to see a bit of the city—on me own, you know. So I can have me own ideas. And if I run into trouble, then I run into trouble. A girl's got to have some time for thinking and dreaming. I canna' do that with me ma telling me how fierce bad everyone do be here in Speakinghast. Oh—what be the use?" Yafatah added miserably. "Even when she doon't be with me, I hear me ma's voice warning me about this and protecting me from that."

"Some protection is good, Ya—"

Yafatah whirled on Barlimo. "Not when it means I canna' buy a pastry in a shop because the shopkeeper will take advantage of me, or worse, the cream filling might be bad from sitting out too long. By the time I think all these things, I doon't want to eat the pastry. I want to toss it at me ma!"

Barlimo nodded. "So your mother needs to change. Aunt and Doogat are trying to help her do that right now, Ya. You must not foil their good efforts by sulking. You must come inside and teach your mother how to let you grow up."

Yafatah's eyes filled with angry tears. "*She* be the ma—not me. She should know these things already." Yafatah crossed her arms over her chest. "I do be the child here."

"Oh. I thought you were a girl growing up—a young woman taking on responsibilities of caring for others besides herself."

Yafatah's face blotched with fury. "That doon't be fair. You put me in a corner. I canna' win. I canna' be a child, and I canna' be a woman. That doon't be fair."

Barlimo chuckled. "Welcome to that celebrated malady called 'growing pains.' It's when you aren't one thing or another for a while. And you feel real uneasy inside all the time. You don't know where to stand with yourself. You get a little scared. Then you take it out on everybody around you. You want them to make the scare go away. But they can't, see."

"Why not?" retorted Yafatah.

"Because," said Barlimo kindly, tousling Yafatah's dark hair, "if they take away your scare, they take away your struggle. And they want you to have your struggle."

"*Why?*" demanded Yafatah.

"Because they want you to be that young woman you so deeply wish to be. Sulking is for children, Ya. Helping your ma become a better person is for adults. Now which world do you want to live in? The one that leashes you to your ma like a toddler, or the one that trusts you to explore the city streets using your good mind and clear eyes?"

Yafatah put her head in her hands. "You're mean, mistress Barl."

Barlimo laughed heartily. "When *I'm* mean, child, believe me—you'll know it. Now come on—stop being bored out here by your lonesome and have dinner with some of the strangest, most talented people in all Speakinghast. You want to see the city sights? Well, *we're* one of them. Ask the Saämbolin Housing Commission—they have all kinds of words to describe the Kaleidicopia. The house is famous, Ya. And you're privileged to be spending the night with us."

Yafatah regarded Barlimo warily, her grudge against her mother starting to weaken as her interest in the Kaleidicopia's residents increased. "Well, maybe I might have a little bit of dinner."

"Good," said Barlimo, getting to her feet. She ushered Yafatah through the brilliantly painted front door. By the time Yafatah and Barlimo returned to the dining room, Fasilla had collected herself. Barlimo smiled at all the curious faces before her and said, "Sit down, please, and we'll have grace."

Timmer rolled her eyes. "Greatkin lover," she muttered grumpily.

Doogat smiled.

As dinner progressed at the Kaleidicopia, Kelandris of Suxonli wandered the city streets, Zendrak's Kindrasul clutched tightly in her fingers. She left the Saämbolin Quarter and crossed the line into the Jinnjirri portion of the city, squinting at a large lime green and hot pink sign. It read: "Abandon normalcy all ye who enter here!"

Kelandris pondered the meaning of the sign and decided that this sector of Speakinghast might be more to her own liking. She fingered the new veil on her head that she had poached from someone's clothesline in a narrow alley. This veil, although black as usual, was not of the homespun variety. It was made of soft, shining silk and crowned Kel's head with elegance. She moved through the evening shadows silently as the full moon above cast soft, silver light on Kel's shoulders and broad back. Her formidable size coupled now with her burgeoning Mythrrim consciousness caused passersby to gape at this physical and spiritual giant of a woman. Kelandris was vaguely aware of their assessment of her, but she found it largely uninteresting. Her attention was focused on the steady heartpull of the Kindrasul that she carried in her left hand. Acting like a homing device of the soul, the Kindrasul brought her closer and closer to the man who loved her—to Zendrak of Soaringsea.

Without hesitation, Kelandris turned down a narrow street that would take her to Wise Whatsit Avenue—the location of the Kaleidicopia. The pull from the Kindrasul increased, and Kel stopped briefly, her hand clutched to her chest, her head bowed. She shut her eyes under her veil, puzzled by the pain she felt in her chest. It was not violent, nor was it particularly unpleasant. Still, it was uncomfortable—and she wished to relieve it. Should she continue following the pulse of the Kindrasul? Although Kel was no stranger to pain—emotional or physical—she had no liking for it. Yet, this pain—this ache—seemed different. It was as if something were straining to be born inside her, and as the pressure intensified, as the demand for emergence accelerated, Kel winced, aware of a bearing down sensation in her whole body—particularly her womb. She wondered at this. How could she feel pregnant when she had not made love for sixteen years? She took a deep breath, fighting off a new wave of pressure. The Kindrasul glinted in the pale moonlight. She held the obsidian beads in front of her face, her hidden green eyes studying the queer markings on each piece of glass. She wished she understood what they meant. Or why she felt it so necessary to follow the pull that they emitted. It seemed like it would be a whole lot easier to just throw the beads away and be done with this queer pain. Much easier. . . .

Kelandris considered lobbing the beads into a nearby watering trough. As she raised her hand, the beads poised for throwing, Zendrak's face flashed before her eyes. His expression was calm, but she could read sorrow in his dark eyes. Terrible sorrow—the kind born of desperation and need.

"And loneliness," she whispered.

Kelandris shrugged. Loneliness had been her constant companion since the Ritual of Akindo. She was used to the feeling; she accepted its continued, unrelenting presence in her life. The thought of living without loneliness struck her as a quaint fantasy—an idle impossiblity. To admit that she might now be faced with a true opportunity to mitigate her own loneliness by joining her life with that of Zendrak's was unsettling. Even as a Mythrrim, Kel experienced loneliness—perhaps more intensely now. She was not surprised by this or dismayed; Kel's loneliness was so integral to her personality that she was almost fond of it—as one might be of a long-time friend.

Still, she hesitated to throw the Kindrasul away.

Without knowing why she did so, Kelandris began to move in the direction of the Kaleidicopia again, the flash of Zendrak's sorrow haunting her. As she rounded the corner, the Kaleidicopia came into view. Kelandris gasped—not from the wild chaos of the building's construction—but from the burning she now felt in her heart. The hand that grasped the Kindrasul trembled. She felt lightheaded and deeply, deeply afraid of what lay just across the street from her. Kelandris jumped, as the front door to the three storey house opened abruptly. A man dressed in blue stepped out, his dark eyes turning in her direction almost immediately. Kel's heart pounded. She met the gaze of the man uneasily. She did not know who he was, but she felt like she should.

Doogat stepped off the front porch of the Kaleidicopia, walking toward Kelandris slowly. He approached her as one might a wild animal, aware that she stood ready to run from him at any moment. He stopped about six feet in front of her, his hands at his sides. His breathing was as ragged as Kel's was, his palms just as damp with the sweat of anticipation and fear. Doogat cleared his throat and asked, "Are you lost? Perhaps looking for a certain street?"

Kelandris shrugged, unsure of what to say. The power of the Kindrasul had her tongue-tied. She felt certain that she should flee from this man, and simultaneously she could not, would not leave. It was not that the black beads had paralyzed her will; rather, they had opened her to a possiblity that she could not ignore—namely, heart's peace. Kelandris frowned under her veil. Finally, she, too, spoke—clearly and without the rhyme of madness.

"I think I'm where I'm supposed to be."

Doogat nodded slowly. "Are you—are you meeting someone?"

Kelandris shrugged again. "Maybe."

Doogat's eyes fell on the black glass beads in Kel's hand. "You hold a Kindrasul," he said conversationally. "I haven't seen one of those in a long time. They're quite special."

"Oh," said Kelandris, wondering who this man was and why he insisted on speaking with her.

Doogat smiled. "Those aren't made for just anybody. You have to have attained a certain level of spiritual insight to cause a Kindrasul to open the Doors of Remembrance for you. A Kindrasul is a little like a universal translator for certain things."

"What kind of things?"

Doogat shrugged. "A greater understanding," he said quietly.

Kelandris snorted under her veil. She didn't like this man's cryptic remarks. They made her feel stupid—as if she *ought* to know exactly what he was talking about but didn't because he was deliberately withholding the connecting pieces of information that would make his comments intelligible to her mind. It was most irritating—and compelling. Again Kelandris considered leaving the presence of the man in blue and again decided to remain where she stood. There was something about this man that pressed her for recognition. Something about the eyes, she reflected. Suddenly, she realized that Doogat's eyes were the exact color and shape of Zendrak's.

Kelandris took a step backward, staring at Doogat's face. He was the wrong height, skin color, age, and build to be Zendrak—yet he smelled like her lover of sixteen years ago. Kelandris inclined her head as a dog might, literally sniffing the air to see if she could make sense of her visual confusion. She was aware of Doogat watching her intently. Kelandris swallowed, still unsure of what she was perceiving. No answers were forthcoming, however, so she gave up in frustration.

"Would you like a greater understanding?" asked Doogat, his voice still quiet. "One that might answer your soul ache?"

Tears started in Kel's eyes under her veil. The man's question had touched her unexpectedly. She pressed her lips together, praying that the man in blue wouldn't notice how much her hands were shaking. A tear slipped down her cheek. Her breath caught.

"Would you like a greater understanding?" asked Doogat again. This time his voice was a little more forceful, a little more direct.

Kelandris said nothing, another tear spilling down her cheek and dampening her veil. The man's question was like a gong. Every time he asked it, she felt a stronger answering resonance deep inside herself. It was terrifying. She felt emotions now that she thought were long dead. Stay dead, she told herself wildly.

For Presence sake—*stay dead*! If you don't, it's going to hurt. It's going to hurt bad—

Doogat watched her with disguised compassion. He could see that he was having exactly the effect he wanted to have on Kelandris: a thaw. Doogat pursed his lips and said drily, "Every cold spell needs a spring, Kelandris."

She stiffened at the unexpected mention of her name. "Who *are* you?"

Doogat ignored her query. It was his opinion that Kelandris needed to figure out the answer to that question without any help from him. If Kel realized that he was Zendrak, than he would know that her Mythrrim consciousness was fully operant—and that he could at last speak freely to Kel of their shared Greatkin heritage and mortal destiny. Until that time, Doogat dared not risk it. Too much information too soon could frighten Kelandris, thereby undercutting the trust he wished to develop with her. Doogat shrugged, and said, "You could let me be that Spring."

Kelandris crossed her arms over her chest. "I'm not a wasteland!"

Doogat arched an eyebrow. "Oh. My mistake. That black veil confused me. I thought you might be barren or something."

Doogat hit his intended mark—Kel's sorest point—the loss of her unborn child at the Piedmerri border. All of Kel's most savage emotions piled to the fore: rage, resentment, self-pity, and soul-wrecking despair. The emotions were so violent that—like the evils flooding out of Pandora's Box—they obscured the quiet, radiant voice of hope that now quickened in her heart. She railed in silence against Doogat's thaw.

Doogat reached into his pocket, pulling out a folded yellow piece of paper. It was one of Janusin's invitations to the Kaleidicopia's annual Trickster's Hallows. Doogat opened it slowly, saying:

"Well, if you're through mourning—perhaps you'd consider coming to this. It'll be held at that house," he continued, pointing to the fuschia door of the Kaleidicopia with his right hand. "Invitation only, you see. It's a masquerade. You won't get in without a costume—the more outrageous, the better," he added with a small smile.

Kelandris grabbed the invitation out of his hand, reading it swiftly. She stiffened as soon as she realized it was a Rimble's Revel. She threw the paper on the ground and replied haughtily, "I'm *akindo*. I don't get invited to parties. I'm alone in the world."

Doogat picked up the paper, watching that Kelandris didn't try to kick him as he leaned over. When he had straightened, he said matter-of-factly, "Then, you *are* a wasteland."

Kel's eyes blazed. She saw that this man—whoever he was—had cornered her expertly. If she agreed that she was a wasteland, she felt as though she would be giving in to the horror of the Ritual of Akindo all over again. Suxonli Village had tried to kill her and failed. Their failure had been a source of compensation to her over the years—and a source of perverse, stubborn pride in her ability to survive no matter what the conditions. On the other hand, if Kel agreed to the possibility of a real Spring, she agreed to the possibility of change. And two-legged contact again. The Mythrrim in Kel balked at this.

"I have no need of kin."

"All beings have need of kin, Kelandris," replied Doogat evenly. "Murderers and prophets alike. Why, even Mythrrim Beasts have need of kin. We are the creaturely source of kinhearth for the world. We are the ones who light the sacred fires. We tell the stories of Remembrance, hmm? Like the one about Trickster's Daughter?"

Kelandris stiffened. Although she had spoken the Mythrrim of *The Turn of Trickster's Daughter*, she had done so in a trance state and now recalled precious little of it in her conscious mind. Kelandris eyed the man in blue warily. "What is this *we* crap?"

"Oh—did I say we? How silly of me. Everyone knows Mythrrim don't exist."

There was a stunned silence.

Kelandris narrowed her eyes under her veil, watching the play of shadows on Doogat's face. The veil made it difficult to see him clearly, so she raised it. Doogat gave her a startled look but said nothing. Kelandris stared at Doogat, unable to figure out how it was that this short, round-bellied man could possibly remind her of raven-haired, six-feet-six Zendrak. Perplexed, she again sniffed the air. The scent of her lover filled her senses. Without warning, the Mythrrim in Kel took over. The woman in black snapped at Doogat playfully. It was a lover's nip—invitational and rowdy.

Doogat took a step backward. He longed to respond in kind, but he wanted Kelandris to realize who he was from the perspective of her conscious mind as well as from the purely instinctual. Otherwise, the power Kelandris commanded as a Greatkin might remain out of her control. She had already killed eight people during her last "turn" in Suxonli. Doogat did not wish the same to happen at the Kaleidicopia three days from now.

"See you at the party?" he said amiably.

"What?" asked Kelandris, bewildered by the sudden change of subject.

"Remember—wear a costume," he continued. "Makes it so much more fun for everyone, I think. Oh, and by the way—Zendrak will be there."

Before Kelandris could respond, Doogat whirled away from her. He walked swiftly to the Kaleidicopia. The door slammed shut behind him. Kelandris stared at the startling color of the door. Feeling disoriented and in some mild state of psychic shock, Kelandris pulled her veil down over her face again. Then, swearing softly, she slipped into the shadows. She would watch this house, she decided. She would watch it closely.

Chapter Thirty-Eight

BY THE TIME Doogat returned to the house, dinner was almost over. A few of the denizens of the Kaleidicopia sat sprawled in the commons room, their stomachs warm and full. Conversation was minimal as Janusin stoked the fire in the hearth, his handsome profile silhouetted against the dancing flames. To his right, Timmer strummed her lotari softly humming a lilting melody to herself and scribbling the notes down on paper as soon as she had them figured out. Feeling contrary tonight, Po decided to do the opposite of what people expected of him; he decided to be magnanimous. In truth, this was less Po's decision and more the growing influence of Greatkin Phebene upon Rimble's Nine. Still, it was a pleasant change and all welcomed it. Po walked into the room carrying a tea service for the entire dinner party. He set it on the round, low table in the commons room just as Doogat closed the front door to the house. Catching Doogat's strained expression out of the corner of his eye, the little thief turned to his Mayanabi Master and said, "You look lousy. Are you feeling all right, Doogs?"

Doogat nodded and ducked into the first floor bathroom. He

shut the door swiftly. Po's eyes narrowed. He poured tea for everyone, and, when he was satisfied that all had been served, he crossed the room to the bathroom. He knocked gently, saying, "Hey, Doogs—you want mint tea?"

Doogat's answer was unintelligible.

"Doogat?" asked Po, suddenly becoming concerned for the old man. In his opinion, Doogat had been acting extremely nervous all evening. Extremely tense. Perhaps Doogat was ill? Po tried the door. It opened easily. Po's eyes widened in surprise.

Doogat sat hunched against the wall of the bathroom, his sixty-two-year-old face streaked with tears. Doogat raised his head sharply. "Get out of here, Po!"

"Nope," replied Po, coming into the bathroom and shutting the door behind him softly. "Something's been eating you all night. I want to know what it is."

"Not now."

Po hesitated. He knew he was treading dangerous ground. He wondered if he felt up to being punched out by Doogat tonight. Deciding that he and his ear could take it, Po pursued his line of questioning firmly.

"Doogat—I'm not a *total* ass you know. I got eyes. Come on," he said squatting beside the Mayanabi, "even masters need friends. Talk to me."

Doogat rested his head against the bathroom wall, his dark eyes shut. "It's a very long story, Po," he whispered.

"Your stories are always long, Master Doogat. And I got all night."

Doogat opened his eyes slowly, genuinely touched by Po's unexpected concern for him. He smiled at the little thief through his tears. "You know, Po—you might make eighth rank yet."

Po scowled at Doogat. "Don't change the subject."

Doogat chuckled. " All right," he whispered, his voice hoarse. "The problem is very simple, Po—I'm in love with the woman who ripped up your right hand."

There was a short silence.

Po cleared his throat. "Simple," he said drily. "Interesting use of the word, Master Doogat."

Doogat smiled, wiping the tears off his face with the sleeve of his blue robe. "As I'm always telling you, Po—things are not what they seem on the surface. Someday, you may consider the scar across your knuckles an honor. Proof, as it were, of your direct contact with the divine."

Po took a deep breath. "I doubt it."

Doogat was silent. "I wonder," he said finally, "what would you do if you came face-to-face with a Greatkin?"

"Run like Neath."

Doogat smiled. "What do you think the others would do?"

Po cocked his head. "This a test?"

Doogat shook his head. "No. I'm just curious to hear your opinion."

"Well, *that's* a first," grumbled the little thief. Then, sitting down beside Doogat, the Asilliwir contemplated each member of the household. "Okay," he said, "I think it would go this way. I think Barlimo would take it in stride. She's a funny one, that Jinn. Nothing ever seems to unseat her. You may be the owner of the 'K,' Master Doogat—but you and I both know who really runs the place. And we're a pretty rowdy bunch of people to deal with on a daily basis. So I don't think a Greatkin would do much more than cause Barlimo to smile. She told me once that her life was touched by grace—that's why she insists on saying it at every meal."

Doogat nodded. "She told me that, too."

Po pursed his lips. "Let's see—Timmer. That's a rough one. Her music is very, very inspired—I mean, the stuff she writes and won't play for anyone. I caught her out in the studio one day, singing her heart out to the Presence. Greatkin, she was pissed. It was like I had caught her having sex or something."

Doogat raised an eyebrow. "Was she singing to a particular Face of the Presence?"

Po nodded. "Yeah. Jinndaven—the Greatkin of Imagination. It wasn't a petition or anything like that. She was just singing his praises. I think she'd just written a song that had popped out right on the first try. And she was thankful for the inspiration. Anyway, I'm not sure *what* Timmer would do is she suddenly found herself in the company of an actual Greatkin." Po grinned. "Course, if it was Jinndaven—she'd probably invite him to her bed. But I digress."

Doogat smiled.

Podiddley scratched his dirty earlobe. "Now, Janusin—I think Janusin would go all to pieces. The way he's worked on that Trickster statue day and night—talk about pure out and out devotion to his craft. Or perhaps even to Trickster himself. I know *I* wouldn't have worked on that statue like that."

Doogat chuckled, agreeing. "Hard work isn't exactly your most intimate friend, Po."

Podiddley scowled at Doogat. "That's *not* the reason I wouldn't have worked on the statue. *I* wouldn't have worked on it because it wears Cobeth's face. And if I had loved Cobeth as much as Janusin did, I wouldn't have had the heart to complete the fucking piece. But Janusin did. He finished it despite his grief. And it's not even a half-assed job, you know. I mean, Jan's so good he could've *done* a half-assed job, and the Great Library would've bought the statue anyway. Cobeth's a jerk for ever leaving Jan."

"I don't think Cobeth wants to be a sculptor, Po."

Po shrugged. "Yeah—that's how Janusin explains it, too. But just learning the craft isn't the whole picture, see. Janusin had other things to teach besides the right placement of a chisel."

"Like what?"

"Oh—devotion. Commitment." Po averted his eyes suddenly from Doogat's intense gaze. "The kind of shit you're always trying to teach me, Master Doogat." He coughed, adding, "Anyway, I think Janusin would start bawling like a baby in the presence of a Greatkin. He'd probably change gender a lot, frost his hair, and start sketching like mad."

"Sketching?"

"Sure. The face of the Greatkin—for his next statue." Po started to pick his nose, but Doogat interrupted him with a handful of privy paper.

"Disgusting habit, Po."

The little thief glared at Doogat. "Hey—I wasn't planning to eat it. At least not with you sitting here," he added impishly. He blew his nose with great fanfare.

Doogat rolled his eyes, thinking how much Po reminded him of Trickster at this moment—with a difference; Trickster *would* have eaten the contents of his nose. With great lip smacking and delight, no doubt.

Po cleared phlegm out of his throat and spat into the nearby privy. Then he continued with his evaluation of the Kaleidicopia's reaction to discovering a Greatkin in its midst. "Rowenaster. Shit—he'd probably have a heart attack, Doogs. And go out smiling. The old professor's loved the Greatkin all his life, I think. How else could he stand to teach first year students for fifty years? I mean, first year students are nice and all—but let's face it, Doogs, Rowen's an intellectual genius, and not one of those students can keep up with him. Not one. So he's got to be teaching for some other reason. I think it's out of love for the Greatkin."

Doogat nodded. "Yes."

Po licked his lips, counting off the house members on his fingers. "Let's see—did I miss anyone? Oh, yeah. Treesono-vohn." Po winced. "Boy, that's a hard one. Tree's a weird sort of fellow. Even for a Jinn. Tell you the truth, Doogs—I think Tree would handle it the worst. I think he'd come undone. He's funny around surprises—he doesn't like them much. Must be because of that accident in Jinnjirri—the one where everyone in his family got swallowed up by an earthquake. Everyone except him, of course. He told me he climbed a tree during the shift—that's why he looks like one. Kind of an homage to the one that saved his life. Anyway, I think Tree would be scared to death." Po paused. "On the other hand, Tree *has* been different recently. Ever since Mab got better. In fact," added the little thief, "in some ways, *everyone's* been different recently."

"How so?" asked Doogat, starting to feel a little calmer.

Po shrugged. "I'm not sure. This is going to sound crazy, I suppose, but it's almost like we've all been waiting for something to happen. And now it is—something, I mean." Po shrugged, running his grimy hands through his unkempt hair—what there was of it. "But see, I don't know what the 'something' is. Maybe it's the Trickster's Hallows. Maybe we've all been a little tense, and now that the thing is almost upon us, we can afford to relax. Except I don't remember it being like this last year." Po shrugged. "Janusin should've had an all-out Jinnjirri fireworks display of temper at the table tonight. And he didn't."

Doogat frowned. "What're you talking about?"

"Oh, yeah—you were outside when it happened. Well, seems that old biddy who visited her this afternoon made off with Janusin's invitations to the party. You remember how edgy he was when the hag kept fingering them in the kitchen? I mean, wouldn't you expect Jan to blow up when he found out they were missing?"

Doogat inclined his head. "Yes. I wonder why he didn't?"

"I asked him that very question."

"And?"

"And he said it was in Rimble's hands. Weird, huh?"

Doogat said nothing. Something about this interested him—something about the synchronicity of Janusin's relaxed response occurring at the same time he was talking to Kelandris outside in the street. Could it be that she really *was* going to turn after all?

Doogat's heart filled with a wild hope, his previous mood of despondency slowly lifting. He regarded Po with undisguised affection, thanking the presence in silence for Po's unwitting reassurance.

The little thief squirmed under Doogat's steady gaze. Then Po said, "That only leaves Mabinhil. Oddly enough, Doogs—I think she'd be overjoyed to see a Greatkin. I don't even think she'd cry—except maybe from happiness. I don't know what you did to her back at your place, but she's really different. I mean, I know you said you were just telling her bedtime stories every night, but I think maybe you might have been doing something more. Some kind of healing thing."

Doogat smiled. "It's very possible," he agreed cryptically.

Po rolled his eyes. "So did I pass?"

"Pass what?"

"The test?"

Doogat gave the little thief a hug. "Yes, Po—you did. Welcome to seventh rank, thirtieth degree."

Po stared at Doogat. "Uh—Doogs—now don't get me wrong, but aren't you *skipping* a bunch there?"

"Am I?" asked Doogat with a gentle smile. "You would've been seventh rank long ago, Po, except for one thing—your own spiritual ambition. As you progress in rank through the Mayanabi Order, you are given a certain amount of power—and with that power comes responsibility. Until tonight, you had not demonstrated to me that you were willing to serve anyone but yourself. I could not let you advance until you gave without thought of reward—O My Thief," he added formally.

"Oh," said Podiddley, his face scarlet with embarrassment. "Well—uh—thanks, Doogs. I mean for the new rank."

"Yes, but don't let it go to your head, will you?" said Doogat drily.

Po swallowed. "Yessir. What I mean is—I'll try not to. Well, you know how I am." Doogat nodded, and sighed.

Chapter Thirty-Nine

THE NEXT DAY, as Janusin and Timmer wheeled the statue of Greatkin Rimble out of the studio toward the brick patio behind the Kaleidicopia. Timmer asked Janusin to stop. She inclined her head, listening intently. She scanned the row of hedge between the property of the main house and its private stable. Janusin watched Timmer for a moment, frowning.

"What is it?" asked the sculptor impatiently. The Trickster's Hallows would begin in less than three hours, and he still had some last minute stitching to do on his lavender costume. He wiped sweat off his brow. "Timmer—come on. I want to get this statue in place."

Timmer ignored him, walking toward the bushes. She knelt down. The startled cry of a hurt dog soon followed. Janusin forgot his hurry and went to investigate. Timmer looked up as Janusin came up behind her.

"Looks like a stray—maybe a year old at best," said Timmer.

Janusin peered into the hedge. Before him lay a medium-sized hound with brindle markings, ugly ears, and pied eyes—one yellow, one black. The dog was panting heavily and seemed to be protecting her left front paw.

"Careful he—oops—she doesn't bite you, Timmer," said Janusin as the bitch showed her teeth when Timmer tried to examine the hurt leg.

Timmer nodded. "Aunt's a healer—think she's any good with animals?"

"I'll go ask."

While Janusin ducked inside the Kaleidicopia, Timmer soothed the dog with a gentle song. The dog's ears pricked up. The bitch made a feeble attempt to wag her striped tail. Timmer smiled at the dog, her eyes drifting toward the statue of Trickster. Having nothing better to do, Timmer talked to the dog about the upcoming party.

"Your timing sucks the royal," she informed the bitch. "We're having a *huge* party here tonight. So, where are we going to put you? The stables will be filled to bursting, as well as every guest room in the house. And I don't dare put you in the library or the greenhouse. Pups like you eat books and dig holes. And there'll be nothing but strange people about, dog—which'll just make you nervous." Timmer pursed her lips. "We don't want you to bite someone—assuming that we even get you into the house without you sampling one of *us* first."

The dog started panting again. Someone laughed behind Timmer. The Dunnsung musician looked up to find Aunt standing a few feet from her. Janusin, Mab, and Tree followed closely. Timmer frowned at Aunt.

"What're you laughing at?"

Aunt knelt beside Timmer. "This dog smiles when she pants. Look at the upturn of her lips. I've never seen anything like it." Aunt reached toward the brindle hound.

"Careful—" Timmer started to say.

The dog did not growl this time. Aunt lifted the dog's injured paw, feeling it expertly. The dog whimpered but did not resist the examination. Timmer was impressed at Aunt's skill and said so.

The Jinnjirri healer smiled. "Truth is, I'm more partial to animals than I am to two-leggeds. But the Presence seems to send me mostly two-leggeds to help. This bitch is a welcome change."

The dog's tail wagged.

Aunt smiled at the brindle stray. "*Look* at those wild eyes. Maybe we should call you Pi, eh? Short for pied? How would you like that?" Aunt asked the dog. Trickster—for of course it *was* Trickster—wagged her tail with more enthusiasm.

"Pi it is," said Timmer.

"Okay," said Aunt, slipping her hands under the fifty-pound body of the stray and lifting her carefully. Glancing at Janusin and Tree, Aunt said, "You Jinnjirri gents finish putting the statue in place. Timmer, you go and make a strong poultice of green patchou bark and sirridian. There's a jar of each in the pantry— Barl gave me the grand tour yesterday. Mab, honey, you fetch that stinking bottle of black antiseptic."

Mab's eyes widened. "Hope this mutt's not rabid, Aunt. She'll for *sure* bite you when you put that stinging stuff on her paw."

"Let's act positive, shall we?" replied Aunt with more confidence than she actually felt. Working with animals was always a risk, and Aunt had endured her share of bites, kicks, and scratches in her time. The Jinnjirri eyed Trickster and whispered, "I want to have a good time at this party tonight, old girl—so I'd appreciate it if you didn't reward my efforts to help you with a nip or worse, hmm?"

The dog's lips curled back into a smile.

Aunt, Mab, and Timmer walked slowly back toward the Kaleidicopia, Trickster nestled in Aunt's strong arms. Tree and Janusin watched the women disappear into the house. Tree sighed.

"Shit," he muttered. "I think we've just been adopted."

"*If* Barlimo says it's okay," replied Janusin, crossing the grass toward the statue of Greatkin Rimble. "Come on, Tree. Let's put this fellow where he belongs."

"In full view of the city street?" asked Tree drily. "Cobeth will love this. He'll take it as a compliment. Can't wait until he's installed in the park at the Great Library. Cobeth will become legend then," added Tree with a sour smile. "Why you had to use *his* face for a model, I'll never understand."

Janusin shrugged. "The ways of the artist are inscrutable."

"Not to mention those of Trickster himself," retorted Tree, recalling his encounter with Kelandris three days earlier. "You know—by having a Rimble's Revel, I think we sort of *invite* Trickster into our midst—if you know what I mean."

Janusin nodded, sighing deeply. "Working on this statue has been more trouble than you can imagine, Tree. There were some mornings when I could hardly bring myself to sculpt it. And not because of Cobeth, either."

"Why, then?" asked Tree starting to push the statue.

Janusin shrugged. "Rowen talked to me about it once. He says that whatever Greatkin his class studies, the force or the patronage of that Greatkin enters into his life and that of all his students. So if it's Phebene or something, everyone starts having torrid love affairs. When it's Trickster—nothing goes according to plan." Janusin paused. "That's how it's been with this statue. And some mornings, I *needed* for things to go according to plan. And of course they never did. Trickster's a bitch of an archetype to work for," he added, wheeling the statue into place in the center of the brick patio.

"Funny," said Tree wryly, patting the erect penis on the black marble from Tamirring, "*I* would've said Trickster's a prick."

Guests began arriving as much as two hours ahead of time. Barlimo swore as the doorbell rang for the third time in fifteen minutes. She told Rowenaster to answer it, as she was not yet done with food preparations in the kitchen. Janusin stopped in briefly to sample the punch that Fasilla was making. As the sculptor poured himself a ladleful of orange and pommin juice, Barlimo paused from cutting brown bread.

"Jan—do you realize those invitations must've traveled as far as *three* counties? There's people coming from *outside* the city to this thing. And they all have an invitation in hand."

Fasilla looked up. "Yafatah says Old Jamilla do be a Mayanabi Nomad. This means, she do travel far and wee."

Janusin complimented Fasilla on her punch and turned now to Barlimo. "Well—like I said. It's in Rimble's hands. Should be interesting to see who turns up."

"Yes," said Doogat, coming into the room. He had just been thinking about Kelandris and was again wondering if she would indeed come. He refused to think of the consequences if she didn't.

"Hey," said Po, walking out of the pantry, his arms laden with cheeses. "Doogs—you're not in costume."

Doogat looked over his shoulder. "Neither are you."

"But I will be," said Po, beaming. "Mine's a surprise."

Barlimo nodded. "I think I'm going to be sick of that word 'surprise' by the end of this evening." She backed away from the bread. "This bread's not cooked all the way through. And that, my friends, is impossible."

"Rimble-Rimble," said Rowenaster as he also dropped in to sample the punch. "Mmm—sweet. Very nice, Fas. Very nice." He wiped his lips and asked, "Where's Yafatah?"

Fasilla shrugged. "She's not speaking to me at the moment."

"I see," said Rowenaster. "Sorry."

"Doon't be," replied Fasilla evenly. "The child do be going through fierce bad times—that be all. It be her age."

Po dumped his load of cheese on the cluttered kitchen table, making everyone jump. He started to unwrap one of the yellow bricks, but Barlimo stopped him. She wagged a finger in the little thief's face, saying, "Wash you hands."

Po gave her a disgusted look and went to the sink. As he turned on the water, he looked back over his shoulder and said, "So, Doogs—how come you're not in costume. Aren't you coming to our little carnival?"

"No."

All motion and conversation in the kitchen came to a full stop. Rowenaster was the first to speak. "You're *not* coming? You said you thought that woman in black might show up. What're we to do if she does?"

"You'll know."

Barlimo said nothing. She was the only one of Rimble's Nine who knew that Doogat was in fact Zendrak. She did not know, however, that Zendrak was Trickster's son. Barlimo intentionally dropped a pan on the floor. The attention shifted to her. As it did so, Doogat smiled at her and ducked out of the kitchen.

Rowenaster turned back to speak to Doogat. "Where'd he go?"

The front door to the Kaleidicopia slammed.

Doogat stood for a moment on the front porch of the Kaleidicopia. His Mythrrim senses told him that Kelandris hid nearby. Doogat had come and gone from the house freely for the past three days. The fact that Kelandris had not approached him during this time did not bode well. Doogat stuffed his hands in his pockets. It was imperative that Kelandris recognize him as Zendrak while he still wore Doogat's "face." Kelandris must not be unconscious when she turned tonight—*if* she turned tonight, he reminded himself sourly. He shut his eyes wearily, his head bowed. Kelandris was strong, stubborn, and committed to survival—her own. What *else* did he need to do to convince the woman in black that more was at stake here than her personal pain and grief? Would she ever stop wearing the clothes of mourning? Doogat swore softly. He was angry with Kelandris now. Very. The woman's narcissism was beyond belief. If she had been a mere mortal, he would've been more sympathetic toward her. But Kelandris of Suxonli was Trickster's daughter. *And* my sister, thought Doogat. He scowled, thinking that Kel's raging self-pity said little for the family bloodline. At the very least, it was undignified. At the very worst, it was selfish.

The sound of boots on cobblestone made Doogat open his eyes abruptly. Heart pounding, he watched Kelandris—still in damnable black—cross the street to approach him. Doogat went to meet her, his steps purposeful, his face a lie of calm. Kelandris bowed to Doogat, her veil fluttering in the early evening breeze.

"I have a question for you," she said, her voice quiet.

Doogat nodded, gesturing for her to continue.

"Who am I?" she asked.

"That's an excellent question."

There was a short pause.

Kelandris frowned under her veil. "One you're not going to answer?"

Doogat crossed his arms over his chest. "I cannot answer it."

"Why not?" she demanded angrily.

"Because you do not know who I am."

Kelandris swore. "Who *cares* who you are. I need to know who *I* am!"

Doogat lost his temper. "Is that all you can think about, Kelandris? Yourself? What about me?" Gesturing wildly with his hands, he said, "What about Mnemlith? Or Suxonli?"

"Suxonli!" she yelled. "You expect me to care about *Suxonli*?"

"Yes."

Kelandris blinked. Who *was* this man? How could he say such a thing to her? Suxonli was the setting for her every nightmare, her every sorrow. Kelandris lifted her veil, intending to spit in Doogat's face. As she revealed herself, she was again caught by the black of Doogat's eyes. Kelandris shuddered, her resolve to harm Doogat wavering. Doogat's white hair suddenly seemed to darken to blue-black, flying back from his face like raven wings. The features of his face became lean and angular, his smile slightly wry. Kelandris took a step backward, shaking her head. Terrified that she was going crazy again, she turned to run.

Doogat grabbed her arm. "You're sane, Kel—you're sane," he said softly in her ear.

Kelandris turned, giving Doogat a wild look. "You left me in Suxonli!" she cried at him. "You left me in their hands! Why didn't you stay? Why didn't you come sooner?" Kel's voice caught. Sobs wracked her body. "You left me," she whispered, her face so full of pain that Doogat had to look away.

There was a short pause.

Doogat swallowed, feeling ill with guilt. "I came as soon as I could, Kel. As soon as I heard your call." Tears started to his eyes. He paused. "You have been in my thoughts every day since that time. And I have never been able to forgive myself for not coming sooner—for not preventing the death of our destiny."

"Prevent it!" cried Kelandris furiously. "*You* caused it! *You* took me over the border to Piedmerri."

Doogat took a deep breath. "Physical children are not the only ones that exist, Kelandris. I wonder if you know this."

"What are you talking about?" she snapped.

Doogat shrugged. "Physical children die. So do mental ones. You distorted the speaking. And so you got confused."

"I *what*?" she retorted.

"In that one place, you distorted the speaking." Doogat

grunted. "Happens sometimes—especially if the emotions are very charged around an issue or event. Which yours are."

"What're you saying?" snapped Kelandris.

Doogat took a deep breath. "I'm saying, Kelandris, that you lost the 'child' during the Ritual of Akindo. At the moment that Yonneth raped a young woman named Fasilla. There was a death and an exchange. . . ."

Kelandris stared at Doogat.

"The *draw* was responsible," he said.

"For *what*?" she cried in frustration.

Doogat met her eyes evenly. "For giving our child into the keeping of another woman's body until such time that this child came to us and asked to be our daughter." Doogat paused. "I did not find this out until recently, Kel. I have lived with the pain of our loss for the past sixteen years, and it has scarred me just the same as if I were truly responsible for the child's death. As it is, we may be given a second chance. We may be given an open door—"

"Yafatah!" whispered Kelandris, suddenly remembering her encounter with the young Tammirring girl in the northwest border of Jinnjirri. "Yafatah is *our* child?"

"Yes and no," replied Doogat. "She was born of the union of Fasilla and Yonneth. She is their flesh and blood in purely animal terms. However, the *draw* took from you and I both, Kelandris. The *draw* that I cursed in Suxonli gave that child a terrible need for a future, a future that only you and I can provide for her."

"Don't be absurd," said Kelandris cooly. "Only Greatkin can create futures."

"That's right."

There was a long pause.

Kelandris stared at Doogat. Was he saying that *she* was a Greatkin? The words of *The Turn of Trickster's Daughter* came pouring into her mind, the repeating one line refrain at the end of each stanza searing her thoughts. Kelandris swallowed. She suddenly understood: *she* was the daughter of Greatkin Rimble. And this man dressed in blue standing beside her was really, truly Zendrak. Could it be that her years of insanity were finished?

Kelandris touched Doogat's cheek tentatively. "Why—why do you look like this?" she asked, "you're so old—"

"It serves me," he replied, taking her hand and kissing it. "It's hard for mortals to accept that they're in the presence of a Greatkin, Kel. They're easier to talk to when they think they're just speaking with an old Mayanabi Master. This face," he added, patting his apple cheeks, "calms them a little." He smiled at Kelandris. "You see, dearest beloved, I am your brother. I am Trickster's son. A Greatkin like yourself."

Tears sprang to Kel's eyes.

Doogat smiled kindly at Kelandris and whispered, "Welcome home."

At that moment, the autumn wind gusted over Kel's back. It snatched her veil and lifted it into the twilight sky. It fluttered out of sight behind some crimson and gold trees. Kelandris said nothing, feeling as naked with Doogat as she had with Zendrak when they had made love in the forest grove in Suxonli. Her hands trembled. Doogat smiled at her reassuringly and took her hands in his.

"Come with me," said Doogat quietly.

"Where?" asked Kelandris, her voice betraying her nervousness.

"Back to my place. There's a Hallows on tonight, and we must dress the part. Otherwise," he added, his dark eyes twinkling, "how will they recognize us?"

"Who?"

"Oh—the world." Doogat grinned. "For starters."

Chapter Forty

THE KALEIDICOPIA'S ANNUAL Trickster's Hallows officially commenced at eight bell-eve, but at least ninety people had arrived before the bells of the city sounded the hour. Those who Trickster had included on his elite guest list dressed in the spirit of the evening. There were buffoons, fools, raggedy men and women, animal headed masks, fops, pranksters, and imposters of all kinds—each wearing a costume that expressed his or her particular outrage or outrageousness.

On the surface, Podiddley's attire seemed the exception to the rule. Of course. The little thief poked his head outside of his first floor bedroom. Making sure that no other house members were nearby, he stepped into the fray of the party. No one recognized him. And why should they? Podiddley was spotless. Furthermore, he was wearing an Asilliwir tailor-made tunic and flare pants of white silk. He was clean from head to toe and smelled like yellow roses.

Twirling his brown mustache, Po sauntered up to Timmer who was busy tuning her lotari for the party. "Is there a thief from the south living at this abode? Podiddley is his name."

Timmer pointed toward the room out of which Po had just come. "Yeah. He's in there. But you'll have to hold your nose. Po's a foul housekeeper."

Po grinned. "Thank you."

"Sure," said Timmer, going back to her lotari.

Insufferably pleased with himself, Po decided to see if *any* of his housemates could recognize him tonight. As Po approached Janusin, he told himself that it was a good thing Doogat was gone—the Mayanabi Master never missed a trick. No point in having all the fun spoiled before he even had a chance to have any!

"Master Janusin," said Po formally, "I want to commend you on that lovely statue of Trickster outside. I've always thought that Greatkin Rimble was a little taller than conventional wisdom would have him be. And the balance of the pirouette is remarkable."

Janusin warmed to the praise. He stuffed his hands in the pockets of his lavender silk tunic and looked as modest as he could. The sparkle in his eyes betrayed his pleasure, however—as did the spreading lavender of his hair. Like Po and Timmer, Janusin was dressed simply and elegantly. Barlimo had commented earlier to Po how odd it was that everyone in the house had opted to wear a solid color costume. She had expected them to wear bangles, mirrors, and ribbons—especially Tree. But Tree had surprised them all and selected a robe of startling orange-red. The Jinnjirri makeup artist joined Janusin and Po now.

"'Scuse me," said Tree politely to Po. "This'll just take a minute." Turning to Janusin, he said, "You seen our beloved thief anywhere?"

"*Beloved* thief?" said Po in genuine surprise.

"Yeah—his name's Po. He lives here in the house. Most of the time he's not beloved," continued Tree. "But tonight I'm feeling generous. I'll get over it," he grinned.

Janusin shook his head. "No. In fact, Tree—I haven't seen Po since we set the feasting table. Did you try his room?"

"No answer."

"What does this Po look like?" asked Po, unable to resist.

"Can't miss him," replied Tree. "He's a regular scum-bum."

"He's got a good heart, though," said Janusin. "You just have to get beyond what he looks like in order to see it."

"And that takes some doing," said Tree, nodding vigorously.

"True," agreed Janusin.

Po frowned privately to himself, unsure if he'd just been complimented or insulted. "What's his *draw*?"

"Same as yours," said Janusin. "In fact, you look a tiny bit like him—hair color and physique, you understand. We'd never catch Po in clothes like yours. Or with his hair clean," he added with a good-natured chuckle. "I've often wondered if the meaning of Po's name is 'slob.'"

Po sniffed haughtily. "Podiddley, gentlemen, means 'steadfast dancer.' It's an old name, and a proud name."

"Oops," said Tree with genuine embarrassment. "I think we've insulted our guest. Sorry." Tree paused. "Actually, sir—if you want to know the truth—Podiddley's got something real special about him. It's just that he doesn't use it much, and it's a waste, you know? Makes him hard to live with sometimes. So we try to—uh—improve him every now and then. But it's only because we see that special thing that he won't share with us, see. I mean—well, I guess I'm trying to say that we kind of love our 'steadfast dancer.'"

"We just wish he'd be a little more *openly* steadfast, that's all," remarked Janusin. Then, with eyes twinkling, the sculptor added, "Be nice if he'd stop dancing around the rent, too."

Po's face colored. He looked away, unexpectedly touched by their warm feelings toward him. "Well, I hope you find your Podiddley," he said quietly and walked into the teeming crowd of costumed people.

The two Jinnjirri said nothing for a few moments.

Then Janusin commented, "Maybe now Po will see that we're not as blind as he thinks."

Cobeth and Rhu entered the Kaleidicopia by the back door of the kitchen. Mab looked up from arranging vegetables on a platter just as Cobeth crossed the threshold. She backed up, her face pale. Cobeth ignored Mab. She had been nothing more to him than a possible lay. When that hadn't panned out, he had lost interest permanently. The Jinnjirri actor grinned at Barlimo—who did not return the salutation.

"What's the matter, Barl—Housing Commission still on your ass?"

Barlimo's even-tempered green hair streaked with red. "Not at the moment, Cobeth. I'm hoping it'll stay that way."

"We'll see," he replied, his eyes cool.

Mab cleared her throat. "What have you got against this house? I mean, why do you hate us *all*?"

Cobeth regarded her in silence. Then he shrugged. "Something to do, I suppose. Besides, it keeps you on your toes. Keeps you creative."

"As if that were something the people in this house needed," remarked Rowenaster drily as he walked into the kitchen. He was dressed in cool gray. The color blended calmly with Mab's tunic of blue-toned pink and muted the glaring brilliance of Barlimo's fuschia attire. "You know, Cobeth, it's only by Barl's good graces that you're allowed here. *I* certainly have no love for you," he remarked, referring to his stolen library card.

Barlimo pressed her lips together. It was Doogat's good graces that allowed Cobeth here tonight—not hers. If she'd had her way, she would've reported the Jinnjirri bastard to the Great Library authorities for suspicion of theft. Never mind if they ever got it proved. A Jinnjirri under suspicion like that would have a hard time in this Saämbolin city. Might force Cobeth to leave altogether, she thought wistfully.

The Jinnjirri actor smiled sweetly at the professor. "The feeling's mutual, old man."

Then, without further conversation, Cobeth ushered Rhu out of the kitchen. As soon as they passed through the swinging door, Cobeth's yellow hair turned a violent red-black.

"Cocksucking assholes!" he said in a low voice. "I'll fix them, I will!"

Rhu frowned. "What're you going to do?"

"Take them on a little journey to Neath." He pulled out a vial of holovespa powder and walked toward the feasting table.

Moments after Cobeth and Rhu entered the Kaleidicopia, the brindle hound escaped from the confines of Aunt's second floor room. Limping, the pied-eyed bitch made her way down the stairs toward the commons room. She stopped on the second floor landing to survey the general chaos and gaiety below. Timmertandi, who was dressed in soft aqua, took to the cleared dance floor and began singing a raucous medley of bawdy Jinnjirri songs. The Jinnjirri in the audience clapped their hands. A few Dunnsung and Asilliwir joined hands to circle dance. A spiral formed, broke, and formed again. As the drumming grew louder, Timmer sang a Tammirring favorite.

Suddenly catching sight of Cobeth, the dog named Pi trotted down the rest of the stairs, reminding herself to limp. She crept over to where Cobeth stood with his holovespa vial, avoiding the crush of feet around her. Cobeth pulled down his mask. It was the same one he had worn on the night he had raped Fasilla—black and yellow and studded with mirrors. Trickster ducked behind a curtain. She sat no more than two feet from where Cobeth loitered with Rhu. She pricked her ugly ears, listening to their conversation.

Rhu put her hand on Cobeth's arm. "Do you think spiking the punch is such a good idea, Cobeth?" She looked about herself nervously. "There's no telling who's here tonight. Not with all these masks. Professor Rowenaster and Master Janusin know some people in some pretty high places—Saämbolin-wise. I've already had my house raided for drugs once. I'd hate to invite a repeat performance. Might hurt the playhouse, Cobeth. Might hurt your work," she added.

Cobeth snorted. "The people who live in this house hurt my work," he retorted. "They all think they know something about Trickster. And they don't. None of them grew up in Suxonli. None of them."

"Yes, but—"

"Stand aside, Rhu. Trickster's going to teach these folks a lesson!"

As Cobeth announced this, Trickster slunk toward him on her dog belly. Then the brindle bitch positioned herself close to Cobeth's yellow-booted feet. There Trickster waited to be stepped on.

Opening the vial of yellow holovespa powder, Cobeth poured it into Fasilla's fruit punch with a flamboyant sweep of his arm. The amount, as usual, was excessive. There was enough holovespa in Fasilla's pommin and orange juice mix to set the entire Jinnjirri Quarter of Speakinghast turning for a week.

At the moment, Fasilla walked through the swinging door of the kitchen, carrying cups and saucers. The Asilliwir woman didn't see Cobeth until she was practically on top of him. The mask gave Cobeth away. Fasilla swallowed and all but dropped the cups and saucers on the feasting table. The clatter was violent. Cobeth looked over in her direction. But, as in Mab's case, Cobeth did not acknowledge Fasilla. It was clear to the Asilliwir herbalist why this was; he did not recognize her. She, on the other hand, had never been able to forget him. Not his mask, his mannerisms, his smell—or his cruelty. She debated what to do. Then she saw the empty vial on the feasting table. She picked it up when Cobeth wasn't looking and sniffed it. Fasilla recognized the bitter smell of holovespa instantly. Her eyes narrowed as she realized where Cobeth had dumped the contents of the vial. She was speechless. All the outrage she had ever felt about this man came to the fore now. Catching sight of Yafatah walking toward her, Fasilla's outrage swiftly turned to protectiveness for her child. She did not want Cobeth to know that Ya was his daughter, nor did Fasilla want Yafatah to know that Cobeth was her father. Without thinking of the consequences, Fasilla pulled out the Asilliwir akatikki she kept hidden in her belt. She set a dart tipped with fast acting poison inside the blow tube. But as she raised the akatikki to her lips, Cobeth fell over the brindle stray, stepping directly on the bitch's bandaged front paw.

Trickster let loose with a scream of pain that silenced the party.

Aunt came running—as did half the residents of the Kaleidicopia. Aunt reached Fasilla first. Aunt stared, her jaw dropping. Recognizing Cobeth from Fasilla's description of his carnivale mask, Aunt stepped between the Jinnjirri and the Asilliwir. Aunt's only thought was to stop Fasilla from ruining her life; the dog's pain could wait. Without saying anything to Fasilla, Aunt tackled her from the front and sent the Asilliwir flying backward into the heavily laden feasting table. Plates and platters of rich foods crashed to the floor. Glasses shattered. House members of the Kaleidicopia did what they could to rectify the damage. Po did his best to separate the two women, but his hurt hand hindered his attempts. Aunt finally ended the skirmish herself by planting her fist soundly in Fasilla's lower back. Fasilla gasped for breath and doubled up in pain, her kidney in agony. Finally, the bedlam subsided. Conversation resumed.

Cobeth, who *still* did not recognize Fasilla or the mortal danger he was in, watched the fisticuffs with amusement. Then, offering a cup of punch to everyone standing near him—including young Yafatah—he drank a glass himself. Yafatah accepted the punch from Cobeth mutely, her eyes troubled. Why had her mother and Aunt started fighting? She didn't know. The dark-haired girl raised the cup of hallucinogenic poison to her mouth mechanically. As she did so, the brindle bitch slammed into her from the side, knocking the punch out of her grasp. The cup broke when it hit the floor. Trickster fell into the shards, carried forward by her jump. The dog yelped and whined piteously. Blood soaked the carpet.

During all the commotion, no one noticed Kelandris and Zendrak enter by the front door. As soon as the two Greatkin walked in, however, the air became charged with power. Kelandris wore red tonight, and Zendrak wore his habitual greens. Kelandris had considered carefully whether or not to dress in the traditional yellow and black of her Suxonli heritage, but when Zendrak had pointed out that such costuming would be amply represented by her brother Yonneth, Kelandris had decided to abandon the wasp-queen motif in favor of Trickster's Blood Day scarlet. As soon as she had made the decision, her bloodcycle had started. This had startled Kelandris—the cycle was one week early—but Zendrak had assured her that she could not turn without it. They had not made love. Her *he* was fully operant, said Zendrak—and had been so for the past sixteen years. She did not need to make love to trigger it this time. Perhaps later, he had added with a smile. . . .

The red and green robes of Kelandris and Zendrak shone with the simple elegance of silk. They looked like a queen and king. Heads turned to watch them pass. Kelandris held her head high, but Zendrak could see the tremble of her lip. Kelandris glanced nervously at him. She could sense Yonneth's presence in the crowd.

"He's here," she whispered. "Yonn's here."

Zendrak shook his head. "He calls himself Cobeth now, Kel. He's not the boy you grew up with. He's not your beloved brother turned renegade. He's lost what heart he had. Don't be deceived by your good memories of him. He may one day become a better person, but you don't count on it tonight."

Kelandris laughed harshly. "Doubtful with a name like Cobeth." She paused. "I can't believe he picked that old name. That's the one I gave him once when he was being a stinker. It's a Tammi word—means cold breath. That's what we call a fire flue that's been left open when there's no fire burning. It's kind of a back door for winter—sneaks in the house and sucks up all the warmth."

Kelandris stopped speaking; she had just caught sight of Cobeth.

Kel's throat went dry. Kel knew only one thing; she didn't want to be anywhere *near* Cobeth. Kel swallowed, her hands breaking out in sweat. She stopped walking.

"I can't," she said to Zendrak in an agonized voice. "I can't do this. I should never have come. It'll happen all over again. Something will go wrong. It has to—it's Rimble's night. They'll beat me—"

Kelandris backed up, her face pale and her green eyes stark with fear. She whirled away from Zendrak and ran for the door. Zendrak caught up with her immediately. Grabbing her arm firmly, he demanded, "What're you *doing*, Kelandris?"

"Leaving," she snapped. "This whole business about turning is stupid. It's a dead ritual. I've already turned once, I don't need to do it again. Suxonli refused me. Let it stay that way," she cried, tears of terror springing to her beautiful eyes.

"Then you condemn the whole world to spiritual decay!"

"You exaggerate," she replied, her eyes becoming glassy with fear. "You do. I'm just a simple village girl from southern Tammirring. What I do has no bearing on the world at large. It affects no one but myself—"

Zendrak slapped her; he slapped her awake.

"How *dare* you!" Kel screamed at him. "After all I've been through—"

Zendrak slammed her up against the wall. "Now you listen to me, Kel. There's no time to treat you gently. Hear this clearly: *if you don't turn tonight, you will be crazy again*—"

"No, I won't!"

"You *will*! And so will the rest of the world. How dare you even contemplate wishing such a fate on all the people in this room—myself included." His eyes bored into hers, full of desperation. "Have you no tenderness for me at least?"

Kelandris started to renounce her love for him, but before she could get the words out, Zendrak shook her. "Don't make yourself into a liar," he hissed. Then, without warning, he kissed Kel deeply. Mythrrim passion ignited between them instantly. Kelandris started to sob as she recalled what it had been like to kiss Zendrak. The man in green held her close, whispering loving things in her ear.

"Hold me," said Kel hoarsely. "Just hold me."

"I will, Kel. And for many years to come—if you'll just give those years to us tonight." He stroked her blue-black hair. "Don't deny the world our love. Don't let Suxonli rob the world of the

• 285 •

fertility of two Greatkin. Give up your resentment and turn. Turn for Trickster, Kel. Turn yet again."

Kelandris hid her face in Zendrak's shoulder, her breathing ragged. Zendrak could feel her tremble. Kel choked back her sobs, her eyes shut tightly. Finally, she raised her head. She met Zendrak's inquiring glance, her emotions unreadable. Then Kelandris gave Zendrak the one thing he had despaired of receiving from her again—a tentative smile.

Forcing herself to be brave, Kel walked shakenly to the center of the room. Seeing Cobeth stiffen as he recognized her, Kel fought back the horror of Suxonli. Taking a deep breath, Kelandris crossed her arms over her chest, palms flat against her red robe. Ignoring Cobeth completely, Kelandris bowed in Zendrak's direction. Holding her head slightly to the side, she shut her eyes. She appeared to be listening to the strains of a faraway music. She hummed a single note, planting her left foot firmly on the floor as she prepared to make her turn. The note sang from her lips cleanly and purely.

Timmer, who happened to be standing nearby, handed her lotari to a member of her quintet. Instructing the fellow to make a D-major chord from Kel's one note, Timmer added a vocal harmony of her own. Startled by the unexpected sound of the lotari's drone, Kel's eyes met Timmer's curious, smiling face. In that moment, Kelandris realized that there *was* another family for her—apparently right here in this house. She smiled hesitantly at the blonde Dunnsung musician. Timmer winked at Kel and continued improvising off of Kel's single note.

Zendrak walked slowly toward the two women. As he did so, Po cut across his path. Zendrak stared at Po's white silks in surprise, his dark eyes delighted. Po, who had never had any dealings with Zendrak, ignored the man in green. Po smiled at Kelandris—instead of running as he had predicted he would do if he ever met a Greatkin face-to-face. Po added another harmony to Kel's continuous note.

One by one, the rest of Rimble's Nine drew toward Trickster's daughter. Kel watched them approach. Barlimo stopped in mid-sentence with an architect and made her way hurriedly in Kel's direction. Mab followed the Jinnjirri shyly, her step light with the pleasure of joining Kel. Tree clamored down the second floor staircase, pursued by the nipping brindle bitch. Seeing the tiny group dressed in solid colors slowly positioning themselves around the woman in scarlet, Tree cried, "Wait for me!"

Janusin, who was outside standing in front of the statue of Greatkin Rimble, wiped away his sorrow over Cobeth with a lavender handkerchief. Stuffing it in his pocket, Janusin answered Kel's summons. As he walked through the kitchen, he was met by Rowenaster. Neither man said anything. Rowen put his silver bifocals in his pocket and followed Janusin into the commons room. Each contrary took his or her place in a circle around Trickster's daughter. It was a rainbow of color. The man in green was the last to join the group.

As Zendrak approached Kelandris, Yafatah broke free of her mother's strong grip on her arm. Fasilla had been in the process of leading Yafatah out of the Kaleidicopia. Aunt's interference in her attempt to kill Cobeth had infuriated Fasilla. She had decided to return to Asilliwir. Tonight. As Yafatah wrenched free of Fasilla, the young girl gave a cry of recognition to Kelandris and Zendrak. The young girl tore after the man in green. Fasilla started after her daughter, her expression horrified. Before she could grab Yafatah, however, Aunt intercepted Fasilla, saying, "Let her go, Fas! Let her go to them!"

"*I* be her mother!" cried Fasilla. "And she'll do as I say!"

Apparently Yafatah overhead this remark, for she turned in her flight toward the Nine and walked back toward her mother. Yafatah and Fasilla faced each other in silence. Then Yafatah said slowly and clearly, "You do be me ma—this be true. But Kelandris of Suxonli do be mother to us all. And I must go to her now."

"You'll do no such thing! Ya! Ya, come back here!"

But the young girl would not heed her mother. Running lightly through the crowd now, Yafatah arrived in time to see Kelandris begin her turn. Yafatah slowed, her attention fixed on the tall woman wearing scarlet silk.

Keeping her head slightly tilted, Kelandris began to turn in a smooth counter-clockwise direction. Her left foot remained firmly on the floor as her right moved around it. Like the Winterbloom for which Kelandris was named, Kel unfolded her arms like the petals of a flower reaching for the warmth of the sun. Kel's left hand pointed to the ground. Kel raised her right, palm upward toward the ceiling. Kel's black hair swung out behind her as her face suffused with an inner incandescence. Her gaze was distant, her green eyes focused on a radiance only she could see. Kel's mouth opened slightly, a slow, full smile spreading across her lips. Sparks of an electrical blue-black charge crackled around her body in an eerie nimbus of the Fertile Dark. And still Kelandris turned. Her scarlet robe became a blur of effortless motion. Now the power of Kel's sixteen-year dormant *he* rose through her body in a double helix of spirals. She gasped with pleasure. As she did so, the rest of Rimble's Nine began to turn likewise. Their synchronous movement steadied the pulse of the Greatkin electrical current coursing through Kel's bones and cells.

On the far side of the room, Cobeth screamed, *"No!"*

He ran toward Kelandris, determined to break through the group of eight surrounding his sister. Kel should not be turning, *he* should! He must break her concentration! He must stop this desecration! She was *akindo*! She was cursed! What would Trickster say? What would—

Something grabbed Cobeth by the scruff of the neck. Cobeth struggled to free himself. He whirled around, swinging at whatever held him. Cobeth missed and fell forward. A tall man dressed in black and yellow rags crouched over Cobeth and whispered in his ear:

"You believes in me, Coby-boy—so you makes me large. And for *such* a good show of faith, we've got something special in mind for you, eh?"

Cobeth truned his head and found himself staring into the pied eyes of Trickster. Cobeth began to laugh wildly. "Something for me?" cried Cobeth gleefully, visions of personal power making him giddy. "Finally, something for me?"

"Something for you," repeated Trickster coldly. Then, without warning, Greatkin Rimble plunged his left thumbnail into the soft flesh of Cobeth's forehead. Like a wasp's stinger, two lancets shot out filling the wound with poison. Cobeth screamed in silence, his face contorted in agony. Trickster withdrew the thumbnail, whispering, "Now we'll see how you like *your* journey to Neath."

Cobeth buried his face in his arms, his body hunched in a fetal position on the floor. Rhu came running over to him. She shooed a brindle dog away from Cobeth's torso. Cobeth was unable to speak to her, his brain on fire. Rhu peered into his dilated pupils. It looked to her like Cobeth was having an unexpectedly bad reaction to the holovespa in the punch. She called for healers. Several came over. Their diagnosis confirmed her own; Cobeth had overdosed. He was having a toxic response. Antidotes were tried, but nothing worked. With each passing moment, Cobeth sank deeper and deeper into an emotional miasma with no bottom. All of this occurred while Rimble's Nine turned contrarywise.

In the center of the room, Kelandris increased her spin once more. She spread her arms, lifting them like wings. Softly she whispered, "So turn the inside inside-out and be sanely mad with me. Master Trickster's turnabout, and come to my ecstasy!"

As Kelandris finished speaking, power exploded among the Nine and was grounded into the *draw* of Saämbolin through the capacity of Trickster's daughter for change. The charge rippled outward. The guests of Rimble reacted according to *their* capacity for change. If they were rigid and afraid, they wept. If they welcomed change, they responded with smiles and joy. Overwhelmed, Cobeth entered a catatonic state of mind. Several healers took him away.

Now Kelandris lowered her hands. She folded them once more against her chest, the movement simple and clean. Then Kelandris came to a standstill. The other eight did likewise, and the turn was complete. Yafatah walked slowly toward Kelandris, tears streaming from her eyes. Now the young girl ran headlong into Kel's waiting arms. She clung to the tall woman, her face suffused with a radiant peace. The future of the world was assured now. The Wild Kelandris had bloomed.

Kelandris kissed Yafatah's forehead. As she did so, Kel's eyes met Zendrak's briefly. Zendrak nodded.

Then the two Greatkin shared a secret smile.

The Panthe'kinarok Epilogue

THE GREATKIN FINISHED the third course of their potluck feast with general merriment and banter. Phebene wiped her lips daintily with the corner of her napkin and belched. Jinndaven looked at her in surprise. Catching his expression, Phebene pointed at the little Greatkin who sat between them, saying, "It's *his* influence."

Jinndaven grunted. "Can't say that it's very flattering, Phebes."

Trickster, who was getting tired of being talked about as though he were not there, started swearing. "*My* influence, she says! What about what she did to *my* plans!"

Phebene picked her teeth with the prong of her fork. "You

haven't a corner on improvements, you know. Love has every bit as much a right to change people as you do, Rimble."

Jinndaven watched Phebene's table manners deteriorate with dismay. "For Presence sake, sister dear—try to be a little more civilized."

"I beg your pardon?" asked the Greatkin of Civilization. "Did you say something to me, Jinn?"

The Greatkin of Imagination shook his head. "Nope. Just complaining about Rimble's bad influence on Phebene. I think we should reconsider the seating arrangements."

"I agree!" replied Rimble hotly. "You've meddled enough, Phebes. Meddled and muddled. Zendrak's losing his edge! He doesn't mind me when he should. And Kelandris—she's gone all sweetness and light. It's disgusting!"

Phebene blew her nose into her sleeve. Referring to Rimble, she said, "Don't pay any attention to his bitching, Jinn. He loves it. Don't you?" she asked, kissing Rimble on the top of his head.

Rimble sank into his chair, putting his napkin over his head like an old woman wearing a newspaper hat. "Love better not be catching."

Jinndaven started laughing. "I think it would be an improoove-ment if it was, Rimble. You'd be ever so much more manage-able."

"Never!" snorted Trickster under his napkin.

"Just think of it, Phebes," continued the Greatkin of Imagina-tion, "Trickster in love—"

"Sick, sick, sick," muttered the pied-eyed little Greatkin.

"Say, Rimble," yelled the Greatkin of Humor at the far side of the round table. Her name was Nessi'gobahn. She wore bells in her hair and had an infectious laugh. "Is it my imagination, or have you grown some?"

Jinndaven investigated. "If it's your imagination, then it's mine, too," he called back. "Rimble's at least a foot taller than when we sat down at the table."

"What do you think it means?" asked Phebene.

The Greatkin of Civilization smiled at them all, her eyes twinkling. "It means, my dears, that Rimble is starting to matter again."